NO WHERE TO HIDE

AL-QAEDA'S ASSAULT ON AMERICA

A NOVEL BY

HERBERT F. PANDISCIO

Herbert F. Pandiscio
67 Old Mill Road, Avon, CT 06001
860-673-5827 (Home) 860-614-1637 (Cell)
hpandiscio@comcast.net
Word Count: 167,028

ISBN: 1481131796
ISBN-13: 9781481131797
Library of Congress Control Number: 2012922948
CreateSpace Independent Publishing Platform
North Charleston, South Carolina

DEDICATION

The book is dedicated to all law enforcement men and women, members of the military and first responders who risk their lives in the fight against terrorism.

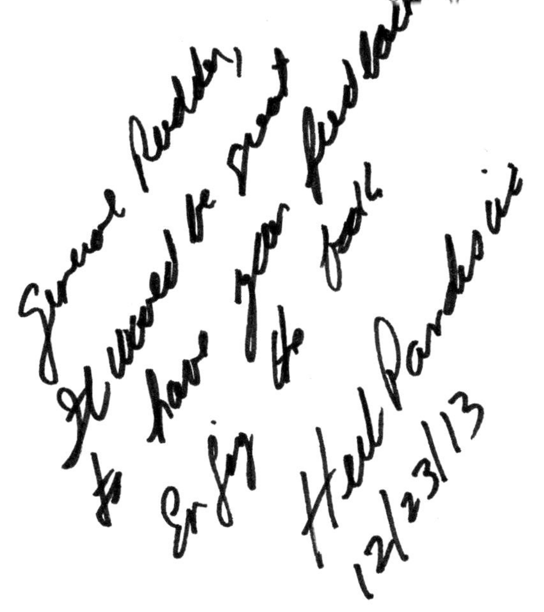

ACKNOWLEDGMENT

I thank my wife, Ruth, for her help and support in bringing this manuscript to publication and who had to endure the challenging work of proofing and editing the early drafts. She followed the credo that there is no good first draft. Or, for that matter, no good second draft.

Thanks to friends, each of whom edited a section of the manuscript and who provided valuable feedback: Dorrie Bean, Lib Blucke, Connie and Tom Heytink, Bob and Lee Karwoski, Claire and Bob McCorry, and Peggy Shanks.

PROLOGUE

The lights in the barrack were at half power as the ten men prepared to move out. They were powerfully built, agile and stood between five ten and six four. They were Seals and Special Forces, enlisted men and officers, each chosen based on ability to complete the mission. They wore cargo pants with multiple pockets, black T-shirts, vest type jackets, black high-top soft sole boots, helmets with night vision goggles and communication capability. They wore no body armor. Each man carried a Colt M4A1 assault rifle, a P228 9mm automatic pistol, a Marine KABAR knife, two hand grenades and multiple gun magazines. Two of the men carried back packs, one contained medical equipment, the other explosive charges. The men were prepared to deploy rapidly, assault with overwhelming firepower, complete the extraction and be out of the area in less than twenty minutes.

These were men of APET, the Advanced Penetration and Extraction Team, commanded by Captain Vinnie Pagano, an experienced combat veteran of the Iraq and Afghanistan wars. APET's mission this night was to penetrate deep into a Taliban stronghold in the Wardak Province and extract, dead or alive, two Rangers captured the previous night. The Taliban commander of the province was a brutal terrorist who first tortured and then beheaded his captives. APET had only a few short hours to extract the men. At dawn, the Rangers would be beheaded in front of villagers.

The men of APET had been briefed earlier as to how the mission would unfold. If the Taliban commander followed his usual pattern, he would have a contingent of twenty to twenty-five combatants with him. The others in his force would have returned to their safe haven in the mountains. Using satellite imagery, APET identified the location of the village chief's house. Behind the house was a shed the size of a large garage. Satellite imagery further indicated that the Rangers were being held there. APET would mount its attack at three forty five a.m. when the combatants would be sleeping. What Captain Pagano did not know for certain was where all of the combatants would be located.

The stealth helicopter would drop the team approximately one and a half miles from the village at three thirty a.m. in a landing area selected by Pagano, after conferring with ground commanders. Fifteen minutes after landing APET would attack the Taliban and rescue the Rangers.

When the men completed a check of their equipment, Pagano walked through the darkened barrack, stood at the door and motioned each man to move out into the night. Silhouetted against the dark sky was a Sikorsky UH-60 stealth Blackhawk helicopter. Liftoff would be in four minutes. With its modified tail boom, noise reducing covering on the rear rotors, and harsh angles and flat surfaces, it resembled a machine out of *Star Wars.* To increase its speed and provide room for the injured or dead Rangers, the Blackhawk was stripped of its guns and extra weight.

Once the last man was aboard, Pagano climbed in, slid the door shut and gave a thumbs up to the pilot. Captain Donna Chang, a decorated veteran pilot of the Iraq campaign, powered the engines and the stealth helicopter lifted into the night sky. Her co-pilot was Charlie Foley. This was his first combat mission at night. It was three a.m.

At three twenty eight a.m. the Blackhawk settled on to the ground. In less than two minutes, the APET team was out of the helicopter and moving rapidly in single file behind Lieutenant Timothy Ryan who had plotted the route to the village. Pagano was second in line.

Once Donna Chang was convinced the operation was successfully under way and there were no enemy combatants in the area, she cut the engines and silence filled the night. It was time to wait. She and Charlie unhitched their seatbelts, crawled back to the main cabin where each picked up a Colt M4A1 assault rifle. They sat on opposite sides of the open cabin and would guard their aircraft while they waited for the pickup call from Captain Pagano. Once that call came, Chang would be airborne in five minutes and at four a.m. she would land her bird in the field between the chief's house and the one next to it.

The APET team arrived at the village a minute ahead of the scheduled time. In the pre-flight briefing Pagano had instructed his men to fan out on both sides of the shed and the house and to stay under cover if possible. He did not want any enemy combatants behind his men.

The shed was dark. It had a double door on one side and a large window on the opposite side. Using night vision goggles, he identified two men sitting on crates next to the door armed only with hand guns. Both appeared to be dozing. He then shifted his gaze to the house were the Taliban commander was sleeping. A guard stood on each side of the door. They were talking quietly. Their casual stance and the fact that their AK-47 rifles were leaning against the door led Pagano to believe they were not expecting visitors. Another dozen or so combatants would be in the house. There was no back door. The distance to the house nearest to that of the village chief's was approximately seventy-five yards with an open field between them. Pagano checked his watch. It was time to repeat instructions for the final deployment of the men. Once that was completed, he would contact Donna Chang. She would lift off five minutes later, head for the village and fifteen minutes later would be on the ground for a pickup of the APET team and the Rangers.

Speaking softly into his microphone, "We go with the original plan. Ed and Jake will cover the front of the house. Lou and Karl, the back. Sharif, you are to take a position between the chief's house and the next house in the event we have combatants sleeping in the second house. Lou, cover the side of the shed with the window. Timothy and I will storm the shed and take down any combatants inside. Pete and Alex, you will follow us in and bring out the Rangers. Jason, secure the path into the village. Everyone, hang on a second."

He switched his microphone frequency. "Donna, go airborne in five."

"Airborne in five."

Back to his team, "Listen up. No prisoners. Repeat, no prisoners. When you hear the first shot, take out anything that moves. We don't leave without the Rangers. Let's move."

Vinnie and Timothy, pistols in one hand and knives in the other, moved slowly and quietly towards the two dozing guards at the shed hoping they would remain sleeping at which time they would have their throats slit. When they were within ten feet of the sleeping guards, one woke and started to raise his gun. There was not sufficient time for either Vinnie or Timothy to reach him with knives drawn. Responding to the situation, Timothy shot him between the eyes. Vinnie shot the second guard in the face. Once the two shots were fired, a barrage of gunfire erupted in front and in back of the house. Vinnie and Timothy, in unison, smashed into the flimsy door to the shed with their shoulders. The door shattered as it was forced inside the shed. Although they were prepared for combatants inside, what they found was a single guard with his arms raised over his head and his AK-47 rifle lying on the floor. He was prepared to surrender and live. Timothy shot him twice in the face.

Both Rangers were tied to chairs, stripped to the waist, mouths bloodied, eyes blackened and partially closed, faces swollen, knife cuts on their chests, necks, and arms and body bruises everywhere. Pete and Alex were behind Vinnie and Timothy and immediately went to the Rangers and cut them loose. The Rangers fell out of the chairs and into the arms of the two big men who, without waiting to see if they were dead or alive, picked them up, held them in their arms and carried them out of the shed towards the edge of the woods where they placed them gently on the ground.

Both Rangers were alive. Pete removed the medical pack he was carrying and removed two battlefield blankets. Alex raised each man's upper body and Pete pulled the blankets behind each man and then wrapped them around each man's upper body. He reached into the pack and brought out a bottle of water that he handed to Alex, who gently lifted the head of each man and gave them a sip. Pete ripped open several gauze packets and wiped what blood he could from the face of each man. There was little else that could be done for the Rangers until the Blackhawk airlifted them out. Pete and Alex checked their automatic weapons and moved closer to the house as back-up, prepared to join the fight if Pagano called for reinforcements.

The minute Timothy shot the first guard, Ed and Jake had opened up with assault rifles and sprayed the front door and windows of the house and took down the guards. Within seconds, combatants inside the house began to appear in the front and back windows, firing wildly into the dark night, unable to see the APET team members. They had not expected an attack. Ed and Jake fired rounds into the front windows and door. In the rear of the house, Lou and Karl continued to target the windows. They reloaded time and again and continued their assault on the rear of the house. Sharif, located between the two houses, watched as ten or twelve men ran out of the house next door and sprinted across the open field toward him. While firing, he called to Pagano. "Vinnie, it's Sharif, I have a shit load of them coming at me."

"Hang steady. Be with you." He and Timothy, firing while they ran around the house, joined Sharif and the three of them knelt on one knee and formed a wall of firepower. Without cover, the enemy charging across the field had no chance of survival. As the three men fired at the combatants, a window broke in the top floor of the house behind them. Vinnie turned and fired at the gunman in the window, but the gunman returned the fire and caught Sharif in the leg. Timothy turned and fired at the same window and the gunman fell backwards into the room. Sharif yelled, "Go for the commander in the house. I'm good."

Vinnie and Timothy ran to the front of the house where Ed and Jake had peppered it with their assault rifles. All was quiet on that side. There was still sporadic firing on the back side. "Lou and Karl, are you ok?"

"Vinnie, either the enemy is dead or hiding in the house. It may be time for a room-to-room."

"Not yet. I want to force the combatants out of the house. Set up a perimeter between this house and the next. There may be more of the enemy in that house. Sharif needs cover until we can move him. Once our transport arrives, I don't want a delay."

"Done."

Vinnie called out, "Timothy, Ed, and Jake, cover the windows while I get grenades into the house."

"Vinnie, I'm closer, I'll do it." It was Ed who broke with protocol.

Before Vinnie could react, Ed ran to the house and threw a grenade through the front door, and then heaved a second one inside. He turned and ran full speed back to where he started and then threw himself flat on the ground to avoid shrapnel from the blasts. After the eight second delay, the first grenade went off followed shortly by the second. The house shook on its foundation as the explosives did their work. There was screaming and yelling as men ran out of the door in an attempt to flee from the smoke and the fire that erupted from the grenades and the exploding oil fired stove in the kitchen. As the bloodied men ran out of the house, the three APET men killed them with a barrage of gunfire.

The last person out of the house was an old man, the village chief. He stood in the doorway with his hands over his head in a gesture of surrender with a white rag hanging from one hand. He was bleeding from facial wounds. He called out loudly, "I am unarmed. Everyone is dead. The commander is dead. I don't wish to die."

Vinnie whispered instructions to Timothy who then disappeared. Next, he called out to the chief while pointing a gun at him. "I want you to show me where the dead commander is. If you make one false move, you are dead." In the background, Vinnie could hear the first sounds of the approaching Blackhawk. Donna Chang would be on time.

Vinnie walked slowly toward the chief. When he arrived at the front door he motioned the chief to move inside. Fire was consuming the left side of the house but the right side was still intact but filling with smoke. When the chief arrived at the door to the room where the dead commander was located, he stopped, hesitated, and then pointed to the room. As Vinnie turned towards the door, the chief flung himself to the floor thereby giving the Taliban commander, who was lying on the floor very much alive, a clear shot at Vinnie. Before the commander could pull the trigger, he was struck with a bullet to the back of his head fired by Timothy who was at the rear window. The Taliban commander took a bullet in the throat from a fast reacting Vinnie, who then turned and looked down at the chief who was still on the floor. Vinnie stared at the chief and fired one bullet into his forehead. He then whispered, "You fucker. That's for the Rangers."

The gunfire had ceased and the men began to assemble in the field between the two houses. All was quiet except for the pulsating noise from the Blackhawk that Donna Chang had set down between the two houses. The flames erupting through the door and windows of the house cast sufficient light for the team to see the dead and dying Taliban combatants lying around them.

Sharif had been picked up by Ed and carried to the helicopter. Pete and Alex carried the two Rangers and carefully lifted them into the Blackhawk. They were still alive. Vinnie remained on the ground, and once everyone was accounted for he climbed aboard and slid the door shut. He gave Captain Chang a thumbs up to go airborne. As she lifted the stealth aircraft into the air, villagers began to fill the street. They were greeted with death all around them.

The Blackhawk turned east and flew at maximum speed towards medical help for the Rangers. Once the Rangers and Sharif were left at a field hospital, she would return the APET team to its barrack.

Having completed what they had come to do, the men sat quietly. Later, when the official debriefing was completed, there would be a celebration but for now they reflected on the mission. Vinnie crawled back to the Rangers who were lying next to each other and whispered; "We're going home, guys, we're all going home." One of the Rangers smiled through his swollen face and performed a weak high-five. The other Ranger, in serious condition, simply nodded. Tears rolled down his bruised and blackened face.

Captain Vinnie Pagano took a seat among his men on the cabin floor and prepared a mental stat sheet; for the enemy, twenty or more Taliban dead, including one commander and one village chief. For APET, two Rangers extracted alive, no dead, one wounded. Mission accomplished.

He rested his head against the vibrating bulkhead of the helicopter as it flew east toward the approaching dawn, looked with pride at his men, with relief at the rescued Rangers, then closed his eyes and wondered how many more times he could do this.

CHAPTER 1

THE AD

The newspaper, opened to the classified ads, was on Vinnie Pagano's desk when he arrived for work. It was Monday, the beginning of another week at Global Insurance. The job opening was highlighted in yellow. "Private Investigator Wanted. Must meet requirements Connecticut Public Act #04-192. Send resume to Ms. Gretchen Iverson, Iverson & Hunt Investigations." The ad listed an email address and phone number.

His first reaction was to question why the ad was on the desk. He had not mentioned to anyone at Global he was looking for a career change. New to the area, he had no close friends or family in whom he could confide, thus ruling them out as the source of the ad. Glancing around the outer office he did not observe anyone who took any particular interest in his arrival. His boss wasn't in so he couldn't have left the newspaper. It was today's edition. His shared secretary was at her desk and didn't so much as glance his way.

Curiosity got the better of him. He booted up his computer, connected to the Internet and pulled up CT General Statute 04-192. Following a careful reading of the statute he concluded that in spite of his distinguished military career, he barely met the requirements for the position of detective in Connecticut.

Nevertheless, “barely” may be sufficient. He thought about the ad for a few minutes and then sent a short email with an attached resume to Gretchen Iverson expressing an interest. If nothing came of his inquiry, nothing would be lost. His job at Global was secure. On the other hand, Hartford, Connecticut was not where he wanted to be.

There remained the nagging question of who left the ad and why? He finally put the thought out of his mind and opened his calendar to check his schedule for the day.

CHAPTER 2

PAGANO

He was the youngest of three children born to Italian immigrants. His parents developed a passion for America and the opportunities it afforded them. They passed their passion on to Vinnie.

His father was one of five boys, all of whom were married. The five brothers lived in the same neighborhood in the small industrial city of Fitchburg, Massachusetts. The Pagano clan was large in number with Vinnie being the youngest of the many male cousins. It was a happy and cohesive group of boys who walked the two miles to high school through two tough neighborhoods, one north of the church on Water Street and the other just below the high school on Pritchard Street.

Primo was the oldest, biggest and toughest of the cousins and his physical presence on the walk to school deterred anyone from threatening members of his extended family. With Primo being the oldest and Vinnie the youngest, a special bond developed between them. It was Primo who taught Vinnie how to box and use the heavy bag and speed bag that Primo had in his cellar.

Their neighborhood was called the *Patch*. If you lived in the *Patch* you were either an Italian whose family came from the mainland, or a Sicilian. The distinction was clear. To the Italians who lived in the *Patch*, Sicily was a country, not an island and all Sicilian men were Mafia. The Sicilians lived on the north fringe of the *Patch* that bordered the railroad tracks. Their turf was close to the river and the coal fired power plant. The Italians in the *Patch* avoided the Sicilians.

Between the Italian and Sicilian neighborhoods there was a narrow strip of land, two city blocks deep and five or six blocks wide where the Shanty Irish lived. South of the *Patch* was the "south side" neighborhood, home to the Lace Curtain Irish who spoke neither to their poor Irish brethren, nor to the Italians until much later when the Italians wrestled control of the city government from the Irish. Then everyone talked to the Italians, including the Sicilians. Vinnie's father was influential in working behind the scenes with the non-English speaking Italians to help elect the first Italian mayor.

Vinnie's high school experience was dismal except for athletics. Big and fast, he earned six varsity letters in football and track. It was while in high school that he received his first experience with prejudice and bias. The athletic program was managed by old line Yankee families and coached almost exclusively by Irish men. It was an uphill battle to earn a starting position if you were Italian. Ethnic bias was always present in the classroom. Italian boys were often seen as children of ignorant immigrants and not capable of academic success.

Vinnie graduated on time but with no plans to attend college. The only guidance counselor at the high school suggested he get work in one of the many factories in town. That dismissive and ethnically poisoned suggestion was sufficient to motivate Vinnie to advance his education. In late August of the year he graduated from high school, he applied for and was accepted at a two year community college. He excelled academically and after the first semester of his second year was admitted to the main University of Massachusetts campus in Amherst, Massachusetts. He majored in psychology and Italian and graduated with a 4.0 grade point average. It was while he was at the University that he was first approached by the CIA. He declined an offer to join the agency and, instead, joined the Army.

The family was not surprised Vinnie joined the Army. Both his father and brother had served in the military. The Italians in the *Patch* loved America and they figured what America had given to them and their children in the way of opportunities must be repaid in some way. Military service was one avenue. Another way was to be a good citizen and stay out of trouble. The Pagano family stayed out of trouble. Vinnie stayed out of trouble, but when trouble sought them out, the elders took care of it. If they couldn't, Primo would.

Like his cousin Primo, Vinnie Pagano grew to be a big man standing six feet two with a solid frame, weighing in at one hundred eighty pounds. With his dark eyes, black hair, smooth olive skin, Patrician profile and beautiful body, he was a handsome Italian man to whom women were instantly attracted. His "height" gene came from his mother's side. She was a tall, beautiful woman from northern Italy. All five of her brothers were stone cutters who worked in the pink marble quarries in New Hampshire. Vinnie inherited their strength and work ethic.

When he transferred to the University of Massachusetts from the community college, he was too late to compete for and earn a varsity sport position. His interest in boxing provided an alternative outlet for his athletic interest. He joined a boxing club in Northampton, a small city near the University and home to Smith College. It was while working out at the boxing club that he was first approached by the CIA. The recruiter was a professor at the university and a regular at the club. He was shorter than Vinnie, physically fit and weighed in at around two hundred. It turned out that he was a powerful and graceful boxer. Once a week, prior to the time the professor first approached Vinnie about the CIA, they would step into the ring and go a few rounds, eventually working their way up to ten. Vinnie thought the professor was tough even by the standard set by his cousin Primo. In some ways the professor was another Primo. A mutual respect formed between the two boxers. Vinnie was to learn later that the professor was a retired CIA agent with a distinguished record as a covert agent.

After their weekly workouts, the professor and Vinnie would have a beer at a local bar. It was during this time that the professor learned whatever there was to be learned about Vinnie who would not be a typical CIA recruit from a prestigious college with historic ties to the agency. What the professor observed was an academically bright, physically tough, ethically strong young man from a patriotic, hard working family who was outstanding at self defense and willing to go on the offensive when victory was required. His potential recruit was fearless in the ring. By the time Vinnie graduated, he was the premier boxer at the club.

The professor believed what Vinnie had demonstrated in the ring would be helpful during his training cycle with the CIA. He would have a head start on the other recruits having had the benefit of growing up with cousins who taught each other the art of self-defense. The professor gave Vinnie high marks for the fact that his family taught him never to look for trouble but never to back off when it came your way. Especially attractive to the recruiter was Vinnie's independent streak and his not needing anyone around him for support. This was a man who was not afraid of the dark and not afraid of being alone. He had the makings of a covert agent. The CIA offer was still on the table when he graduated but Vinnie was not interested until he had completed a tour of duty in the Army.

Vinnie appreciated his Army experience; the discipline, the focus, the attention to training, the camaraderie, working with the combat experienced men and women who were drill sergeants and mentors, the iron will of the men and women on his team to complete a mission and bring back the wounded and the dead. He knew from his negative high school experience that Army education, unlike that in most city high schools, is capable of teaching all young men and women something of value, something they can take home after their tour of duty. It knows how to encourage and promote cooperation under the most stressful of conditions. He believed it would serve teachers and administrators well to have been in the military. When they returned to civilian life they would be more sympathetic in dealing with the kids who were struggling in school, the same kids who risked their lives so teachers could exercise freedom of speech. Once educators served in combat they would not automatically swing politically to the left. It would put some balance in their lives and the lives of their students.

Following a battery of tests, Army brass decided that Vinnie Pagano would attend a special operations school. He was given no choice. The physical and psychological training was brutal with demands and goals beyond anything he could imagine or thought he could endure. Bravery was put to the test each day. It was during this training that he learned the art of killing. It was only when he completed the course that he was told of his assignment to APET, the Advanced Penetration and Extraction Team, whose primary charge was to penetrate behind enemy lines to find and bring home the dead and wounded following a battle. The secondary objective was to abduct enemy combatants, Taliban fighters and al-Qaeda terrorists and bring them back for enhanced interrogation.

Vinnie spent five years with the unit, four of them as leader, earned the rank of Captain, completed two tours of duties in Iraq, one in Afghanistan and had several cross border assignments into Pakistan. His work was deemed heroic and the reputation of the team was known throughout the combat zones. His team left no one behind. Five years of living in hell and the prospect of still more tours of duty in combat zones was enough to signal him that it was time to move on. With the current administration and Congress in power and the Department of Justice firmly against enhanced interrogation, he knew the country would never again achieve victory wherever it fought. In his mind, liberal education from kindergarten through graduate school had institutionalized weakness throughout the society. The military was proficient in starting wars, but was a failure in completing them because of political interference. He passed up a two step promotion and retired from the army.

It was not without considerable regret that he retired. Five years of hell and horror also included leading courageous men and women. It was not easy to severe the relationships. He thought about the professor and the CIA when he was discharged but decided to put it on the back burner. There would be time enough for that down the road. He was still a young man.

A college acquaintance who stayed connected with Vinnie during his time in the Army, worked for Global Insurance in Hartford, CT, a major player in the international insurance business. The friendship resulted in Vinnie being interviewed for the position of staff psychologist. Following a short recruiting cycle he was hired. His primary responsibility was to assess regional managers for their potential to successfully handle leadership positions at the officer level. He went from leading kids younger than himself into combat against some of the cruelest enemies the world has ever encountered to making shrink talk with some of the dullest people on the planet. His secondary function, given his military career, was to determine if men and women in critical and sensitive positions within the company were psychologically and emotionally suited for the decision making responsibilities that went with the job; i.e., did they have the stuff to intimidate subordinates and increase the bottom line.

With less than a year under his belt as an insurance shrink, he needed to escape before he found himself lying on a couch talking to another shrink. It had become a challenge for him to be associated with a business that employed as many manipulating bastards as did the insurance industry. In his mind they were a step down from Wall Street investment bankers.

Then, on that Monday morning the ad appeared on his desk. Little did he know the chaos it would create in his life.

CHAPTER 3

APPOINTMENT

Gretchen Iverson's secretary, Darlene, called. As he was to learn later, the secretary was not a secretary.

He enjoyed receiving calls from women he did not know and then envision what they looked like based on voice alone. Without exception, he wanted to believe they were tall, blond, blue eyed, leggy, busty, sexy and dying to meet him. That is what he dreamt about. All men thought this way so he never considered himself weird. He told himself that it was a guy thing. Given his recent bad luck, he figured his dream would be popped and she will be short, dumpy and anything but sexy.

"Mr. Pagano?"

"Speaking."

"This is Darlene from Iverson & Hunt Investigation."

"Hi. What can I do for you, Darlene?"

"Actually, it is what I can do for you."

At this point he really wanted her to be blond, leggy, busty and sexy. His breathing had already accelerated and he had yet to meet her.

"Before I die of anticipation, it would help if you told me what this call is about."

He had the sense she did not enjoy his humor.

"Miss Iverson reviewed your resume and is interested in meeting with you. She has scheduled interviews with candidates for this Friday and has an opening at 10 a.m. Are you available?"

He did not like the sound of candidates referred to in the plural wanting to believe that he would have no competition given his service record. But, better to be in than out.

"If you give me the address, I'll be there."

"The office is located in Simsbury at the Metro Plaza on Hopmeadow, third floor."

"Where on the third floor?"

"Iverson & Hunt is the third floor." So much for a stupid question.

"See you Friday."

"We look forward to meeting you."

He hoped he was mistaken when she noted "we" will be looking forward to meeting you, not "I" am looking forward to meeting you. So much for his dream of landing a blond, if not the job. He hoped that Ms. Gretchen Iverson would be more enthusiastic than Darlene.

As Friday approached, he gave thought as to what he would wear to the session. He knew how to dress for a military interview; full dress uniform. But in business everyone dressed as though they were on vacation. At Global, if you were not meeting face to face with a customer, you dressed casually. Some of the women dressed for beach volleyball. He decided that Gretchen may as well see the authentic Vinnie Pagano. He chose tan slacks, loafers, blue blazer and a dress shirt open at the neck. Casual, dull like an insurance executive or a vacationing lawyer on Cape Cod in August.

The drive to Simsbury was a short one from his home in West Hartford. Metro Plaza was new, only a year or two old. It did not appear to house many businesses. It was an expansive three story building, shimmering glass and bright stainless steel, set out by itself on a beautiful parcel of manicured land with a spectacular view of Avon Mountain and Heublein Tower to the East. The tower was built by Gilbert Heublein, a German born hotelier and restaurant innovator as a summer home.

Vinnie knew, from living in the area, that Avon Mountain was in fact a ridge approximately nine hundred feet above sea level that ran from New Haven, Connecticut north for fifty or sixty miles up into Northampton, Massachusetts, the home of that female bastion of liberal education, Smith College. The Avon-Simsbury-Bloomfield sections of the ridge were well known because of Gilbert Heublein's Tower which was built at the highest elevation of the ridge. On a clear day you could see as far as Boston from the top of the Tower. During World War II there were rumors that German agents secretly used the tower to communicate with Nazi Germany. During the cold war the ridge housed a launch bunker for intercontinental missiles which were secured in silos in other parts of the country.

Vinnie parked close to the building and walked to the entrance. The expansive parking lot was more than half full. In addition to Iverson & Hunt Investigations, there were two other names discretely listed in smaller font in gold leaf on the glass doors. The first was Private Security Services, LLC. The second was Advanced Technology Systems, Inc. The names raised questions at the outset of Vinnie's foray into the world of civilian investigation.

The lobby was expansive, open, with a polished white marble floor. On three sides glass walls soared from the floor to the full ceiling height of thirty feet. On the fourth side of the lobby the first twelve vertical feet of the wall was solid and then glass reached to the ceiling. Set approximately forty feet back from the entrance were two elevators, one on each side of a large, expensive, chrome and glass reception desk with an equally expensive looking receptionist. She was smiling at him as he entered. He smiled back and was already in love with Iverson & Hunt. With the exception of two upholstered side chairs without arms, one on each side of the desk, there was no other furniture in the lobby. Visitors to Metro Plaza were not encouraged to sit. The impression was one of cool, orderly, clean, quiet and understated. It was an updated art deco scene. It could be a little intimidating to someone the least bit insecure.

Missing was any apparent sense of security. There was no guard and no surveillance cameras that Vinnie could detect. He thought this odd for a new building that housed an investigative firm, a security business, and a high tech operation. What he did observe was an attractive, smiling, friendly looking receptionist. He approached her desk and before he could utter a word, she said, "You must be Mr. Pagano. Ms. Iverson is expecting you."

"And, what would you say if I told you I am not Mr. Pagano?"

"There is no chance you are not Mr. Pagano."

He flashed his best smile, "How can that be since you have never seen me before? And, I certainly would have remembered any encounter with you."

"I have your photograph on my computer screen and have looked at it from time to time since you made your appointment with Ms. Iverson."

"And what did your looking tell you?"

"That you are who you say you are."

"And that is?"

"Mr. Vinnie Pagano."

"Would you have a problem showing me what is on your screen?"

"Not at all."

He made his way around the desk and could not help looking at her. She was gorgeous. All he could think about was seeing her without any clothes. His stare was obvious.

"You did want to look at the screen?"

He would have preferred to say, "No, I would rather look at you," but he didn't. He needed to be on his best behavior. This was a job interview and he knew from experience that the assessment made by the first person you meet is an important step in being judged. Iverson & Hunt would confer with her. Instead, he stuttered, "Yuh."

He was on the screen in full Captain's uniform. It was his official U.S. Army photograph. It was taken at the ceremony when he was promoted as a result of his work in Afghanistan. He stared at the screen and had to admit that he looked pretty damn good. Could see why this receptionist would be impressed. He had to acknowledge that Gretchen Iverson knew her business and she did not hesitate to demonstrate it to him before they met. She was prepared for this interview. Yet, having lived for five years in situations where security was a number one concern, twenty four hours a day, he was puzzled as to why there was no security in the lobby considering the three businesses in the facility.

He returned to the front of the desk. It was then he took notice of the name of the receptionist. Debra Johnson.

"Debra, thanks for allowing me to see the screen. I should tell you that I look more impressive in my combat uniform than I do in that dress uniform."

"You look quite impressive in your dress uniform, Mr. Pagano."

"Please, call me Vinnie."

"I'm sorry but the firm has specific protocols as they relate to clients."

He thought about her using the designation "firm," but moved on. "But, I am not a client. Just an ex. Army officer looking for work."

"In that case, Vinnie, I will call you Vinnie."

"Perhaps a drink after work?"

"I believe you will be late for your appointment with Ms. Iverson if you don't move along. She does not suffer well those who are late."

He did not hear any response to the invitation for a drink and she was not wearing a wedding ring.

"By all means, we do not want her to suffer."

"Correct, you do not want her to suffer."

"Where to?"

"Elevator on the right."

"What floor?"

"The elevator is programmed."

"Smart elevator."

"Very smart."

"And once I get to wherever it is I am going?"

"Darlene will be there to greet you."

"I look forward to meeting her."

With no response from Debra, he set off for the elevator wondering what her silence indicated. Was there something about Darlene he should know? He was soon to find out.

CHAPTER 4

LADY IN CHARGE

The elevator on the right only lifted to the third floor. It meant that Private Security Services and Advanced Technology Systems shared the elevator on the left. Which company was on the first floor and which was on the second? Vinnie made a mental note to remind himself to ask Debra about that when he returned to the lobby.

The elevator had no floor buttons. As soon as he stepped in, the door closed and in ten seconds or less the doors opened and a woman was standing there. He assumed it was Darlene. He was in love! Again. She was without a doubt a beautiful woman. Not sexy, not leggy, but beautifully classic. She was wearing an Armani suit, Jimmy Choo shoes and a cream colored blouse. Her makeup was discrete, quiet, and soft. Vinnie judged her height at five foot nine or ten, weight about one hundred twenty five. Her physical condition spoke of daily workouts and a regimented diet. Men must line up to be with her. This is what he hoped Ms. Gretchen Iverson would look like. Darlene would be hard to beat.

"Captain Pagano, I am Darlene."

No last name. Just Darlene. Safer that way. No kooks checking her out. Her first name was enough for any guy. Perhaps it was only a stage name to throw everyone off. Her voice was silken, smooth, and disarming.

"It's no longer Captain, Darlene. I retired and am now simply Mr. Pagano. Vinnie if you like."

"The firm is respectful of retired military personnel and insists that we use official military titles even if the person is no longer in uniform." She was the second person to use the terminology, "the firm." Was there more here than is seen?

"I commend the company. Ex military are not often respected." He chose not to use the term "firm."

"All former military personnel, whether federal, state or local are given status with us."

"Pleased to hear that."

"Ms. Iverson is ready to meet with you. Please follow me."

You would have to be out of your mind not to follow Darlene hoping that at some point she would stop, turn, and invite you into her bed. However, it was clear to him that this scenario was but a dream. They turned right and passed several offices situated on one side of the central core. The walls in the corridor were floor to ceiling glass so that anyone working in the offices was visible from the corridor. Each office looked out onto open space; each was a first class facility and each was occupied. It was obvious that Gretchen's office was at the far end of the corridor and, given the orientation of the building, it must have a spectacular view of the ridge line and the tower to the east. He wondered who had the office at the opposite end of the corridor. But, who or what was Private Security Services and Advanced Technology Systems?

When they reached the end of the corridor, the wall looking into Gretchen's office was floor to ceiling glass and a woman was visible at her desk. The organization literally operated in the open. Darlene stopped. Vinnie stopped. She said, "I will leave you here. Enter and introduce yourself to Ms. Iverson." The she turned and returned the way they had come. He detected smugness about Darlene as though she was enjoying herself at his expense, which she was.

He opened the door and entered. Ms. Iverson rose from her desk and came forward. "Captain Pagano, I am Gretchen Iverson. It is a pleasure to meet you. Your credentials are impressive. Please, have a seat."

He immediately took a liking to her. She gave a positive and professional impression. There was a quiet and refined graciousness about her.

"Thank you."

She came around her desk and they sat across from each other in matching chairs. As formal as she appeared in her greeting, this meeting was structured as an informal conversation designed by her to learn as much as possible about Vinnie and to share with him as little as possible about the organization. This was to be a contest between two intelligence agents sparring intellectually with one another. He liked this woman. It was a great way to start.

In spite of the casual setting, he initially had trouble concentrating. The military taught him to maintain focus, never be distracted and here he was in the role of the nervous interviewee. Why? Iverson was as polite and welcoming as any job candidate could want or expect. It was only when she spoke again that he regained his composure.

"I read your short email expressing an interest in Iverson & Hunt Investigations. I also read your resume. You have had an interesting career for such a young man."

He couldn't help but take note that she emphasized "young" from the resume. How old is she?

"I don't know if it is interesting or simply atypical."

"Well then, let's talk about it. First, you struggled to graduate from high school and then had an outstanding community college career. You went on to graduate magna cum laude from the University of Massachusetts with one major in psychology and a second one in Italian. Then, you made what appeared to be an irrational jump into the Army. You completed several tours of duty in Iraq, Afghanistan and Pakistan as an intelligence officer with the military police. And now you are on a new tour of duty with those you referred to in your email as 'the walking dead' at Global Insurance. Is that about it?"

"Sounds like an endorsement for a best seller."

"Who knows?"

"What I do know, Ms. Iverson, is that I am bored at Global and miss investigative work."

"Tell me about your work with the military police."

"I will share with you what I can. The military police designation was something of a cover because of the nature of my real assignment."

"And what was your real assignment?"

"I led teams of young men and women into situations where only the brave and well trained survived. It was what we refer to as extraction work."

"And exactly what is extraction work?"

"Most Americans know that our combat troops, in all branches of the military, have had a long history of always attempting to bring back their wounded and dead. It is a tradition that encourages our troops to risk their lives knowing that if anything happens to them, they or their remains will be brought home to their families. Soldiers need to know they will not be left behind. As traditions go, it sounds great. I emphasize that an 'attempt' is made. We did not always succeed."

She asked a question the answer to which she knew. "And, what happens to your comrades if you did not succeed?"

He had to stop for a moment as he thought of his team members risking their lives and facing death to uphold this tradition. They knew that in attempting to extract others that they could be the ones left behind.

"There are some aspects of failure it is best you do not know, at least not yet."

"I accept that. Please tell me what you are cleared to talk about."

He continued. "There are times when it is impossible for a combat unit to bring out its dead and wounded. War is not scripted, there is no playbook. The enemy has its own plans. All too often the surviving troops are so badly injured they are unable to help themselves let alone their wounded buddies. They have all they can do to remove themselves from danger. Other times, there is no easy way for troops to move their dead and wounded because of the conditions of the battlefield or because there are no land vehicles, helicopters, boats or whatever transport is required."

He hesitated as he remembered the two members of one of his teams who died while on an extraction mission. Two members in twenty seven missions did not sound statistically bad unless it was you who did not make it. Carlos was twenty and Roberta was twenty two. Both were high school dropouts who found a home in the Army. They had survived the demanding training cycle and between then had participated in fourteen missions. Vinnie had personally carried Roberta's body two miles to safety and his second in command, Timothy Ryan, had done likewise with Carlos.

He continued, "When this scenario plays out, the military assigns special teams to move in and extract men and women who cannot help themselves and whose buddies are unable to bring them home. Timing is critical. These teams, small in number, are on alert whenever an impending battle or engagement was to take place. They were able to move into combat zones, often in a matter of minutes, depending upon where they were located. Those who volunteered for this work had special training in extraction, hand to hand combat and the use of a variety of weapons. They were physically fit, able to lift and carry a wounded or dead soldier a great distance and willing to risk their own lives for others. The work was not for the faint of heart. The public has little or no knowledge of units like those I led. They usually heard about the system the military used to extract downed pilots. Every American has seen movies dealing with helicopter rescues, especially during Viet Nam. Rarely did any of my teams have that luxury."

He stopped and looked at her. There was nothing more to add.

"And, was that the sum total of your work?"

"It is a fair description."

"What haven't you told me, Captain?"

He hesitated before responding. "I shared with you what I am authorized to talk about."

"I believe that 'extraction' work is somewhat more expansive and dangerous than you have described."

He did not respond.

She continued. "Did you not 'extract' those other than your comrades?"

"I told you what I did in the Army, Ms. Iverson. There is little more I can tell you."

"Fair enough."

"Can we talk about Iverson & Hunt?"

"Certainly. What would you like to know?"

"I understand from your secretary that you are interviewing or have interviewed several others for this position. I am curious as to why you decided to interview me? I barely meet the State of Connecticut criteria for 'detective'. "

"You are right about barely qualifying for 'detective' but your military experience is impressive. You are modest, Captain, regarding your work. You were something of a hero. Had you remained in the Army you were scheduled to jump two pay grades and be promoted to full Colonel. That is not a typical promotion route."

"Few knew of that promotion."

"Our firm is well connected with leaders of the military/industrial complex. We have friends in high places. I made several inquiries once I read your resume. I liked what I saw and I liked what I heard from those who worked with you or knew of your work, including some members of your teams."

Again, he did not respond.

"You were a hero to your men and to those whose lives you saved. Not to mention the gratitude of the government for extracting enemy combatants. Your work is legend in the military."

"My team was made up of both men and women."

"I stand corrected, Captain.

"I prefer to be called Vinnie. And you?"

"Gretchen will do nicely."

"Given that you are now enamored with my background, am I'm hired?"

"Not yet. Until my partner has an opportunity to meet you and form a second opinion, we will make no decision."

"And just who is 'we'? Is there a Hunt?"

"There is a Hunt."

With that, Gretchen rose from her chair and headed out of the office. He followed without comment. As they walked the length of the building in the opposite direction from her office, he noticed that the offices on the periphery were occupied by "management looking" men and women who were casually dressed. The middle section of the floor was literally filled with wall to wall computers, hundreds of them. There was more to this than Gretchen had let on.

Time would tell.

CHAPTER 5

THE PARTNER

The wall at Hunt's office was similar to that of Gretchen's, all glass. Visitors were able to look in and observe the occupant. Each end of the building was a mirror image of the other. The expensive executive chair behind the expensive executive desk was occupied, but the occupant had a back to Vinnie and Gretchen and there was no way to see who was sitting quietly looking out to Avon Mountain.

Gretchen stopped outside Hunt's door and spoke. "Vinnie, I will leave you here. Ms. Hunt is waiting for you. She and I are the principal partners. She is as tough and ruthless as she is beautiful. Should things work out such that we hire you, don't make the mistake that most men do and let your testosterone run ahead of your brain when dealing with her. In many important ways, she is more experienced than you. And while it is none of your business, I will say it anyway. She has a partner."

For one of the few times in his career, he was left speechless. What in hell was that about? Gretchen gave him a warm smile, turned and left. Vinnie realized that he had not made any judgments about her, Gretchen, that is. And that was unlike him. He knew he needed to do this. Soon, before he was offered the job, a job he knew would be offered.

He opened the door and entered.

Before he could utter a word, the chair slowly swiveled and Darlene, the off limits Darlene, stood and came forward. "Welcome, Captain, I'm Darlene Hunt." With that she extended her hand. He found it cool and strong to the touch.

Holding her hand and looking directly at her, Vinnie hesitated and then spoke. "Do you always pretend to be someone other than who are when greeting candidates?" He released her hand.

"I did not pretend to be anyone other than an employee of Iverson & Hunt when I greeted you. That temporary role did not exclude my being someone or something else."

"If you say so." He had a definite edge to his voice. He was not happy with the turn of events.

"Please have a seat." She sensed she had a tough guy in her office.

Darlene's office was a mirror image of Gretchen's. The building was a large rectangle with the entire length of the structure running parallel to Avon Mountain in the rear and the parking areas in the front. Offices were located on both sides of a central corridor. Between the rear of the building and the mountain was a large manicured field of grass interrupted only by discretely placed and beautifully manicured flower gardens.

The two corner offices occupied by Gretchen and Darlene were located at the rear of the building, one at each end. They had glass walls on all four sides. One side faced the mountain, the second faced the corridor, the third faced either north or south depending upon which office you had, and the fourth faced the adjoining office. In the case of Gretchen's office, the fourth glass wall faced north toward the town of Simsbury. Darlene's fourth wall faced south onto farmland in Avon. The view from the huge windows at the rear of both offices was magnificent. It must be nothing short of spectacular in the winter when snow covered the field and the ridge line.

The summer months brought warm air currents to the valley. Occupants of the rear offices could observe colorful hang gliders sliding off a wooden platform anchored to the ridge and floating down into and around the valley like beautiful butterflies. Once the warm air began to cool in the late afternoon, the gliders would make graceful landings on the property close to Gretchen and Darlene.

"Gretchen made it clear that you had to pass judgment on me before any hiring decision was made." Once again, there was a hard edge to his voice. He was unable to mask his displeasure with Darlene.

"That is correct."

"On what basis will you make your judgment?"

"What do you suggest?"

"How about starting with the only matter that must be important to you?

"And what is that?"

"Since you know what I did in the Army, the only quality you seek in me is the ability to take on a job and destroy anyone who stands in my way to accomplishing an assignment for you. And if necessary, to kill them."

"What makes you think we are interested in that skill set?"

"Skill set? Let's not play around with semantics, Ms. Hunt. It was not the fact that I barely qualified for the Connecticut detective license that interested you in me. You and Gretchen read my resume, made a few phone calls, were both shocked and pleased when you learned of my unique military experience and immediately knew you had the person needed for your next adventure whatever it may be. You lied about having other candidates. You had no intention of interviewing anyone other than me. We can forget the ad in the paper in which you advertised for a run of the mill detective. You need me. I do not need you. So, if you are finished with the theatrics, let's get down to business."

"And what is that?"

"To start with, let's talk compensation."

CHAPTER 6

WALKOUT

"What makes you think we have anything in mind for you?"

He spoke softly. "As I just said, you and Gretchen did not go through this charade just for the hell of it. While I have already grown to dislike you, I also appreciate the fact you are smart and ruthless. Gretchen? She may be even smarter. Ruthless, I do not know. But whatever the case, you have discussed my background and decided you need me. So, what do you have in mind? An extraction? An assassination? A kidnapping? We can discuss these possibilities after we settle compensation."

She wanted to smack Vinnie but stayed on course. "We know what your salary is at Global. If you are hired, we are prepared to match it plus a twenty five percent increase and a small signing bonus."

He looked at her with distain, got up from his chair and walked slowly toward the door without any comment.

She called to him. "Where are you going?"

"Where does it look like?"

"I do not understand."

"Of course you do. You can't play good cop bad cop with a real cop."

"And what is that supposed to mean?"

"It means that you make a ridiculous offer, I walk out. Gretchen calls later today or tomorrow and offers a substantial increase over your offer and apologizes for your staged conduct and rudeness."

"You really are an insolent son of a bitch."

"At the moment, I am an insolent son of a bitch. Goodbye Ms. Hunt."

With that he left the office, walked the half length of the corridor, entered the elevator and floated down to the lobby. He gave Debra his best smile and left the building. Once in his car, he realized just how pissed he was. But he was also controlled. He had two entrepreneurs playing good cop, bad cop with a guy who had lived through the worst shit one can imagine. Four tours of duty, death waiting at every step, shattered bodies and blood and guts over your hands and body. Brave young men and women sacrificing their lives while Gretchen and Darlene polished their nails back home. And, now, they were trying to play with his head. He smiled knowing they had finally met their match. They had no idea they were playing with fire.

Vinnie left the parking lot and headed back to Global in Hartford. He'd taken half a personal day in the morning and figured to return for the afternoon sessions that were scheduled with three national Directors who covered the mid-west, far-west, and southwest for Global. Essentially, they were highly paid con men and women whose job was to sell insurance and then find every excuse under the sun to refuse to pay legitimate claims. Regardless of their title on the organizational chart, job one was to terrorize subordinates who had sales quotas to meet. Either they met them or they walked the corporate plank.

That afternoon he met separately with the three walking dead. While in the Army, Vinnie supervised nineteen and twenty year olds with more common sense than any of these stiffs. Not to mention that his men and women developed more leadership ability after twelve weeks of military training than these three possessed after several years of indoctrination by Global instructors. He knew first hand that the military knows how to train men and women. No bullshit, no fancy resorts with two short lectures a day, no golf lessons, no spas for the mistresses and no cocktails followed by dinner and a night of screwing. In the Army, schooling was serious business.

Vinnie was convinced that by the time he returned to the office Gretchen would have called. She did. He did not return the call.

CHAPTER 7

SHARON

He worked until after six which was later than usual, especially for a Monday. When leaving, he took note that Sharon Rizzo, secretary to his boss, Evan Knight, was still at her desk. He had to pass by her to reach the elevators. Vinnie found her to be pleasant enough whenever they had business to conduct, which was seldom. She was always willing to help. There was no talk about her in the office, none of the unusual gossip that was the mainstay of any large organization. Whispering about each other at the water cooler was part and parcel of business life. And, so it was at Global.

The only talk he did hear was that Sharon had been married for a short time to a super star in the company's investment department. She had come to Global after earning an associate degree from Tunxis Community College and within a few weeks had met and fallen for Tim Whitlock. In addition to being wealthy in his own right, he was a fair haired boy in the company and a top investment officer. He was considered a catch, sex wise and business wise, both in the company and out. What Sharon didn't know was that he had a reputation as a philanderer long before she met him and he continued the practice after their marriage. Once she discovered that he was sleeping around she filed for divorce, ended up with a world class settlement, took back her maiden name and continued as a secretary at Global. Other than formal contacts with her when he had to see his boss, who was also her boss, there was limited contact between them. The word was that her divorce settlement was such that she did not have to ever work again. She loved her work, however, and decided to continue at Global.

After he shut down his computer, turned out the lights and locked his desk, he headed for the elevators. Sharon heard him and looked up. She offered a bright smile and a "good night Vinnie." He looked at her and offered his own "good night Sharon." Looking at her, he judged her age at twenty two or twenty three. "See you tomorrow."

He headed for the elevator, pushed the down button and waited. While he stood listening to the elevator rising in the shaft he decided that it had been one hell of a day and what he really wanted and needed was company, pleasant company unrelated to his job search. He turned and walked back to Sharon's desk. She looked up somewhat surprised, but with her lovely smile. "Forget something?"

"As a matter of fact I did."

"Anything I can help with?"

"I would really like it if you were to close up shop and have dinner with me."

She looked straight into his eyes, briefly looked away as though she was thinking, and then returned her gaze to him. "Is this an invitation for a date?"

"No. It is an invitation to have dinner with a colleague who could use the company of a lovely woman, no strings attached."

"Bad day?"

"Real bad, but I could recover nicely with you as my guest at dinner."

"You have been here over a year and have never so much as had a social conversation with me. Now dinner?"

"I have not had much to say with anyone while here."

"Why is that?"

"I'll give you the answer at dinner."

"Give me five minutes to close up."

"Sharon, where are you parked?"

"On the fifth level. Why?"

"It will be late when we return from dinner, not a good hour of the night to enter the garage alone. Let's walk downtown to dinner. When we get back, I will pick up my car on the first level and drive you to yours. I'll feel better if I know you are safely on your way. By the way, dinner is on me."

"Sounds good to me."

CHAPTER 8

TROUBLE

They made their way to Adriana's restaurant. Vinnie had eaten there a few times and always had a good experience. It was a pleasant setting and tonight it had a small but vibrant crowd in the dining room. The bar, however, was wall to wall humanity. Most of the patrons looked under thirty five with men outnumbering women at least three to one. The odds favored the women if they could stand the pawing. Everyone looked like they either practiced law or sold securities. Vinnie considered both to be on a par with insurance salesmen.

He asked the hostess to seat them in either a booth or a quiet spot. She obliged and elected a booth. A booth on one side of them was occupied. The booth on the other side was vacant. Perfect for talking. Sharon drew more than a few complimentary stares from both men and women as they were shown to their booth. Walking in front of Vinnie, he took note that she was five nine or five ten, a hundred twenty five pounds, blessed with a lovely figure, nice legs, tight ass and a naturally attractive stride.

Once seated, "You owe me an answer to the question as to why you have had little to do with me and most everyone except Evan. A year is a long time to be detached from your colleagues."

"Sharon, they are not colleagues. I do not like my work, find most days a trial and have not found anyone with whom I wanted to spend any serious time with. Tonight being the exception."

They were interrupted when the waitress returned to take orders. Sharon ordered a cosmopolitan. Vinnie ordered a Knob Creek on the rocks.

"You have not had much to do with me other than when you have an appointment with Evan."

"That doesn't mean I haven't noticed."

"And what is it that you noticed?"

"It is what I failed to notice until now. Astonishing brown eyes, great features, lovely complexion, beautiful smile and a demeanor that is welcoming and friendly. Not to mention a man stopping figure."

She changed the subject.

"Why don't you like your work? You seem to be doing well. Personnel I have spoken with have been impressed with you. If you were not effective in screening senior staff for leadership qualities the company would have let you go."

"The truth is, after my previous life, this work is boring, actually mind numbing. I need more excitement in my work."

"Why don't you look for that work?"

"The fact is I am looking. Thought I had something wrapped up today but one of the partners was playing games with me. I walked out on her."

"Do you always walk out when things do not go your way?"

He wanted very much to tell her about his military career. Not only did he never walk away from action he did not like; he sought out the tough assignments. When you have the skill you want to use it. How do you tell that to someone you really just met and who knows nothing about you. He looked into her deep brown eyes and told himself that one day I would tell her more. But, not tonight.

He decided that it was his turn to change the subject.

"How about you, why do you work here? You must have had other opportunities. Working for an insurance company can be boring as the devil."

"I met my former husband here. Our marriage was a mistake. After the divorce it was comforting to return to an environment that I knew. I wouldn't have done so if my ex hadn't been transferred to Global's British subsidiary in London. It is unlikely he will ever return here. As far as I know, no one in the department has had anything to do with him since he left. He has a prominent position at the London office. When he was here, he and Evan were colleagues, but not friends. How about you? Ever married?"

He had the feeling that Sharon was about to change the subject again.

"I went directly into the Army after college. Military life is not conducive to marriage. It isn't conducive to any relationship except with members of your team. Since I returned to civilian life the opportunity to meet women has been limited."

"You are surrounded by women, the percentage being three or four to one. It would not be difficult to find any number who would be attracted to you or you to them."

"When you are not happy in your work you tend to lose interest in most everything within the environment. Once out of here and settled into a new job there will be a better balance to my life."

"We had better order. It is getting late."

He got the attention of the waitress and they ordered a light dinner. They chatted throughout and the time flew by. It was close to nine thirty and Sharon signaled that it was time for her to head home. The walk back to the office building and parking garage was comfortable with little talking and a lot of thinking by both of them. Without saying so, it was clear they had a pleasant evening. He wanted to see her again and believed she felt the same.

His car was parked on the level reserved for executive personnel. She slid into the passenger side and closed the door and he drove her to the fifth level where her car was located. In spite of the late hour there were many cars on that level. It was then Vinnie realized that Global ran three shifts in some departments, especially information technology, billing and international market trading. He pulled into an empty spot several spaces down the ramp from Sharon. They got out of his car and, together, walked up the ramp toward hers. She was pleased with his concern for her safety.

He wanted very much to kiss her goodnight, but thought the better of it. What he didn't know was that if he had made a move on her, she would have willingly accepted. She liked this man. "Vinnie, I had a nice time this evening. Thanks for asking me to dinner."

"Thanks for accepting. Let's do it again."

"Yes, soon."

Just as he reached to open the door to her car, they heard the sound of breaking glass higher up on the ramp on the opposite side from where Sharon was parked. Vinnie waited a minute and then started to walk up the ramp to see what was happening just as two guys came out from behind a car carrying a briefcase and a laptop computer that they had stolen from the car. Sharon had also walked up behind Vinnie. The smaller of the two men was holding an automatic pistol in his right hand. He was five seven or eight, slight build, pockmarked face and had a pony tail. He wore a black t-shirt, dirty jeans, heavy black boots and sported a tattoo on his right arm.

The second guy was much bigger and taller. Vinnie figured him at six one or two, one hundred ninety to two hundred ten pounds, muscular. His hair was a dark greasy brown combed straight back, no part. He wore a long sleeve denim shirt, khaki pants and cowboy boots.

As the two guys walked slowly toward Vinnie and Sharon, the smaller guy with the gun spoke to this partner. "Tommy boy, look at what we have here, Barbie Doll and Ken. She looks ready for fucking and he's about to shit his pants."

"Ritchie, I think you have it right. Since I'm running this fucking show, I get to fuck her first. You get leftovers. From the looks of her there will be enough." Tommy then put the briefcase and computer on the ground. Sharon, having read Vinnie's file and aware of his war record was nervous, but not alarmed. She knew that without the gun these two thugs were no match for him. Distracting Ritchie who had the gun was the key. If she could do that for Vinnie, they had a good chance of getting out of this unharmed.

Ritchie slowly headed for Vinnie, all the time making threatening gestures with the gun. Tommy, the big guy, headed for Sharon. When he was in front of her, he reached out with his left hand and grabbed her right breast. Ritchie called out, “Go for it man!” At that exact moment Sharon let go a strong kick to Tommy’s left shin. The sharp point of her Jimmy Choo high heel shoe punctured his skin and drew blood. It was a strategy that she had learned from a seminar on self defense that Global required of all employees. Before Tommy could react, she delivered two more swift kicks to the same area, this time hitting bone. He bent down from the pain and yelled, “You fucking bitch, I’ll kill you for that.”

Ritchie, having heard Tommy yell from the pain and swearing at Sharon, was momentarily distracted by looking at his partner. Vinnie reached out, grabbed Ritchie’s right wrist and savagely twisted it to the left until he heard the elbow being separated and the gun drop to the floor. While Ritchie screamed with pain, Vinnie drove his right hand into his face breaking his nose and crushing teeth. Ritchie flew backward on to the pavement where he moaned in excruciating pain. All of this happened in fifteen seconds.

Tommy turned toward Vinnie and seeing Ritchie lying in pain on the pavement with blood all over his face and chin was about to call it quits when Vinnie drove his right fist into his chest with the power of a heavyweight boxer. Ribs cracked and Tommy doubled over, his hands pressed against his chest trying to quell the pain from the blow. Vinnie then coupled both his hands together, intertwined his fingers, and drove his hands up and under Tommy’s chin. There was the sound of a jaw braking and teeth disintegrating. A final blow to the nose and blood was everywhere. Tommy fell to the ground.

Sharon looked both in awe and in horror at the human destruction Vinnie inflicted on the two thugs in only a minute or two. Vinnie spoke first. "Are you okay?"

In a whisper she spoke. "I'm okay but did you have to hurt them this much?"

"Once they raped you until they had no more to give, they would have either kept you for a daily gang rape or killed you. And next week another woman and then another. The answer, Sharon, is yes I had to hurt them so they'll never assault any woman again."

"What now?"

"Now you get in your car and go home. Be careful to stay on the other side of the ramp. I don't want any blood on your tires. I'll call tomorrow. And, Sharon, that was gutsy of you to take on Tommy and give me an opening."

"I read your resume and knew they were no match for you if I could distract them. What are you going to do now?"

"I'm going to clean up the mess."

"Vinnie, I'm sorry for that comment about hurting them. It's just that I have never seen men fight before. Thank you for saving me from being accosted or worse." With that, she gave him a kiss on the cheek, got into her car and drove off.

Vinnie picked up the gun lying on the ramp, released the magazine, put it in his pocket and walked over to the three foot high concrete barrier that formed the wall of the garage. He turned the gun upside down, held it by the end of the barrel and slammed the slide several times into the concrete rendering the weapon useless. To be absolutely certain it would not be used again, he held the gun in a normal position in his right hand and smashed the bottom of the barrel into the concrete barrier. Next, he wiped the gun clean with his handkerchief, walked over to the guy called Ritchie who was still on the ground, leaned down and stuffed the gun into his pant pocket.

He stood, walked over to the second guy, Tommy, who was also on the ground. "I heard you tell your buddy that you are the man in charge. Well, man in charge, get on your feet."

"I can't. I'm hurt fucking bad."

"You don't know what bad is, Mr. Man in charge. Get on your feet, drag your buddy into whatever you drove to get here and head out of town."

"I'll get you for this." That was a mistake.

By now Tommy had struggled to his feet, unsteady but standing. Vinnie walked over to him, looked him in the eyes and with his left hand grabbed him by the throat, squeezed and held tight. Tommy's breathing slowed, he coughed, and his eyes bulged and began to glaze over. He lifted his arms in a gesture of helplessness but Vinnie held on until Tommy was close to unconscious. Then he released his grip and Tommy began to breathe again but the look of absolute panic and the dreadful fear of death did not leave his face. He knew with certainty that this guy called Vinnie Pagano would like an excuse for killing him and Ritchie for threatening the woman with rape.

Without a word Tommy staggered over to Ritchie, pulled him to his feet and they both stumbled to their car. They were human wrecks. Tommy got behind the wheel and drove down the ramp and out of the garage. And out of town for good. Vinnie went to his car, opened the trunk, searched around and finally pulled out the handle to the tire jack. He walked over to where the stolen goods were sitting on the ground and inserted the jack handle carefully into the handles of both the briefcase and the laptop computer case and carried them over to the car they were stolen from. He reached through the broken rear window on the passenger side and placed both cases on the rear seat. The only fingerprints on the cases were those of Tommy and the owner.

Returning to his car Vinnie placed the jack handle back into the trunk. In spite of the heavy human damage there was little evidence of the fight. Most of the blood was absorbed by the dirt on the ramp. What little evidence remained would quickly be ground down and contaminated when cars left the garage after the night shift and when employees arrived in the morning. Sharon was safe, the briefcase and computer were back where they belonged, Tommy and Ritchie were on their way out of town, the gun was rendered useless, the police were not involved and Vinnie was back in action. It felt good.

He left the garage and went home. Afghanistan all over.

CHAPTER 9

IVERSON & HUNT

Tuesday had been a long day and sleep came easily. He was wakened with a call around eight a.m It went on to the answering machine. It was from Gretchen. "Vinnie, this is Gretchen. I know you are upset. I would like to explain. None of what occurred was by accident. We used a protocol that has been used with many of our interviewees. This was poor judgment on our part. It failed to consider your experience, your maturity and military background. Please call."

He had planned on thinking about Sharon for a while, reflecting on last night and the comfort level they had in being in each other's company. Nothing happened, yet much happened. He needed and wanted to see her again. But, not today. Today he needed to think about Gretchen's call.

Iverson & Hunt. It was rich sounding like a Fifth Avenue art gallery, nice flow to the words, the gold leaf lettering on the lobby door, two statuesque partners. He wondered if Iverson was Iverson and if Hunt was Hunt. The names sounded manufactured. They were names that a clandestine federal agency would create. And, of course, they would develop all of the necessary paperwork to prove they were who they purported to be. Iverson had a Nordic, stately ring to it, smooth like a boat ride on an Amsterdam canal. Hunt sounded intriguing, strong and formidable, projecting a sense of security.

Iverson & Hunt needs you. He recalled the military slogan, "The Army Needs You." But who left the ad? Someone at Global suggesting he leave? Wrong desk? Was it for one of the other administrators? Insurance companies have a shit load of investigators, most of them dealing with trivial insurance claims. The ad had a nice ring about it and would be attractive to many investigators and detectives who wanted to deal with more exciting matters and for greater compensation. The night cleaning crew, the maintenance guys?

He spent the morning looking for information on Iverson & Hunt. When he visited Gretchen and Darlene there was much activity on the third floor. At the time he didn't think to visit the first and second floors where Private Security Services LLC and Advanced Technology Systems, Inc. were located. He would have to enter the building illegally at night since there was no way to discretely check those floors during the day. Nothing prevented him from asking Gretchen. But that could wait until he learned more about Iverson & Hunt.

He called Sharon at Global. She answered on the second ring. "Sharon speaking. May I help you?"

"Sharon, this is Vinnie. I decided to take some personal time today. Wanted to let you know in case Evan asks for me. I have some business to tend to. It is possible that I could be in by late afternoon but I don't want anyone to plan on it. My calendar was for in-house paper work. There are no appointments."

"Evan is also out today so I do not think you will be missed."

"So much for being important."

"Meant nothing by it. I hope you have a profitable day with whatever it is you are up to."

"This is a business call otherwise I would ask you out. Not a good idea to mix business with pleasure. But if you were to give me your home phone number I will call tonight and ask."

She gave it to him and he promised to call.

The first stop was at the Simsbury Town Hall. When he asked the town clerk for the name of the owner of Metro Plaza, she referred him to the tax collector. Rachel Blackstone, who he later learned had been the collector for more than twenty years, took the question in stride and immediately retrieved the tax information card for Metro Plaza. She was a young looking veteran of municipal government. Must have started right out of high school.

The owner of Metro Plaza was a Bermudian corporation named Highland Properties located in Hamilton, Bermuda. The contact name on the tax information card was a law firm, also in Bermuda, that handled Highland Properties legal matters and their overseas investments. The tax bill was sent to Bean, Choate & Whitehall, Solicitors, thirty five Front Street, Hamilton, Bermuda. Bills were paid on time and there was never an issue with the property or taxes as far as Rachel Blackstone knew.

He asked Rachel if she knew what type of work Iverson & Hunt Investigations was involved in. She responded with a slight smile, "Investigations." He said, "Thanks" with an engaging smile and then asked, knowing the answer beforehand, "Do you know the nature of the business for either Private Securities Services or Advanced Technology Systems that are tenants at

Metro Plaza?" Her prize winning smile brought forth, "I do not know." He had the impression she was playing cat and mouse with him and he was the mouse. But, her mischievous smile signaled that she liked this young, handsome man. He was the most interesting person she had dealt with for some time.

She asked, "Is there any particular reason why you are interested in Metro Plaza?"

He lied. "I represent a global company with offices in the United States that is interested in purchasing prime office buildings. Once I learned of the property and had the opportunity to examine it, I knew it was exactly what my company would want in its portfolio. It is an outstanding facility. Before I approach the owner it is important that I learn as much as possible beforehand. Given the prestige of your community and the fantastic location of Metro Plaza with its astonishing view of Avon Mountain, it goes without saying that this property is a prime asset."

"We think so. Simsbury has no problem with limited foreign ownership of properties as long as the property is not degraded in any way."

"I have just one more question if you have the time."

"I have the time. But thanks for asking. Most of my out of town visitors assume I have the time. It is their impression that government employees do not work very hard."

"Having been a government worker for many years, I can appreciate what you are saying."

"The question?"

"In looking over the property this weekend when the building was closed, I noticed there were three tenants; Iverson & Hunt Investigations, Private Security

Services, and Advanced Technology Systems. Since Iverson & Hunt is the only company using personal names, I wonder if you know if there is an Iverson or a Hunt, and if so have you ever met them?"

"I have met Iverson and I know there is a Hunt although I have never met her."

"I know I used up my one question but is there anything you can tell me about them?"

She hesitated for just a moment or two and then responded, "I just realized that you never told me your name."

"Sorry. Did not mean to be evasive. I am Vinnie Pagano and have a driver's license to prove it." She smiled. He immediately wondered if it was a mistake to use his real name. She waved her hand in a gesture to mean that she had no interest in his driver's license.

"Lovely name. As I said, I have not met Ms. Hunt but have heard rumors that she is all business and an accomplished tennis player. She also owns an impressive sailboat in Essex that she uses frequently during the season. On her second husband or was. Miss Iverson is occasionally seen in town during the lunch hour. Like Ms. Hunt, she does not live in town. If I am not mistaken, Iverson lives in West Hartford. No idea where Hunt lives."

"Do you know if Ms. Iverson is married?"

"Do not know that. Have you noticed that you are getting personal about the two partners?"

"Well, I plan on meeting both of them. My company will make an offer for Metro Plaza. It helps to know the players."

"If you have finished with your questions, I should be getting back to work."

It was clear that the inquiries about Iverson & Hunt were at an end. The truth was that he learned more than expected.

"Rachael, I really appreciate your help. If I do extend an offer for my company I will be back to town hall. Lunch will be on me."

"Offer accepted. And, good luck." As he turned to leave, she said to him, "Vinnie, Be careful. The two women about to enter your life didn't get where they are without being talented. And tough, and whatever else it takes to get to the top. You are much too young to get hurt."

"Thanks. I'll be careful."

Vinnie Pagano had the distinct feeling that he had made a friend in Rachel. .

CHAPTER 10

SECURITY AT THE PLAZA

When Vinnie returned to his car he made a cell phone call to Jason Rabinowitz. Jason headed the technology unit for the battalion he and Vinnie were assigned to in Iraq. He left the service shortly after Vinnie and took a job with a software development company in California. Being a mega company, it took several minutes and multiple phone hand-offs before Jason came on the line.

"Don't tell me you want to re-up and take me with you?"

"There are times on this job when I wish I were back with the team. But, at the age of thirty, I am too old. Could not keep up with the youngsters."

"Never too old, Vinnie. If they called, we would be in the air in short order."

"I would rather not think about it just now. Look, Jason, I am being considered for an investigative position and am doing some digging about the company."

"You want me to dig too?"

"Not really. I need something else. On the other hand, let me give you the name of the company and the two partners. The company is Iverson & Hunt Investigations. The partners are Gretchen Iverson and Darlene Hunt. If you have spare time and want to do some 'quiet' research, it will help. But my real purpose in calling you is to ask about security systems."

"I'm listening."

"The office building is two or three years old. Three stories in height. It has wall to wall and floor to ceiling glass. It is basically a glass house. The glass has a slight tint to it, probably for esthetic reasons and, I assume, to reduce glare. The ceiling is hard finished rather than a suspended construction. It has a glossy white painted finish. Recessed lighting, sprinklers and heat and smoke detectors. Nothing else visible. The floors are marble and there is a decided absence of furniture. Two elevators, one only goes to the third floor, the other goes to the second. The whole place is modern and quiet. OK so far?"

"OK."

"What is missing to my eyes or touch are any security devices. No visible cameras, no electric eyes, no pressure pads, no obvious laser or microwave sensors, no old fashioned peep holes, no sensors on the door handles, no retina scans, no anything that I can see. The absence of cameras is the most obvious thing. So what am I missing?"

Jason hesitated for a few seconds. "Tell me about the receptionist. I assume there is one?"

"The receptionist?"

"Yea, the receptionist. Where was she located and what was she wearing?"

Jason was not only a talented techie, but he was a buddy so Vinnie was not about to get into his head.

"She's lovely, her name is Debra, single, located in the center of the lobby behind a clean desk, between both elevators and armed with a phone and computer. When you enter there is no way to miss her and no way would she could miss anyone who entered. She is located dead center in the lobby against the back wall. As I recall, she was simply dressed, little jewelry except for a pendant worn around her neck. Oh, she had a picture of me in dress uniform on the computer which is how she recognized me before I introduced myself."

"Vinnie, were there any doors in the lobby other than those at the elevators?"

"As you look at the receptionist area there is a door to the right of the right side elevator as you are looking at it. It had no signage. I assume it led to a back office. To the left of the receptionist and to the left of the other elevator was a door that had a small sign indicating rest rooms. To the left of the rest room door was another door that was marked, 'First Floor'."

There was a delay in his response. He was thinking.

"Tell me about the glass. Was there any texture, any design?

"Christ, Jason, I wasn't there as a building inspector. How often do you inspect windows?"

"Did you not tell me a minute ago that you wanted to be a sleuth?"

"As best I can recall the glass was clear except for the tint but it may have had a texture."

"One last question. Were there seats for visitors and, if so, where were they located?"

"There were two chairs and they were located just off to either side of the receptionist and angled toward her."

Again, there was a pause. He was pondering over the data.

"The answer to the security question is quite simple. The receptionist is a camera and an effective one at that. My money is on the pendant she wore on her neck. Some of the sprinkler heads are real while others are cameras. She and the sprinklers are the security cameras you did not see. The owners took care to position her desk in the center of the lobby. My guess is that the camera in the pendant probably has a hundred and eighty degree sweep of the lobby. The chairs for visitors are placed to the side so as to not obstruct her view. It literally had you or anyone else in view all of the time except when you went to the restrooms. Anyone's guess what they had there for security. The door to the right of the right elevator most likely led to a locked guard room with monitors and you can rest assured there was a rent-a-cop or two."

"So when she is not in the lobby there is still a back-up security system?"

"My guess is that she is the backup and the sprinklers are the first line of defense. One or more of the heads are cameras. Believe me, Vinnie, if this organization is worth its salt they had you covered one way or the other. The best test is to break into the place and see what happens!"

"Easier said than done."

"Vinnie, are you on something?"

"Not on something, but on to something and not certain what it is. Before you hang up, I have a question about the glass."

"What's the question?"

"It just struck me as unusual that there was so much of it. Not being here it is difficult for you to get a sense, but when I entered, I had the feeling that a thousand eyes were watching. Is that possible?"

"I will do some research to see if the glass could possibly have been a gigantic camera. But if it is, for what purpose? There has to be a simple answer. Unless of course Iverson & Hunt is something other than what they say it is. If that's the case then the glass may be important. I just do not know. But, I will get on it."

"If Iverson & Hunt is something more than advertised, I will find out."

"Listen, I need to get to work. If I am correct about the receptionist, the next time you are in the building she will be wearing either another pendant or some type of label pin that serves the same purpose."

"Thanks Jason. Talk soon."

CHAPTER 11

HIGHLAND PROPERTIES

If you are an investigator or work for the IRS, it is prudent to assume that every company doing business in the states and which has its headquarter and legal counsel off shore has something to hide. There could be a thousand reasons why Metro Plaza and Iverson & Hunt Investigations are the exception but Vinnie was not about to hold his breath. He knew he needed more information.

Tuesday was turning into a very long day for him. But he forged ahead. First he placed a call to Highland Properties in Hamilton, Bermuda. Once the receptionist answered he asked to be put through to the person in charge of property acquisitions. He had no idea if they had an acquisitions officer, but he would soon find out.

"We do not have an acquisitions administrator," answered the very British voice, "but Tony Eden is in charge of capital projects. I will put you through to his office."

Another female British voice answered and he asked to speak to Tony Eden.

"May I tell him who is calling and the reason for the call?"

While driving back to the office he had debated whether to use his own name or a fictitious one in making the two phone calls to Bermuda. There also was the issue of just how much information he should provide. Did he want Gretchen and Darlene to know that he was making inquiries? He had lied to Rachel at town hall as to what he was doing although he did use his own name. Until he could satisfy himself that Iverson & Hunt is what it claims to be, the lying would continue. He felt uncomfortable lying to Rachel but promised himself he would make it up to her. But, for now, he would use a fictitious name.

"My name is David Wilde. I represent a global investment trust that purchases property worldwide. We have an interest in a property in Simsbury, Connecticut that is owned by Highland Properties and would like to make an offer to purchase it."

"Thank you. I will inform Mr. Eden of your interest."

A few minutes passed. He was not optimistic the charade would work. One never knows until one tries. Finally, a male voice answered.

"This is Tony Eden, Mr. Wilde. I understand you are interested in the Simsbury, Connecticut property. I must tell you at the outset that Highland Properties is not interested in selling any of its assets. The Simsbury property is of special interest to our investors."

"I understand you have worldwide holdings only a few of which are in the United States. Surely a single small property in Connecticut cannot be a significant part of your portfolio. Our company has many properties in the states and this would be an addition to our substantial portfolio. We are prepared to offer a generous premium over current market value for the property."

"It is not for sale at any price, Mr. Wilde. But I appreciate you interest. Good day."

With that the line went dead. "Not for sale at any price." Only property in the U.S. and of special interest to their investors. Before Tony Eden could get off a call, Vinnie made his next call to Bean, Choate and Whitehall, attorneys of record and who were also located in Hamilton, Bermuda.

The same routine was followed and finally he spoke to a Mr. Freddie Blair, chief counsel.

"Attorney Blair, my name is David Wilde calling from the Unites States. My firm, international in nature, is interested in a property that has your firm's name listed as the official contact. My company would like to discuss a possible purchase. It is located in Simsbury, Connecticut."

Blair hesitated before responding. "Why do you have an interest in this property? As I recall, it is a small facility hardly worth the attention of an international group. What company did you say you represent?"

"I didn't but it is a private equity group in which the partners wish to remain anonymous until such time as a purchase is about to be consummated. I'm sure you understand. We are prepared to make a very generous offer, well above its market value. It is a property that will fit nicely into our portfolio."

Vinnie waited while Freddie Blair prepared a response. Neither he nor Highland Properties had an interest in selling. There had to be a reason. It did not smell right. Finally the pieces were beginning to fall into place.

"I am sorry Mr. Wilde but the property is not for sale. We appreciate your generous offer. However, Highland Properties considers it a choice asset for its investors. You must excuse me, I have to take another overseas call."

There was a call but it was not from overseas. It was from Tony Eden whose office was down the street from Highland Properties. A sense of panic was in the air in Hamilton, Bermuda. In the meantime Vinnie had two more calls of his own to make.

CHAPTER 12

RACHEL

"Hello, this is Rachel. May I help you?"

"Rachel, it is Vinnie Pagano. Sorry to bother you again but I wanted to know if you could tell me who previously owned Metro Plaza."

"There was no previous owner. Highland Properties had it built."

"Who was the contractor?"

"It was a company from Delaware. Newark, Delaware. The selection seemed odd at the time. There was some talk about it because no local contractors or sub-contractors were used, nor were there any local workers on the job. Construction took place around the clock, seven days a week, holidays, without let up. All of the workers were housed in motels on the Berlin Turnpike. The contractor provided transportation to and from the motels each day. There were rumors the company bought three or four small run-down motels for use by their workers. Once the construction ended they were to be sold. I never did follow up to determine whether or not they were sold or to whom. The construction was completed in record time. There were two local building inspectors supervising the construction. One of them suspected that some aspects of the construction were kept from him but he never found anything out of order. The other inspector never expressed any concern."

"Anything specific with the first inspector?"

"The concrete for the foundation was purchased in the region but poured by the out-of-state workers and always at night. The arrangement was that the cement trucks stopped at the entrance to the site and the contractor had his own drivers take over the trucks during the poring. The cement company drivers waited at the gate until the trucks were returned to them. The inspector thought the night poring to be unusual but there was nothing in the local building codes to prevent it. The swapping of drivers was certainly unusual. All of the building materials were prefabricated elsewhere and shipped here for installation."

"What about the glass for the exterior walls?"

"Same thing. Brought in by out of state trucks and installed by the company workers."

"Anything else?"

"There is one other thing. This can be verified. A friend of mine who works for the regional power company that supplies energy to Simsbury told me that the contractors installed utility lines to handle far more electrical power than is normally used for a building the size of Metro Plaza. It was four or five times what is usually required for an office building."

"Was that ever questioned by the inspectors?"

"Not that I know of."

"Do you recall the name of the general contractor?'

"Yes, I do, since they were in my office several times. It was Myers and Moore. I should mention that they had the site secured day and night. The only persons allowed on it were their employees, the building inspectors and town officials on official business."

"Thanks again, Rachel. I owe you."

"Perhaps during the promised lunch you'll tell me what you are up to. You know, tell me the truth."

"I told you my name."

"Tony Pagano. Nice name. I like it. It fits you.

"Talk to you again."

CHAPTER 13

NOT WHAT IT APPEARS TO BE

He called Gretchen. The receptionist put him through without delay. She had been instructed to expect a call. By this time Vinnie had collected sufficient information to have a productive discussion with Gretchen. There was also little doubt in his mind she knew what he had been doing and why he had not returned her call sooner. It was possible that Tony Eden and Freddie Blair did not talk to each other until after each of them had called Gretchen and Darlene about the phone calls they received from David Wilde that were related to Metro Plaza. Once the women had the information it logically followed that other calls were made to each other. Tony Eden and Freddie Blair now knew that David Wilde and Vinnie Pagano were one and the same.

"Hi, Vinnie."

"I'm in the neighborhood and could be there in a few minutes."

"I will be expecting you."

When he arrived at Metro Plaza, the first order of business was to take careful note of the glass. He did so. The second was to see if Debra was wearing a pendant or pin or some sort. She was. He waved casually to her and headed directly for the elevator on the left, the one that only went to the second floor. He didn't attempt to look carefully at the sprinklers but reminded himself to do so later.

"Captain Pagano. Excuse me but your elevator is on the right."

"Thanks Debra but there has been a change of plans." With that he rang for the elevator on the left. As he stepped into it, he glanced back at Debra and saw her frantically reaching for the phone. No doubt she was calling Gretchen. But it was too late to hinder his mission.

The elevator stopped at the second floor. When he stepped out he was surprised by what he saw. The entire outside perimeter of the second floor was a series of offices with floor to ceiling walls that allowed for spectacular views of the mountain or fields. The office walls that faced the interior corridor that ran around the entire floor were also of glass. The center of the second floor was a maze of hundreds of computer and servers tended to by a significant number of technicians. The walls that formed the outside of the center area of the floor that housed the computers and servers were made of glass and had the same texture and tinting as those in the lobby. The design of the second floor was such that everyone had a view of the entire area and of the work being performed.

Vinnie knew there was no need to look at the first floor. It would be a duplicate of the second floor, of that he was convinced. Private Securities Services, LLC and Advanced Technology Systems Inc. only existed on paper. Metro Plaza was the CIA Center for Communication Intercepts, or, CCI. It was the primary communication monitoring center on the East coast with the one at Langley being the back-up. That realization had barely registered with him when he heard the elevator stop. Both Gretchen and Darlene exited. Darlene looked pissed and Gretchen looked upset that her cover had been discovered by a man she hardly knew and who had done so in record time. As angry as she was she also knew she had her man.

"What the hell do you think you are doing?" It was Darlene.

It would have been easy to ignore her. The more he saw of her the more he disliked her. Discretion being the better part of valor, he politely suggested that they retire to one of the offices for a chat.

Almost in unison they turned on their heels and headed back to the elevator. They held the door open, he entered and briefly wondered if he was about to be accosted. He tried to determine which of them was the most stunned by the turn of events but decided that they were both a little frightened that their cover story had been pierced. He thought that if they were among the best the CIA or some other domestic intelligence agency employed as spies, the country was in deep shit. He had seen what he was not supposed to see and Gretchen and Darlene would have to answer to someone.

The elevator stopped at the third floor. When they exited the elevator the three of them turned north and walked in single line, Vinnie bringing up the rear. They went to Gretchen's office at the far end of the building. She was clearly the head honcho for this operation. While Darlene made a great first impression with her beauty, it was Gretchen who had a presence. This was the first time he really noticed her. Equally as tall as Darlene, she was graceful in her stride and had an attractive but not overly sexy body.

As she walked her short brunette hair swayed. Her suit fit her slender body perfectly.

There was a conference table in the office that sat six, two on each side and one at each end. Vinnie quickly took a seat in one of the end chairs. Darlene did not make a move for the other end chair yielding to Gretchen. Darlene looked angry that Vinnie had taken what was obviously her power chair. Both women were used to being in control of meetings. They were about to meet their match. Darlene took a seat to the right of Gretchen with her back to Avon Mountain. The show was about to begin.

Vinnie knew that Iverson & Hunt Investigations would be on the defensive following Gretchen's conversations with Tony Eden of Highland Properties and Freddie Blair of Bean, Choate & Whitehall. The two women would have figured out that David Wilde and Vinnie Pagano were one and the same. They probably determined that Vinnie learned that the law firm was the contact entity through the town hall in Simsbury.

His strategy was to allow Gretchen and Darlene to take the initiative and for him to remain quiet, as he did in Afghanistan, and let the enemy make the first move before he struck. He was holding the high ground and had the line of fire when needed. The Army teaches well. Darlene made the first thrust.

"Just what right do you have to fake a name and then contact businesses in Bermuda regarding Metro Plaza?"

"Why are you so concerned about my having an interest in buying a building? It is owned by a trust in Hamilton, Bermuda and you're a tenant. I can do what I wish with my money. This is a great facility and it could generate a handsome retirement income. It pays to look ahead. Not to mention that in the meantime I could be your landlord. I would be around to check on things, to make certain you are satisfied and have no complaints."

They had anticipated a denial. Considering what they did for a living, the truth or what passed for the truth, was often difficult to handle. Most of the folks they dealt with were accomplished liars. Darlene was flushed and ready to kill Vinnie. Gretchen was expressionless, allowing her partner to take the lead. Vinnie wondered how an Iverson got brown hair and brown eyes. She looked lovely from the front and he remembered what she looked like from the rear. He liked her but the meeting was still young.

Once again Darlene took the initiative. "Why did you lie to Tony Eden and Freddie Blair?"

"Why did you and Gretchen lie to me about your intentions in recruiting me? Why the phony ad in the Courant? Why the 'good cop, bad cop' routine? Why the phony businesses on the first and second floor? Why was Metro Plaza built under the cover of darkness with an off shore contractor that just happened to be the defense department's number one 'go to' company in both Iraq and Afghanistan? Why a lobby filled with visual detection systems disguised as sprinklers? How come one of the Simsbury supervising building inspectors can afford Bermuda vacations twice a year on his salary?" He didn't really know if the building inspector had been on the take but figured it wouldn't hurt to throw it in.

By now Gretchen was beginning to look uncomfortable, Darlene had the bearing of defeat.

"I haven't figured out just which government agency you are associated with, but I soon will. The creation of your front organization was one sloppy job and left enough trails for an amateur to follow. When I get to the end of the trail I will also know why you have been fucking with me. But what I do know is that I have something you need."

They looked at each other. There was a short period of uncomfortable silence. Gretchen took over. "Darlene, it is time we leveled with Vinnie. He unraveled our operation faster than we had thought possible. In fact, we did not think it possible. We need to talk."

CHAPTER 14

OWNING UP

Darlene initiated the discussion but her anger still had an edge to it. "When the ad was placed we had not anticipated that someone with your background would apply. It was straightforward. We needed an experienced detective for routine work. He or she would not have worked out of this facility. We also wanted a 'civilian' for the work we had in mind. That did not diminish the fact that we also needed a highly qualified and experienced agent for a totally different assignment. We are an arm of a government agency but are not at liberty to disclose its name until we have identified the person we are looking for. No formal effort has been made to hire such a person. You simply fell into our laps."

If the conversation was not so serious he would have suggested that he'd be happy to fall into their laps. The timing was wrong.

"I have two questions. First, why did you leave the ad on my desk?"

"We are not aware of any ad that was left on your desk. Tell us about it."

Vinnie told them about the Courant ad and how he found it when he arrived for work on that Monday morning.

"Vinnie, no one associated with us placed the ad on your desk. We did not know you existed."

"Anyone you are associated with could have left it."

"Take our word for it. It did not originate with us or with the only other person who has knowledge of this operation."

He thought about that for a minute. If it wasn't Gretchen or Darlene who had left the ad it had to have been someone at Global who thought he was not suited for his job as a staff psychologist. It had to be either Sharon or Evan. This still did not sound right. He intended to pursue it when he returned to the office.

"Second question. If you work for a government agency, you have access to the records of hundreds of active agents working in other agencies who would be interested in and be highly qualified for whatever it is you are attempting. In addition to active agents, the country is awash with ex military and retired agents from Special Forces, Green Beret, Delta Force, Navy Seals, treasury, homeland security, national security agency, in addition to the FBI and CIA. You literally have your pick of the best."

Gretchen took over. "That is true. When you asked if you had the job you were referring to the detective position. Darlene and I were considering you as a candidate for a totally different assignment. Frankly, we had planned on looking at ex military to fill it. After reviewing your background we thought we had the person but put a decision on hold until we could dig a little deeper into your career. We were convinced that you had not told us everything. As of now you are the only person we interviewed for a position for which we have not yet officially recruited."

"Gretchen, when you left the message for me on Monday you said that you 'needed me.' That was before I stirred up a hornet's nest with my inquiries. Once I made that first call to Bermuda you must have realized the potential for me to unravel this operation, whatever it is. Now you have to come clean and hope that I cooperate. The other option is to call some of your clients and have me eliminated. Since you and Darlene obviously know your way around the military that should be no problem. You can tell me the truth or you make a call for a clean- up squad. Does that sound about right?"

"Something like that."

There was silence. He learned a long time ago to never fill a vacuum. Best to wait it out, much along the lines of a client-psychologist session. Take a deep breath and wait. Look them in the eye. They exchanged glances and made the first move. He wondered if they had a rehearsed script that they were about to act out.

"While we technically did not lie to you, we deliberately avoided full disclosure which is somewhat short of telling the truth. On the other hand you were not entirely truthful with us. We did not know this when we met with you the first time. After your Bermuda inquiries it was essential that we learn more about you. Our second round of phone calls was noteworthy for what individuals did not want to share with us. It would be an understatement to say most people we spoke with were evasive when we attempted to dig deeper into your background. Finally we called in some favors and put the puzzle, your career puzzle, together."

He waited. They were silent for what seemed a very long time. The only sound was the movement of cold air flowing through the air conditioning vents and the slight noise of their bodies moving in the leather chairs. Still he waited. Darlene broke the silence.

"You told us you used the military police as a cover for your real work in extraction. Is it not true that you were army but assigned to an altogether different agency?"

"I'm listening."

"The fact is you were Navy Seals not army. It is also true that you did not volunteer for the Army but were recruited during your sophomore year in college by the CIA. The professor you boxed with was a recruiter and he saw the potential in you for clandestine work. You were ethnic, independent, smart, a loner, inquisitive, bi-lingual, street savvy, tough and shared little about yourself with anyone. You had a series of girl friends, none serious. The fact is you were the perfect public university candidate for the CIA, someone to mix it up with recruits from the Ivy League. The Director had sent word out to recruiters that his agents all profiled the same way and a diversified mix was needed. You underwent training at the Farm for approximately six months and were so damn good at what they asked of you that they recommended that the Seals take you on for extraction work. You were assigned to an extraction unit, trained for another six months, graduated at the top of the class after which you which you were sent to Iraq. A year later you were promoted to captain and put in charge of several extraction teams. About the only thing we do not know is what the hell you are doing at Global."

"Safer than combat, sleep better at night."

Gretchen stepped in. "Vinnie, you enjoy acting like a grown up version of the tough neighborhood kid but you are one clever son of a bitch. In two days you unraveled this operation, even if you do not know the specifics. We have no doubt that in another day or two you would know most of what you want to know. However, you are a retired military hero and a patriot. There is no way you would undermine us especially when we tell you what we need you for."

It was getting late, Vinnie was emotionally spent and both of the women had themselves been through a stressful day. Darlene spoke up. "Gretchen, why don't we leave the details to tomorrow when we are sharper than I feel right now? Whatever we wish to share with Vinnie can wait another day."

Gretchen was not certain what Darlene was up to, if anything, so she decided to go along with her. "Vinnie, are you ok with an early morning meeting?" Vinnie looked at Gretchen and told her it was fine. He, too, wondered if there was more to the delay than met the eye but he was tired enough to go along.

Gretchen spoke, "Then that is it. We meet here at nine a.m."

CHAPTER 15

LEON'S

Vinnie took the elevator down and was greeted by Debra. "Good night Vinnie." She said it with a smile and somewhat of an invitation now that he was in the good graces of Gretchen and Darlene. Vinnie, thinking of Sharon, offered a big smile and a "See you in the morning."

About now he could have used a good friend and a big drink. He had made no close friends while working at Global and was not inclined to stop at a singles bar by himself. It was four ten p.m. and he remembered he promised Sharon he would call this evening. Since she would be leaving work in less than an hour he decided to call her at the office and try to convince her to meet him for a drink and dinner. If she agreed he would have time to stop off at his apartment in West Hartford and be in town by five.

She answered, "Sharon, how may I direct your call?"

"Hi, it's me, Vinnie."

"I recognized the 'me' voice."

"It is nice to know you have not already forgotten who I am."

"No chance of that."

"I have an idea but don't hesitate to tell me if it doesn't work for you. I planned on calling tonight but since you will be leaving the office in a few minutes, I wondered if you would like to meet somewhere for a drink and dinner?"

"Um. I'm not sure that a woman should say 'yes' so quickly with someone she hardly knows."

"You probably know more about me than just about anyone since you have friends in personnel. And, if you have dinner with me tonight you will know me that much better."

"The answer is 'yes'. Where do you suggest?"

"Let's make it close to where you live so you will not have far to drive. So, where do you live?"

"West Hartford."

"No, I live in West Hartford."

"I know exactly where you live."

"You've been spying."

"I figured that someday I may need a ride to work."

Changing the subject, "How about if we meet at Leon's around five thirty?"

"Make it six. That will give me time to run by my house and change into something more comfortable."

"See you at six."

Perfect. He decided to stop at his apartment and change.

Vinnie arrived early so as not to keep Sharon waiting in the event she arrived before him. He was happy to wait. It was a lovely summer evening, mild temperature, clear sky and a slight, lazy-like breeze. Even at this early hour Leon's was jumping as were the other restaurants on LaSalle Street. All of the outside tables at Leon's were taken except for the one being held for him. He was a frequent customer and, while they do not reserve outside tables, Vinnie told the hostess know how important it was tonight.

He parked across the street adjacent to the bank assuming Sharon would do likewise. It was close to six fifteen and he was looking across the street at the parking lot to see if he could spot her driving in or walking across the street. To strangers, it looked as though he was pacing.

"Looking for someone, mister?" The voice was from behind him.

He turned towards the voice and looked into her beautiful brown eyes as she whispered, "Hi Vinnie."

She was more beautiful than he remembered from yesterday. Her Mediterranean complexion glistened, and her smile had warmth that would ignite a man's heart. Yesterday she had her black hair pulled back in a ponytail, today it was falling freely to her shoulders and in front it framed her face as if in a portrait.

He was so surprised to see her he moved back a step and took her in. She no longer was a secretary but a picture of youthful beauty. Her conservative office attire was replaced with a pale yellow dress by Giorgio Armani, cut discretely low in front to display bosom without offending and of a length that displayed slender, shapely legs. She wore a simple but elegant necklace and matching gold bracelet by David Yurman. Her Jimmy Choo high heels, colored to match her dress, afforded her the height to look directly into Vinnie's eyes that acted as magnets. Both were thinking of an embrace, both wanted one but this was not the time. He feared this moment may not be repeated.

"You haven't said a word, Vinnie."

He remained quiet for another moment or two. "You are the most beautiful woman I know. It's a bit like the class beauty agreeing to go to the senior prom with the class nerd."

"You are anything but a nerd and if you ask me to the prom, I will accept."

Vinnie smiled at the comment. At this moment, he was as happy as he could remember. This was a planet away from the horrors of Iraq and Afghanistan. The college age waiter, who was unable to take his eyes off Sharon, managed to compose himself enough to let Vinnie know their table was ready.

Vinnie ordered an Absolute martini up for himself and a pinot grigio for Sharon. After the waiter left, Sharon spoke, "You look quite dashing, Vinnie. You appear to have left the Global wardrobe at home."

After he had spoken to her on the phone to arrange dinner, Vinnie had gone to his apartment, showered, shaved and changed into tan slacks and loafers from Nordstrom's and a Ralph Lauren blue blazer. He wore his shirt open at the collar and wore no tie. He looked like a real catch himself. While the men in the vicinity of their table had given Sharon approving and lecherous glances, the women did likewise with Vinnie. They made for an elegant, handsome couple.

"I wanted to make a good impression on my first date."

"This is an official date?"

"I think."

"Vinnie, what is it that you really want to do now that Global holds no interest? Does what occupied you all day today have anything to do with your future plans?"

"Before I answer your questions let me ask if you know what I did in the service?"

Sharon lifted her glass and took a sip of her wine. "I read your resume when you first arrived. Evan had asked me to return it to personnel so I took the opportunity to examine it. I looked at it again today. A friend in personnel smuggled it to me. It would be immediately obvious to anyone who read the resume that you gave but the barest of details and personnel does not have access to military records. Knowing many of the employees in that department, they would not have conducted a serious background check once they learned you were a decorated hero. I was impressed the first time I read it and more so after reading it again today and filling in some of the blanks."

Taking another sip of her wine, she asked, "What did you do?"

"On this beautiful evening in a pleasant setting, I would like to make a suggestion. This being our first date, let's defer this discussion for another day when we can have a serious talk over coffee. That way, I am guaranteed I will see you again and we avoid any possible upset when I share the details of my work. I promise to tell you all that I am authorized to talk about. Unless, of course, you have the highest level of clearance provided by the government."

"I love your suggestion and I accept. Now shall we order? I am starved."

Vinnie called the waiter and they placed dinner selections. She ordered veal francais with roasted potatoes and asparagus. He ordered the same but had them hold the asparagus. It was pleasant dining outside, with laughter and conversation emanating from the other tables. The setting sun added to the romantic atmosphere. By the time dinner was over, darkness had set in, the subdued lighting was turned on and strains of Elton John music softly permeated the air. With each passing moment, Vinnie felt himself being drawn into her sphere, vacating the tough guy role he played earlier in the day with Gretchen and Darlene. He had dated many women in college and a few female officers during various deployments, but never was he so happy to be with a woman as tonight. He sensed that Sharon could read his thoughts.

CHAPTER 16

BERMUDA

Tony Eden was on the phone with Freddie Blair. "Fuck, Freddie, this guy saw right through Gretchen and Darlene's cover story. Whoever had this hair brained idea to use Iverson & Hunt Investigations as a cover should be shot. In a couple of days this guy wipes out an entire year of planning."

"Tony, you think maybe that someone who competes with the best of Navy Seals for courage and toughness is capable enough to outsmart the pussies who man the decision-making desks at Langley? Some desk jockey will soon be on the way to an outpost in Somalia. Fortunately, our guy still does not know what agency the women are assigned to nor does he have any idea what they want him for. For that matter neither do we."

"Either you have burned out your brains fucking your secretary or you've been in the sun too long. This guy will have all the pieces in place in twenty four hours. And, why would he want to consider working for Gretchen and Darlene knowing what fools they look like after this fiasco? Their operation will look to him like a Disney movie. Jesus Christ, Freddie, among his other talents this guy is a fucking assassin. These women must look to him like Nancy Drew and her kid sister."

Freddie thought about this for a minute. He reflected about the two women, both of whom he would like to make. So far it has been wishful thinking. While they were two entirely different personalities, they both were beautiful women. Gretchen was a classic professional, groomed to display but a hint of her sexuality. Freddie knew she had an affair with the chief of station in Russia while on assignment with the American Embassy. She also had a brief fling with the former Director until his wife put the community property divorce settlement option to him. Since then there has been no word of her love life. Freddie made a mental note to do some research. There could still be an opportunity for him.

Darlene was a different case. She was a hard ass beauty who had a number of affairs with powerful men both in and out of government, including some of the most influential players in the defense industry and the military. She had spread her legs and her talent around. Unlike Gretchen, who was somewhat standoffish, Darlene loved to tease any guy she came in contact with. Then she would decide which she would take to bed. But, she made a decision only after determining there was something to gain other than just another orgasm. Given her connections, she could have any assignment within the agency she desired except those of Director and Deputy Director. In fact, she could name any number of civilian, military and government positions in and around Washington and she would get them. Freddie knew she always retained the upper hand in her relationships. She could be very effective at "kiss and tell" and there were many men who could be compromised including those at the highest levels of government.

What Freddie did not know was that Vinnie Pagano had so pissed her off that she lost her poise and called him "an insolent son of a bitch." He had never known her to lose her cool. If Freddie knew about this encounter between Darlene and Pagano, he would not be happy. Vinnie might just be the type of guy she would fuck for pleasure. That would push Freddie back another notch in the wishful thinking line.

"Tony, I think you underestimate the women. They may appear to be bedding every prominent politico but they are two smart operators. Put them together and they are among the best front line intelligence officers in the agency. You are mistaken if you think a public university, blue collar wop is going to get the best of them."

"You are out of your fucking mind labeling this guy this way. If he ever heard you refer to him as a wop, he'd stuff your penis up your ass. That is after he slit your throat and gutted you. One on one you would be red meat for him. Have you read his file? I suggest you stay a continent away from him. From what I learned of his background, he will see you as the enemy during your first handshake. You can bet he will be paying us a visit. You had better put in for vacation time the minute you hear he is traveling."

"Why would he visit us? If the situation has been blown, he will be talking to Gretchen and Darlene."

Tony ended the call. He needed to think. Freddie could be a problem and may need "counseling."

CHAPTER 17

ROME

She was walking on Via V. Veneto towards Palazzo Barbarino to meet Carlton Richardson. The Louis Vuitton bag on her left shoulder swayed in rhythm with her stride. Hanging from her right shoulder was a Gucci leather briefcase that contained working documents. The spiked heels gave her a sense of being tall when in fact she was five foot two in stocking feet. Her fashionable shoes, combined with her finely cut and extravagantly expensive suit, gave her the look of a successful professional. To the passerby she was another business woman rushing to keep an appointment. Rome was filled with such woman now that international conglomerates recognized how effective females were in developing new business. Fluency in two or more foreign languages gave European women an advantage in dealing with foreign businessmen. Times had changed such that business men would rather be in the company of women when conducting business away from home, especially beautiful and attractive women. Like many Italians, she was fluent in English. It would be difficult for the average American to detect her Italian dialect.

Bettina Falaguerra was the business development Director of the Economic-Commercial Section of the Italian consulate in New York City. Her public role was to assist Italian companies in promoting Italian products and services in the United States. The position afforded her the opportunity to travel extensively, connect with important business leaders and return to Italy on a frequent basis. Her position at the consulate provided her with diplomatic immunity and the use of its diplomatic pouch when traveling abroad. Unknown to the American intelligence community was that Ms. Falaguerra was the Director of Italian intelligence gathering on the East coast of the United States.

She had left JFK on Monday and arrived at Leonardo Da Vinci shortly after 8 a.m. Tuesday. Her limousine was waiting. The embassy driver held a card with her name. Once in the limousine, she instructed the driver to take her to the Parco Dei Principi hotel on Via G. Frescobaldi. She checked in shortly before ten a.m. and used the first day adjusting to jet lag and enjoying the Olympic size pool on a warm and sunny July day. Following her swim, she spent two hours in the late afternoon walking in the Villa Borghese which was across the street from the hotel. Following a quiet dinner at a small trattoria near the hotel, she returned to her room, watched the evening news and fell asleep around eleven p.m.

The wake-up call stirred her at eight thirty after which she showered, selected the proper attire and went to the dining room for breakfast. As expected, she drew the attention of both the wait staff and business men who were already in the room. She was attractive even at this early hour. Following a breakfast of juice, espresso and a sweet roll, she went to the front desk to retrieve the briefcase she had placed overnight in the hotel safe. The doorman hailed her a cab. Once again, she attracted the attention of several business men waiting for cabs when her skirt was drawn up and showed a good deal of gorgeous legs as she entered the cab.

Wanting her meeting with Carlton to appear casual to anyone who may be observing them, she had the cab driver drop her off at the corner of Via Bissolati and Via V. Veneto. She walked the short distance to Piazza Barberini.

Carlton Richardson was attached to the American Embassy in Rome as Director of the Economic Section. The work of the section was to facilitate U.S. exports and investments in Italy and to provide advocacy on behalf of U.S. business interests operating in Italy. His title and work expertise was not unlike that of Bettina Falaguerra. His meeting with her would be seen as a professional one that addressed common trade interests shared by the two countries.

Much of the American Embassy Economic Section business in Rome was usually held in a social setting and, in this case, away from any possible electronic bugging of the Embassy. The restaurant, Casa Mia, was located on Via Avignonesi a few steps from Piazza Barberini. It was a favorite of embassy personnel being a small family run business, quiet and the most unlikely place for intelligence gathering or dissemination. The menu was limited but authentic Italian.

Carlton saw Bettina approaching and couldn't help thinking that if she was assigned to the Italian Embassy in Rome he would make every effort to seduce her. All of the major embassies in Rome were choice assignments and, by design, were staffed with attractive and talented women, in that order. The social network between embassies was well developed and there was a great deal of international fucking. Carlton always had two or three liaisons in operation simultaneously. His current bed mate was Gisela Rudenschroder of the German embassy. She was a typical German beauty; tall, blond, busty, leggy and the best fuck he had every encountered. She was also an accomplished agent for the German intelligence service. There was little that Gisela had yet to discover about sex and was happy to share what she did know with whomever she was currently bedding on behalf of her employer. Carlton was aroused just thinking about her. As experienced as he was, Gisela always had another surprise for him. Oral sex with her was the most erotic experience Carlton had ever encountered. Sitting in the sun waiting on Bettina but thinking about Gisela, he could feel his penis expanding in his pants.

Carlton's position as Director of the Economic Section was a cover for his real job as station chief for the CIA. His assignment was a direct one made by the Director of the CIA in Washington. He was a replacement for the former station chief, Max Rietsema, who was now an international fugitive wanted by the Italian Prosecutor General for his involvement in the adduction of Abdu Khalid, who was allegedly seized by the Americans and sent to Egypt for enhanced interrogation. At the time, Khalid was under heavy surveillance by the Italian government and was suspected of recruiting men to fight against the Coalition Forces in Iraq and Afghanistan. Prosecutors for the Italian government also alleged that Italian intelligence officials assisted the CIA in the abduction.

Carlton's assignment as Director of the Economic Section in the American Embassy was officially known to the Italian government, in particular, AISES. It was required that new members of all embassies in Italy be registered with the appropriate government agency. It was assumed that some percentage of foreign embassy employees is in the intelligence gathering business. None of Carlton's actions to date gave rise to any suspicion that he was a CIA operative. He worried that the meeting with Bettina Falaguerra would raise the threshold of suspicion. Unknown to him or Bettina Falaguerra, there was justifiable reason to be concerned.

CHAPTER 18

FLIGHT FROM ITALY

Max Rietsema stopped momentarily to look out over the expanse of Baxter State Park. The trees displayed the vivid colors of late summer. The views looking out over the Appalachian Trail to the south and the International Appalachian Trail to the north were spectacular. He had climbed the Knife Edge trail to the top of Mt. Katahdin and was taking a brief rest before he began his descent. He was the only one at the summit and the quiet and beauty were intoxicating.

It was early afternoon and the weather had a serious bite to it, not uncommon in northern Maine, especially at the higher elevations. The weather report was for a changing pattern with a cold front moving in. The temperature at the summit was hovering in the low forties and there was a threat of precipitation later in the day. A gusting wind of fifteen to twenty miles per hour out of the north created a wind chill factor of between twenty five and thirty degrees on his face and neck. He pulled the collar of his parka up tight. Max had chosen a mid weight parka knowing he would be doing a fast climb and not lingering long at the summit. It was the parka a professional climber would choose for a climb when the temperature was around the freezing point. He was surprised that no other climbers had been ahead of him on the ascent given that it was an excellent day for climbing.

Baxter Peak, where Max was sitting, is the northern most point on the Appalachian Trail that extends two thousand one hundred and seventy nine miles south to Springer Mountain in Georgia. The trail was one of the three triple crowns of long distance hiking in the United States, the others being the Continental Divide and the Pacific Crest Trail. These were serious climbs. Kahtadin had claimed many deaths either from exposure in both summer and winter or from hikers falling off the Knife Edge and down into one of the glacier-formed cirques that surrounded the mountain.

His thoughts changed briefly from enjoying the vista to his concern about the trip down. Two young, strong looking East European men were waiting somewhere on the lower portion of the mountain. Not knowing who they were and how they located him caused a level of anxiety. For a moment, he thought that he was being overly suspicious. Elizabeth was the only person who knew he was in Maine, and he only used the documents she provided him. He knew that it was only a matter of time before he would be discovered. But, this was too soon. Elizabeth certainly did not reveal his locations to anyone. There existed, however, the possibility that he had been compromised by the pilot who flew him here or the lab technicians who prepared his false documents. Anyone who knew of his new credit card number would have instant access to his movements. He wondered if secure cell phones could be compromised and his location easily discovered.

His mind was racing through other possibilities. His plane out of Rome had traveled between Corsica and Sardinia, and then traversed northernmost Spain across the Pyrenees staying just south of the French border. While Spain did not have much in the way of an air force or sophisticated radar systems, it was possible that the plane had been detected, but that in itself would not have led to his being compromised in Maine. Once out over the Bay of Biscay and then the Atlantic, neither the Spanish or Portuguese military forces had the equipment to track the aircraft as it turned south to the Azores flying only a few hundred feet above the water.

There was the possibility that the other three CIA aircraft that refueled in the Azores had created interest in the countries from which they left. Max assumed they would have come from secret airfields in Western Europe, located close to the coastlines to minimize the time they would be on radar screens. Sooner or later he would need to know how he was comprised and by whom. Someone would need to be eliminated.

He pulled the pack off his back and dropped it next to him, then reached in for two energy bars and a bottle of water. He ate the two bars and then drank slowly from the water bottle until it was empty. The bottle and energy bar wrappers were placed back into his pack. When done, he reached for his binoculars, scanned the Knife Edge trail, and then shifted his sight line slightly to the east and examined two other trails that intersected with the Knife Edge about a quarter of a mile below him.

Having taken care to assess all of the climbers who were at the trail head when he prepared for his climb, he decided not to worry just yet about the husband and wife team or the family of four. On the other hand, his many years with the CIA taught him things were not always what they appeared to be. He would exert caution with all of them. Stored in his back pack, in addition to his hand gun, was his CIA issued KABAR knife made of high tensile carbon steel. It has been a standard issue of the USMC since World War II and was now in use with almost all front line troops. It had a handle made of six compacted leather discs and slid easily out of its dark leather sheath. The blade was seven inches long and the overall length was twelve inches. It was a manual killing machine. It was also an all purpose tool used to cut a path through brush, dig foxholes and hack away at any obstacle, including human ones. It would remain in his pack on the descent until he entered the tree line at which time he would strap it on his belt.

The climb today was the third he had made up the Knife Edge. Originally from California, he had heard about the two great peaks in the East, Mt Washington and Mt Katahdin. Since moving East he had climbed Mt. Washington three times from different trail heads. While the mountain was considered to have the worse weather in North America and record setting low temperatures, it was Katahdin that held his interest today. Unlike Mt. Washington, where most of the trail heads were located at the base of the mountain, you had to do some serious trekking to reach the trail heads of Katahdin. The mountain was not a serious technical challenge for Max what with his having climbed many of the fourteen thousand footers in Colorado and both Mount Blanc and the Matterhorn while stationed in Europe. Today was to be an enjoyable hike with few natural challenges. It was the human challenge he was concerned about.

He had viewed the mountain for the first time in Freeport, ME while he was shopping at the L.L. Bean outlet store, a required stop for anyone visiting the state. As Max climbed the stairs to the second floor of the store and reached the wide landing half way up, he looked directly at an enormous and highly detailed photograph of the mountain that displayed the spectacular Knife Edge and both Baxter Peak and Pamola Peak. Once he saw the photograph, he decided to make his first climb. That was several weeks ago. He was back for the third time.

While he was enjoying the quiet reward at the summit that comes from a successful climb, he reminded himself he was an international fugitive from justice. The Italian government was determined to bring him to trial in Rome along with twenty two other Americans who were alleged to have taken part in the abduction of Abdu Khalid. For most of his sixteen years with the agency Max pursued the bad guys. Now he was the pursued.

Three months earlier Abdu Khalid was seized by American CIA agents in Rome and secretly moved to Egypt. The seizure was planned and carried out by Max Rietsema as head of station in Rome. Prosecutors for the Italian government also alleged that a number of Italian intelligence officials had assisted the CIA in the abduction.

At the time of Khalid's abduction, he was under heavy surveillance by the Italian government and suspected of recruiting men to fight against the Coalition Forces in Iraq and Afghanistan. At the time, Italy had several hundred troops fighting with the Coalition. Arrest warrants were issued for the Americans who were to face trial. They did not appear; instead, the Deputy Director of the Central Intelligence Agency, without the knowledge of the Italian government, removed the agents from Italy. By leaving Italy the agents became international fugitives. Had they remained, they would have been imprisoned while awaiting trial. The Italian government was embarrassed internationally because the CIA agents were not apprehended.

It was not the fact that the Italian government was opposed to enhanced interrogation that led to the arrest warrants being issued. What had officials upset was that CIA agents abducted a Yemen citizen on Italian sovereign soil without the knowledge or approval of the Italian government. They were also concerned that the Americans were operating a major spy ring in Italy.

The Italian government, angry that the twenty three Americans fled Italy before they could be tried placed a high priority on the apprehension of the one member of the team who made the decision to send Khalid to Egypt for enhanced interrogation. The Italian external information and security agency (Agenza Informazione e Sicurezza Esterna or AISA) decided that for maximum publicity and to save Italy from further embarrassment, it would attempt to take into custody, Max Rietsema, the former CIA head of station in Rome and the person responsible for the abduction.

AISE's monitoring of the situation after the Americans fled Italy revealed that Rietsema was no longer on active duty. His whereabouts were known only to Elizabeth English, the Deputy Director of the CIA. For political reasons, the Director of the CIA did not want to know where Max Rietsema was in hiding.

The Italian government was one of two parties interested in Max's whereabouts. An Islamic terrorist group based in Italy was also on the hunt for the CIA Agent. Unlike the Italian government, which would imprison him, the terrorist group meant to execute him. This would send a statement to the world that if you bring harm to any Islamic fighter, you will be found and executed. The terrorist group intended for this to be a mirror imagine of the George Bush philosophy, whereby, if you bring harm to America, the government will eventually find you and prosecute you. Eluding the Italian intelligence service was one thing, avoiding detection by Islamic groups with worldwide tentacles was quite another. Max knew that not one, but two foreign groups had an interest in apprehending him.

Fortunately for Max, a friend inside the Italian government had alerted him that he and his colleagues were to be apprehended and charged with kidnapping a foreign national on Italian soil. It was then that the Director of the CIA directed that Max and all of the targeted agents leave Italy immediately. He left it to Elizabeth English, his deputy, to deal with their exit. She provided the agents with fast, radar deflecting clandestine air transportation out of the country in order to avoid alerting the Italian government at any of the border crossings. Twenty two of the agents were to be dispersed into three groups. Max, the twenty third agent, would travel alone. Four agency planes were waiting to transport them to their new secret locations. The three planes shared by the twenty two agents were flown to destinations known only to the Deputy Director of the CIA and the three pilots. Max, on the fourth plane, had no idea that

Bangor, Maine was to be his first stop on a constantly changing itinerary.

A half hour before he was to land, the co-pilot went into the cabin and handed Max a briefcase that he said was given to him by Deputy Director English. Gus was to immediately examine the contents. The co-pilot also asked that Max hand over all identifications he had on his person. Max was also handed a letter signed by English authorizing the co-pilot to retrieve the documents. Once that was done, Max also handed the letter back to the pilot. He kept his secure cell phone.

Once the co-pilot returned to the cockpit, Max opened the briefcase. There was a letter from English instructing him to destroy the letter once it had been read and the contents understood. Enclosed was a complete set of identification documents for James Parmeter, Max's new persona. The documents included a passport, a Maine driver's license, a social security card, a health services card, a credit card, and a road service membership card. A car with a Maine registration was waiting for him on arrival in Bangor and he was given information as to how to identify it. The keys were in a small magnetic container that was attached to the frame of the car directly down from the handle on the rear door on the passenger side. Also inside the briefcase was $20,000 in small denominations, a detailed map of Maine and directions to a safe house in Waterville, a hundred mile trip to the southwest of Bangor.

Thinking about the safe house, Max was in the dark as to where any of the other Agents were settled, but assumed that they were given low profile, temporary assignments in backwater stations in the United

States and provided with new documents. Some of the agents with families would undoubtedly leave the agency and look for private security jobs in the business community. Given the hostile attitude of many members of Congress towards the CIA, the temporary assignments selected by others would end up being permanent. Gus could not help but wonder if it paid to be one of the good guys.

CHAPTER 19

THE CLIMBERS

While resting on the summit, Max reflected back on the three climbing parties preparing their gear as he was about to begin his climb. He had taken the time to pretend to do some warm up exercises and walked in the parking lot to survey the climbers and their cars. He was a fugitive and was taking no chances. Everyone was suspect.

The first party was comprised of a husband and wife team, both of whom looked in great shape and who had the bearing of serious climbers. The man was easily six foot two or three and she was a good five foot nine or ten. Their packs were well worn and their boots were high end and had tramped many trails. Their parkas were premium quality. Their packs, like their shoes, were the best and had experienced many miles on the trail. He took note that they were driving a Subaru wagon with a Maine registration and a University of Maine parking sticker. He smiled at the "No Casino Here" bumper sticker. Max took an immediate liking to them and had the impression that these two would not have to be told to "carry out what you carry in."

The second party was a family of four, a mom and dad and two teenagers. Mom looked a lot younger than dad and was an attractive brunette. She looked athletic but not in a mountain climbing way. He was well built, about six feet two or three and Ivy League good looking. Everything about them was upscale and expensive. Their Navigator bore New York state plates. Probably from one of the New York suburbs and enjoying a long weekend in Maine. Their clothes looked like they had been recently purchased. Their climbing gear was new. The teenagers looked preppy and were well mannered and business like as they prepared to climb. Dad probably was a Wall Street banker making a ton of money and mom did her best to spend it when she was not ferrying her kids from one activity to another. Max thought that, while the family did not appear to have the experience to climb a challenging peak, mom and dad didn't make it to their station in life without being driven and directive. He gave them a better than even chance to make the summit.

The third party was of intense interest to him. It was comprised of two males in their late 20's, early 30's. Both were under six feet, and weighed in between 200-230 pounds. They could be taken for brothers in that they were both solidly built, with large upper bodies, bull necks and large round, shaved heads. Max was awed by the size of their hands. They were not what you would want around your throat. Their clothing and gear was marginal for the climb, obviously put together quickly. They wore no hats or gloves. A bit of bad weather at the summit and they would have trouble descending, especially today, with the temperature hovering around the freezing mark and the possibility of precipitation. They spoke English, but with a distinct East European accent. Max recognized the accent having served in Moscow and St. Petersburg.

Their car had a Massachusetts registration with a Hertz sticker on the windshield that identified it as having been rented at Logan International in East Boston. An alarm went off in Max's head. Why would you rent a car at Logan, drive two hundred miles to the north, trek in 3-4 miles to reach the base, to climb one of the toughest peaks in the East with equipment that provided no margin of safety? They bore watching.

With the exception of the two men who remained next to their car, everyone made casual talk for a few minutes while preparing their gear. They were all anxious to begin the climb. Max made an assessment as to what he thought the order of departure would be. Being alone, in great shape, with his gear in place, he would move out quickly and keep a steady three miles per hour pace, something the others would not be able to match. The family would move out next but would be passed in the first mile by the husband and wife team that would be slower to move out in order to have everything in order. His sense was that they were experienced climbers. They might just be of assistance to him. Once on the trail, they would move steadily and be only a half hour of so behind him. On the descent, they would be behind him since they both had expensive looking cameras and would be taking pictures. He would have to plan on them being an hour behind him.

The two east Europeans would be last. If Max's hunch was correct, they would be in no hurry, would not hike very far, and would be looking for a secluded spot within the heavy brush. Having sized up the situation, they knew that Max would be the first up and the first down and well ahead of the others. That scenario appealed to them.

Sitting on the peak, Max Rietsema was now James Parmeter, his new cover name. He never shared his vacation destinations with anyone except the Deputy Director of the CIA, Elizabeth English. Maine was as secure a hide-a-way as any, or so he thought. Until the issue with the Italian government was settled, he knew that the Deputy Director had no intention of allowing him to go active or public. The Prime Minister of Italy would not be likely to pardon Max given the uproar over the abduction. It would be some time, maybe too much time, before the two countries would reach an agreement to drop the charges against Max. On the other hand, an invitation to the White House might soften the Prime Minister's stance. Max would have to speak with Elizabeth.

Once the issue of a pardon was settled for Max, there still remained the matter of the terrorists literally wanting his head. There would be no negotiating with them.

He thought about Elizabeth a great deal during his unplanned and unwanted hiatus. They met in Cambridge, Massachusetts when she was at Radcliff and he was at Harvard. It was not long before they fell in love. Unknown to each other, both were recruited by the CIA while in undergraduate school and would go active pending successful graduate work that was to be funded by the agency. They never mentioned this fact to each other. They were separated after graduation when she attended Stanford for graduate work and he went to Wharton. Her graduate work was in Western European history, Italian and Spanish; his work was in Organizational Planning, with language training in Russian, Italian and French. They communicated during graduate school and met twice, once in Philadelphia and once in San Francisco. While they still were passionate about each other, they were driven to complete their graduate work and be assigned to overseas posts with neither knowing what the other was up to.

Once graduate school was completed they, along with many other recruits, were ordered to Washington, DC for orientation. It was then that they were reunited. Their love affair blossomed.

While he was not a top covert operative, Max was sufficiently successful to be assigned to some of the premier capitols of the world in an embassy position while working for the CIA. What he lacked as a field operative was more than compensated for by his ability to make sound decisions in the middle of chaos. He possessed the intellectual qualities to use any crisis as an opportunity, always able to clear away the unnecessary and focus in on solutions. This decision- making ability, coupled with his political acumen and charming personality was sufficient to bring him to the attention of the Director of the CIA. It also helped that he was tall, had rugged good looks, and spoke Russian, Italian and French. Those qualifications earned him the postings in major cities. It was his work in Rome as head of station that led to a decision which resulted in his being an international fugitive on the run from Italian justice and Jihadist revenge.

He brushed aside these thoughts and focused his binoculars on the Knife Edge trail. It was time to start down and he needed to get a fix on the lay of the land. As he had anticipated, the husband and wife team was only a half mile from his position and moving at a strong, steady pace with the woman in the lead. They made the climb look easy and enjoyable. He would soon meet them on the way down.

Setting his sights lower, he could make out the family team spread out into two groups. They had just cleared a shoulder and were in full view. Given the reservations he had had about their stamina, he was surprised to see that all four were only a quarter mile or so below the husband and wife team. The teenage boy was in the lead followed closely by his mother. Back a hundred feet or so, the daughter and father pulled up the rear. All in all, it was a commendable effort by all of them. He reckoned that all four family members would make it to the summit by two thirty. It would be an hour or more before they passed each other. It was best that they not be anywhere near Max for long.

As expected, the two men were nowhere to be seen.

CHAPTER 20

FIRST KILL

The distance from Baxter Peak to Palomar Peak was just under a mile, at best a forty minute descent. He would pass the husband and wife team in approximately twenty minutes and the family group in forty minutes. The more he thought about it, he did not want to involve any of them in what would or could take place further down the trail.

As the husband and wife approached, Max spoke first. "Hi, great day for a walk."

They smiled, "Somewhat more than a walk, but still great."

"I spotted you from Baxter Peak and admired your strong, steady pace. I gather you have been here before."

"I try to get a winter climb in with a group of friends. Betsy and I manage at least one early summer climb, and a second one in late fall. How about yourself?"

"I'm just here for a few days and heard about Kahtadin from friends. It is all that it was cracked up to be. A bit of a challenge and a great view of Maine. Different than European climbing."

"Have you climbed either of the two big ones in Europe?

"Yes, both the Matterhorn and Mount Blanc and several smaller but challenging ones in Germany. If you can handle this one in winter, you can manage the European peaks. You will have to try them someday, both of you. You are strong climbers and look accomplished. If you do have the opportunity to climb in Europe, keep in mind that the Matterhorn is a national park and you can only climb with a paid guide and it is expensive. I didn't know that the first time and had to settle for a lesser challenge. Also, if you get into trouble in Switzerland while climbing and need help, you also pay for that. Everything is business with the Swiss. Well, I had better start down. While I think of it, I haven't seen the two male climbers that started out last. How about you?"

Betsy spoke, "Thanks for the tip on Europe. As for the two male climbers, we don't believe they made it out of the tree line. Given the way they were dressed, it seemed odd they would be here at all."

"Well, nice talking to you. Safe trip."

"Likewise."

Max started down. It was three miles from the time you enter the tree line to when you reach the trail head. He was certain that he was under observation and would be until he reached the tree line and was well into the forest at which time he would be temporarily out of view. Placing himself in their shoes, he would not attack until his prey was closer both to the trail head and the cars which would make for a quick escape. He figured that around the quarter mile mark he would encounter them. The fact was that he still did not know who they were but was confident as to why they were here.

A little below Paloma Peak he met up with the family. He stopped and spoke to them. “How’s it going?”

The young girl spoke first. “We were watching you with our binocular and were impressed with how fast you walked and how quickly you made the summit. You are going down and we have yet to get to the top.”

“Likewise, I was watching all of you and was also impressed with how well all of you are doing. You should be very pleased. This is no easy climb. Just be careful when you get over the shoulder just past Paloma Peak. The Knife Edge is just that, a razor thin path.”

The mother spoke up. “Given the time of day, does it make sense for us to continue? We are all a little tired.”

“You have ample time. Just watch the weather and keep a steady pace. The slower your pace, the less energy you expend and the longer you can climb without rest. The forecast is for possible rain later in the day. If you see a change in the weather, then turn back. But right now it looks good for the rest of your climb. Just don’t linger on the summit.”

“Thank you.”

“You’re welcome.”

With that they went their separate ways. Mom said, “That is one hunk of a man, let me tell you. I’d climb with him any day. I can imagine being rescued by him.”

The kids and the husband smiled with that one and happily started for Baxter Peak.

CHAPTER 21

THE HUNT

Max had two options to stay alive. With the first option he could create a flanking move, basically a half circle around the two men using compass directions and end up at the trail head and then get out of the park. The option did not solve much in that they would still be on the hunt for him. The second option was to kill both of them and drag their bodies into the heavy brush where the other climbing parties would not discover them. With that accomplished, he would head back to his safe house and call Elizabeth for help. When the other climbers returned to the parking lot at the trail head, they would simply assume that the two men were lost somewhere in the forest. That would not surprise the climbers. The problem for Max was how to separate the two men since taking on both of them at the same time was not an option. If they were assassins, he had to assume they had both hand guns and knives. The best bet was to draw them into the forest, let them get a fleeting look at him moving deeper into the woods and then disappearing so as to force them separate to look for him. One on one, he was confident of his ability to kill them.

Max moved down the trail with a steady but slow stride and made good time. Shortly after entering the woods, he stopped and removed his back pack. He lifted his KABAR knife out of the pack, removed it from the leather sheath and slid it inside his belt on the left side so he could quickly get at it with his right hand. Next, he removed his MK23 pistol, screwed on a sound suppressor, checked the magazine, chambered a round, put the safety on and slipped the gun inside his belt in the small of his back. He removed the binoculars and placed them around his neck and put his compass in his pocket. Then he flung his backpack deep into the woods.

He continued slowly down the trail until he heard voices. He stopped, looked carefully and then spotted both men walking up the incline towards him. They were about seventy five yards away. One of the men spotted him, pointed and said something to the second man who moved quickly up the path followed by the spotter. The spotter was carrying what looked to Max like a sniper's rifle. He had not planned on that.

Max moved quickly off the path to his right and headed deeper into the forest at a right angle to the trail so he was moving away from them. Because they would now turn into the woods towards him, the distance between them lengthened as Max had planned. Geometrically, they were moving along the hypotenuse of a triangle toward a point in the woods where Max was standing. He then started to run knowing they would do likewise. Since he was in excellent physical shape, thanks to a mandatory fitness program in the CIA, Max knew that they could not reach him until he wanted that to happen, which was part of the plan. He continued on the same line and by the time he dipped down into a swale, he had opened up sufficient distance so they lost sight of him. He quickly removed his parka, placed it on the ground, then removed his sweater and placed it on a branch and placed his navy blue cap on top of it. Putting his parka back on, he turned back up the mountain walking parallel to the trail. The men ran towards the sweater and hat which, from a distance, resembled a human. When they realized that they had been deceived, and with Max nowhere in view, they knew they had to split up if they were to have any chance of finding him.

They each chambered a round in their automatic pistols and decided that it was not likely Max would return to the original trail, thereby leaving three possibilities. One was for him to travel on the same line as he has been moving going deeper into the woods; the second was to turn left and head down towards the trail head and his car; and the third was to head back up the mountain. Since they were veterans of the Serbian conflict, they understood Max was engaged in a divide and conquer strategy, but they had no choice but to split up if they were to assassinate him. There was no way they could report to their superiors that they had failed.

They decided that one of them would head down towards the trail head to cut off Max's access to his car and thus his escape. The other would travel up the mountain remaining in the forest believing it unlikely that Max would return to the trail when other climbers would be returning from the summit. That he would move deeper into the woods made little sense to them since he would be further from his car. They consulted and decided that Max went back up the mountain in order to create a greater distance between them and give him an advantage of dealing with only one of them at a time. But, they had no option. One would have to retreat and cover the parking lot. With his binoculars, Max observed their decision and was pleased with himself. He had altered the odds in his favor.

By now, the receding sun was casting a lengthening shadow in the woods. This worked to Max's advantage since it would make it more difficult for his pursuer to see him in the dense brush and undergrowth. Given his early assessment of the two men, he decided not to engage in any hand to hand combat if it could be avoided. The plan was a simple 'shot to the head' since he did not know if his pursuer was wearing a flak jacket.

Max broke a path in the heavy underbrush as he climbed making it obvious to his pursuer which way he was moving. He came to an area of shoulder high boulders that forced him to make a right angle. As he did so, he noticed a depression off to the right side. There was substantial underbrush in it that provided cover for Max. He crouched low into the depression and pulled some of the brush around him. Darkness was setting in. He remained quiet, listening to the grinding of leaves as the assassin walked slowly up the broken path, looking to the right and left as he did so. From his position Max would not have a view of the man until he made his turn at the boulders. Until then, he had to remain quiet. He crouched still lower into the depression. The crunching of the leaves stopped and there was complete silence as the assassin stopped and took stock of the situation, believing that his prey was near. Satisfied that Max was not among the boulders, he moved cautiously on. As soon as he passed the depression, Max stood, pointed the MK23 at the back of the assassin's head and spoke. "Stay right there." The assassin stopped.

"Put the rifle on the ground." The man hesitated and then slowly slid the rifle of his shoulder, stooped over and placed it on the ground.

"Good so far. Now, raise your hands in the air. If you make a sudden move, I will shoot you." The man did as he was told. Max learned by the way the assassin had held the rifle that he was right handed.

"Why are you pointing a fucking gun at me? I am here hunting. Put your damn gun down." Max could hear the accent, however slight.

Max ignored him. "If you do as you are told, you will live. Now, with your left hand reach into your jacket and lift out your pistol and place it on the ground."

"I have no hand gun."

"Once again, use your left hand and take the pistol out of your jacket and place it on the ground."

"Fuck you."

The silenced bullet flew over the right shoulder of the assassin, exactly where it was intended to go. "The next one goes into your shoulder. Now, who hired you to kill me?"

"I have no idea what you are talking about. So, fuck off and leave me alone."

"Once again, who hired you?"

Silence.

"Let's start again. Take the pistol out of your jacket with your left hand and place it carefully on the ground."

Since the assassin was right handed, it was difficult for him to reach into his right hand pocket with his left hand to remove the gun. Finally, he took it out and started to bend down to place it on the ground. He had three options. The first was to put the gun on the ground and take his chances later. The second was to keep it in his left hand, turn quickly to the left and attempt to shoot Max with his left hand. The third option was to rapidly transfer the gun to his right hand, and turn either way to get a shot off. He chose the second option. He took the gun out of his pocket, turned to his left, and started to pull the trigger when a silenced 45 caliber bullet blew a hole in his head. He looked with hatred at his killer in that split second between life and death, and then fell face first on to the ground.

Max picked up the rifle and made certain the chamber was clear. He went through the pockets of the assassin and found six bullets that he put in his pocket. The only papers on the dead man were for the car rented at Logan International. There was no passport, license, credit card, hotel or motel keys, receipts or other identification. His was carrying several thousand dollars American in 50's and 20's and a cell phone. Max took the rifle, gun, cell phone and money and left the assassin where he had fallen but not before he picked up the two spent shells from his hand gun.

It was now time to kill the second assassin. Max took a compass reading and headed back to the main trail. He held the automatic pistol in his right hand with the sniper rifle slung over his left shoulder. It was a beautiful crafted .338 weapon with a Schmidt and Bender scope and a five round magazine. It was not for amateurs. The cell phone that he had taken from his first kill was in the outside pocket of his parka. It would not be long before the second assassin would be concerned that his partner had not returned or that he did not call to confirm the kill. When there was no response to the call, the hunt for Max would begin anew.

CHAPTER 22

DRINKS AND MORE

Vinnie motioned for the waiter to bring the check. He and Sharon had passed on dessert and were ready to leave. They both knew that the way this evening ended would say something about their future relationship. This was an exceptional woman and Vinnie did not want to make a misstep.

She put an arm through his as soon as they left the restaurant and without a word they headed to her car that was parked in the lot across the street. The car was at the very end of the lot where there was limited lighting. It faced high bushes that helped shield the lot from the adjoining neighborhood. The overhanging limbs of trees provided a visual barrier for the houses adjacent to the lot and made for a shadowy canopy over the end of the lot. There was a car on both sides of hers and the lot was full. Vinnie was pleased to see the relative seclusion hoping that the night might end with a casual embrace in the privacy of the darkened lot. He longed to hold her in his arms but resisted the thought so that he would not be disappointed.

As they walked quietly, he could feel the warmth of her breast against his arm and was aroused. They walked slowly, intimate strangers, not wanting to let go. They both understood the secret, unspoken and mysterious language of love and passion. She looked up at him and smiled and he pulled her arm closer to his chest. There was a mutual shivering that comes from wanting each other, but that carried with it the worry of one or both miscalculating.

They reached her car. She turned to look at him. "Vinnie, I had a beautiful evening. I saw a different person than the one who works at Global. I like this edition much better. I hope you ask me out again."

"Anyone who has one date with you would be stark, raving mad not to want to see you again. You are not only beautiful, but you are just lovely. I hate to see the evening end."

"Vinnie, I have the feeling that both of us would like to keep the evening going, but something special has happened tonight, something quite wonderful. I want to hold on to it for a while. Do I make any sense?"

"Sharon, anything and everything you tell me makes sense. I'll treasure this night and accept your need to save it. It is amazing that I feel like a teenager on a first date with the most popular and beautiful girl in the class."

She turned from him and started to reach for the door handle of her car and bring this wonderful evening to a close, but then hesitated as though changing her mind. She turned and looked up at Vinnie. He worried that she was about to speak words he did not want to hear; that he had been too obvious in his lusting after her. Looking at him appraisingly, she raised her hands and placed them against his cheeks. Vinnie was surprised at the gesture and felt an urge to hold her. Before he could move, she stood on her toes, slid her hands around his neck, drew herself up to him and kissed him. He placed one arm on her back and the other on a buttock and softly and tenderly pulled her tightly to him. She willingly folded herself into his body and could feel his erection pressing against her. Her tongue was soon into his mouth searching, inviting him to take her. He carefully slipped the straps of her dress off her shoulders and placed his hands on the see through bra that highlighted her ample breasts. He felt her nipples harden at his touch. She reached down and squeezed his penis. He quickly hardened and moved his hands under her dress and between her legs. She wore no panties and he could feel the smoothness, warmth and moisture of her vagina. She moaned with pleasure as his finger probed her vulva. With each of his movements, she tightened her grip on his penis and rocked her body to the rhythm of his finger movements.

He turned his body so his back was leaning on the car door and she pressed herself into him. Wanting still more, she unbuckled his belt and together they unzipped his pants. She pulled down his jockey shorts and grabbed for his penis. With his hands under her buttocks, he lifted her higher on to his body and then gently eased her down and as he did so, she slid his penis into her warm and wet cavity. He then lifted her body up and down and with each downward release of her body on to his penis he experienced the moisture and trembling of her orgasms. She cried with pleasure when he erupted inside her.

CHAPTER 23

ROMAN ASSIGNATION

Bettina Falaguerra and Carlton Richardson performed beautifully as two executives discussing business. Anyone observing them would assume this was a meeting and not an assignation. Their initial greeting and conversation was designed only for those who may have had an interest in their meeting.

"Bettina, you look wonderful. Your job must agree with you."

"Thank you Carlton. I do love my work and I especially look forward to returning to my native country from time to time. And, thank you for the compliment. You, as always look, what do they say in English, dashing and debonair? "

"Now, you are too kind." As he said it, he could not help but imagine being in bed with this striking woman. Her fluent English with an Italian accent gave her a cosmopolitan, sophisticated air, qualities Carlton loved in his women, qualities he saw in himself. He also knew that most women were drawn to his good looks, athletic physique, and his subtle and inviting lusting. The question in his mind was whether Bettina Falaguerra was drawn to him. But, there was time to pursue that later. Now, important business had to be conducted.

"I think, Carlton, we should order. I have a meeting at the embassy in an hour."

It was early so they both ordered a light lunch of bruchetta with diced tomatoes, parmigiano, chopped asparagus along with a glass of pinot grigio.

As soon as the waiter had taken their orders, they got down to business. "Bettina, are you certain that no one followed you?"

"For a moment or two I thought there was someone. Now, I am not so sure. But, it makes no difference since we are representatives meeting on behalf of our countries. As long as we act the part, avoid names and talk softly we are in no danger of being compromised."

"I will go first with my news. The American embassy, usually hot with rumors, is unusually quiet. The action of the Italian government in issuing arrest warrants for Max Rietsema and his twenty two agents sent shock waves throughout the delegation. I'm not certain about the Italian employees and what they know. Perhaps you can speak to that. Officially there is no news, but unofficially we have reason to believe Max is out of Europe. Exactly where is anyone's guess. It will be a well kept secret until such time as the Deputy thinks otherwise. Essentially, I have little corroborated information to share. But, no news is good news."

"Carlton, I am afraid I am the one with the bad news. I insisted on meeting face to face in order not to run the risk of having a call intercepted. Security at my embassy in New York and also here in Rome is like a sieve. No phone is considered secure and the walls have ears. To the matter at hand, I have no idea where he is, but I do know that his whereabouts may be known to Abdu Khalid and his followers."

"I don't believe that. Security has been tight and information impossible to acquire. How can this be?"

"A week ago, Italian custom agents at Fiumicino detained two male Serbs who were in transit from the Ukraine to Logan International Airport in East Boston. They were flying with Lufthansa, had a layover in Rome and had to go through a passport check. Their papers were in perfect order along with the Delta tickets to Logan. When asked the reason for the trip to the United States, they both gave what the agents thought was a rehearsed response. They said they had never been to the states and wanted to see Boston in particular and meet other Serbs who had established a small community in Waltham, Massachusetts. When asked to see their hotel reservations, they had none and said they would most likely stay with members of the Serb community."

"So far, I see nothing suspicious, Bettina."

"There are three concerns, Carlton. First, they had no return tickets to the Ukraine. Instead, they had reservations on a United Airlines flight from Logan International via Chicago to San Diego dated three days after their arrival in Boston. This made little sense if they had wanted to visit Boston and stay with the Serb Community. Second, all of their baggage consisted of a single soft pack carry-on and a briefcase. Their luggage was identical as though it was issued by the military. Third, between them they were carrying over ten thousand U.S. dollars. I almost forgot. There is a fourth problem. We learned later that there is no Serb community in Waltham."

"Then what happened?"

"While they were detained, Italian customs contacted the Italian intelligence service. It ordered that the two men be held at the airport until notified otherwise. They were to be told there was a question about their passports. The Italians contacted the CIA, MI-6, the Mossad, and the French Generale de la Securite Exterieura. Within hours, everything came back negative. With no reason to continue holding the men, they were allowed to leave on the next available Lufthansa flight to Boston."

"How did you come by this information?"

"We have no intelligence operation in Boston. Being Director of Italian intelligence in New York, I was immediately contacted and requested to dispatch agents to Boston to determine more about the men. My agents, being Italian, have no law enforcement standing in the United States. We could not demand that the Lufthansa operation in Boston share the surveillance tapes of all passengers deplaning in Boston. There was another delay as my superior in Rome had the Italian government contact the CEO of Lufthansa. Whoever spoke with the CEO explained the situation and stressed that the two Serbs could be terrorists intent on detonating a bomb on one of their planes. Permission was granted. My agents had the passport photos and compared them with the surveillance tape. The Serbs were on the Lufthansa tape. It showed them exiting the area and heading for the baggage and ground transportation area. Since they only had carry-on luggage, the agents assumed they would either be met by someone or would rent a car. My agents, having no authority to check every car rental company, did the next best thing. They went to the cab and limousine station and found the supervisor. Acting like American police, my agents flashed their Italian Agent I.D.'s and followed with the passport pictures. The Serbs had not taken a cab or limo. The assumption was that they had rented a car. When the head dispatcher was asked if he was on duty at the time the Lufthansa flight arrived, he said he was. Having done as much as they could, the agents returned to New York."

"Why didn't you contact the Boston CIA office and request that its agents deal with the car rental?"

"If I had done that I would have disclosed my role in intelligence services. The best that could be done was for me to contact the Italians and let them take over. I did so. I do not know if they contacted the CIA."

Carlton spoke, "I'll talk to the Deputy Director to see what she knows. It is possible the Boston Office was contacted and decided this was not important enough to report to her. It could have been lost at the bureaucratic level. As soon as I know something, I will get back to you. When do you return to the United States?"

"I will know that after my meeting with my superior but, I believe I will be on a flight tonight."

"Bettina, why were you unwilling to disclose to Langley that you are station chief of intelligence in New York, since I know it."

"Carlton, for the same reason I have not revealed to the Italian intelligence service that you are the new station chief in Rome. If I were to reveal your position, you would be removed by your Director and recalled home. I have good reason to believe you would miss what Rome is currently offering you."

"I wish you a safe journey, Ms. Falaguerra."

CHAPTER 24

THE MEETING

As promised, coffee and Danish were awaiting Vinnie's arrival along with a large serving of Gretchen and Darlene. The meeting was in Gretchen's office. Both of the women sat across from Vinnie.

"You look a little tired this morning. Late night?" It was Darlene.

If he didn't know better, he'd have to believe they had a tail on him last night. Whoever conducted that surveillance would have had an exciting story for Gretchen and Darlene. The more he thought about it, the story would have served to earn him some points with one or both of them.

"I had a restless night. Recurring nightmares about combat. You tend to replay events hoping to change the outcome. Never works."

"Sorry to hear that." Gretchen with sincerity.

"Thanks, but lack of sleep won't interfere with whatever it is you want to discuss. So, why don't we begin?"

"Good enough. Darlene, why don't you begin with Max and work back to the event."

"I thought, as a starter, you were going to discuss who the two of you work for."

"We need to discuss that and we will but, as Gretchen has suggested, the most effective way to get into what we do is to begin with the person who was at ground zero in our story. His name is Max Rietsema. He is a career CIA operative and a quiet hero. On paper his resume looks quite average and that is because his visible work has been mostly administrative while behind the scenes he is an outstanding agent and diplomat. He has been chief of station in multiple countries including several in the Middle East. It is difficult to recount how many explosive situations he has harnessed through his diplomatic skills while always protecting his agents. If not for Max's work, the head count of dead agents around the globe would be significantly higher. There is not a head of state in the Middle East who has not been the focus of Max's demands."

While Darlene spoke Vinnie noticed the sadness in Gretchen's eyes. She looked momentarily forlorn, deep in thought, distant. Was Max a lover from the past, a friend in need, a colleague in trouble, a success story gone bad? Perhaps all of the above. In time Vinnie would learn of the relationship if there was one to be found. She caught him staring at her and quickly looked interested in what Darlene was saying.

"Vinnie, have you heard the name Abdu Khalid?"

"Hasn't everyone? His story was carried by literally every media outlet, including Al Jazeera."

"Especially Al Jazeera, Vinnie. He is a hero to al-Qaeda and the millions of Muslims around the world who pray for the demise of western civilization, in particular, the United States. Do you know of the circumstances that led to his notoriety?'

"He was high on our hit parade of terrorists, the kingpin behind many bombings, suicide attacks, the marine barracks holocaust, several beheadings of newspaper reporters, support for the Twin Towers bombers and a host of other atrocities committed against both military personnel and civilians."

"Correct. That is only the beginning of the story. The guy is an evil son of a bitch who must be killed. The main plot began with the fact he was hiding in Italy with the assistance of high level Italian government officials. The CIA learned of his exact location and, with the help of certain officials in the Italian intelligence service, kidnapped Abdu Khalid and transported him out of Italy to Egypt for alleged torturing. To better understand the complexity of apprehending him and moving him to Egypt, twenty three CIA operatives were involved, some of whom were official and some off the books. The Italian government was so angered and embarrassed by our abducting a Yemen national on Italian soil that it issued arrest warrants for twenty two agents, plus the head of station. The government was dead serious about prosecuting the agents. By doing so, it hoped that al-Qaeda would spare Italy any grief. How stupid can a government be?"

"And, the head of station was Max Rietsema," said Vinnie.

"Yes."

"Darlene, this is a story that has played out over the decades. Different names, different situations, but all involving black operations which almost always are the most effective way of gathering valuable information. Then, the good guys are crucified by bad guys. Nothing new. An honest to God hero goes out on the limb to help save his country from the 'Evil Doers' as George Bush labeled them, including many evil doers in our own government and in the general population who believe you can jawbone your way to security with those who hate us for our democratic ideals. They are basically homeland terrorists with mainstream media as their megaphone. I assume that they, along with the Italian government and Khalid's friends, have this guy on the run. Worse, the Director wants no part of him, the agency does not know what to do with him, powerful senators on the Hill who detest the CIA want his head and experienced operatives in the agency think him a hero. And then there are you two and a group of rogue agents, both on and off the official organizational chart, who want and must save his ass by apprehending and terminating Abdu Khalid. And, somehow or other, you want to drag me into the story. Right?"

The women looked at each other knowing that Vinnie Pagano was one smart son of a bitch. Darlene spoke, "Something like that."

"Wrong. I have enough bad memories dealing with the most evil people on the face of this planet to last a lifetime. I did my thing. It's someone else's turn."

"That is bullshit, Vinnie." Gretchen finally spoke up, with anger. She was back. Whatever had caused her earlier disconnect had passed. "Every one of us who has been on the front line fighting the terrorist movement both understands and has the responsibility to protect Max and bring him home. He may never be a front line operative again, but his knowledge and understanding of terrorist operations is one of the most valuable commodities the agency possesses. He is one of the few agency leaders who has the balls to confront the Unites States Congress and not give a damn. He needs to be saved, not for himself but for our country."

"If he is so valuable an asset, why doesn't the Director bring him in? If anyone has the resources to accomplish it, he has."

"Officially, the timing is bad. Powerful forces in the Congress are intent on controlling all intelligence agencies, especially the CIA. It is in no mood to save Rietsema. He is too outspoken and uncontrollable as far as they see it. There would be no tears shed if the Italian government incarcerated him."

"Those bastards!"

"Vinnie, there is a long history of conflict between the many Directors of the CIA and certain elements within the Congress. It continues unabated in spite of the foreign threats against us and the need for our intelligence agencies to be ruthless in the pursuit of valuable information by any means at their disposal. If the truth be known, the Congress does not want smooth coordination between the numerous intelligence agencies, and it especially does not want a single coordinating agency even though it has one. It wants turmoil and miscalculations so it can step in and take charge. While Congress distrusts all of the agencies, the CIA is its primary target. The Director is walking a tightrope. One major misstep and he is out and the fools on the senate intelligence committee will demand a lap dog as a replacement. Those of us who know the Director understand that he is very much aware of what has to be done in Max's case and will make certain that it is done, but it will be off the record and coordinated by someone else. Field agents trust him to bring them home when the need arises. He is the only Director we have ever had who has impressive field experience. The same goes for his deputy."

"Officially, he is on the sidelines. I buy that but who runs the show?"

"Vinnie, her name is Elizabeth English. She is someone we know personally. Or, more accurately, she is someone who has worked with Darlene in the field. I'll fill you in on her credentials later. What is important is that she is the Deputy Director and has been given the Director's unofficial support to use any and all agency resources, both human and material, to bring this to a successful conclusion. She is the only person who knows where Max is at any given moment. They have secure communications. By whatever means she needs to employ, she has been instructed to bring this matter to an end. That means killing Abdu Khalid."

"Unless I missed something, there is no successful conclusion to be had. There is a world-wide arrest warrant out on Max Rietsema and a major terrorist on the hunt for him, not to mention Khalid's network across the continents. Our government may be able to compromise the Italian prime minister and get him to pardon your guy, but I don't see any way out of the al-Qaeda hunt. Or, is that where you plan on my entry into the story? Before you answer that, please tell me how the CIA was able to locate Khalid in the first place."

Gretchen spoke, "The answer to your second question is that we do not exactly know how he was located."

"Gretchen, you may not know technically how he was located, but the agency knows who gave the location. Unless you fess up, this little chat is over."

It was Darlene who spoke. "We're reluctant to share some information without knowing if you are on board."

"You will never get me to commit to being on board without sharing everything you know. Even at that, you may have to look elsewhere for help. The fact is that if you do not trust me with information, whether or not I am on board, it doesn't say much for my reputation. I'm a decorated hero, remember?" He found himself smiling at his comment.

The levity in his response was sufficient to lighten the air.

"Here is what we know. The informer is a female in a high level position in the Italian government, a position that affords her easy and unquestioned access to resources allowing her to travel freely between Italy and the U.S. We have been led to believe that her American contact works for the embassy in Rome, but that is rumor, not fact. The American embassy in Rome employs more than one hundred American citizens and over seventy five Italians. Less than half of the Americans speak Italian, and almost all of the Italians read, write and speak English. Little goes on in the embassy that the Italians are not aware of. At this point, it is anyone's guess as to who her contact is other than the fact that it is someone in the embassy. Since many of the Italians understand English, it means that her contact could be any one of the more than a hundred employees. We can also assume that one or more of the Italians are intelligence agents, not only for the Italian government, but for other governments with representation in Rome. You can turn most low level agents with either money or sex."

"Darlene, thanks for that. Having conducted a few investigations in my lifetime, it occurs to me that it would not take the agency long to determine who the high level female is that has the contact in the embassy. Once that is known, identifying her embassy contact should be relatively easy. Why hasn't that been done?"

"For one thing, it makes little difference to the United States now that our agents are safely out of Italy. The information has little value for us. If anyone needs to know, it is the Italian government since it has a high level mole in its midst."

"I do not agree. Every country is potentially an enemy. You know as well as I that we spy on all of our friends and they do likewise. It is a constant battle to stay ahead of them politically and militarily. The question is who has the best intelligence and counter intelligence capabilities. Italy is as much an enemy as any of the other unfriendly nations. The truth is Italy loves us for tourist dollars. It long ago forgot we saved their asses. If not for us they would be serving kaffee mit schlag and not cappuccino. I'm sure it has not gone unnoticed that its government is unstable and its Muslim population is large and growing. Having a high level informer within its government is a valuable asset to us.

He hesitated while the women had a chance to absorb what he was telling them. Then, he continues. "It is essential that we know who she is, what she does and then determine what help she can be in bringing Max home and assisting in future operations. Second, don't you think it important to know who, within the embassy, either received or learned of such vital information? It means that either that person or the woman has a sympathetic contact within the Italian intelligence service. If necessary, we should kill to learn her identity."

Darlene took over. "Are you able to find out who she is?"

"If I wanted to. But that leads me to my first question which you so smoothly slid by. What is it that you really want from me?"

"I'll try to answer that." It was Gretchen. "Truthfully, we are uncertain. As we told you earlier, we simply stumbled upon you. Our ad was for a journeyman detective for our cover operation. Who shows up, but a war hero in the prime of his life and with the self confidence of a tiger looking for it next meal. Then, for good measure, add in the fact that he is of Italian heritage and speaks fluent Italian. A background check tells us little of what you did to earn two jumps in rank only to refuse the promotion and go to work with an insurance company as a staff psychologist. Suddenly, we have a cocky, wise ass, talented ex-military on our hands for a vital job that is yet to be fully defined. You are what we need, Vinnie, and truthfully, we do not have a definitive plan going forward. If you agree to work with us without knowing all the details, except that the mission is critical, then we need to have you meet someone."

He asked with skepticism, "Who might that be?"

"We need an answer first. Are you with us?"

"Maybe. I need to think about it. I'll let you know."

"When?" It was Gretchen.

"Soon."

"We do not have much time, Vinnie. So, when?"

"Tomorrow."

"Tonight. We need to know tonight. Pack an overnight bag. If you agree to join us, you'll be flying. Casual attire on the plane, slacks and jacket for tomorrow, and informal wear for Saturday. A car will pick you up at your apartment at seven tonight. Call Global now and tell them you are taking a personal day. Tomorrow is Friday and you will be back to work on Monday morning. In fact, we could have you back by noon on Saturday in time to have the weekend to play. Be advised, however, that when you step into the car at seven p.m. you will be a contractor to the CIA and subject to the secrecy act. Don't bother asking where we are going and who we are meeting. You will know when you board the plane. Both Darlene and I will be traveling with you."

He looked at his watch. "It is ten thirty. I will call you before six tonight with an answer. I need time to think."

"Vinnie, under no circumstances are you to discuss this with anyone. Use any excuse you want to be out of work tomorrow, but do not discuss what went on here this morning. Understood?"

"Understood." He left the room with the distinct feeling they knew about Sharon.

CHAPTER 25

SECOND KILL

The husband and wife team were off the peak and making their way down. Whatever it was that Max had to do, he had to complete it and be clear of the parking lot before they were within hearing distance. That meant quickly killing the number two assassin and disposing of his body. The car would have to remain in the lot to be discovered by park Rangers when they arrived for duty the next morning. He could not allow that to happen. The car had to disappear. Elizabeth would have to be contacted for assistance. She will not be pleased to have to send a cleaning crew, but she would not hesitate.

The assassin was not about to let Max leave Baxter State Park alive. His partner would have called if Max was dead. There was no call. He was now the target. The assassin knew that Max had the sniper rifle but was not concerned since he was not a sniper expert and would not risk using it, missing his target and exposing his position. The chances were good that he would attempt a close-in kill. The assassin liked the odds since he was a full time killer and Max was not.

The killing game was about to continue. The assassin had the choice of taking cover in the wooded areas on any of the three sides of the parking lot. Max, on the other hand, had to reach the far side of the parking lot and use the parked cars for cover. He determined that the gunner would have his best advantage by taking cover on either side of the trail well before it emptied into the parking lot. Max believed that the ambush would take place approximately a hundred yards up the trail from the parking lot. He had other plans.

Assuming an ambush, Max turned right off the trail and walked a path that was perpendicular to the trail and parallel to the parking lot and the road leading into it. He continued in the woods away from the assassin until he could see that the access road curved sharply away from the far end of the parking lot. By crossing the road after the curve he would not be seen and would be able to make his way back behind the cars from a different direction than the assassin expected. Once behind the cars, he would have to flush him out in the open. Time was of the essence in that the sun was casting long shadows, darkening the lot and impairing a clean shot. If he removed the suppressor for greater accuracy, the husband and wife team would hear the shots and that would lead to complications. He made his decision and then quickly but quietly crossed over the road above the curve, moved into the woods and made his way back towards the parked cars. The suppressor was on the gun and the safety was off.

Still walking in the fringe of the woods, he reached the assassin's car. The front end faced the woods. He needed a strategy to force the assassin, who was on the trail on the opposite side of the parking lot, out into the open. Distracting the enemy was the key to killing him. A gun was far preferable to hand to hand combat. Once again Max checked to make certain that the safety was off. Quietly as possible he emerged from the woods, went to the window on the passenger side, removed his parka, wrapped it around the KABAR knife handle and smashed the glass. It splintered into thousands of crystals some of which fell inside the car and some outside. He put his parka on and waited for two or three long minutes to see if there was any reaction to his breaking the glass. There was none. He kicked some the glass crystals on the ground under the car and reached inside the window and unlatched the door and opened it. More glass crystals fell outside and he kicked them under the car with his right foot. Sliding into the passenger seat with the KABAR still in his hand, he depressed the horn and jammed the knife into the crevice between the horn pad and the steering wheel. The horn blew continuously. He ran to where the other three cars were parked and took cover behind the family SUV which was first in line and the closest to the trail head. He checked the fully loaded clip, made certain a bullet was chambered and waited.

Hearing the blare of the horn, the assassin leapt from his cover and, as fast as his feet could carry him, raced out of the trail on to the parking lot. He knew the blaring horn was coming from his car and made a run for it. The last thing he needed was for witnesses to be present when he made his kill. He had to turn off the horn. Max's calculation that the horn would expose the killer was a stroke of genius on his part. Unfortunately for his assailant, it would prove deadly.

The gunner's car was the last in line and he ran towards it. Max waited a moment and then moved out from behind the SUV onto the parking lot. The assassin, as he was running toward his car, saw peripherally that there was movement behind him and to his left. He began to turn and saw Max taking aim. Before the assassin could complete his turn and get off a clean shot, three piercing missiles struck him; the first in his right shoulder, the second and third in the chest. His legs began to weaken and he lost his balance. As he saw Max coming towards him, he struggled to stand upright. In spite of the pain in his right shoulder where the first bullet struck, he raised his arm to fire. Before he could get off a shot, three more forty five caliber bullets tore into his chest. The assassin struggled to remain upright as the force of the bullets propelled him backwards.

Red foam bubbled from his mouth and ran down his chin and on to his throat to mix with the dark blood oozing out of holes in his chest. He touched the blood on his chest with his left hand and then held it up in disbelief. The wrong man was dying. The gun fell from his right hand on to the ground. His eyes, those of a paid killer which were once filled with confidence, glazed over and closed. Death came quickly as he slowly fell backwards on to the pavement. Max picked up the gun. He then ran to the car, jumped into the passenger seat and removed the knife and silenced the horn. Once he had sheathed the knife, he returned to the body with a change of plans.

It was far too risky to move the body in his own car as previously thought. The better option was to place the dead man in the trunk of his own car. By the time the ranger arrived in the morning, the body would be gone along with the car, thanks to Elizabeth. Max would be back in Waterville.

He grabbed the man under his shoulders and dragged him across the parking lot to the car. As he did so, scuff marks from the assassin's shoes were left on the pavement. Max reached in through the smashed window, opened the passenger side door, leaned over and opened the driver side door. He went around to the driver's side and used the remote button on the lower part of the dash to spring open the trunk. He went through pockets and found the car key but nothing else that would be of help in determining how he had been located. He wrestled the body into the trunk and slammed the lid shut. Blood from the body stained Max's shirt.

He went back to where the kill took place to make certain there was no blood on the ground. By falling backwards, the only blood was on the body. Even if there was blood, the setting sun was casting long dark shadows on the black pavement. By morning it could be animal blood. Six empty cartridges from his gun were on the ground and Max scrambled to find them in the twilight of the evening before the climbers returned. Once he had retrieved them, he placed them in his pant pocket.

Max walked back to the fringe of the woods, picked up his parka, went to his car, unlocked the door and slipped into the driver's seat. He removed a cell phone from his parka, dialed a secure number, gave his exact location and requested a level one extraction of body and car to be completed before daylight. That done, he turned the key, started the car, backed up, turned and headed out of Baxter State Park.

He had outsmarted and outmaneuvered two assassins. They were dead but he was still the hunted.

CHAPTER 26

TRAILHEAD CONFERENCE

Twenty five minutes after Max had driven out of the parking lot, Glenn and Betsy Wilcox, the husband and wife team, emerged from the trail head and entered the parking lot. Darkness was setting in. Three cars were parked at an angle with the front ends facing the woods. Their car was the second in line, followed by the crossover belonging to the family. Max's car was next in line. The car belonging to the assassins was last and the broken window was not visible since it was on the passenger side and angled towards the woods. Unless you had a reason to approach the car, Max's secret was safe until morning, by which time Elizabeth would have extracted the car.

Glenn looked around the parking lot and was the first to speak. "Betsy, the lone climber seems to have left. Not a surprise in that he was clearly accomplished and moved with confidence. I couldn't help thinking when I saw the speed with which he climbed that he was a loner. Not many climbers would be able to keep up with him. No question that he has climbed a peak or two. I'm surprised that he didn't hang out to talk to us."

"He may be a man with a mission. No time to waste. I thought he was very nice, not to mention being quite handsome."

"Even I agree with that. He was a handsome devil. But, alone? There may be more here than we understand."

"I have no idea why anyone climbs alone but it is none of our business. It is getting dark and late. We need to get home and prepare for tomorrow."

With that, they packed their gear in the wagon. By the time they were ready to leave, they could hear the family laughing happily as they descended the trail. Soon thereafter, the four family members came out of the woods, entered the parking lot and went to their car. Glenn and Betsy had not left. Climbers, having a lot in common, easily engage in conversation and so it was with the six of them, standing next to their cars comparing their climbing experiences that day.

The teenage boy spoke. "I wonder where the two gorillas are."

"Ben, behave yourself."

"Mom, did you see the size of those guys. Their necks and arms are twice the size of dad's. When they walked, they looked as though they were stomping over bodies. I wouldn't want to meet them in a dark alley."

Ben's sister, Alex, spoke up with the certainty that only a teenager possesses, "Maybe no one else noticed but from watching Matt Damon in all those spy movies, I knew they were up to no good. Their oversized jackets told me they had guns under them."

"Alex, you have watched too many movies," said her dad.

"Maybe so, but I bet we all agree they weren't here to climb."

Glenn and Betsy looked at each other and he spoke. "I agree with Alex that my first and last impression was that they were up to no good. But that still does not answer the question as to what they were up to and why they were here in the middle of nowhere."

Stan added to the mystery, "If they were not here to climb and given the fact that they are not equipped to camp out and that there is nothing here for a saboteur or terrorist to destroy, I figure they were looking for someone. And, clearly, since we are all here in one piece, it figures that they were not after us."

There was a moment's hesitation before Lee entered the conversation, "The only other person in the park was the lone climber. Since his car is gone, we can assume that he was not involved."

Glenn disagreed. "That is not necessarily true. The only thing we know is that he is gone and two guys are still somewhere in the park based on the fact that their car is still here. After the lone climber entered the tree line on his descent, did anyone see either him or the two guys?"

No one answered and Glenn continued. "I thought not. Therefore, we have no credible information regarding the three of them. For all we know, they all could have driven off in one car. Or, the climber is still in the woods and the two guys took his car. What I do know is that I am tired and ready to call it a day."

Betsy responded. "As we all saw, the lone climber was experienced and there is no way he would be wandering around in the woods with night fast approaching. I say he is on his way to a happy hour with friends. There are probably women waiting for him. If I were single, I certainly would be waiting. The two others are somewhere in the woods and, for what reason, I don't know. It is always possible that one could be injured, but highly unlikely that both are. If they are lost, it is not a problem since they never stuck their heads above the tree line and therefore are not exposed to the elements. Even the dumbest climber lost in the woods knows enough to go downhill. If they needed help, they would have called out. Tonight's temperature is to be in the 30's. We can assume they will not perish by freezing to death. If, as Alex believes, they are after our local Matt Damon and carrying guns, they can protect themselves. In any event, the Ranger will find the car here in the morning. He will probably search it for clues and if convinced they are lost, will mount a search party. So, let's assume that Ben's bozos are lost in the woods and go home."

With that, they climbed into the two cars and left Baxter State Park, passing by the car with the broken window and a body in the trunk. Ben was the only one of the six who took a quick glance at the assassin's car as they passed it. Although unspoken, none were satisfied with the multiple suggestions as to what the two men were up to or where they were. All wondered about the lone climber.

CHAPTER 27

SAFE HOUSE

Max drove slowly so as not to draw attention to himself. The last thing he needed was to be stopped for speeding with his unregistered gun and that of the assassin in his possession. It was a two hour drive back to the safe house giving him time to think about the day's happenings. He knew that his secure phone call to Elizabeth would result in the car and body being extracted from the park in the next few hours. It was essential that Elizabeth move quickly. If by chance the car was not out by dawn all hell would break loose.

Max believed that the second body in the woods would not be found for some time. It was far enough off the trail. The chances were that by the time it was discovered, it would have been mutilated and torn to pieces by animals and decomposed. There was no way it would be identified.

He was convinced that neither body would be discovered by authorities. Once that issue was settled in his mind, his first order of business was to get to the safe house in Waterville, remove any evidence he had brought into the apartment and discard it and his climbing gear when and where it was safe to do so. He planned on traveling light with only his cell phone, gun, wallet and phony identification papers, including a Maine license. There were two other valuable possessions he had that Elizabeth would want; the key to the killer's car and gun. Both, forensically, would help find the source of the attack on Max.

When he entered the safe house he made a thorough search of each room looking for any evidence that they had been violated. None of the traps he set had been activated. Satisfied that the apartment was clean, he removed his clothes, showered, shaved and put on fresh clothes. He placed his climbing gear into a plastic bag. All items that he used were also placed in the bag. It would be discarded at his next stop. Finally, he wiped down all surfaces he had touched. This was not necessary because Elizabeth would have a cleaning crew in the apartment early the next day. It would undergo a far more extensive cleaning than Max had performed. Max would be the last person to use this safe house. It was damaged goods and of no further use to the agency. An agency shell real estate company would get rid of it.

When Max made his call to Elizabeth, he included an urgent second request for transportation out of Maine. Elizabeth was ahead of him and informed his that an agency jet would be waiting for him at the private plane area at Bangor airport. His instructions included how he was to dispose of the car and anything he removed from the apartment including any clothing and equipment he had worn to make his climb.

He closed and locked the door to the apartment, threw the plastic bag on to the back seat of the car, made one last survey of his surroundings and, satisfied that the area was secure and that he was not under surveillance, got into the car, turned the key in the ignition and began still another odyssey.

It was late and he was tired and faced the long ride to Bangor where his transportation was waiting. Everything was under control. Then, out of the blue, a shock wave ripped through his body. His mind panicked over a detail he had left behind that would start an FBI investigation as early as the next morning when the Ranger arrived at the trail head. He had made a serious mistake. How could he have been so careless? No, not careless, stupid! His stupidity would accelerate and mobilize multiple agencies into action and compromise his well being and that of the CIA. How could he have missed the sniper rifle that he placed on the grass next to the asphalt when he emerged from the woods? Intent on breaking into the car, he put the gun down to free up his hands. He actually stepped over it when he returned to the car later to pop open the trunk and wrestled the body into it. The extraction team would never see the rifle lying in the grass on the fringe of the parking lot. Going back was out of the question. There was no time. His ride would not wait.

He dialed a secure number, waited for a password request, entered it and left a message with Elizabeth for the extraction team detailing where the gun was located. Satisfied that he had done all he could, he stepped harder on the accelerator and sped towards Bangor feeling vulnerable and exposed. If they could find him in Bangor, literally in the woods, then they could find him anywhere. Someone in the agency has betrayed him or so he thought.

As he made his way to his rendezvous, a Dassault Falcon 2000 LX was being fueled. With a range of 4,000 nautical miles, Max could be moved anywhere in the continental United States. He had no idea as to his next destination. He also forgot about the shattered window glass lying next to the ground and the information it would yield.

CHAPTER 28

WITH RESERVATION

"Hi, it's me."

"I know."

"Sorry I didn't call earlier but I had an appointment to keep."

"Are you coming in today or do you usually start your weekends so early?" She was mildly upset with him. Her voice was strained and he hoped she was not crying softly. He was uncertain if it was his conduct last night or the fact that he did not call her later in the evening or this morning.

"Something has come up and I have to be out of town tomorrow. Please leave a note for Evan letting him know that I am taking a personal day. I leave tonight and will return on Saturday morning. I was hoping that I could see you before I leave."

"I'd like that. What did you have in mind?"

"Can you leave a little early, around three or four? I'm going back to my apartment to pack and deal with some other business. I could stop at Whole Foods on the way and pick up a bottle of wine and the fixings for an appetizer. You could come here or we could meet at your apartment. I have to leave by six. What suits you best?"

"I will leave here at three. Evan is away and Karen can handle the phone. You do the shopping and I will do the prepping. Come by my condo around four. And Vinnie, I know you don't know how to handle discussing last night, but I loved every minute of it. Whatever happened was at my initiative. Your honor is still intact."

He couldn't help smiling at that comment. "Thanks. See you at four."

He had several hours before he had to respond to Gretchen and Darlene. He was questioning why he would want to get involved in an operation that, in his mind, had less than a fifty-fifty chance of success. Maybe when he knew more, he could alter the odds. As he assessed the situation it was clear to him, if not the two women, that there was no way the president of Italy was going to pardon Max and the others without a substantial payoff. On the other hand, with Berlusconi out of the picture, negotiating with the new Italian president would be easier since the scandal did not occur on his watch.

He was certain that Gretchen, Darlene and the Deputy Director would have ideas as to how to approach the Italians. The more he worked with the two women the more he liked them personally and the greater his appreciation for their talents. What he did not know was how they felt about him. Nevertheless, a professional bond was forming and he would trust their judgment on the Italian side of the issue. He also knew that the high ranking female at the Italian embassy would be in the equation, although uncertain as to her role. First, he needed to learn her identity.

As for Khalid, Vinnie needed more information before he would express an opinion. What he did know was that he had spent most of his time in Iraq and Afghanistan killing the likes of Khalid and would not fail if called upon now.

Max was another one of the good guys being victimized by the bad guys. It was that simple. He may be operating in a sphere that was foreign to Vinnie, but they were on the same side and believed in the same principles and values. They believed in the goodness of America and were committed to saving it from those who were relentless in wanting to bring the country to its knees. If Gretchen and Darlene really understood Vinnie, they would have simply said, "One of ours is in trouble and we need you to save his ass." That would have been the end of it. His mind was made up.

He dialed Gretchen and she picked up. "You're early."

"Little sense in delaying when I know what to do."

"And that is?"

"I am on board for the time being but reserve the right to change my mind after whatever occurs tomorrow. If that does not work for you, then I am out."

"That works perfectly. See you at seven. And, Vinnie, we really appreciate what you are doing." She hung up and then dialed a secure number. The phone was picked up at the other end after three rings and Gretchen spoke, "Estimated time of departure is seven forty five p.m. Will update once we are airborne." With that she hung up.

When Vinnie arrived at Sharon's she had changed into loose fitting warm-up pants and a man's button down shirt. The first two buttons were undone and the cuffs were folded up. Her hair was pulled back in a ponytail and she wore minimal make-up. She had discretely applied a light and expensive perfume. The contrast with the night before was stark. From

Giorgio Armani to Nike and Gap. From sophisticated and elegant to youthful and wholesome. But still beautiful.

When she opened the door, both of Vinnie's hands were full. She leaned forward and gave him a light kiss on both cheeks. Liking it, he nodded approval and encouraged her to do it again, which she did.

Her condominium was contemporary and light. It reflected her bright personality. It was a happy setting that Vinnie entered. With the bottle of wine in one hand, he stood in the middle of the open great room, looked around, turned to her and said, "It is as lovely as you Sharon. Thanks for asking me to share it, if only for a couple of hours."

"I'm happy you came. I missed you today. The office is not the same when you are not there. But why do I have the distinct feeling that you will not be there long?"

"Let me open the wine and then we can talk. OK?"

"OK."

With that, he opened the wine and poured it into glasses Sharon had placed on the kitchen counter. She unwrapped the package Vinnie brought. In it were four pieces of prepared bruschetta. She put them in the microwave for fifteen seconds and then placed them on two china dishes. Together they walked to the sofa and sat. He handed her the glass of wine and clinked her glass.

"Vinnie. May you return safely from wherever it is you are going." They both took a sip of their wine.

"The truth is that I have no idea where I am going, what I am doing once I get there and who I am seeing. For reasons I cannot share, I believe it is vital that I go."

"Does this have anything to do with your being out of the office the last few days? It is obvious you had a mission."

"Sharon, this all started simply enough. I walked in one day and there was a help wanted ad on my desk for a detective position with an investigative service. From there, events took over and eventually led to my being out of town tomorrow. If not for the ad, I would be at my desk this very moment."

"It is all my doing. If I hadn't left the ad, none of this would be happening."

"You left the ad? Why?"

Sharon turned on the sofa and looked directly at him and spoke. "On the one hand, I really did not know you even after your being at Global for a year. You are there, but not there. It was obvious you didn't belong, as you put it, with the walking dead. On the other hand, I had seen many employees come and go with the company. The salary and benefits are great and they help recruit talented employees. Invariably, they all end up as drones, pushing paper, watching the clock, stopping off every night for a drink or two before heading home. They wind up mixing with the young women, many of them gorgeous, who are looking to move up in the company. What the women do not understand is that the only position for them is usually prone! It is not long before the affairs start, marriages go to hell, demotions begin, transfers are initiated and assignments are made to windowless offices in the basement. You have to believe me when I tell you that unless you are 'recruited' to join Global by members of the executive committee, you are destined to always be second tier. Two groups possess the power at Global; the really old money that quietly owns controlling shares and the new breed of young financial vultures who will eventually bury the company after they have looted it. The former put their kids in the top jobs and the latter put their mistresses there. Those two groups decide who will be promoted and successful. You would not have been one of them."

"I don't get it. Given all that, why would you be concerned for me? As you just said, I was there but not there. You hardly knew me. There was no reason to worry about me."

"Vinnie, I read your resume, several times in fact. You are what every parent wants for a son; an American hero, smart as the devil, fluent in three languages, a modern warrior, strong, handsome, successful and above all, a man who cares about his country and has been on the battlefield to prove it. Should I go on? In fact, you are what every sister would want for a brother, every wife for a husband. I decided that Global could not have you." Her words were spoken with passion and love.

"And what every girlfriend would want for a boyfriend?"

"Something like that. I will hate not being able to look at you every day, but I know that there is something larger at play. Some men are born to families that love America to the core; they are different in that they are not distracted by current events. They are not swayed by political rhetoric. They always know what the end game is and are willing to risk life and limb to get to the goal. They love as fiercely as they fight. If not for them and their willingness to take on the establishment, there would be no hope for our country. You're one of them Vinnie and I admire you for it, will miss you while you are gone, and will pray for your safe return."

With that, he leaned over, kissed her gently on the lips and nudged her into his arms. They remained quiet and still for a moment or two and he could feel her heart beating against his chest. She felt secure and safe in his reassuring arms.

When finally he released her, he said, "Sharon, if I didn't know you, I would think you were pushing my candidacy for the joint chiefs-of-staff. I love your sentiments and your beliefs. In a couple of hours I will be operating temporarily under the secrecy act and will be forbidden to speak to anyone about what I know. Until then, I will tell you what I can. Truthfully, I do not know what the 'end game' is. Until I do, I have reserved the right to decline the offer of employment. The most I am able to share is that a good man needs help, a bad man must be found and that some members of a government agency believe I can help. That is what I know."

Acting like a couple who had been in a long term relationship, they occasionally kissed, embraced and touched, sipped the wine and nibbled on the bruschetta. It was six when he released her and said it was time to leave. At the door, they embraced and kissed. "Vinnie, I didn't chase you out of Global to put you in harm's way. Please be safe." With that she cried softly. Wiping the tears from her cheeks, she wrapped her arms around him and buried her head in his chest.

He kissed her gently, turned and left. She watched as he walked to his car. Her love for him was overwhelming and she was frightened to death for what awaited him. She believed him when he said he would be back, but in her heart, she knew it would not be for long.

CHAPTER 29

CARLTON'S CALL

On the short walk back to the embassy following lunch with Bettina Falaguerra, Carlton pondered what she had shared with him. He reviewed in his mind the points she had made. First, the Serbs were leaving Boston for San Diego three days after their arrival from Rome, although their stated purpose for coming to the states was to spend time in Boston and connect with their Serb community. Second, their luggage and briefcases were identical, indicating that they were issued by some agency or military unit. Third, they carried an unusually large amount of American cash for such a short stay. Fourth, it was determined that there was no Serb community in Waltham. It was obvious to Carlton that the Serbs were traveling for another reason and he was determined to find out what it was. As station chief in Rome he was worried he had allowed two terrorists to slip through his fingers. He and Bettina were on the same page as far as saving Max's ass, but he was also concerned about saving his own.

Carlton had to admit that the facts indicated further investigation was necessary. He knew that the American Embassy in Rome had not been contacted by either Italian customs or the Italian intelligence agency regarding the airport questioning of the Serbs about their subsequent flight to Boston. He had no idea if Langley had been alerted by either agency. A phone call to Elizabeth was in order.

When he arrived at the embassy he went directly to the secure room and placed the call to Elizabeth's cell phone. She knew his call would come sooner or later and answered on the third ring, prepared with a fabricated story for his consumption. "Carlton, I wasn't expecting to hear from you. I assume there is a problem." Her phone was only to be used in an emergency.

Elizabeth never wasted words with Carlton. Over her strong objections, he had been appointed by the Director to run intelligence operations out of the American Embassy in Rome after Max had fled from Italy. From her perspective, he spent too much time in the bedroom and not enough in the field. He was also a snob and drank heavily. She also believed that his cover position as Director of Economic Section was poorly developed and limited his access to high level Italian politicians and intelligence agencies. Elizabeth also knew that the position had a positive side from his perspective in that it connected him with Bettina Falaguerra, his beautiful counterpart in the Italian Embassy in New York and head of Italian intelligence in the northeast United States. Unfortunately for Carlton, Elizabeth was his boss.

Although often tempted, he had never gone over Elizabeth's head. She could be as ruthless as she was attractive.

"Actually, I am calling to see if there is problem. I lunched today with my colleague, Bettina Falaguerra. She shared some interesting facts about two Serbs. Before I waste your time with the details, it would be best if I asked if you have been updated on this matter by either the Italian intelligence service or your agents in Boston?"

"I was informed by our Boston field office. The agent in charge was sufficiently concerned to move it up to me. We learned they rented a car at Logan. The car was paid for in cash and they used one of their passports as identification. They asked for a map of the Boston area. The Hertz personnel detected nothing unusual except the fact that they spoke limited English with a distinct accent. They thought it could be Russian or Slavic but they were not certain. Other than that, they were not much different from other foreigners renting a car."

"Did they return the car to Logan?"

"Carlton, I have the president on the other line. I will have to get back to you." With that, the phone went dead. At that moment, POTUS was hosting a state dinner for the President of France and was not on the phone. Carlton looked at the phone in his hand and swore, "The bitch knows more than she is telling me." He slammed the phone down.

Elizabeth stared at her phone and was uncertain if she was correct in not sharing more with Carlton. She suspected almost everyone in the agency as being capable of betrayal, often for money, occasionally on principle, mostly for sex. Still fuming because he was appointed to replace Max, one of the few agents she trusted without reservations, she was not going to bring the Rome office into play unless necessary. Carlton's lusting after every beautiful pussy made him a security risk. Every woman who slept with him and worked at a foreign embassy was most likely a spy who wanted to get into more than just his pants. From her perspective, he could not be trusted with state secrets.

She never understood why the Director chose him. One day she would raise the question.

She thought about Max and the mess he was in and was dispirited thinking she could eventually lose him as a field Agent. He was one of a select few who acted on principle. That thought reminded Elizabeth that she needed to speak with Gretchen and Darlene, two of the trusted agents, to receive a status report on their efforts to find a qualified team member.

Elizabeth learned from her agents in Boston that two Serbs had rented a black Chevy Impala at Hertz for three days, paid in cash and asked for a map of New England. At the check-out gate, they asked the attendant for directions to Bangor, Maine. The attendant confirmed the East European accent and thought they were Russian. They grunted a "thank you" to him and were on their way.

She glanced at her watch and knew that the Falcon 2000LX was at that moment approaching Bangor and Max would soon board it for his flight south. His message about the rifle had been forwarded to the cleaning crew and within hours the evacuation of car and body would be complete. The second body, still in the woods, posed a problem. That was for another day. She just had time to change into an evening gown and get to the White House to try her fluent French on the President of the French Republic and his wife.

CHAPTER 30

AMOS TRUMBULL

The sun was beginning to make its ascent in the eastern sky, one of the earliest points to lighten the horizon on the eastern seaboard. It was a phenomenon that thousands of Maine residents experienced every day. In a few minutes the sun would lift itself above the tree line to the east and shoot rays of sunlight onto the western end of the parking lot at Baxter State Park. Along with the sun would come the first climbers of the day, hoping to reach the summit of Katahdin and return safely.

The park Ranger was driving a four year old Ford 250 pick-up, the standard vehicle for the park service. Great for driving and great for hauling, all seasons, all weather. Amos Trumbull had been with the service for twenty two years, having been accepted right out of high school, long before the days when you needed a college degree to be employed. Formally uneducated as compared to new recruits, Amos had the common sense of a down easterner and an uncanny ability to sense when all was not quite right. He also knew how to handle a variety of guns.

Born into a family that had been among the early settlers in Maine and who remained in Maine, Amos was Teddy Roosevelt's idea of the man born to nature. His daddy had him in the woods as soon as he could walk, and placed a gun in his hand when he was eight years old, much to the chagrin of the then local chief of police, Horace Browning, who believed that Clint Trumbull gave his son a gun at age eight only to piss off Horace. In spite of it, Clint and Horace were friends. So it goes in Maine.

The truck had a second occupant. It was Annie, Amos's new Springer Spaniel. Annie was a high spirited animal, smart and adorable as dogs go, although that is not a description that a Maine dog would want. Amos always had a dog and when one died of old age or accident, he quickly got another. "Man and his dog" pretty much described the two of them. Annie was three years old, could ran like hell and was a good hunter.

Amos pulled into the parking lot and, as was his routine, he drove to the western edge and parked his Ford at the trail head. He turned off the engine and stepped out of the truck. Annie flew out before Amos was fully on the pavement. Always one to press his luck against bureaucratic rules, Amos supplemented his brown Ranger outfit with a comfortable black and red plaid wool Woolrich jacket. It felt comfortable against the morning chill. Until the sun got higher, the frost would continue to cover the landscape. A quick survey of the parking lot indicated that yesterday's climbers had pretty much picked up after themselves. Except for a few scattered papers and wrappers, the lot was clean. He found, over time, that experienced climbers were much better than novices about carryout out their garbage.

As he surveyed the parking lot, Annie was running around letting off some steam from having been in the truck for twenty minutes. The sun had risen just enough to begin to cast long shadows over the parking lot. In an hour or so it would be high enough to bring sunlight to the entire lot, but for now it only touched a portion of the western edge. As it did, Amos caught a glimpse of reflective light on the north side of the lot.

As he started to make his way to where the reflection was seen, Annie let out a small growl followed by barking. She repeated the growling and barking. Amos turned and walked over to Annie. She was pawing at the ground. He moved her aside with his hand and gave her a command to sit, which she did. He bent down and looked closely at what she was pawing at and observed the red stain. As first glance it looked as though a bird or small animal had been attacked. Amos had seen this same scene a hundred times if he had seen it once. He was about to let it go when he noticed the two scuff marks on the pavement just ahead of the red stains. Alone, that would not have caused any concern since large animals usually drag their prey into the woods. But these were not animal marks. The two scuff marks turned into two lines that stretched across the lot towards where Amos had seen the reflection. He got up and followed the scuff marks until they ended. He looked down at what appeared to be a scattering of glass crystals and immediately knew that it was shattered glass from either a car or truck window. Over the years there had been a number of vehicles broken into and he had witnessed how the new tempered glass disintegrated into thousands of crystals when smashed. He stood for a quiet moment with Annie sitting at his side and pondered what he had just seen, what it meant, and what the next step should be.

Horace Browning was no longer chief of police but he still lived close by and, contrary to what city folk think about rural law enforcement officers, Horace was one smart cop. It was early but then old folks got up early, especially in Maine. Amos took out his cell, found Horace's number and dialed.

It rang. "In trouble again, Amos. You never should have been given a gun at seven."

"I was eight and you never should have been chief of police. Damn lucky you never had to fire a gun since you couldn't hit a turkey if it was at your feet. That said, you did have a good head and I need you to use it for me, now. "

With that, Amos shared his observations. When he finished, Horace asked, "Do you think the marks were made by the heels on shoes and that a body had been dragged across the lot?

"I do. Given the broken window, one might logically conclude that a car was broken into and the body put into it and driven away. That, however, is pure conjecture. There were only a few climbers yesterday and there is no way of immediately knowing who they were. If they had seen anything, they would have reported it to the Ranger station. Maybe I'm making too much of this."

"Amos, red stains, drag marks and broken glass do not make for nothing. Something occurred and it needs to be pursued."

"I guess I didn't want to think that an assault or murder could take place in our park."

"This is not time for sentiment. My suggestion is that you immediately close the gate and secure the parking lot for the rest of the day. Place a sign on the gate indicating that it is closed until further notice.

Direct climbers to another trail head. Then, you call this into the state police and follow that up by notifying Chief McCorey what you have done. He is the local law enforcement officer and he can be difficult to deal with if not kept in the loop. Then call the Ranger station and get another Ranger over there pronto to stand guard at the gate. As soon as the state police arrive and conclude that there may have been a murder, the Bangor office of the FBI will be called in. They have the resources to test the stain and determine who manufactured the glass which will lead them to the vehicle manufacturer, perhaps even a model. Then the investigation will run its course. The vehicle had to come from someplace and the red stain belongs to someone or something. If it was the stain alone, I would think animal. Coupled with the drag marks and the broken window, there is more to think about."

"Horace, what if I were to get something into the papers with the hope that one of the climbers would have seen something that may help?"

"Unless you want your ass in a sling, do nothing of the kind. At best, the feds are friendly enemies. They want their way. There are several other federal agencies that do equally good work but the FBI has the muscle and the reputation. They also have the best forensic laboratories in the world. I'm thinking the feds will want to know who the climbers were yesterday. Let them figure out how to find them. And, Horace, be sure to shave. You may be on CNN or Fox. Don't want to look like a country hick."

"Thanks, Horace." Amos hung up and made for the entrance to close the gate, thankful that Horace was at home when he called.

CHAPTER 31

DEPUTY DIRECTOR

The black Cadillac SUV arrived precisely at seven p.m. The driver got out and rang the doorbell, Vinnie answered. Without a word, he picked up his overnight bag and pulled and locked the door behind him. As he walked to the car he had an opportunity to assess the driver who was ahead of him. Military bearing, six three or four, one hundred ninety five pounds, lean with a strong upper body, broad shoulders, long gait, short haircut, quiet shoes and an oversized jacket. He took Vinnie's bag and tossed it on the back seat and then opened the front passenger door and motioned for Vinnie to get in. "It's a thirty minute ride. May as well be comfortable. Before you ask, we are headed for the private aircraft area at Bradley. To be precise, we're going to World Wide Jet Service where you will be met by Gretchen and Darlene. There is nothing more to tell so don't ask."

"Thanks. I'll enjoy the ride, but there is one question that I'd like to ask. What are you carrying?"

"That obvious?"

"Takes one to know one."

"Glock 19."

"Nice." With that, they settled into silence until they arrived at World Wide Jet Service.

Thirty two minutes later, the SUV pulled up in front of a low slung, modern building with a lot of glass. Vinnie stepped out, opened the rear door, grabbed his bag and followed the driver into the building. The interior was a work of art. Everything about it suggested money, lots of money. Those with private jets or who lease them expect the best and World Wide Jet Services provided it. As is always the case with money environments, there was a classy looking receptionist, even at this hour. Apparently the clock never stops for those with big plans. What Vinnie did not know was that World Wide Jet Services was a successful front operation for the CIA in the New England region. It ran a legitimate and financially successful jet service for business men and women and for the general public, while providing transportation for its agents operating in the Northeast. It also owned or leased only the very best in private planes. Its inventory included the newest Gulfstream 650 and the older, but perfectly maintained and the favorite of many, the 450. The agency also knew where those clients of interest to the CIA traveled to, when they left and with whom. If they didn't know why, they would soon find out.

The driver let the receptionist know that Vinnie had arrived and he then left the building and drove off. The receptionist picked up the phone and spoke, "Captain Pagano is here." Gretchen and Darlene trained the receptionist well. Almost immediately Gretchen and Darlene emerged. Both had changed into casual traveling clothes and looked somewhat younger than they looked in their corporate uniforms. "Hi, Vinnie." It was Darlene.

"Hi, Darlene, hi Gretchen. This is a fabulous and luxurious facility. I have the feeling that this is about as much of it I am going to see." With the words hardly out of his mouth, the deep hum and purring of beautifully engineered and well maintained jet engines just outside the lobby interrupted any further thoughts. The three of them turned to see a Gulfstream 450 approach the building and then turn so as to place the door to the plane facing the lobby. Talk about pampering. This was a far cry from his transportation in Afghanistan.

The door opened, stairs unfolded and gently touched the ground. The women headed for the door, climbed the stairs and Vinnie followed. One of the two pilots greeted the women by name and welcomed the three of them aboard. The stairs were drawn up, the door retracted and locked, and a minute later the 450 turned and headed for the tarmac. It took its position at the end of runway and, after being given clearance from the tower for takeoff, the pilot moved the throttles forward. The two whining, powerful Pratt and Whitney engines were fighting the brakes. When the engines attained optimum power levels for the race down the runway, the pilot released the brakes and Vinnie was propelled to a new destiny, somewhere, for some yet unanswered reason, with Gretchen and Darlene, both of whom he was now in love with.

The Gulfstream rose sharply, banked to the left, made a pass over Hartford gleaming in the night, then headed south for the Virginia countryside.

CHAPTER 32

OUT OF BANGOR

Exactly fifty two minutes earlier another jet lifted off in Bangor, Maine. The Dassault Falcon, powered by two Rolls Royce engines, flew a routine pattern out of Bangor airspace and with ease climbed to 40,000 feet. The pilot turned south for a trip that would take them to the Virginia countryside with an estimated arrival time approximately the same as the Gulfstream 450 carrying Vinnie, Gretchen and Darlene. Other than the two pilots, Max Rietsema was the only person on board. It was a moonless night and there was little to see except the lights from communities far below and barely discernible from this altitude. Ordinarily Max, like any capable agent, would be determining the compass direction and generating alternate destinations, changing them each time the plane altered its heading. The agency spent a great amount of time having agents practice this routine in the event of abduction. It was difficult to do so in a plane where you lacked street noise and different road surfaces that would be present if you were abducted by car. Tonight, he was exhausted and he knew he was in good hands, heading towards safety with Elizabeth in charge. He slept.

CHAPTER 33

ELIZABETH'S RENDEZVOUS

In the covert worlds of the many American intelligence agencies, there have always been secrets kept from those in charge. It was best they did not know so they would not be culpable in the event of public disclosure.

In the rich Virginia farmland fifty miles from Washington there was a thirty thousand acre farm, the ownership of which was registered to John Winslow Burnett. Mr. Burnett existed only on paper. The farm was one of many 'off-the-books' properties owned by the CIA. The farm produced neither crops nor animals. It consisted of the land, several barns of varying sizes scattered across the vast holding, an impressive mansion and eight stand alone cottages within walking distance to the mansion. Five of those cottages would be occupied this night.

To the rear of the mansion was a very large and relatively new garage capable of housing ten vehicles, four for visitors, two for the caretakers and four for the security force. Next to the garage were four additional cottages for use by security personnel. The caretakers, all of whom were employees of the Central Intelligence Agency, had sleeping accommodations in the mansion. Except for the barns, all of the physical facilities were clustered in the most remote part of the farm, almost dead center, where the tall oaks provided a canopy that shielded most of the light and activity from prying eyes in the sky.

Adjacent to the facilities was a broad meadow that stretched for seven eighths of a mile and was forty yards wide. Two oversized barns were located at the west end of the meadow. One barn housed ground equipment for servicing aircraft; the other could shelter two large aircraft from prying eyes.

On each side of the meadow, at ground level, small low intensity landing lights were located fifty yards apart and ran the entire length of the meadow. They were activated by incoming aircraft. Every hundred yards there were two sets of directional lights in the shape of arrows, each pointed in the opposite direction. The lights were controlled from the ground and acted as a windsock for the aircraft since ninety five percent of the flights into and out of the farm were at night.

The Director of the CIA, Anthony Mallory, had no knowledge of this facility. It was used for two purposes; the first being the debriefing of agents coming in from clandestine operations. They were brought to the farm under darkness and taken out the same way with no idea as to where they had been. They could be there for a few days or a few weeks. The fewer who knew of this location the better it was for the agency. The second purpose was to provide a safe site for Elizabeth English's covert operations such as the one about to begin.

Elizabeth English, Deputy Director, was continuing what had already been a long and challenging day. The best had been kept to last. Shortly after her brief conversation with Gretchen, she had received a secure communication prepared by her and Darlene that provided a complete work-up on Captain Vinnie Pagano. Elizabeth could not have been more pleased. Early in his career, he had been one of their own without their knowing it. She had to smile when she thought about his turning upside down both Highland Properties in Bermuda and the solicitors Bean, Choate & Whitehall and to have done it in two days. Her two agents in Bermuda, Tony Eden and Freddie Blair, would be expecting a call from Elizabeth any day. She would also have to have a word with the ladies for being out-maneuvered by Pagano. He had outsmarted both of them.

An informant in the Simsbury Town Hall had reported Vinnie's visit to the tax collector's office and related how he had charmed Rachel on his way to collecting information about the construction of Metro Plaza and on the private lives of Gretchen and Darlene. She liked this man without meeting him and was pleased the search was over. He would be one of a group of four, the others being Max, Gretchen and Darlene, in whom she would have complete confidence. If anyone at the agency was to find and kill Khalid, it would be one or more of the four.

The lights from Langley faded as the helicopter's powerful engines lifted it into the night sky to reach cruising altitude. The twin turbines screamed and the fuselage vibrated and shook. Elizabeth had never gotten used to the deafening noise and the cold touch of metal. She held fast to her seat and said her usual silent prayer as she did each time she flew in a helicopter. In less than forty five minutes, it reached its destination and prepared for landing. Had the helicopter been equipped with a rear view mirror, Elizabeth would have seen that three minutes behind her a

Dassualt Falcon 2000 was headed for the same meadow and that four minutes behind the Falcon a Gulfstream 450 was also approaching the landing area.

The pilot of the helicopter triggered the landing lights and a security agent on the ground immediately activated the directional arrows which indicated an east west landing. The helicopter made a turn and settled into the required flight pattern and two minutes later settled on the field. Both the landing lights and directional arrows remained on for the Falcon and Gulfstream. A car was waiting to greet the helicopter's only passenger.

As her car idled on the grass, the Falcon glided quietly down the meadow, turned and made its way back to the holding area and parked next to the helicopter. Max emerged and was pointed to Elizabeth's car by his pilot. He entered and the car drove away. The Gulfstream, quieter still, touched down softly, turned and moved back and parked next to the Falcon. The door opened, the stairs were lowered and three passengers emerged. A second car approached the plane and the three passengers got in. The car moved off.

The door to the large barn behind the three aircraft opened and a fuel truck approached the Falcon and the Gulfstream. The Falcon was fueled first, taxied to the end of the runway, turned into the wind and jetted down the runway and into the darkness. The Gulfstream, fueled, taxied to the end of the runway, turned and with full throttle rocketed down the runway and catapulted into the night sky. The landing lights and directional lights were extinguished.

Serious business was to be conducted this night by some of the brightest minds in the agency. Two men, three women. No glass ceiling for this venture.

CHAPTER 34

KHALID ARRIVES

Khalid was a man on the run, but not at so fast a pace that he could not enjoy the finer things in life. Tonight he was ensconced in a plush and luxurious cottage on the grounds of the Remy Plaza Hotel in Palm Beach Gardens, Florida. So confident was he of the incompetence of Homeland Security that once he had bought his way out of Egypt, he headed directly to the United States, via Saudi Arabia, with a new identity. He made this bold move believing that the several intelligence agencies looking for him would assume he had headed to a mountain hideout in Pakistan where most terrorists hid from American intelligence agencies. Egypt, an alleged friend of the United States for more than thirty years, allowed Khalid to leave the country for a mere ten million American. So much for America buying the loyalty of brutal regimes. The CIA, the guardian of Khalid while in Egypt, had been double crossed by powerful and influential forces within the Egyptian government.

Khalid was a free man who was on the hunt for Max Rietsema. He wanted to inflict as much pain as possible when he killed Max. It would be many times worse than what the American believed Khalid would have suffered in Egypt. But mostly, Khalid needed to terrorize the entire population of the United States. He would do so by implementing catastrophic events.

His new identity was that of a Saudi prince, Hamil Zahid. Zahid was one of dozens of princes related to the royal family, but not among the well known or recognized. Zahid was selected because his overall build was similar to that of Khalid and, being of the royal family, was free to travel in and out of the country with no questions asked. Like most of the men in the royal family, he was a womanizer. Khalid's men had been observing his pattern of behavior for several weeks. Almost like clockwork, he spent every Wednesday afternoon and evening with his mistress. On this particular night, Khalid's operatives waited until he left her apartment, then abducted and murdered him. Because time was of the essence, the prince's passport and other documents were taken and, within four hours, Khalid's picture was expertly substituted. By mid- morning the next day, Khalid was on his way to the United States. Until he cleared United States customs and security, he would remain Prince Hamil Zahid.

His point of entry into the United States was Los Angeles where the TSA was far more interested in tourists who were attempting to board aircraft with oversized tubes of toothpaste and shampoo than in apprehending terrorists who posed a threat to national security. His entry went smoothly and when he exited the airport, a car was waiting for him. The driver was a young female and seated in the back was a white male. Khalid seated himself next to the stranger who handed him a sealed envelope and spoke in a clipped business-like manner. "Everything you requested is enclosed. The documents were perfectly prepared by the Iranian Ministry of Intelligence and Security and flown here two days ago in a Pakistani diplomatic pouch. You will not have a problem with the documents. The photograph used is the one you sent us and that we forwarded to Tehran. There are three sets of documents, two as an American citizen and one as a British citizen of your age and characteristics. You will have no trouble. The envelope contains your round trip ticket to West Palm Beach, Florida. Your plane departs from here in approximately two hours. Hotel reservations in Palm Beach Gardens are also enclosed. Now, if you please, give me all of the documents you possess so they may be destroyed. When you leave this car you will be Jonathan Drew. Allah be with you."

Khalid handed him all of his documents. The car, which had made a circle of the airport, pulled up to the curb and Khalid got out and left without so much as a word. His planning had been perfect. His work was about to begin.

An early morning breeze filtered through the lanai into the bedroom, accompanied by the first light of day. They stirred as the tropical breeze washed over their naked bodies. He was lying on his stomach with this face buried in the soft pillow. One arm was tucked under his chin and the other stretched out on the bed. After dinner at the elegant Restaurant du Village on the Inter-coastal Waterway, they returned to the bungalow for a night of lovemaking after which he slept soundly. Khalid was solidly built, muscular with small amounts of hair on his chest. He was thirty six years of age. Tall by Yemen standards, he was five foot eleven and weighed in at one hundred and seventy pounds. His complexion and facial structure was not unlike that of a west European or American. Women would consider him extremely handsome and sexy. To the hotel staff, he was Jonathon Drew.

Marta, on the other hand, was Dutch and looked every inch the part. Now twenty one, she had been spotted by Khalid when she worked as a guide at The Hague while he was there for a conference two years earlier. At the time she was only nineteen. He seduced her the night of the first day he saw her. Khalid was an expert at seduction since he came from a culture which encouraged the seduction of women. These were men who held the Koran in one hand and Playboy in the other. Their societies were built on seduction.

Marta refused to travel anywhere near or in the Middle East. Her arrangement with Khalid was that she would be his mistress; he would provide her with a luxury villa in Paris to complement the one he owned in London and that she would travel first class anywhere in Western Europe and the United States when he was on either continent. For two years it had worked well. Marta had flown into West Palm Beach the day before Khalid arrived. When alone, she constantly fought the urge to have sex with men who invariably pursued her, but shuddered at what might happen if Khalid learned of it. She loved sex, was good at it and had an insatiable appetite. She was young and needed more than most women. Some day she would be rid of Khalid and fold herself into the arms of a very rich westerner. For now, her work was with Khalid.

She rolled over onto him, her breasts bearing down on his back, her warm vagina nestled on his buttocks. He began to stir as she pushed her hands under his thighs and groped for his penis which became alert and growing. As she fondled it and then stroked it, he came alive. He lifted his head off the pillow and reached back around her and placed a finger into her anus. As she moaned with pleasure, she removed one hand from his penis and placed it on his hand and pushed his finger deeper within her. She cried with ecstasy. He released his finger and rolled over onto his back with his enormous penis standing erect. Without any encouragement, she slid down his stomach and took him in her mouth and began to masturbate him fiercely. When he was close to orgasm, she removed his penis from her mouth and slid it into her. Her plunging up and down on him was bringing him close to ejaculation, and he added to the physical pleasure by pushing up each time she plunged down on to him, all the while his hands kneaded her hardened breasts. His warm semen flowed into her like fuel and powered her continued attack on his body until she had no more to give. All movements stopped as she removed his penis and fell onto his body and finally rolled over on her back. Khalid fell sound asleep.

It was close to nine when he woke. Marta had showered and was having a continental breakfast on the lanai when he came up behind her and gave her a kiss on the neck. "You were wonderful last night and again this morning."

"It is your doing Khalid. You bring out the best in me."

He stiffened at the use of his name. "Marta, need I remind you that for my work in Florida, I am the Englishman, Jonathon Drew. Khalid does not exist until we leave here. Understood?"

"I shall remember and Jonathan Drew will have the time of his life this evening."

"He will be a very fortunate man, indeed. But you must not kill him at his young age. He has important work to do."

"And what might that be my love?"

"It is man's work and of little interest to you. I have to spend the rest of the day with associates. You are free to spend the day as you wish. Anwar will drive you anywhere you want. If you wish to charter a private plane to see Key West, he will arrange it. Never having been there, you may find it fascinating. It will be a look at a degenerate country. I ask only that you be dressed and ready for dinner at nine."

"Thank you, Jonathan, but I think I will go to West Palm, walk on Worth Avenue and do some shopping. I will be waiting for you when your business is done. Perhaps, before we dress, we could conduct some business of our own."

"I will return in time for our business." With that, Jonathon Drew started for the shower. He was to meet his co-conspirators in less than an hour.

As he was about to enter the shower, Marta spoke up. "Jonathon, I would love to see Key West but I prefer to go with you."

"Then, before you leave for Europe, we will do so. Would you like to shower again?"

CHAPTER 35

BLOOD AND GLASS

Amos called the state police, identified himself and asked for the duty officer in charge. He was passed through to Captain Steven King.

"Captain King."

"Captain, this is Amos Trumbull, park ranger at Baxter State Park."

"Good morning Ranger Trumbull. What can I do for you?"

Amos described in detail the red stains, the drag marks and the crystals from the broken window.

"What else do you have in the way of evidence?"

"That's it, Captain."

"You expect the state police Criminal Investigation Division to commit resources to this with so little evidence?"

"No offense, Captain, but this is not just a little evidence, as you suggest. If the red stains turn out to be human blood, we have the possible makings of a homicide. There were other climbers here yesterday and you should attempt to reach them in the hope they possess some other information. The fact there is glass at the exact spot where the drag marks end gives reason to believe that a body had been dragged to a waiting car. I am suggesting that you initiate an investigation, sample the stains, try to determine the type of vehicle the glass came from and attempt to find the other climbers. You have the resources to test the stains and a call from your office to the FBI would help in analyzing the glass crystals."

"Look, Ranger Trumbull, I will decide when and if an investigation is warranted and from what you have told me there is no justification to conduct an investigation. Do you understand?"

"What I understand, Captain, is that if you insist on sitting on your ass hoping that I am just a hick park ranger who is over his head, then let me be as clear as possible. Immediately after I hang up, I intent to call the regional office of the FBI in Bangor and provide them with the details. And, regardless of what you decide to do, I am then going to call the local chief of police and put him in the loop. When this story breaks and the public and the state legislature learn of your bureaucratic bullshit, you can spend your retirement pondering what might have been had you acted like a cop and not like an asshole."

With that Amos hung up and quickly called Police Chief McCorey, who thanked Amos for putting him in the loop and who volunteered to call the FBI, an offer that Amos readily accepted. "And, Amos, don't worry about the State Police. They would be of limited assistance since they do not know the area. You followed the correct protocol in informing them. Until the FBI arrives, we have the authority to do what we want, other than disturb the possible crime scene in the parking lot. Why don't we work our way up the trail, stretch out two to three hundred feet each side and see what we can come up with. I will meet you there in twenty minutes with four officers. If you can spare two rangers we could cover a good distance before the

FBI arrives. You most likely have Annie with you and I will bring Nellie. Will has his two dogs. Together we can cover a lot of territory. There may be nothing or there could be something of importance out there. It doesn't help that we do not know what we are looking for. Let's find out."

"Chief, that sounds good. See you in twenty. And thanks."

CHAPTER 36

ELIZABETH

The first car took Max directly to his cottage. On the way he handed Elizabeth the small package that held the automatic pistol, the car key and the bullets for the sniper rifle. "These may be of help."

She took the package and placed it inside the large shoulder bag she was wearing. "I will get these delivered to a lab tonight. The helicopter is on standby now. Max, I am glad you are safe and back with us. The attempt on your life was a blow to me. There is a leak and we need to find it before we can make any headway in finding Khalid and eliminating him."

"Make no mistake, Elizabeth, we will find whoever is dirty. I understand you have brought reinforcements to help."

"You will meet them tonight."

They entered Max's cottage and he put down his bag. "Max, before we meet the others in about forty five minutes, we need to talk. Rather, you need to talk. Walk me through the events from the time we placed you in the safe house until now. Take your time and skip no detail." For the next thirty minutes he related every moment of his existence in Maine.

When he finished, she spoke. "Here is the way I see it, Max. First, if the rifle is still there, and we have to assume it is, the extraction team will find it. By morning the car will be on a flat bed on its way to a lab in Washington along with the rifle. Second, if there is any evidence on the ground in the parking lot, the Ranger will find it. These are usually old timers who know when a rock is disturbed. If they find something suspicious the local chief of police will be called in. That is the protocol in the back country. Like the park rangers, these back country law enforcement people are good. If he or she suspects a possible homicide, a call will be made to the state police. They, in turn, might bump it up a notch to our friendly competitors. Then, all hell breaks loose. Think of it, Max, the FBI investigating a CIA matter. The Director will be bullshit and I can see some of our favorite Congressmen cheering from the sidelines."

"Any way to change directions?"

"None that I see, except to do everything we can to temporarily interfere with and confuse their investigation. We know far more than they do about the Serbs and the car and we need to be careful not to share any of that information with them at this time. That is why we need to discover the leak and do so fast."

"I know you Elizabeth, you have someone in mind."

"I do. I'll get out of here and let you freshen up. See you at the house in fifteen minutes."

In the meantime, Vinnie, Gretchen and Darlene had been taken to their cottages and informed to be at the house for dinner at eight thirty at which time they would meet Max and Elizabeth.

CHAPTER 37

THE BODY

Chief McCorey, four of his men and the three dogs met Amos, the two Rangers and Annie. Amos felt comfortable that the chief was in charge. He learned that McCorey had more bark than bite. The chief and Amos took the left side of the trail accompanied by two of his men and Annie and Nellie. He assigned his deputy, Will Hansen, to the right side with another of the chief's men along with two Rangers and two dogs. The chief gave himself two hours before the FBI arrived. He instructed the Ranger manning the gate not to let anyone in or out and send any climbers to other trail heads. If the state police arrived before the FBI did or before the Chief returned from the search in the woods, they were to be told that Chief McCorey had declared the parking lot a crime scene and they were to wait outside the gate for fear of contaminating the scene. The chances were great that Captain King would arrive with his men.

The Chief and Will agreed to keep in contact with their cell phones and to report anything unusual to each other. The plan called for the eight men to spread out thirty to forty yards apart and to walk up both sides of the path for approximately one hour after which they would turn and start back down covering the same area a second time. The dogs were to be set loose to go their own way. If they found animal or man, they would be heard from. The men were specifically instructed to pick up any shell casings they might find and place them in evidence bags. With that, they all set out. The time was eleven a.m. They were not at all certain what they were looking for.

The men, all experienced hikers and woodsmen, walked steadily and easily with little talking. They kept their distance from one another and formed a relatively straight line. It was a cool day but the men perspired under their late summer clothing. One by one they shed their jackets and tied them around their waists. The only noise was the sound of their heavy shoes crushing ground cover and the breaking of limbs being pushed back to make a path for the men. There was also the occasional rustling of leaves on the ground as small animals ran through the brush. The four dogs were running every which way, some crossing the path but always returning to either Amos or Will. Annie and Nellie were man's best friends but they were not hunting dogs as were Will's. They dogs were. They were pointers and from the same litter, four years old and experienced in the woods. One was Rachel and the other Martha, named after Will's grandmothers.

It was close to noon and nearing the time to turn when Nellie started to bark, then howl, then barked again. Soon Annie joined in. Rachel and Martha raced across the trail and joined the other dogs. Four dogs were sounding the alarm and running in circles. The barking and howling was deafening. Amos and the others ran towards the dogs.

The Chief called Will. "Will, we may have something but keep your men where they are until we can confirm. I'll call back as soon as I know what is going on. With that, he ran towards the dogs and joined Amos and the others. The Chief and Amos called off the dogs who circled their find. Lying on the ground was a Caucasian male with a bullet hole in his forehead. He was dead. "Will, you had better get over here."

While waiting for Will, McCorey and Amos talked. The other men stood aside and listened while holding on to the dogs. "Amos, your gut instinct was correct. There is more here than first thought. I'm no coroner, but this guy hasn't been dead for more than a day or so. That would place the time of death in the same time frame as the event below. When all is said and done, the two events will be tied together by some common thread. This was no coincidence. What's surprising is that the body was not discovered by a bear. Forensics will at least have a full body to examine."

"What now chief?"

"Now, we make that call to the State Police and another to the FBI to update them. The FBI will put a copter in the air with field agents and forensics. This is not going to be a pretty picture. Amos, I think it best if two of my men officially secure this scene. Will, take your men and Rachel and Martha and search the area above the body. Fifty yards should to it. If you find anything of interest call me. In the meantime, the rest of us will go back down and direct traffic."

Six hundred miles away Max was under the impression that the Serb in the woods would not be discovered for several days or weeks, perhaps never.

CHAPTER 38

CONFERENCE

Dressed in Palm Beach wear consisting of lightweight tan gabardine slacks, white silk shirt open at the collar, pale blue linen jacket and tasseled loafers, Khalid looked like any other wealthy playboy out on the town. He called for a cab from the Remy Plaza Hotel and gave the driver directions. A block before the intersection of route A1A and PGA Boulevard, Khalid asked the cab to let him out at the Fitzgerald Blanding Business Park, a small office complex on A1A that surrounded a carefully manicured park. He paid and tipped the driver the standard fifteen percent, got out of the cab and walked towards the door of what was labeled Building A. He walked slowly, wanting the driver to observe him headed towards the door. Khalid learned to be careful. Once the cab turned right on to PGA Boulevard and was out of sight, he reversed his direction, walked to a waiting car and got into the front passenger seat. "Hello Ibraham. Let us get on with it."

Ibraham Malik was born in Yemen and he and Khalid were childhood friends. They remained close throughout high school after which they both were sent abroad by wealthy parents to take advantage of British and American universities. Not being outstanding scholars, their parents bought their way into the

London School of Economics for Ibraham and Stanford for Khalid by contributing millions to their respective endowments. Both spoke perfect English with no hint of their native language. They spent more time in England and America than in Yemen but maintained close times with families who remained there.

Ibraham continued south on A1A for four miles until he reached the gated community of Presidential Estates, one of the most prestigious names on the East coast of Florida in addition to being one of the most expensive addresses. The car stopped at the gate, Ibraham gave the security guard the name and address of the home being visited, his name and the special entry code provided Khalid by the homeowner and without which you could not enter. As soon as the car was waved through the gate, Khalid used his cell to call the host who immediately used a remote to raise the garage door. Ibraham drove directly into the garage and the door closed behind them. The door from the garage to the house opened and Khalid and Ibraham were greeted by Abua Karsam, in whose name the mansion was leased. Immediately behind him were Suleiman Amir and Abdul Jazier. Behind them was Karsam's bodyguard, Yousuf, who stood well over six feet and possessed typical Muslim features, dark beard and facial hair, prominent nose and barrel-chested. His loosely fitting jacket revealed the grip of a weapon under it.

Once greetings were completed, Abua led the group to a large soundproof library. Once inside, Yousuf closed the heavy reinforced wood paneled doors behind them. He took a seat just outside the door, opened his jacket, took out his gun, checked to see if the safety was off and rested it on his right knee.

Inside the library were three more men, Aba Najdi, Ghani Mohammed and Hafs Karzai. Once again, Karsam made the introductions. The eight Yemeni sat at a rectangular table with Khalid at the head and Karsam, Suleiman, and Jazier to his right. Najdi, Mohammed, and Karzai took seats to his left and his friend Ibraham Malik was at the opposite end of the table. Each man was born in Yemen. Of the eight, two attended college in England, three in the United States, two in France and one in Russia. All were al-Qaeda terrorists and, except for Khalid, none were on the radar screens of any of the United States intelligence agencies. They were al-Qaeda "sleepers" and had been in the United States since shortly after 9/11.

Khalid and Ibraham lived in Yemen but Khalid also maintained villas in Paris and London. Both were registered under cover names. The other six lived in the United States and ran highly profitable and successful companies in multiple states. Abua Karsam operated an import/export firm in Atlanta, Georgia. Suleiman Amir was the CEO of a deep sea exploration company in San Diego, California. Abdul Jazier's firm was located in Dallas, Texas and manufactured large, complex valves used in natural gas pipelines in thirty five countries. Aba Najdi imported wine and liquor from all over the world and was located in Boston, Massachusetts. Ghani Mohammed was the CEO of an international construction company operating out of Seattle, Washington. Hafs Karzai's company had two main distribution facilities, one in Chicago and one in Denver, and sold or leased under a license from its Italian owner, the Silver Eagle X650, a two engine jet comparable in specifications to the French

Falcon 2000 and a competitor to the Gulfstream 550 and equipped with the most advanced avionics to be found in business jets.

The common denominator for all six businesses was the ability of their owners to travel domestically and internationally in private aircraft with few questions asked. The six businesses had a combined total of forty four branches. The forty four branches purchased materials and services from hundreds of suppliers and sub-contractors located throughout the country, including Hawaii and Alaska. The total work force of all of the companies numbered in the thousands. Of importance to Khalid was, by design and agreement among the six companies, that no less than fifty percent of the thousands of employees had to be devout Muslims who believed in the domination of America and who regularly attended daily prayers. All six corporate offices were located in large cities where there existed a substantial Muslim population. And, it was this access to thousands of devout Muslims, the children of Allah, that Khalid saw as the foundation of his ultimate plan.

The symbolism of the seating was not lost on any of them. This was not a meeting of equals. Khalid, being the intended victim of the CIA, took the power seat and was in charge. Ibraham Malik had what he thought was the second most powerful seat because of his friendship with Khalid. In fact, the second most powerful seat belonged to Abua Karsam but he chose, for the moment, to be an equal to the other five. The six had been handpicked by Bin Laden to work with Khalid to execute a series of catastrophic events more powerful than 9/11.Osama was now dead and the question of al-Qaeda succession remained a question mark.

"Friends, we have two items on our agenda. First, Max Rietsema must die. None of you need concern yourself. He will die at my hands. You will stand clear of this in order to concentrate on our larger project."

"And, what is that Khalid?" asked Suleiman Amir.

"To make 9/11 look like child's play."

Suleiman spoke once again. "If that is so, why then must the killing of one infidel consume your time? You are the leader of a new holocaust to fall upon America and you risk it all by concentrating on one man and an insignificant one at that."

"I will waste no time with Rietsema. He will be dead within the week. I will find him with help from our brothers."

Abua Karsam, the host and the more reasoned of the group spoke in gentle tones to Khalid. "Khalid, we all know, we all understand how this man's attempted cruelty to you drives a desire to destroy him. Each of us at this table would gladly kill him for you. Suleiman speaks words of wisdom in questioning, not what has to be done, but when it should be done. Your skill of pursuit is unquestioned as you have proven so many times. If anyone can locate Rietsema, it is you. But in the off chance that something may happen to you, there is no one to replace you. No offence to Ibraham, but while he has the skill of planning and would gladly give his life for Allah, he does not yet have a loyal following. Without you, Khalid, the project will fail."

Before Khalid could respond, Ibraham spoke up. "Khalid, we would all die to ensure that you live to rain death on the infidels, but if you die, so does our dream." There was a nod of agreement from all at the table except Khalid. He paused for a moment, "I have listened to your concerns. For now, we move on to the more important project." The point had been made and he accepted that the killing of Max Rietsema would be delayed.

Little did any of the eight know that the planned killing of Khalid was, that very night, being placed on the front burner by Elizabeth English and her covert team of CIA agents.

CHAPTER 39

THE GOOD GUYS

Elizabeth was the first to arrive at the house. She was greeted by a middle aged woman who ran the household and provided meals for the security detail, members of the agency who were there on business, those on training assignments and "guests." She greeted Elizabeth whom she knew from her many previous visits. The makings for drinks were on a portable bar. Following a short cocktail hour, dinner would be served. Elizabeth had planned that this night would be for the sole purpose of beginning the team building process with work scheduled for the morning.

Gretchen and Darlene arrived next. The three women, all experienced in covert operations, were also friends. They greeted each other warmly and quickly engaged in conversation.

"I want both of you to know how much I appreciate the work you have done in identifying Captain Pagano. I know it was partly good fortune, but your initial assessment of his capabilities made it all happen."

"Before you go too far with the compliments, keep in mind that if he had not seen the ad this never would have occurred. The last time we spoke of it, he was certain we placed the ad on his desk at Global. We denied having any part in it, but we do not think he believes us. Is that still your impression, Gretchen?"

"Absolutely. If we did not place the ad on his desk, who did?"

"My sense, after reading your report is that once you both denied having anything to do with the ad on his desk he would have discovered the identity of the third party. The truth is, I am curious as to who placed the ad. Someone wanted him out of Global. We need to know why. Someone either hated him or loved him."

Darlene spoke. "I am placing my bet on the love angle."

Before anyone could respond to Darlene's provocative statement, Max arrived. He nodded at Elizabeth, whom he met a few minutes earlier and for whom he had worked for many years. Without hesitation, he walked up to Darlene and gave her a hug and a kiss on the cheek."God, it is good to see you."

"Likewise," she responded.

He turned and faced Gretchen and, after a long moment in which his eyes became a camera recording a beautiful scene, he walked to her, held her tightly and then released her with a kiss on both cheeks.

"Welcome home, Max. You had us worried. We can't wait to hear what happened."

The Deputy Director spoke. "Time enough for that later. Now, how about a cocktail while we wait for the final member of the team. Help yourselves."

Back in his cottage, Vinnie looked into the mirror and wondered what he had gotten himself into. Hadn't he told Gretchen and Darlene at the outset that he had all he needed of combat? Two wars were enough for anyone. When all was said and done, who gave a shit? One war never prevented another. You kill one Taliban and two take his place. You destroy his truck and he carries the load on his back. If he is too tried to carry it on his back after a day of fighting, then his mother or sister carry it on theirs. Al-Qaida is like a smoldering fire underneath ground cover; you put it out in one place and it erupts in another. No amount of effort ever extinguishes it for good.

He was beginning to doubt his judgment about agreeing to this meeting. You had to question your decision making ability when you sign on for an undefined mission. He wondered if he was motivated by being told they needed him to help a brother in arms who is in danger or if he lusted after two covert operatives and would risk his life to be near them. This was a moment of uncertainty.

The others would have gathered by now. He purposely waited to join them. They knew each other, had worked with each other and would spend time talking about old times. Vinnie did not want to be the fifth wheel. When the time was right, he opened the door to the cottage, stepped out, pulled the door behind him and walked towards the house. He would be the appropriate ten minutes late.

As he strode to the house, he wondered about the Deputy Director of the agency. How does one acquire such a powerful position in a government which is ruled by men? Is she a token or is there a lot more to her? Where did she grow up, go to college? What kind of work has she accomplished? To whom does she owe a favor? Did she sleep her way up the ladder? Is there a powerful male force that keeps her in business? Why in hell would she want the job to begin with? How old is she? What does she look like? Only a few questions would be answered tonight.

As he entered the old fashioned parlor, she immediately walked up to him, "Vinnie, I'm Elizabeth English and I am delighted to meet you." Her friendly green eyes focused like a laser on his. She smiled warmly at him, placed her left hand on his right arm and with her right hand extended a firm handshake. He didn't know if this greeting was real or bullshit, but he felt himself being drawn to her as though she was a magnetic field.

He held her hand for a moment longer than necessary and while looking directly into her green eyes he had the feeling that this woman could seduce just about any man she desired. Finally releasing her hand, he spoke. "Elizabeth, I'm pleased to meet you. Gretchen and Darlene spoke highly of your work as Deputy Director."

She smiled and said, "Be careful of those two. As you may have surmised, they often have multiple agendas running simultaneously. Now, I want you to meet a very special person." With that she took Vinnie by the arm and led him towards Max. On the way, he gave the two women a nod and smile. They nodded and smiled back, hoping that their work had paid off.

"Vinnie, this is Max Rietsema. And, before you ask, it is his real name and has been since birth. Max, this is Vinnie Pagano who we hope will, after learning what we have to tell him, join our little team."

Vinnie knew that all eyes were on him. He was the new kid on the block. The three women looked with apprehension and interest as the two men gazed at each other as they moved to shake hands. One was a wonder boy in the agency who worked miracles throughout the Middle East, rubbed elbows with kings and shahs, dictators and despots and who was now a hunted man. He was also a cultured man with the correct breeding, attended prestigious colleges and had friends in high places. Max was loved by those who worked for him. Maybe Gretchen's former lover. The other was a neighborhood boy, public education, state university, smart, tough physically and mentally, ethnic background, tried and tested on the field of battle, the guy you want on your side when the going gets rough and the one who never left the wounded behind to be captured. Both were basically the same size and height and both were handsome though in different ways. The visible difference to those who understood human nature, as did the three women, was that Vinnie displayed confidence and cockiness, while Max showed the strain of having been hunted by assassins and having killed them.

Vinnie held out his hand and was the first to speak. "Max, I don't know what the ladies are up to but I am anxious to find out."

Max smiled at the way Vinnie had broken the ice and decided to follow up. "Vinnie, Elizabeth said it best when she noted that Gretchen and Darlene always have multiple agendas. And, only God knows what Elizabeth has in store for the team. What do you say we have a drink and find out?" With that they retreated to the portable bar and poured two healthy Knob Creek on the rocks. Darlene and Gretchen smiled brightly and sighed a breath of relief while Elizabeth gave them a thumbs up that neither Max nor Vinnie observed. Without any game playing, a team was forming. Khalid would not be pleased if he knew. But, then again, the newly formed team did not know what Khalid was plotting.

Almost in unison the three women moved over to where Vinnie and Max were talking. Darlene asked, "What does a girl have to do to get a drink in this place?"

"Darlene, what will you have?"

"The same as you, Vinnie. Thanks."

Max quickly asked Gretchen and Elizabeth what he could get them. Gretchen settled for a scotch and water and Elizabeth requested a vodka martini. When everyone had a drink in hand, Elizabeth proposed a toast. "For Max's safe return to us, for Vinnie who may join us in our efforts and to Gretchen and Darlene who brought Vinnie to the agency. Finally, to the gods who have brought the five of us together. May we find and kill Khalid before he rains havoc on our country."

They raised their glasses and in turn touched the crystal to each other. Then Max added, "And a toast to Elizabeth who risks her career tonight to do what others lack the courage to do. May her God shield her from the enemy within."

Dinner was served at a table set for five. Elizabeth was sitting at twelve o'clock. Clockwise from her were Max, Darlene, Gretchen and Vinnie. The seating was a sociogram in action. Elizabeth engaged Max and Vinnie, Darlene engaged Max and Gretchen captured the attention of Vinnie. This was stage two of team building. It also provided Max and Gretchen the opportunity to have eye contact.

Dinner conversation was light hearted and the meal superb. When dinner dishes were cleared, Elizabeth stood, walked to the door and closed it. "As of this moment, we are in a highly classified conversation. Each of us is now subject to the secrecy act in spite of the fact that we are acting outside of authorized channels. The release of any information to any person or persons other than those of us in this room will be considered an act of treason. Any question on this?" There was no response.

"We have several issues to discuss. The first concerns a major leak that threatened Max's life. He will now explain all of the events leading up to the attempt on his life beginning with the Italian government sentencing him to five years in prison along with twenty two of his colleagues. No detail will be missed. Max, please go ahead."

All eyes shifted to Max. "I was station chief in Rome and running agents in Italy, Sicily and the Baltics. A source within the Italian intelligence community alerted me to the fact that Khalid was in Rome." Max then proceeded to relate every detail of his experience beginning with his abduction of Khalid and up to and including his boarding the flight on the Falcon 2000 in Bangor, Maine earlier in the day. For forty three minutes the others listened intensely. Max was exhausted when he finished.

"I know you have questions for Max but save them for tomorrow. It was important that you heard Max's story before we could proceed to the next step. His story leaves us with many concerns. I will say that by the end of the day tomorrow we will have information on the sniper rifle, hand gun and car key. The autopsy of the body and examination of the car may not be ready until Saturday. Keep in mind that there is a second body on the mountain. Now, feel free to have a nightcap if you wish. The grounds are secure if you choose to take a walk before turning in. The security detail is on duty twenty four/seven and they have been given photos of each of you. There is no chance you will be mistaken for an intruder. Otherwise, breakfast will be served at seven a.m. and we will continue our work at eight. Personally, I am exhausted and headed for bed. Good night." She then turned and left for her cottage.

"I've had a long day and am also ready to call it quits." It was Max who then headed for his cottage. A minute after he was on his way, Darlene said good night to Vinnie and Gretchen and left for her cottage. Vinnie was too exhilarated at what he had heard to end the night without a walk to settle down. He headed to the portable bar and poured himself a Knob Creek. "You can pour me one of those." It was Gretchen. He did so and suggested, "How about a walk before we call it a night?"

"I was about to suggest the same." With that they stepped into the night.

CHAPTER 40

McDonald

Chief McCorey was met in the parking lot by one of the park rangers. "Chief, you had better come to the gate. Captain King of the State Police is there and pissing mad. Said if you do not get your ass over there and give him permission to enter the park he will have your badge. I don't think you want to mess with him."

"Well now, let's just go and have a friendly chat with the Captain."

McCorey could see King staring at him from across the parking lot, hands on hips, chest out and jaw set for combat. The chief walked leisurely to the gate and took the initiative to throw the Captain off balance. In his slow down east accent, "Hello Captain, pleased to meet you. And, thanks for waiting until I got back. I know you appreciate how forensics teams demand that evidence be secured. And, defense lawyers, if they are pulled into this, will look for the slightest contamination of evidence. But, then again, why am I telling this to someone of your experience? As I said, thanks for coming. Now, if you will follow me, I will share what we have. The FBI will be here shortly to officially take over the investigation."

Somewhat mellowed, Captain King asked, "Why was the FBI called when this is a state park and under state jurisdiction. The state police should be taking the lead."

"The park service is the custodian of park and employees of the federal government, not the state government. Even if that were not the case, we know that an out of state car was involved somehow in the murder. About three hundred yards into the woods to the left of the trail head, we found a body of a male with a bullet hole in his forehead. We're assuming that the red stain I am about to show you is blood that belongs to a second body yet to be found. But, back to the car. If it is involved in a murder the chances are great that it is headed out of state and that makes it a federal case. My thinking, Captain, is that before this is over, you, me and the FBI, for starters, will all be working this case. Just a matter of who does what. I think it best to let the suits figure it out. But, you and I could work our end together. Now, let me show you what we have."

The Captain knew a professional cop when he met one. "Chief, thanks for the update. I'd like to see what you have." With that they both headed for the red stain.

Careful not to step on the stain, the Captain was curious about the drag marks. "Chief, is it possible that the drag marks belong to a large animal, a deer for example, that a hunter dragged to a car?"

"That is entirely possible but for the fact that where the drag marks end there are glass crystals that definitely came from a vehicle of some kind. Once forensics complete their work, we will know if the scuffs are from heals of shoes or from hoofs of a large animal. There is also the question of why would a hunter break into a vehicle with a deer?"

The Captain responded, “I understand that this park is usually busy with climbers all year. Do you know if there were any climbers yesterday?”

“Like you, Captain, we also assume there were witnesses to some action here if not to the homicides themselves. We also believe that the FBI will put out a call via the media. Look, if we are going to work together, let’s forget the formalities. My name is Mike. How about you?”

“Tom.”

“Then Tom and Mike it is.”

“Let’s get to work.”

“By the way, Ranger Amos Trumbull is an excellent law enforcement officer. You just pissed him off a little. Fact is he is a professional. His father, Clint Trumbull, was chief before me. If it wasn’t for Amos’s snooping ability we would not be here. Nothing happens in the park that he isn’t aware of. Go easy on him.”

“Thanks for the advice, Mike.”

Together, they followed the drag marks until they ended at the glass crystals, careful not to step on any on them. The captain turned to the chief. “Are you thinking that the person who shot the man in the woods also shot a second person in the parking lot and then removed the second body?”

“That is exactly what I am thinking. I’m also thinking that it is impossible for someone to shoot two men in broad daylight on a busy day in this park without someone having seen something, some element that would give us a basis for a meaningful investigation. We need to find climbers who were here yesterday. Neither you nor I can try to locate them unless we want the Bureau on our backs. We need to leave it to the suits. They will be here soon enough."

The words were hardly out of the chief's mouth when three tall, well built, determined looking men in dark blue or black suits approached them. They came across the parking lot, three abreast, like line backers in the NFL. With each step they took, their jackets opened and the shoulder straps of their weapon holsters could be seen. The one in the middle spoke first. "Is one of you Chief McCorey?"

"I'm Chief McCorey and this is Captain King of the Maine State Police. And you are?"

"I'm Special Agent Stuart McDonald of the Federal Bureau of Investigation, Bangor Regional Division assigned to this investigation."

Never shy about confronting anyone, the Chief asked, "And your companions are?"

"Sorry. This is Agent Donald Brzyinski and Agent Imar Rasan."

After a round of handshakes, the chief took the lead. "I made the call to your office in Bangor and informed the duty officer of the facts in simple terms. The Captain and I understand that you will take the lead in this investigation and we will assist whenever possible and at your discretion. But, to keep the protocol uncomplicated, this alleged crime occurred in my jurisdiction and in that of the captain which means that we will be running parallel investigations. If we turn up information or evidence that is pertinent to your work, we will share it. Now, if you are ready, I'll ask the Captain to show you what we have and let you get to work."

As Captain King led the procession towards the red stains, he could not help smiling to himself as he contemplated how the Chief co-opted the suits by making it clear that he and the Captain were in this to the end and, in the best political sense, deferring to the Captain when it was time to share what they knew with the FBI. There was no way that the Chief was about to let the feds believe that the state police were to remain on the sidelines or that the feds could run roughshod over either of them. Mike McCorey was a cop's cop.

The Captain pointed out the stains and the path of the scuff marks leading to the glass crystals. He then turned to the Chief. "Since you discovered the body in the woods, I think it best that you take over." During the review, the feds listened quietly and said little.

"Thanks Captain. The body is located a few hundred yards into the woods on the left side of the trail head. Without touching the body, it appears that he died from a single shot to the forehead. One of my officers and his dogs will have completed a search of the woods above where the body was found. We will join him as he makes his way down. Since he did not call me on his cell, we can assume that he found nothing of interest. This way, gentlemen." With that, Agent McDonald and his two associates followed the Chief and the Captain into the woods.

Agent McDonald spoke. "What made you initiate a search of the woods since there is nothing in the parking lot that would indicate that some other action had taken place in the woods, let alone a homicide?"

"Good question Agent McDonald. Actually two of us made that decision. Park Ranger Amos Trumbull discovered the stains and the glass. He is a first rate law enforcement officer and you will need to meet him. He is the key to the evidence in the parking lot. This being a climber's paradise, we made what scientists call 'an intuitive leap' and figured that the dispute in the parking lot could very well have started on the trail leading to Mt. Katahdin. Just a guess but it turned out to be a good one. Having done many search and rescues looking for lost climbers, we quickly organized a party and decided to climb for an hour up and an hour down and return to the parking lot to meet you. If we had thought that you would not be here for several more hours we would have gone higher. As it happens, we discovered key evidence. I think I hear Will's dogs coming now."

Will arrived a few moments later. "Chief, we found no material evidence but we did notice that the ground cover just above where the body was found had been trampled. It could have been where the shooter was hiding. We found no shell casing. Either the shooter picked it up or it is under the leaves and debris. If you want, we could use metal detectors, but my gut feeling is that the shooter cleaned up after the shooting."

"Thanks, Will. I want you to meet Agent McDonald of the FBI. He will take on the responsibility for the investigation and we will give him whatever help he needs." Introductions were made after which the Chief led the agent to the body.

"Chief, I appreciate your protecting the evidence. Our forensics team should be here shortly. It will collect evidence and conduct a preliminary examination of the body. The body will be moved to Bangor for an autopsy and the other physical evidence will be flown tonight to the FBI lab in Washington."

"Agent McDonald, does the agency intend to alert the media as to the events here in the hope that some of the other climbers will come forward?"

"It makes sense that we do that, Chief, but the decision will most likely be made by the Deputy Director for Field Operations. He may want to wait until the evidence is examined. I know you are thinking that the sooner the better since the climbers may travel out of the area. If it is any help, I will be speaking with him later today and will urge him to release the news to the media tonight for publication and broadcasting tomorrow."

"Appreciate that. Now, I will withdraw all of my men so you can do your work. I will inform Park Ranger Trumbull to keep the park closed until you approve reopening it. He will stay on duty until you have the time to speak with him."

"Thank you for your work in preserving the evidence. I will thank Park Ranger Trumbull for discovering it and reporting it. I wonder if you and Captain King are able to stay with us while my agents and I process what we have learned and decide on the next steps? We may need your help."

"Captain King and I will be at the main gate with the Rangers. Here is my cell number."

McDonald programmed the number into his cell. "Thanks." He already had in mind what he would ask of the Chief.

CHAPTER 41

FBI

Stuart McDonald Took over the investigation. "Don, I want you to take charge of the body, the evidence and the work of the forensic team. We need an autopsy completed as soon as possible. Imar, we need to continue the search in the woods. The local chief did a great job in the time he had before we arrived. I want you to call the office and pull in as many agents as you can to make a further search of the woods with particular attention to the area between the body and where we are standing. Whoever shot the victim had to come down. Put one of the agents in charge. Try using Tom Wilson. He has some growth capability as an agent. I want you to take one of the agents and personally search the grass and wooded area adjacent to where the glass crystals were found and where we assume a vehicle was parked. In the meantime, I will brief the Deputy and try to convince him to release some data to the press and hope that yesterday's climbers see or hear about it and come forth. Any questions? If not, let's get started."

Agent McDonald called the Deputy in Bangor and briefed him fully on his findings, stressing the importance of locating one or more of the climbers. The Deputy left it to McDonald to make the media contact and to release only the barest of details.

McDonald called the Chief. "Chief McCorey, I have a favor to ask of you and Captain King if he is still in the area."

"He is with me and we will be there in a minute or two."

The three law enforcement officers met in the middle of the parking lot and conversed as equals. They came to an agreement a few minutes later. The Chief would contact the media. He would inform them that an unidentified male body had been found in the woods just off the parking lot by a dog belonging to one of the park rangers. The ranger was making his routine morning policing of the area. There was no identifying information on the body and because it is presumed that a car is missing from the parking lot, the chief thought it best to bring in both the state police and the FBI. Both possessed forensic laboratories that were the best available and would be helpful in identifying the body. If anyone was in the park the day before they should contact the Chief. Phone numbers and email addresses were provided. That was as much information as would be provided. They told no lies and the information given was accurate.

Agent McDonald spoke. "Thank you both for your assistance. To the degree I am authorized to share information, I will do so. Not knowing what we have or what the larger picture is, if there is one, I cannot promise more than that. I'd like to give both of you my cell phone number in the event you need to contact me. Do not provide information on the phone. I will meet with you personally. Again, thanks." Once the phone numbers were given, the meeting broke up.

As the three law enforcement men went their separate ways, each was reflecting on the ease with which they had put aside a potential territorial and jurisdictional dispute.

CHAPTER 42

DESTROY AMERICA

"Let us begin. We must first deal with the political. The western powers have, for as many years as those of us in this room have lived, been on a campaign to secure the rights to precious oil that Allah has blessed us with. While the European nations have plundered our resources, it is the Americans who were and are at the forefront of raping our countries. They accomplished this through their oil companies that stole our oil and sold it on world markets at any price they wished. Then they took the revenue and invested it in the most advanced oil technology in the world in order to extract still more oil from our lands. They made hundreds of billions of dollars while the people received nothing."

Khalid looked at his colleagues and it was clear that they were in agreement. "It was only when OPEC was created that we began the process of developing a collective strength which enabled us to share in the profits through control of our oilfields and partial ownership of the western oil companies. Money was taken from the greedy hands of western powers and deposited into hands loyal to Allah. The Americans, not to be denied their oil, threw billions of dollars at those whose loyalty they tried to buy. Such fools, such stupid fools, to believe that those who hate them and dream of the collapse of America would honor any agreement."

Khalid stopped momentarily to take a sip of water. No one stirred. "The money that was thrown at kings, monarchs and despots never reached our people. Billions in dollars were stolen by these leaders and sent to safe havens around the globe. They looted that which belonged to the people while America looked on and did nothing to stop the plundering of resources which belonged to the masses. Millions of our people suffered while a few lived lives of luxury. The masses were kept under control by armies that were created and armed by the United States."

He stopped for a moment before continuing. "The entire Middle East is aflame because of America's failure to develop alternative fuels. They found it more economical to plunder our resources than to extract oil from the Alaska wilderness, the Gulf of Mexico and the Atlantic seacoast. The harvesting of oil and gas within the continental United States would have provided America with sufficient resources for the foreseeable future and allowed them to depart from the Middle East and leave us at peace. Thankfully for us, the United States Congress has no will, no courage, no vision and no interest in survival. Its members serve only to enrich themselves. Its dereliction of responsibility has allowed us to determine the ultimate destiny of America. Who would have believed that oil would carry with it the power to bring western civilization to an end? My brothers, before we join Allah in our next life, we will be witness to a second holocaust when our people take to the streets, overthrow all western supported governments and assume total control of our oil resources. When that happens, we will force America to its knees along with Israel." He hesitated long enough to catch his breath.

"I ask you, where is it written that all sovereign nations must have democratic governments? Who made the United States the arbiter of governmental form around the world? Why must their laws be our laws? Who gave NATO the right to create 'no fly zones' over a sovereign nation's airspace? What international law allows the president of the United States to send covert CIA operatives, drones, and Special Forces into another country and kill whomever it wishes? We must destroy this imperialistic thinking. If we stay on course and repel American efforts to democratize our sovereign nations, we will eventually force all western democratic governments to govern as we govern. We will demand that they adhere to our laws and not theirs. And, if they refuse, we will punish them as they have punished us. One day we will have the military power and the resources to block their airspaces, bomb their cities and kill their people. Even as we speak, Iran has drones in the sky and is close to developing an atomic bomb."

His throat was dry and he began to cough. The others looked worried that he might collapse from his emotional words. Suleiman poured a glass of water and handed it to him. "We must all believe that in the lifetime of our children the world as we know it now will then be a Muslim world living under Sharia law. When historians narrate how such a thing could come to pass, they will identify America's dependence on foreign oil and the partition of Palestine to create the illegitimate country of Israel as the two causes."

Khalid took a breath, looked around the table at each man and spoke slowly, hoarsely and with hatred in his voice. "America must be destroyed."

Aba Najdi responded. "Khalid, did we not bring America to its knees on 9/11? World economies were destroyed, the worst recession in modern times engulfed the planet and all European nations are now on the brink of bankruptcy. America suffered and has yet to fully recover. Our friends control much of the world's oil reserves and it is our ultimate weapon. Once we drive out the royal family in Saudi Arabia, control Libya and Egypt, rebuild Iraq to our liking and once again control Afghanistan, we will be in control of the world's greatest oil reserves. Then, with vast financial resources, we shall dictate how the world will operate."

"Aba, you speak from ignorance!"

Aba was frozen in place by such a harsh rebuke but was fearful of engaging Khalid verbally at this moment. He saw the evil in his eyes and could feel the unease among the others. They were intimidated by the man at the head of the table and feared for their well being.

Khalid was undeterred by his assault on Aba and continued with harshness in his voice. "All listen to my words. 9/11 was the worst mistake the Muslim world has made in this century. The Saudis, the most treacherous of America's partners, provided the funds for our brothers who perished as they flew aircraft into the Twin Towers and the Pentagon. I have no idea what the royal family was thinking by not stopping that assault on America. We are all fools if we believe that 9/11 was successful."

Those around the table were shaken and speechless on hearing these words. They looked at each other hoping that one or more would break the silence. Ibraham took the lead when he observed the dismay on their faces. "What Khalid says is true. If I may continue, Khalid?"

Khalid nodded his approval. "What he says is true because the events of 9/11 only served to mobilize the American government. It poured billions into their intelligence apparatus and developed the most sophisticated electronic surveillance systems in the world. Citizens supported every initiative suggested by the president and the Congress. Every community, large and small, rural or urban, was put on alert for suspicious activities by anyone who in any way resembled a Muslim. America's allies, both governments and citizens on the street, came to its defense and supported a president who had been labeled a fool and a cowboy before 9/11. After 9/11 he was a hero and set the United States on a course to destroy us. The aircraft killed three thousand Americans and that was the end of our jihad, but it was the beginning of American vigilance. For ten years they pursued Osama Bin Laden and on Sunday, May 1, 2011, thanks to their intelligence apparatus, technological advances, and the best trained Special Forces in the world, they stormed his protected compound in Pakistan, killed him and threw his body into the sea."

He stopped and looked at each man and repeated his prior words in calm and measured voice, "That was the end of our jihad. Every effort to terrorize America since then has failed. The country's heightened awareness and vastly improved electronic surveillance system makes it impossible for us to communicate with our cells except by the slowest of systems." He then looked to Khalid who continued the discourse.

"Ibraham has stated it well. Ironically, our only gain has been the creation of the position of Director of National Intelligence whose job it is to coordinate the work of all of the intelligence agencies in the country. You look surprised? You wonder how the creation of such a powerful position has worked to our advantage? Once again the American Congress, in creating this position in a deliberate attempt to minimize the work and influence of the CIA, has created a monster. Had the Congress asked us, we would have told them that the CIA is the best intelligence organization in the world. The training of its agents, its covert operations, and its world wide support system is the envy of every security service in the world. It is the most feared intelligence service in the Muslim world. When combined with the Navy Seals and other special forces, there is no place to hide from the reach of the CIA. Every other intelligence service, including those of America's friends and enemies are at best second rate. Yet, liberals in the Congress and the Department of Justice despise it and will do anything to destroy its effectiveness. They are fools, all of them. They have pummeled the finest intelligence agency ever created. The fact that the Egyptians betrayed their trust and allowed me to escape does not diminish the quality of its work. If we make even the smallest mistake, I assure you that the Central Intelligence Agency will be first to know."

The others were surprised at his complimentary comments about the CIA but knew what he had said to be true. He continued, "What is so laughable is the fact there are over forty five government intelligence agencies in the Unites States and the Congress expects that the Director of National Intelligence will successfully coordinate the work of all of them. He will have as much success as we would in coordinating the work of forty tribal chiefs in Afghanistan. We in the Arab world are fortunate that one does not have to be intelligent to become a member of the United States Congress. As always, in a democracy, it is money that determines who becomes a member of that body. Listen to my words; we will ride to success on the backs of their ignorance. We will use the lack of coordination between the intelligence agencies to our advantage. Our agents in America will compromise some members of Congress with money and sex, especially those members who sit on the powerful oversight committees. Some members of Congress are notorious for leaking information. Others are lecherous infidels who will compromise the nation's security for sex."

He waited and then continued, "The Congress of the United States is a world class example of where the sum of the parts is less than the whole! Let us pray to Allah that the Congress creates still another intelligence agency and further diminishes the work of the CIA."

When it was clear that he had ended this phase of the meeting, Abdul Jazier nodded and got Khalid's attention. It was time for the others to go on the offensive. "This is all interesting and makes for good listening, Khalid, but what does it have to do with our work this day?"

"It means, Abdul, that we are about to develop plans for a series of suicide bombings across the country."

Ghani Mohammed retorted, "And you consider suicide bombings to be another 9/11? Forgive my impertinence, Khalid, but that is foolishness."

Ibraham jumped in. "Please, Ghani, there is no need to be insulting."

"What is insulting is that those of us hearing this for the first time are being taken for fools. This is an idea conceived out of anger and one that fails to weigh the consequences of the action. If implemented, there would be no place on this planet to shelter Muslims from the wrath of America. Using Khalid's own words, there would be no hiding from the CIA. There would be a world-wide condemnation of the Muslim community. I say it again, Khalid, that suicide bombings are the work of the ignorant who work only for the guarantee of paradise, money for their families and sex with virgins. They have no interest in Islam. We will not ride to success on the backs of such fools. Israel survived such bombings for decades and so will America. I scoff at such a suggestion."

Not used to being challenged, Khalid rosc from his chair and pointed his finger at Ghani and spoke with fury in his words. "You think it foolishness when in each of the fifty states we will destroy schools, churches, hospitals, shopping malls, subways, movie theaters, airport terminals, hotels, medical centers, bus stations, court houses, supermarkets, restaurants, recreation centers, night clubs, college student centers and any facility where people congregate? There are thousands of possibilities. The list is endless. Americans will be afraid to leave their homes. Again, I ask you to listen to my words. The bombing of the Twin Towers was a crushing, lasting and traumatic blow for metropolitan New York and the Pentagon, but the rest of the country quickly returned to business as usual. The average American was temporarily inconvenienced. The only lasting impact has been longer lines at airport security while every ship, bus, train, private aircraft and commercial truck is wide open to us to mention but a few. Homeland Security places marshals on commercial aircraft while thousands of private aircraft fly without restriction. With my plan, every American will fear leaving his home. No place will be safe. The entire country will be in a panic, the economy will falter, security forces will be removed from more critical projects like border control in order to protect the homeland which will be in chaos. The military, unable to field sufficient troops to bring stability to a nation in panic, will have to transfer forces from the Middle East, thereby opening the way for us to fill the vacuum. What is foolish with this plan?" With that Khalid slowly lowered himself into his chair while glancing with bitterness in his eyes at each of the others at the table.

Hafs Karzai, who had been silent, spoke in a challenging voice, "Tell us, Khalid, just how do you plan on recruiting hundreds of suicide bombers. They would easily be detected trying to enter the country. This means they have to be recruited and trained in this country. Is this not so?"

"It is so."

"We do not have a recruiting infrastructure here. The question remains; how will they be recruited and trained?"

"It is now time for prayer when we ask Allah for the courage to continue our work to destroy the American way of life."

CHAPTER 43

GAME PLAN

One by one the cottages came to life, exiting the night and entering the day. The porch lights next to each door went on and their glow was warm and reassuring. Behind the white semi-opaque shades of each cottage, lamps were turned on and occupants could be seen moving about in preparation for the day. As they woke, each wondered if the others had spent the night alone. It had not gone unnoticed that Max left the dinner meeting a short time after Elizabeth and they had a long history. Darlene left alone while Vinnie and Gretchen had remained behind for a nightcap and a walk.

Max, being anxious about the day ahead, was the first to leave his cottage. Shortly after he headed for the mansion, he was followed by Gretchen. They had hardly stepped off their porches when Elizabeth and Darlene appeared. The four were greeted by a cool mist and a dense fog that spread like a white blanket over the farmland and, as they began the walk to breakfast, their shoes settled onto the damp grass with each step leaving an imprint behind. In the distance, the mansion was brightly lit and alive with activity. The light in the windows alternated between dim and bright as waves of fog drifted past.

As though conducting their march to the mansion by an agency protocol, none spoke as they walked. Each knew that the tale Max related the previous evening was about to propel them on a course of action not knowing what the end game would be. The one person who would have a major role in its success was nowhere to be seen. Then again, they all knew that he walked to a different beat. It was this quality that had kept him alive through the most unimaginable horrors he had experienced in the Middle East.

When Elizabeth, the first to reach the mansion, opened the front door, she was greeted with the inviting smell of fresh coffee, bacon, sausage, fried eggs, muffins and Vinnie. The night shift of the mansion security detail had just finished breakfast with Vinnie as a guest."Were you hungry or just anxious to get started?"

"Both."

"I will also assume that you knew the night shift security detail would be here and it would be profitable to have a chat with them about security. Battlefield habits do not dissipate easily. If I were a betting woman, I'd say that you did a perimeter check before retiring last night."

"Truth is both Gretchen and I did a walk-around last night. I did another tour of the area this morning. The immediate grounds are secure and, if I can offer an educated guess, the vast expanse of this farm has more physical and electronic security than the White House. However, Gretchen and I do have a question for you; are our conversations being recorded by the agency?"

She waited until the others had entered the dining room, placed her hand on his arm, looked into his dark and questioning eyes, "Vinnie, everything we are about to discuss and any actions we may take as a result of the conversation do not exist. For the official record, this meeting has been called by me to debrief Max regarding the attempt on his life. Gretchen and Darlene are here officially to listen to the debriefing and provide me with options as to the next step or steps I may consider in identifying the leak that led to the assassins locating him in Maine. The security detail has no interest except to keep us alive. In case you are wondering, the exterior walls of this old mansion has been completely renovated with material that makes it impossible for any sound on the inside to be con veyed to the outside by any means that we know exists at this time. A variation of the material was applied to all of the glass used at Metro Plaza and was applied by the same agency contractor. When time permits, I will tell you how we discovered the material. We have not shared the technology with any other agency."

"And, how do you explain my presence?"

"You are not here. The pilot understands that officially there were only two persons on the Gulfstream that arrived last evening. I have faith that you can convince a friend to testify you were elsewhere if an alibi should be needed. Now, I need breakfast. How about a second cup of coffee?"

"Thanks, but I need a little exercise. See you at eight." With that he left the house. He still had questions as to security and wondered if his involvement with the team would endanger Sharon. Two questions had been answered by Elizabeth; he need not bother Jason about the glass exterior walls at Metro Plaza and the three women knew about Sharon. He wondered how much they knew.

The nine o'clock meeting started on time. The seating arrangements had changed slightly with Vinnie choosing to sit next to Gretchen. Elizabeth took note but moved on to recapping the significant elements of Max's story beginning with the abduction of Abdu Khalid in Rome by the agency and ending with his exit from Maine. "We now have three issues with which to contend. All are off the books. First, we have the need to identify the leak. Second, we need to learn who in the Italian government knew that arrest warrants had been issued for Max and his colleagues and who then forwarded that information to him. Third, we need to find and assassinate Khalid before he can rain havoc on the country."

"I thought we were to find a way to keep Max out of harm's way." It was Gretchen.

"Once we have found Khalid, Max is safe. This is a personal vendetta with Khalid and none of his inner circle will have either the stomach or resources to take on Max."

It was Max who spoke next. "I agree with Elizabeth that once we have Khalid, we will have broken the back of his organization. Without him, there is no number two to take over. Ibraham Malik would die for Khalid but he is essentially a foot soldier and has no following in the Muslin world. Let's get Khalid. For him, 9/11 was just a warm-up."

"Elizabeth, both you and Max have made reference to the fact that Khalid has a plan to create havoc greater than 9/11. Have I missed something? Is there some intelligence that the rest of us are not aware of?" It was Darlene.

"Nothing clean. The threats he made against the United States at the time of his abduction and during the Egyptian episode gives us a reason to be concerned that he is plotting something major. From the time he was extracted out of Egypt by al-Qaeda, he has not been heard from."

"Or, seen." It was Vinnie.

"Correct. We have not had a confirmed sighting. In the past, he spent a fair amount of time interviewing with Al Jazeera where he railed against America. The fact that we have not seen him recently may indicate he is somewhere other than the Middle East."

"As in the United States." Again, it was Vinnie.

"Possibly, but we have no corroboration. Abdu Khalid is on the Homeland Security watch list, but he is fluent in English and does not look any more like a Muslim than does Max or Vinnie. He is well educated and has lived here and in Europe for a number of years. Unless there was a problem with his passport, he could easily gain entry to the states. Money being no problem, he has a wide choice of travel options, points of entry and transportation modes. He has had eleven years since 9/11 to develop a network of devoted followers in this country any one of whom would give his life to protect him."

"Elizabeth, our Simsbury facility has not detected any electronic communications between Khalid and his followers in the states. For that matter, it has been quiet world-wide. We would be the first to know if there was any talk going on. As you know, our equipment and personnel is superior to that of any other agency, domestic or foreign." It was Darlene.

"That doesn't mean they are not communicating. There is another means of communicating that is readily available, usually not detected unless there is some suspicion of wrong doing, is cheap and reliable although a bit slow. It is called the United States Postal Service."

Quiet took over the assemblage. They looked first at Vinnie and then around the table at each other seeking a response to his comments. Darlene was the first to answer. "Vinnie, we have thousands of postal inspectors around the country to examine suspicious mail or suspicious activity. They could be on this fast. It wouldn't work."

Elizabeth and Gretchen remained quiet, but Max responded. "Vinnie is right. This has been under our noses and we have not yet put in place a system for detecting terrorist communications by mail. How about this for a scenario. We have Khalid who looks, acts and dresses like an American business man, takes up residence in an expensive neighborhood, is socially active, engaging to neighbors and country club colleagues and goes to the local post office like the rest of us and deposits and picks up his mail. Who would suspect? And, in case you find a flaw in that it is possible for a first class letter to get lost, he need only send a copy the next day. Now, what are the odds of two letters being mishandled?"

"Does it make sense? Is everyone on board with this idea?"

"Elizabeth, I am on board for the time being, but need more time to think of other flaws. Now, how do we go about locating Khalid?"

"Darlene, I am going to ask Vinnie how he would go about it. He is not yet a victim of agency group think." Vinnie did not know this was coming, but was pleased to be asked.

With that Elizabeth turned to Vinnie. She liked his boldness. This would be a test of his analytical skills. He began. "Darlene is correct in stating that if the agency facility in Simsbury is unable to detect electronic communications, and if Khalid has been absent from Al Jazeera television, then the odds are in favor of his being outside the Middle East. I'm also thinking that if our informant inside the Italian Government had heard anything on the European front, he or she would have contacted us. Since Khalid has no immediate issue with Europe, then it is safe to conclude that he is in the states or on his way. It is Max and the United States that he plans on terminating." He looked around the table and no one was ready to speak. Max looked pensive.

"I'm going to think aloud for a minute or two and place myself in Khalid's situation. His entry point could be anywhere by any means including a private aircraft. His inadvertently getting caught up in border action with the agents along the Mexican American border rules it out as a point of entry. It is too risky for him. Rule out the southern border. Now, let's go north. For years, the Canadian border had more holes than Swiss cheese. The long standing antagonism between our countries did not help. It worsened when they provided amnesty to those who ducked out on serving in Viet Nam. More recently, they provided a safe haven for those who did not want to serve in the Gulf War. After 9/11, Canada finally concluded that it was in its best interest to work with our government in beefing up its border security. The last thing it needed was a border crossing by someone like Khalid that could lead to a national disaster in this country. Such an event could bring down their government. Between boots on the ground and extensive electronic surveillance in place on both sides of the border, a crossing from Canada would be difficult. Given the ineptness of the TSA, Khalid would have a safer opportunity entering from either the East or West coast of the United States. The best place to hide is often in the open. Again, placing myself in his shoes, I would want my ultimate location to be as far away from my point of entry as possible. This brings up four questions; under what name did he enter the country, where was his point of entry, what is his destination and what Middle East country would support him and also have the sophistication to alter a passport and forge several sets of identity documents?"

Elizabeth, "You have a suggestion?"

"I'm pretty certain of the country, but not yet prepared to suggest which coast he entered. We have the issue of a passport, the principle document necessary for him to enter the country. It makes sense, if he makes it safely into the country, that he destroys the forged passport. He takes on a new identity with other forged documents and flies off to his final destination in the United States. Remember, each time he moves from one airport to the other, he increases the risk of detention. On the other hand, if he senses that we are closing in, he will make one or more moves before he leaves the country. But, to continue, my money is on his entering the country with one passport and then taking a flight out of the same airport on the same day to his final destination using another identity. There are the questions of where he acquired the passport and what country has the technical ability to prepare multiple identities. If he is moving around, he will require several sets of documents. If it were me, I would find someone with physical characteristics similar to mine, abduct him, steal his passport, kill him and dispose of the body so it could not be immediately reported as missing. This would buy me a day or two during which time the passport is altered and new documents prepared. Then, I quickly leave that country and head to the United States before the victim is discovered. Now, to answer Elizabeth's question, the only countries in the Middle East with the technical know-how are Iran and Saudi Arabia. Given Iran's highly effective intelligence services and its hatred of the United States, it gets my vote. When Khalid fled Egypt, we know he traveled to Saudi Arabia. Somewhere in that country there is a dead male stripped of his passport. Now, if we can figure out where Khalid entered and the name he used, we can make our next move." With that he placed his hands on the table and sat back for reaction.

"So, all we need to do is find out who is missing in Saudi Arabia and then compare the missing man's photo with the surveillance tapes at all major points of entry in the country. Then, we have a starting point." It was Darlene.

"I don't know if you are serious or not, Darlene, but the fact is the agency has access to every surveillance tape made at all points of entry into the United States that receive flights originating in a foreign country. That is the easy part. I'm trying to determine how we can learn of a missing male in Saudi Arabia who is prominent enough to have a passport without alerting Langley as to what we are doing. Any ideas?"

Max, who had remained silent interjected, "Why assume he entered by plane? Consider for a moment that there are hundreds of private yachts, recreational ships, merchant freighters and boats entering the states every day. Many are flagged in countries that are our enemies. He could be on any of those."

"Elizabeth, before I respond to Max's comments, I need to know if I missed something." It was Vinnie. He kept his emotions under control and spoke in a quiet voice, one tailored to make others listen. "I understand that all initiatives on our part that deal with Max have to stay off the record because he is a persona non grata with the Congress, but why do we have to avoid Langley in trying to locate Khalid? He is a high profile terrorist who has to be eliminated. If you want him dead, I can do it but, I need resources in addition to the human ones in this room. If I decide to join the team and put my life on the line, I need a highly skilled partner, someone who knows how to kill and who knows how not to get killed. Add to that a variety of weapons, transportation, secure communications and a back-up team. We have a long and treacherous road ahead of us. Khalid has infinite resources in this country, including multiple safe havens in literally every state in the union. Every mosque is a potential safe house for him. I need, we need, what Langley possesses."

"I need to hear how Vinnie responds to Max's concern. It seems to me that it is an important question." It was Gretchen.

"I think there is a misconception about our modern day terrorist. The 'enlightened' thinking by our out of touch 'foggy bottom' analysts is that all terrorists endure the most severe hardships to achieve their goals. That may be true of the second team, the believers, the followers and the devout, but it is not true of the Khalids of this world. While the Quran establishes strict standards regarding alcohol, sex, and morality for Muslims, the leaders ignore what is good for the masses. Rome, Paris, London, New York, Madrid and international playgrounds like Nice and Monaco are occupied with terrorist leaders who live the life of luxury complete with mistresses and debauchery. It is a fact that Saudi princes spend more time out of country than in and it isn't for the weather. Underneath the folds of their garments is a penis looking for action. And, before we condemn Muslims, the same is true in the United States where the rich and powerful, the well connected, the leaders of the military/industrial complex and our own Congressional leaders of both parties suck the wealth from middle class America and adhere to a different morality. Just look at the mess in Benghazi. Consider how many legislators, athletes and actors in the past decade have preached family matters only to be caught with mistresses or same sex partners. The powerful in every culture talk egalitarianism but act like monarchs. Khalid long ago left behind the discomforts of the second team. Max, our prey is not hiding on a freighter, playing shuffle board on Celebrity Lines, swimming with kids on a Disney ship, or, making out with his mistress on a yacht headed to Martha's Vineyard. Unless you all have a better argument to offer, I stand by my opinion that Khalid is here, now, and he is plotting a new 9/11. In the meantime, he is living the life of a prince." He looked around the table. "I rest my case."

Elizabeth waited for a few seconds and when no one spoke, she did. "It's time for a break. We have a lot to think about. Refreshments are in the lobby. We reconvene in thirty minutes and at that time we begin to develop a strategy leading to the assassination of Khalid." With that, she stood and headed for the lobby. The other followed, except for Vinnie who remained seated with a worried look on his face.

Gretchen was almost out the door when she turned and saw Vinnie. "I'm buying if you are interested."

He turned towards her, smiled and thought how lovely she was. "I'm interested. But, how about a walk to clear the cobwebs?" They poured themselves coffee and headed for the door. Elizabeth for the second time took special note of their closeness and wondered if a liaison was developing. She made a mental note to be more vigilant in her observations.

"What's troubling you?"

"I'm not certain. Knowing you have been involved in high risk covert operations, you must have experienced, at one time or another, a worry that all the parts don't fit, that something is not right but you are not certain what it is. We all do. It's a feeling that can spook you, put team members at risk and upset an operation."

"What do you think doesn't fit?"

"Max doesn't fit. I mean, why are the three of you so concerned over one agent who, quite frankly, abused his position as station chief to abduct Khalid on the soil of a sovereign nation, thereby putting the entire agency at risk of criminal proceedings and providing the Congress and other enemies of Langley with more ammunition to blow the agency to hell. If you wanted Khalid so damn bad, you should have waited until he entered the United States. Embarrassing a foreign nation was foolhardy. If I may put it bluntly, Gretchen, am I being asked to risk my life for a guy who fucked up, for someone the three of you have had as a lover at one time or another?"

Calmly, she responded, "Not me, possibility with Darlene and, certainly with Elizabeth. That said, Elizabeth would not risk your life for his."

"They were lovers. That is reason enough."

"That's unfair."

"I think it's time to find out. Let's get back to the session."

"Vinnie, I hope you don't intend to deal with this now?"

"Let's see what happens and then I'll decide."

Gretchen spoke. "If we waited until Khalid was in the country, we would not have had the opportunity for enhanced interrogation."

"As it turned out, you lost that opportunity when Egypt set him free. You got nothing while risking everything." He headed back to the mansion.

CHAPTER 44

WHY SAVE MAX

"It is close to eleven. Let's wrap up the session by responding to Vinnie's comments and finalize our work after lunch. The questions on the table are; is Khalid in the United States and, if so, where? Second, what alias is he using? Third, what is he plotting? Fourth, who employed the Serbs to assassinate Max and why? Fifth, where is the leak that led to the attempt on Max's life?"

"I'll go first." It was Darlene. "Unlike the period before 9/11 when the Muslim community was hardly visible, and with most Americans hardly aware that the community existed, it has grown in strength and in numbers. There are in excess of three thousand mosques in the states, many in heavily populated urban areas where any attempt by our government to monitor who goes in and who goes out is next to impossible, not to mention that the liberal press would crucify the government if it tried. The fact is every mosque is a potential safe haven for Khalid. While I believe the vast majority of Muslims are American in their lives, they are children of Mohammad in their hearts and would give their lives to protect Khalid if asked to do so. There is no way an Imam of any mosque would betray Khalid if he sought refuge or asked for their help in other ways. This is all by way of saying that I, too, believe he is in the country. I have no idea where, but Vinnie is correct, Khalid is here."

"Before the question is raised, let me be clear." It was Max. "This is not about me. I am expendable. Our job is to find and eliminate Khalid before he can rain terror on our population. I sure as hell want to know who contracted with the Serbs to eliminate me and who pointed them to me in Maine, but both are secondary to the assassination of Khalid. Elizabeth, I suggest we work as two units, one to find our prey and the other to determine who contracted with the Serbs and why."

"Khalid is here and I say let's find the bastard ASAP. I also agree with the two unit approach as suggested by Max. Personally, I want in on running down Khalid." Gretchen was certain that given her background, she would be teamed with Vinnie.

Elizabeth took charge of the conversation. "The first unit is comprised of Vinnie and Gretchen. They will find and kill Khalid. Max and Darlene will comprise the second unit charged with the responsibility to find the leak and determine who contracted with the Serbs. I'll support both units. I will start by having a conversation with Alexei Dmitrov, my Russian counterpart in the FSB. The Serbs don't make a move that the Russians aren't aware of. Alexei owes me for earlier assistance provided him. I am confident he will know something. As soon as I have information, I will inform both units. If the leak appears to have come from Italy, I will inform unit one since Vinnie speaks fluent Italian. That means that Vinnie and Gretchen could possibly be dispatched to Italy but that remains to be seen. Finally, for unit one, there is the issue of entry into the United States. I doubt if Khalid changed physical characteristics between the time he entered the states and when he boarded another flight to his final destination which I assume was the same day. I realize that this is conjecture but, it is the best we have to work with at this time. We need to examine every surveillance tape made of persons entering the states through every point of entry from overseas and then compare those tapes with those of everyone who then boarded another flight in the same airport on the same day for movement within the continental United States. Langley has an advanced facial recognition program but it lacks the power required for this task. Fortunately, we have friends who have the capability of processing what will amount to millions of photos. We do not need Langley." She looked at her watch. "It's eleven thirty. You have approximately thirty minutes before lunch. We will reconvene again at 1 pm."

"Elizabeth, you originally indicated that we would work tomorrow morning. Is that still the plan?" Vinnie asked the question.

"I was hoping to have the lab results on the car, the body and the gun to share tonight. It is taking longer than expected since I was unable to use our lab at Langley without risking a lead. Our private source has a lab facility that is more than adequate for the task but needs more time. I'll make a decision on our schedule when we return for lunch."

CHAPTER 45

THE ROBERTSON FAMILY

Chief Mike McCorey received the call from the Robertson family within twenty four hours following the public announcement. They had such a satisfying climb on Katahdin, they decided to remain in the area for another day or two. The hotel desk clerk where they were staying knew they had climbed the mountain. He called their room and informed them of the announcement seeking information from anyone who had been in Baxter State Park in the last day or two. They immediately called Chief McCorey who arranged to meet them at the hotel.

"I want to thank you for calling me on this matter. The desk clerk said that you enjoyed your climb and that you decided to stay in the area a bit longer and do more climbing. That is what we like to hear from our tourists. Maine is a great place to vacation. I grew up here and cannot imagine living anywhere else. That said, please tell me what you saw or heard and then I'll want to ask a few questions.

Alex jumped right in. "I told my family that they were up to no good and that they had guns under their jackets." Before Stan or Lee Robertson could say a word, Ben continued Alex's theme. "They were tough looking guys and built like wrestlers with huge necks and arms. I would not want to meet them alone."

"Hold on now. Someone needs to tell me who we are talking about." He looked at Stan and Lee hoping they would join in which they did.

"Alex and Ben are correct in that there were two tough looking men in their late twenties, early thirties who did not look at all like climbers. Lee and I talked about it when we returned to the parking lot after our climb. When we first arrived in the morning to climb there was a youngish couple who looked every part the experienced climbers. Don't know their last names but they called each other Glenn and Betsy. Then there were the two men who did not speak to any of us. Finally, there was the lone climber who, it turned out, was the most experienced climber of all. In fact, he mentioned that he had climbed extensively in Europe including the Matterhorn and Mt. Blanc. He also mentioned climbing in Asia. We never learned his first or last name.

"And, what my husband did not mention is that when we returned to the parking lot, neither the two men nor the lone climber were anywhere to be seen. The car belonging to the two men was parked at the end of the line where the four cars belonging to all of us were parked when we began the climb. No one was near it or from what we could see, in it. The climber's car was gone. That was not surprising since he was a fast climber and finished well ahead of all of us."

"Can you describe the lone climber?"

"My mom thought he was a hunk! So didn't Betsy."

"Alex, please. Chief, to be more accurate, he was handsome, had an athletic build, climbed with seriousness and skill, was pleasant and well spoken and professionally equipped to climb. He looked like a model you would see in a climbing magazine."

"Was he American?"

Stan spoke up. "Definitely American. If he wasn't, then he had to be a spy trained in a high powered language school or someone who learned English early in life. But in my mind he was American. The other men were definitely not American. They had heavy accents. I'd guess eastern European, Russian or Slavic."

"Do any of you remember what model car he was driving?"

"It was a Chevy Impala, new model and black. Didn't really fit the guy. He should have been driving a Porsche."

"Well, son, with a memory like that I could use you on my force. How about the car that belonged to the two men? What was it like?"

"It was also black but I don't think it was a Chevy, but it had the same general body style. What do you think dad?"

"I agree with my son. The cars were black and looked a lot alike. They were not high end. If I had to guess, I'd say they were both rental cars. By the way, the husband and wife team drove a Subaru wagon." The Chief made note of the cars.

"Young lady, you mentioned that you thought that the two men had guns. Can you be more specific?"

Stan and Betsy glanced at each other and rolled their eyes but silently agreed to let their teenager talk, not that they had much choice. Actually, they were impressed with the maturity of both kids in talking to the Chief.

"Well, to begin with, they looked like they were out for trouble. Why else would you be at the base of a great mountain like Katahdin and not have some climbing gear with you? My parents think I'm foolish but when you see bad guys on television or in the movies, they always wear jackets that are too large so they can hide guns. The two men had on big jackets and you could make out a bulge on one side."

"How about the lone climber, did he have on suspicious clothing?"

"No, as my mom said, he was dressed for climbing. Did he have a gun? Could have had one in his back pack, I guess."

"Like your brother, you would make a good detective."

"Chief, my daughter brings up a good point. Lee and I discussed it after the climb when we returned to the parking lot and saw that the lone climber and his car were gone, the two others were nowhere to be seen and yet their car was still here. After 9/11 you begin to be suspicious of anything unusual, like thinking the two men were terrorists or murderers. Since there is nothing here for them to destroy and, because my family and the young couple were unhurt, the two men were obviously not after us. So, we asked ourselves, what were they up to? The only other explanation was that something was going on between the two men and the lone climber. The question is what? At the beginning of the day there were three living men and two cars and, at the end of the day, there was one car, one dead man, and two men unaccounted for." The Chief was not about to tell them that both cars were missing.

"I couldn't have summarized it better. We have a dilemma which is why we are pleased you came forward to provide valuable information. Because this is an ongoing investigation, I cannot provide much in the way of information except to assure you that you are not in danger. I will share what you have told me with the FBI. They are officially in charge of the investigation. The agent in charge, Stuart McDonald, will most likely contact you. Finally, at any time did you observe the two men talking to the climber and did you see the two men on the mountain?"

Ben answered. "The answer to both questions is no. If the two men were on the mountain they would have been in the tree line. One of us would have seen them if they ventured out in the open."

"One last question. Do you have any idea who the other two climbers were?"

Lee spoke up. "Only their first names as we mentioned. Their car had a University of Maine parking sticker. They were too old to be students so perhaps they work there. The university probably would know them if you mention their first names, indicate they are serious climbers and drive a Subaru wagon. They were very nice. Hardly the type being hunted by murderers."

"Again thank you for coming forth. You have provided valuable information. Before you leave, I need to have your itinerary for the next few days and your home address, cell phone and email."

"Chief, something is really bothering me. The four of us were and still are of the opinion that the two men were here on business, bad business. My family is not the target of anyone and it is hard to envision that the couple was being hunted. If they were, the two men would have been waiting for them at the end of the day. None of us would have stood a chance with them. They reminded me of the men we saw in the news who terrorized the women and children in Bosnia and tortured and slaughtered every male they encountered. There was a cruelty about them." At this point the Chief began to listen intently.

Stan continued. "I would bet our house that the body in the woods is not that of the lone climber. I know you will tell me that there is no way of knowing that at this time. But, if you had met the climber you would absolutely understand why I am so sure it could not be him. This was a well conditioned, smart guy, experienced in the woods and mountains, and he had toughness behind his sophisticated bearing. I guess what I am saying is that if I was to get lost in the woods and wanted to survive, this is the guy I would want to be with. He had confidence written all over him. I do not have an explanation for the car being missing, but I make the prediction that when you and the FBI have concluded your investigation, you will find that the climber is alive and the second man is in a ditch somewhere. For my money, they were after the climber and he outsmarted both of them."

Alex added, "I told my family that the climber was like Matt Damon in the Bourne movies and the two guys had no chance. Like my mom said, he was some guy."

The Chief was silent for a moment or two and then spoke. "I've been a law enforcement officer for several decades and this is the first time I have met a family that has four detectives. You have given me a great deal of information, valuable information, with some yet to be proven suggestions. Again, many thanks for your help."

With that, the father gave the Chief the information he wanted and then the family returned to their rooms. They mentioned that they would be there for another day if the FBI wanted to speak to them.

The Chief went outside and used his cell phone to call Agent McDonald. McDonald picked up on the second ring. "Chief, you have something?"

"I do. I'll meet you in the parking lot in thirty minutes."

Agent McDonald arrived a few minutes before the Chief and was leaning against his car when he arrived. The Chief parked next to the agent, got out, shook hands and extended greetings. "Thanks for calling Chief. I appreciate your discretion on the phone. I assume you got a response from the announcement."

"I did and want to compliment you and Captain King for agreeing to the announcement. It worked by bringing out one of the parties. It was a family of four and they had great information and acute observations. We also have a solid lead to the other climbing party. The father and daughter also offered some interesting thoughts on what happened. They are at the hotel through tomorrow. Before I give you all of the details, I want to mention something the father said that I chose not to follow up on. It could be something his children are not aware of or, for that matter, his wife. I also thought it best that you follow up on it. He mentioned that it was possible that the lone climber, their daughter's version of Matt Damon, could have learned his English as part of his training to be a spy. I assume you have access to military records. If, so, it would be worth taking a look at Mr. Robertson's record. Now, let me share the rest."

They sat in McDonald's car and as the Chief talked, the FBI Agent made notes on his iPad. When the Chief finished he turned to McDonald, "There's a lot to run with here. You'll need more manpower than the two agents with you."

"That will not be a problem. The question is where do we begin? What is the logical sequence of events to pursue? Any suggestions?" The Chief was clearly impressed that the FBI would be interested in his opinion and not just the facts he had collected. He liked McDonald's style.

"I think it would be valuable for you to speak with the family as soon as possible. See if they have second thoughts on what they shared with me or anything they may have forgotten. Then, I'd pursue the spy idea with the father. He struck me as a damn smart guy himself, a lot like the climber they described. It is interesting that he believes that the second guy is dead and that the lone climber is safely out of here after having outwitted the two men. It would pay to do a background check on him. He could be one of you for all we know. The spy thing is not so outrageous when you think about the climber having scaled the likes of the Matterhorn, Mount Blanc and some of the peaks in the Himalayas. He got around. If the lone climber is safely out of here, where is he, where is his car, where is the second guy and the second car? But, I'd start with the father and see where that goes."

The Chief thought a minute and continued. "Before I forget, I would also pay a visit to the university administrative offices located on the Maine campus in Orono and try to identify the couple. Based on what the family told me, they looked like capable climbers which means they would have been closer to the lone climber both on the mountain and when they returned to the parking lot. They may be able to fill in some of the blanks. Their names are Glenn and Betsy and they drive a Subaru wagon. The faculty at the university is like a family. Someone will know them."

"Chief, you'd make a good Agent."

The Chief laughed and said, "Thanks for the compliment but I'm used to carrying my gun on my hip and not hidden in the folds of an expensive suit. I'm still a country boy at heart and too old to run around the country dealing with those ornery country cops."

"Well, if you change your mind."

"No chance of that happening. While I think of it, any results from your lab?"

"Nothing yet, but I expect to have something in the morning."

"I just thought of another suggestion since you asked. Would it make sense to have one of your lab geniuses meet the family and the husband and wife team and create a composite of the climber? The Robertson family certainly had some ideas as to how he looked. Chances are the university couple would also add to the identification. I don't know about you, but this case is getting interesting. A composite could help."

"You have jumped ahead a couple of steps. A composite is normal protocol when we have witnesses who met with and spoke with a possible suspect."

"Well, Agent McDonald, it is time I got back to country policing."

With that, Agent McDonald laughed and said, "I'll be in touch chief. I'd appreciate it if you would inform Captain King of what we have. And, thanks again."

"Be pleased to call him. And, good luck with your investigation."

CHAPTER 46

UMBERTO

While the others were discussing team business, Elizabeth walked the grounds of the mansion thinking about the discussion during the morning session. She was impressed with Vinnie's analytical mind, his field experience, his positive attitude and potential to run down Khalid and kill him. It was a combination that few field agents possessed. As effective as Gretchen, Darlene and Max had been in their work with the agency, none had demonstrated the cold and calculating willingness to purse and kill. It was true that each had killed when the situation demanded it, but none had initiated it. Vinnie was determined that Khalid had to be eliminated and would do so if instructed. He was the one person who possessed the skill and will to do what needed to be done.

Of the other three, it was clear to Elizabeth that Gretchen was the best choice of a partner for Vinnie. She was proven in the field, an expert shot with a variety of hand guns, outstanding at self defense, skilled in communications and electronics, possessed good instincts and she was not afraid of the unknown. Being a physically attractive woman, she added an important dimension to any covert operation. Yet, Elizabeth worried that Gretchen had initiated a relationship with

Vinnie that was not completely agency business. She was aware that they had a nightcap together last night and then walked and talked for over an hour. While the security Agents on duty did not observe any sexual activity, they had the sense that there was more than was obvious. It was not unusual for agents to have affairs with co-workers. She thought about herself and Max and their continuing relationship although she was aware that it was coming to an end if it had not already reached that point. What worried Elizabeth was that Vinnie and Gretchen were involved in a fast developing relationship on the eve of an importance assignment. Gretchen also knew that Vinnie had something going with Sharon Rizzo and that was bound to surface as a problem. While she had complete trust in Gretchen as an agent, she also knew that Vinnie was a handsome, virile man and that Gretchen had not had a serious relationship for some time. She was vulnerable, he was available and Sharon was a thousand miles away.

Elizabeth envisioned herself making love with Vinnie, lying on top of him and moving up and down while he caressed her breasts and sucked her tongue into his mouth. Thinking about it made her damp between her legs. She was distracted from her thoughts by the ring of her cell phone. She recognized the point of origin and picked it up on the third ring. It was a secure call from Rome and not from Carlton

"Buon giorno, my friend, and greetings from the Eternal City.

"Buon giorno, Umberto. You have news." It was a statement and not a question.

"Yes, Yolanda and I conducted the surveillance as you requested. It was several days in length and at first we were not optimistic in that each day he drove directly from his office to the apartment of his mistress and remained until one thirty p.m. after which time he returned to his office. Today was different. He walked from the American Embassy to restaurant Casa Mia on via Avignonesi where he met with an Italian woman, a very sophisticated woman who, according to Yolanda, was dressed expensively in Italian designer clothes. Shortly after they were seated, we took a table far enough away as to not be conspicuous but close enough for us to overhear a good portion of their conversation. The woman spoke English but it was obvious she was Italian. When she spoke to the waiter in Italian, her dialect was strictly Roman and upper class. With her label camera, Yolanda took several photographs of her. The woman shared with her luncheon companion the details of the two men and their trip to the states via Rome. From what we could see and hear, the gentleman looked and acted as though he knew nothing of the incident. Of course, he could have been acting. We do not know."

"Do you know who the woman was?"

"Not then, but when their lunch was over, we continued our surveillance. She went directly to the Italian Embassy. She was there less than an hour. When she left, we followed her cab to the hotel Parco Dei Principi. As soon as she entered, Yolanda got out of our cab and walked closely behind the woman to the front desk where Yolanda engaged one clerk in conversation regarding the availability of rooms that evening, all the while overhearing the women who asked a second clerk for her room key. She gave him her room number and he handed her the key. He asked if he could do anything else for her and she told him that a limo would be picking her up to take her to the Alitalia terminal at Fiumicino and she wanted him to call her room the minute it arrived. She then handed him some Euros.

"Good work, Umberto."

"There is more. Once she left the desk, I went up to the clerk who gave her the room key and spoke to him in Italian, of course, and asked if the woman who just took the key was the famous Italian actress, Gina Vacarro who, in Italy, is loved by men and women alike. Her picture adorns billboards all over Rome. The clerk told me that the hotel's guest was as not quite as beautiful as Gina Vacarro and that it would be blasphemous to even suggest it in public. Then, in a hushed voice, he told me the other che bella donna was senorina Bettina Falaguerra and was easily a numero dieci. I apologized for wasting his time, gave him twenty Euros and left. Once I learned she was flying out of Fiumicino, I had two of my associates leave for the Alitalia terminal where Yolanda and I later joined them. I did not want to run the risk of losing her in the crowed terminal. If you have ever traveled on Alitalia out of Rome you know what I mean. Organized chaos. But you are in luck. She boarded a flight to JFK and will arrive on Alitalia, flight number AZ1608 at five minutes past two p.m. your time. As soon as I end this call, I will transmit her photo to your cell phone. Elizabeth, having seen many beautiful women in Rome, Bettina Falaguerra is stunning. She is a number ten plus. Be forewarned that she will easily compromise any man you assign to cover her. One more thing to help you identify her in New York. She is wearing, according to Yolanda, a beautifully tailored, black designer pant suit with a pale blue blouse and carrying a grey Gucci over-the-shoulder bag along with a briefcase. She has no checked luggage so she will be moving quickly to the ground transportation area."

"Umberto, that was great work. Please thank Yolanda for me. Payment will be deposited in your Swiss account this evening. It will include an extra payment for your two associates."

"Gracia!"

Elizabeth dialed Vinnie's cell number. When he picked up she said, "Vinnie, I need you and Gretchen here pronto. First, go to your cottages and retrieve your belongings. You will be traveling out of here within minutes," and hung up. She dialed a second number and when it was answered, she spoke, "I want it fueled and ready to depart for JFK shortly. Prepare a flight plan." She searched her phone for the Alitalia web site and checked flight status for AZ608. Updated arrival time was now two forty five p.m. local time. It was now eleven thirty five. Approximately three hours before it landed. She dialed a forth number that was picked up on the first ring. "Bring a car around immediately. Three passengers for the airstrip." She hung up. The fifth call was to her office.

"Her office phone rang once and it was picked up. "Hi boss."

"Hi. Anyone of importance knocking down the door?"

"Neither the Director nor the President. There are several dozen calls, but you know that anyway."

"I've been monitoring them. Nothing that cannot wait. There is a matter of some urgency. I need you to check the website of the Italian Embassy in New York and get the latest posting of their employees and titles. I'm especially interested in a Bettina Falaguerra and her position. Then call State and get whatever they have since it has oversight of foreign embassies. Ellen, I need this fast. Whatever you get, I want you to email it to me and copy it to the computer on the Gulfstream."

"We can do this officially with state or we can have Julian worm his way into their data base."

"Let's start officially but if you sense that they are withholding data, release Julian. I should be back in Washington later today. Oh, one other thing, Ellen. I want you to wire fifteen thousand dollars to Umberto's Swiss account before you leave work today. Chao." With that Elizabeth hung up.

By the time Vinnie and Gretchen arrived at the mansion, the car was at the front door. Elizabeth motioned them to step into the car. She began to brief them on the call from Rome and finished while the car was parked next to the plane. "By the time the Gulfstream is off the ground, you will have photographs of Bettina Falaguerra on the computer. There is a printer onboard so you will have photos to use as identification at JFK. I will have two agents meet you at the Alitalia check-in desk to help in the surveillance. Vinnie, assuming that you decide to join us, I took the liberty of having credentials prepared for you. You'll need them at JFK. A flight plan is being filed as we speak and you will be cleared to land at the secure area for government aircraft. A car will be there to take you to the Alitalia terminal. If it is of any help, my Rome associate emphasized that our person of interest is stunning, a number ten on the beauty scale. You should have no problem locating her. Once you have her settled at an address, call me immediately. Depending upon what you find, we'll decide on the next step. Vinnie, this is a case where you may be using your fluency in Italian. Other than what I have told you, we know little about this Italian national although the chances are good that she is associated with the Italian Embassy in New York. We will know that soon enough. My office is running down whatever the embassy or the state department has on her. Check the on- board computer for that information during the flight. I want to emphasize that you both need to stay close to her until we learn more."

"What about our afternoon strategy session here?"

"I'll arrange for the five of us to meet again once you have completed this assignment. At the moment, Bettina Falaguerra takes priority. You may be in the city for a few days. Buy whatever you need when you get settled. Gretchen knows the hotel we use. Now, time for you to go."

They boarded the plane, the stairs were retracted, the door secured and within seconds the plane began to roll on to the runway. It was with an element of envy that Elizabeth watched as the Gulfstream, under full power, roared down the runway, sharply lifted its nose, retracted its wheels and shot upwards into the heavens. She looked into the sky until the plane was no longer visible and then stepped back into the car with a heavy heart. How she wished she was Gretchen this day and this night.

CHAPTER 47

DISSENTION

Following prayers in the foyer of the house where the host, Abua Karsam, had placed prayer rugs, the men returned to the meeting room. Yousuf was there to greet them. Once inside, he closed the heavy doors behind them. The recess had served to calm nerves but did little to deter the others from confronting Khalid's suicide bombing strategy. In retrospect, they now wished they had encouraged him to pursue Max Rietsema. It would have temporarily deflected his interest in suicide bombers.

Once settled, Khalid began. "If we are to bring the country to its knees there is a need for both a short term and long range strategy. In the short term, our efforts must be continuous, widespread, easily carried out and not require a high level of technological skill. The goal is to put fear into every home and business in American. The long term goal will take a major effort by us and our supporters to recruit candidates for suicide bombings. I am aware that there are millions of Muslims who are afraid to participate in the destruction of America for fear of being unsuccessful, apprehended by the authorities and convicted and sentenced to Guantanamo. Nevertheless, they still hate America. As we succeed with our first bombings, other loyal Muslims will thank Allah that they can be part of the destruction of America. Small successes will lead to great achievements.

"Again," asked Abdul Jazier, "how will you recruit the bombers? This is America and the vast majority of the Muslim population is educated and not easily willing to give up the luxuries that success has afforded them. They have built a future for their children. Many of the faithful are second and third generation and have established roots in the country. These are not ignorant peasants who can be persuaded that life after death is better than life on earth. The promise of virgins in the afterlife is viewed as a myth by most Muslims. Your ideas threaten the strategic, long range goal of out-breeding the Caucasian population and eventually becoming the majority at which time we will control local and state governments and eventually the United States Congress. It will take time but, as you are well aware, we are on our way of accomplishing that goal in Europe. The United States Department of Justice cannot outlaw the loyalty of the faithful to the writings of Mohammed. Given the country's porous borders and the inability of naval forces to prevent the illegal entry of Muslims by ships along the east, west and gulf coasts, the government is complicit in helping us to accelerate the increase in the Muslim population. Khalid, why in the name of Allah would you compromise a well thought out, long range strategy for a plan that is doomed from the start? We must be patient."

"You say be patient! Patience is the chain that binds us to inaction. Patience discourages us from moving forward to achieve our goals. It is the tool of the weak whose lack of courage insults our Holy One. You asked that I be patient in killing Rietsema and I agreed, but I will not be patient in our quest to destroy America. While we do nothing, millions of our faithful live under the rule of oppressive governments that are supported by the United States. For more than fifty years our people have lived under martial law enforced by the ruling class. The Jews continue to strangle Gaza and the West Bank with weapons provided by the Unites States. How much longer must the Palestinians wait to be free? "

Ghani Mohammed asked, "Who, besides you, Khalid, developed this plan?"

"No others. Why do you ask?"

"Is the wise course not the one that asks others for their thoughts?"

With a flash of anger Khalid asked, "And what thoughts do you think we will get from those who cower before the powerful? What will you tell me except to be patient? I'll tell you what I will get from involving others. Nothing! The weak remain weak because they live among the weak. Once we bring them hope by crippling this country, they will become strong. It is for us, those of us in this room, to give the weak hope. I shall do this one way or the other."

There was an unsettling silence as those around the table desperately sought a way to deflect Khalid's anger and his unwillingness to reconsider the dangerous path he was about to embark on. His last comment was a threat to the group, either they worked with him on his quest or he would take matters into his own hands.

The color had drained from his face as he slumped into his chair from emotional exhaustion. He had not expected the resistance that was forming among the others. They were all carefully recruited by Bin

Laden from among the most anti-American terrorists in Yemen. He wondered what had happened to their resolve. If anything, he was prepared at the outset of the meeting to temper what he thought would be revolutionary ideas coming forth from them! He believed that they were here to carry out the wishes of Bin Laden. But it was clear that his death at the hands of the CIA and Navy Seals Six had weakened, if not destroyed, their resolve. They were resisting the use of violence. The idea was forming in his mind that these were dangerous men who could not be trusted to support al-Qaeda.

It was still early in a day that he initially believed would extend into the late afternoon and result in a single voice. He now knew that that was not about to happen and he had to demonstrate a faked position of compromise to gain time to redesign his strategy, but not his goal. They must not gain the upper hand. The others were also looking for a way to defer any decisions. The uncomfortable silence continued. Finally, Khalid regained his composure, forced a smile on his face, sat erect in his chair and was about to speak when Ibraham came to his aide. He looked at Khalid who gave him a nod of approval so slight that it was not noticed by the others.

"Khalid, you have set forth an unexpected challenge. You believe the long range strategy of suicide bombings is the correct way to proceed. Others, taken by surprise by the strategy of massive and widespread suicide bombings, need time to reflect." Bowing to Khalids's sense of pride without admitting that the morning had not gone as planned for his boss, Ibraham then looked at Khalid and asked, "Would you not consider it wise to provide a day or two to think deeply about your proposal and to pray to Allah for guidance?"

Looking at the others after a moment of reflection, Khalid responded, "I believe that Ibraham has suggested the correct path for us to follow. Let us return tomorrow at one p.m. If you wish to confer with me prior to that time, please use my secure cell phone number that has been provided. Reflect deeply on what must be done and seek the guidance of Mohammed." Then, standing, he looked at each and in a somber tone, "May Allah keep you safe."

Almost in unison and one voice, "May Allah keep us safe."

Ibraham stood and strode to the door and opened it. Yousuf, who had been sitting on the other side, was immediately on alert. Khalid remained seated while the others left the room. Abua Karsam, with Yousuf standing next to him, wished each man well as he left. Ibraham was last and waiting for Khalid. Karsam needed to talk to Ibraham privately. He asked Yousuf to see if Khalid wanted anything. When Yousuf left for the meeting room, Karsam handed Ibraham a piece of paper with a cell phone number. "We must talk soon." Ibraham nodded and placed the paper in his pocket.

CHAPTER 48

Ms. WOOD

Agent McDonald arrived at the university around one p.m. He had no trouble locating the administrative offices. They were located in a three story brick building with white colonnades in the front and several broad stone steps leading to the entrance. He parked the car and entered the building. It was one of the oldest on campus and had a well worn, appealing look and smell about it. Inside, the paneling was dark mahogany with white trim. The floors were grey Maine granite with black grouting. He stood in the main entry way and looked for the appropriate office. There were seven doors off the entry way and each had a wood lower half in the same mahogany color, and the top halves were frosted glass not seen in many buildings today. He couldn't help but wonder how many thousands of students entered this building over the many decades it has been here, some being encouraged to enter the University of Maine and others encouraged to leave.

He found the door he was looking for. Stenciled in black on the frosted glass were the words, "University Personnel Office." Entering the office he was greeted by a receptionist who looked like someone's kid sister and just as cute. He concluded that she was a part timer working her way through school. From what he could see, she had on a tight t-shirt that displayed her ample breasts, blue eyes, short cropped blond hair, delicately applied make-up and a smile that warmed one's heart. What he couldn't see was an all too short skirt, a neat figure and sandals.

She looked up, "May I help you."

"I would like to see the person in charge of the personnel office."

"May I have your name please?"

"Stuart McDonald."

"May I tell Ms. Woods the nature of your business?"

At least the young woman was well trained by Ms. Woods. "If you please, I will explain that to her directly. But, thanks for asking."

"One moment please while I see if Ms. Wood is available."

As she walked from her desk, she did, indeed, have a short skirt and a "knock them dead" body.

She returned shortly. "Ms. Wood will be tied up for the rest of the afternoon and suggests that you make an appointment."

He gave her one of his best smiles, stood tall over her desk and, while holding open his FBI credentials wallet for her to see said, "Please convey to Ms. Wood that I need to see her, now."

A little pale from having met her first FBI Agent, and a damn good looking one at that, she hustled back to Ms. Wood's office. Within a minute of two, Ms. Wood appeared. She was in her early fifties, looked like a 60's person who never left the campus. He thought the FBI probably has her record in an archive from when she was part of some violent college protest.

She approached him in a slightly hostile manner. "What is this about?"

In his business-like manner and employing his well trained, 'how to deal with hostility" voice, he quietly said, "Ms. Wood, we need the privacy of your office. This is official business of the United States government. We can conduct it here or in our office in Bangor. Your choice." A clear threat pleasantly delivered and she understood it. She had been there before.

"Please come to my office."

Once settled in her office, he took the lead. "The FBI is involved in an investigation regarding the homicide of a man whose body was found on Mt. Katahdin a few days ago. Possibly you may have seen the press release we issued. We are interested in speaking with anyone who may have been in Baxter State Park at the time. Information was provided us which indicates that one or two persons from this university were climbing in the park on the day in question. The information consists of their first names, Glenn and Betsy. Our source suggests that they appeared too old to be students, are experienced climbers and they drive a Subaru wagon that has a UMaine sticker. We need your help in locating them."

"Are they suspects?"

"They are not. They are of interest to us in that they may have witnessed something that, together with other information we have gathered, will help solve this homicide."

She looked at him for a moment, her thoughts wandered and soft tears appeared behind her tinted glasses. "You have to excuse me but my eyes have been giving me trouble lately. Time for new glasses." She removed them and dabbed at her eyes with a tissue. In that split moment of reflection Stuart McDonald so reminded her of her first and only love at the age of twenty two that all of her hostility towards the FBI simply dissipated as she looked at him. Many years ago, as a campus anarchist, men like McDonald were her enemies. If only she had said yes to the proposal of marriage instead of choosing the life of a protester and anarchist. Flag burning, occupying campus administrative offices, sex with just about anyone and doing drugs all seemed so wonderful at the time. It was a high that she thought never would end. But it did and when it was over, she had nothing to show for the wasted years. It ended as a bitter experience. She lost Andy and his love, is now an old maid imprisoned in a mind numbing job far beneath her intellect, in a tired old building in the wilds of Maine, far away from Radcliff and the intellectual community she found so nourishing. She whispered silently to herself, "Don't let your woman say no to you Agent McDonald."

She composed herself, "You need go no further. I know the couple. They are Glenn and Betsy Wilcox, both scientists here at the university. He is a physicist and she is a biologist. They are experienced climbers and they drive an old Subaru."

"How is it that you could identify them so quickly?"

"Everyone on campus knows the Wilcox. Fabulous people, volunteer for everything, self assured, great teachers, loved by students, a bit independent but always there when you need them. Let me check their schedules."

She turned to her computer and punched in a few keys. "As it happens, they are both off today. Let me give you their home phone and address. If they know anything, I assure you they will be most cooperative."

She wrote down the information and handed it to Agent McDonald, touching his hand as she did so. He placed the note in his breast pocket and stood.

"Agent McDonald, as they say, I hope you find your man, or woman."

"We usually do Ms. Wood. Sometimes it takes longer than we like but we never close a file. No matter how old."

She thought about his last comment and knew that somewhere in the bowels of a building in Washington there is a file on Amanda Wood. "This is a little late, but thanks for caring enough about our country to do the work you do. The students on this campus, actually most campuses, have no appreciation for the work of our intelligence agencies. I know I did not when I was their age. I was among the many on campus who despised the FBI and the CIA. Thankfully, some of us grew wiser as we grew older. "

"Change is never too late. Thank you, Ms. Wood, for your help and the kind words. Now, I must be going."

As he walked toward the door, she called to him. "Agent McDonald."

He turned but before he could say anything, she did. "Thank you." And once again, tears surfaced ever so slightly behind her tinted steel rimmed glasses as she turned back to her office.

For a reason he could not determine, he felt a sense of sorrow for Ms. Wood. He was confused as to the message she was giving him. He thought that perhaps he had some unfinished business with her.

Using the directions given to him by Ms. Wood, he easily found the Wilcox house. He rang the door bell and was greeted with the happy and pleasant face of Betsy Wilcox. Without any sense of alarm in being faced with a total stranger, she said "Hi, what can I do for you? If its Glenn you want, he is out back."

Holding up his credentials, he introduced himself. "Hello Mrs. Wilcox. I am Agent Stuart McDonald of the Bangor office of the Federal Bureau of Investigation. I need a moment of your time. May I come in?"

With a smile on her face, "You really mean the original FBI? The guys from Washington? Should I call my lawyer?"

Confronted with what only could be describes as a fun loving woman, he laughed aloud and said, "Actually, I am from Bangor and we are on the same side Mrs. Wilcox. It's your help I need, not your lawyer."

"Please come in. I will call Glenn." She then proceeded to the back door and called Glenn. "Honey, the FBI is here and they will haul my you know what to Guantanamo if you don't get your butt in here, pronto!" McDonald could only smile.

In no particular hurry, Glenn entered through the back door and asked, "Just what is it that you want. Every minute I spend in here those nasty weeds continue to invade my tomato plants."

"Be serious, Glenn. We have company. Agent Stuart McDonald of the FBI is here and wants to interrogate us."

"Betsy, the politically correct terminology is interview, not interrogate. They do the latter at Guantanamo, not in the home of the Wilcox family where patriotism is the order of the day. Now, where is J. Edgar Hoover?'

She tugged at his sweater and pulled him into the living room where he was greeted by McDonald. "Hi, I'm Glenn and I swear on my family bible that I am not a member of the Brink's hold-up gang of 1982. Betsy, please tell the man I was in Europe at the time."

McDonald wondered what he had gotten himself in for. "Actually, Mr. Wilcox, it is Betsy that the bureau is interested in for that historic heist, but the statue of limitations has kicked in. She is free to try another robbery!"

After they had a good laugh and settled down, McDonald explained why he was there and asked them to share what they had seen or heard at the scene.

"He was an excellent climber, strong and fast. In fact, he told us that he had climbed extensively in Europe. Betsy and I have seen many competent climbers in Maine, but this guy was really good. We pride ourselves on our stamina but we were no match for him. He was pleasant but was all business. Great equipment and the perfect clothing. As I said, he knew what he was doing. As for the other two guys, they were out of their element. They were thugs by any standard and not the type of men you would want to cross."

"Glenn is correct in that the two men were there for reasons other than climbing. Forgive the hyperbole, but they are what are depicted in the movies and fiction as assassins. I know that may sound outrageous but it is accurate. I can't imagine why anyone would want to injure two scientists who are working on routine matters. The same goes for the family of four on vacation."

"What did you see when you returned to the parking lot?"

"It was getting dark. We were the first down followed shortly thereafter by the family. I said first down but that was after the lone climber. The six of us talked about the fact that the lone climber was nowhere to be seen. His car was gone. The car belonging to the two guys was still in the lot but they were nowhere to be seen. Betsy and I talked about the climb and agreed that the two men never went above the tree line. We saw the lone climber ahead of us on the ascent and talked briefly with him on the way down. But, we never saw the two men."

"Did you hear any gun shots at any time?"

"I didn't. How about you Betsy?"

"Nothing."

"Did you notice anything suspicious about the car the two men were driving either before you climbed or after?"

Betsy, "I didn't."

"Nor I."

"Knowing what I have shared with you and based on your own observations and instincts, what do you think the two men were doing at the mountain?"

"Considering that the men could have been robbers, terrorists, killers, molesters, slave marketers and God knows whatever else, there apparently was no one or anything in Baxter State Park to interest them. That is, other than the lone climber. If they wanted to rob someone, business would be much better in Bangor. I don't think Glenn and I would bring much on the slave trade market and who in heavens would want to kill any of us? Besides, if they had wanted to rob us, kill us, or abduct us why didn't they do so? They certainly had ample opportunity. Glenn and I talked about all of this on the ride home. The only option left had something to do with the climber."

"What do you think that was?

Glenn added his comments. "To begin with, you need to have met the climber to appreciate what

I am about to say. He could be a poster boy for the Sierra Club. Tall, good looking, great physique, strong climber and, from the brief conversation we had with him, well educated. On one hand a guy you would gladly spend happy hour with and enjoy his meeting your friends. But on the other hand, and this is only a gut feeling, a man you would not want to mess with. He had a worldly bearing. Something deep about his personality. Had the stature of someone who had seen a lot of life including the dark side. Don't misunderstand this, Agent McDonald, but you have some of the same traits."

McDonald, a skilled interviewer, remained quiet waiting for either of them to continue. He was particularly interested in Glenn's comparing the climber to himself, McDonald. It had the same undertone as the comment made by Stan Robertson when the latter said that the climber may have learned English when training to be a spy. He asked the two of them, "At any time when you were with the family, did anyone mention that the climber could have been in law enforcement?" He carefully avoided mentioning spy or intelligence services believing that the law enforcement angle would bring out more information if there was any to get.

"It never came up in the discussion. We were more interested in the fact that the two guys were still in the woods since their car was still there. I'm sorry now that we did not take a look at the car. It may have held some answers. But, I knew Glenn would be upset if I nosed around."

"Before I forget, I want to mention that it was Ms. Wood at the administrative offices who identified you immediately from your first names and the fact that you are expert climbers and drove a Subaru. We spoke in private so no one else in the office is aware of why I was there. You may want to thank her for helping me find you. The information you have provided will be useful in working this case. I believe she was initially upset with my being on campus but she ended up being quite pleasant. Thanks for your help. Now I must get moving." He stood and started for the door.

"Agent McDonald, for what it is worth, the teenager may have gotten it correct when she said that the climber was like Matt Damon and that the two men were no challenge for him."

"Thank you Betsy. I will keep that in mind. Now, I have one more thing to ask of you. I'm certain you know, from TV or media, that law enforcement agencies attempt to develop a picture of a person by creating a composite based on descriptions given by witnesses. Until recently, we'd ask you to come to our offices and work with a technician. Times have changed and we can work with you through a computer and a phone. If you are both available tomorrow between nine and eleven, I want you to go to the web site noted on this card and then dial the phone number listed on the card. A technician will pick up and, together, you and he will work on a composite on the computer. I'll also ask the family to do the same. Once we have a composite, we will run it through a facial recognition program and hope for a match."

"That works for both of us in the morning. In the afternoon, Betsy has a class. We will connect with the technician in the morning."

"Great, I will alert the technician."

"Please let him know we are excited at the prospect of identifying the climber."

"Him is a her."

Betsy spoke up. "There is one other thing we forgot to mention. While we were still above the tree line, we both heard a car horn blowing. It lasted for a couple of minutes and then stopped. Sounded like it came from the parking lot but we have no way of really knowing that. I suppose it could have been the car the two men were driving since they were the only ones we could not see. But, that is only a guess. And why would they blow the horn in the woods of Maine?"

Agent McDonald made a note of it and then they walked him to the door and he left.

"What do you think Glenn?"

"It's hard to believe that Amanda Wood would not to be nice to someone as pleasant as Agent McDonald."

"She may have a reason not to like the FBI. We know little about her."

"Maybe we should ask her."

"We will do no such thing."

When McDonald got into his car he used the cell phone to call the Robertson's at the hotel and made arrangements to meet them that same evening. He arrived around seven and they were sitting comfortably in what is referred to in Maine as a parlor. They were anxious to meet him and he immediately took a liking to them.

"Thank you Mr. and Mrs. Robertson, Alex and Ben for meeting with me. I feel as though I know you after having talked with chief McCorey. What I would like to do is go over the same ground as he did. Often, in reviewing earlier statements, additional bits of information emerge. The smallest detail often points us in a new direction. So let me begin by asking to you share a narrative about the climber and the two men."

For the next hour and a half, all four members of the family basically repeated what they had shared with Chief McCorey. Agent McDonald did not learn anything new other than the fact that Ben thought that the car belonging to the two men looked different but he could not tell why. When pressed on the matter he said that when they left the parking lot, the car was angled so that the driver's side was hidden but you could see the trunk and the passenger side. When asked if that was different than when he had first seen it in the morning, he said no.

"Ben, this is important. Please think carefully about what you saw. What was different?"

He was silent for a moment and said, "There was something shiny on the passenger side. When we passed the car on the way out of the park, I only had a quick glance of the passenger side and I remember thinking that there was something reflecting on the ground. I didn't mention it to the family since it didn't seem important."

"Ben, let me ask you, what do you think you saw?"

"Being a parking lot, it could have been a can or a broken bottle. More likely a broken bottle. Careless climbers often leave that stuff around."

Agent McDonald could see why Chief McCorey was so impressed with the family. "Did any of you hear a car horn blowing while you were on the mountain?"

Stan spoke. "We all heard a car horn blowing. It lasted quite a long time before it stopped. It could have come from the parking lot or the access road. We didn't think much about it."

McDonald took note and then explained the new method the FBI used in creating a composite and that the husband and wife team would also be working with the technician. They were excited to be part of the continuing investigation.

"Thank you all for your help. Now, I have to be on my way."

When he left, Lee spoke up. "Did anyone else get the impression that Agent McDonald and the climber had many of the same characteristics? Like maybe they went to the same school?"

"He is another Matt Damon."

"Alex, there you go again. What is your fixation with the Bourne hero?" It was Ben.

"It is not a fixation, Ben. It's like mom just said, there is something similar about both guys. Didn't you get the feeling that they are smart and tough?"

Stan joined in. "Alex and Ben, I am really proud of the way you handled yourselves with the Chief and with Agent McDonald. You gave accurate descriptions of all three men and offered a couple of ideas to be pursued. I think all of us were helpful and objective except your mother who couldn't take her eyes off of the climber. Her testimony will have to be carefully vetted."

Lee jabbed him in the ribs and laughed along with Alex and Ben.

"Stan, for making fun of me in front of the children, you can take us out for ice cream!"

CHAPTER 49

LAB RESULTS

After seeing Vinnie and Gretchen off, Elizabeth returned to the house. On the way, she received a cell call. "You have something?" She listened and told the caller that she would return the call in a few minutes and to stand by. She then called Darlene's cell phone. When she answered, "Darlene, I need to see you and Max as soon as you can get to the house."

"We'll be there in five."

Once they arrived, Elizabeth explained that Vinnie and Gretchen had left for New York and explained why.

Max responded, "I thought that Darlene and I were to pursue the leak. Since there is the possibility that the Italian national may be involved, why are Vinnie and Gretchen doing what we should be doing?"

"Max, it was logical to send them because Vinnie is fluent in Italian and is Italian. It may be that the only way we will find what we need is for him to ingratiate himself with Bettina Falaguerra in her native language. Do you have a problem with that?"

Max looked dismayed at the turn of event but decided to avoid a confrontation with Elizabeth. "I think it makes good sense."

"Good. Now let's address the bigger issue. Who hired the Serbs and why? That job, Max, is for you and Darlene. We have a lot to do so let's not get territorial. I am about to return a call to the Director of the private lab who called a few minutes ago. I deferred the call until you were here. It will be on speaker phone so both of you can hear what I will hear for the first time. Vinnie and Gretchen are also plugged in via satellite."

She dialed the number of the lab. The phone was picked up on the second ring and she activated the speaker phone. "This is what we have for you, Elizabeth."

"First the body. Whoever took this guy down was a decent marksman. The shot to the shoulder disabled the dead man's shooting arm. Then he took five bullets to the chest. All six rounds were 45 caliber. The car is a black Ford Taurus, late model. It was clean except for glass crystals from the broken window on the passenger side. The key was for the car and it did not have a chip in it. The papers were for a rental from Logan. It had the name of the person who rented it but it was bogus. That is a dead end. There were two used coffee cups. We ran them for prints and found nothing.

"Anything else?"

"I saved the best to last. The rental papers had the starting mileage. We compared that with the mileage when we received the car from you. The reading was approximately one hundred ten miles greater than the distance from Boston to Baxter State Park in Maine. If you think of Bangor as being a straight line along the shore from Boston on Interstate 95, then this car was driven to the west before heading north. Which leads me to the gun. We know that it is virtually impossible to get a gun on board any overseas flight into the United States. Yet the dead guy had a gun, but not just any gun. This is a Yargin PYa .380 Russian semi-automatic pistol. Not many of them around."

"Where are you taking this?"

"I'll make a suggestion and you can run with it or ignore it. The only Russian community of any size with more hit men than the mafia is located in Brooklyn. If you run a line from Boston to Brooklyn and then north to the mountain, it fits within 10-15 miles of the recorded mileage. As I said, only an idea."

"And, a good one at that. Clean up what you have. Total disposal is required. I'll email authorization. If you turn up anything else, let me know." With that, Elizabeth hung up.

She kept the line open with Vinnie and Gretchen and Max and Darlene were still on speaker phone. "You heard the man. A possible Russian connection. Vinnie, any experience with the Yargin in the Middle East?"

"It was in widespread use in Afghanistan. The Russians had a great market with the Taliban. It's a military issue and was used by the Russian forces when they took on the fight in Chechnya. It wouldn't be my choice but it is a sturdy weapon and does the job at close quarters. The military liked it because it held a seventeen round clip. It works well in extreme weather conditions."

"The challenge is how we track the source of the weapon. It is just another one of millions in circulation." It was Elizabeth.

Vinnie chimed in, "There is one possible way. Max, if I recall your comments last night you said the weapon you retrieved had a silencer. The lab did not mention it. I assume it was an oversight. Anyway, Vladmir Yargin did not design the weapon to take a silencer. That being the case, the barrel of the gun the assassin used had to have been re-machined by an expert and the firing mechanism altered. If, as the lab suggested, the assassins made a detour, it stands that the detour was to someone or someplace where expert machinists and gunsmiths are available. Something doesn't fit. Why go through all the bother to refit a Yargin with a silencer when they could have picked up any number of weapons on the street. Unless, of course, someone wanted us to track the weapon back to its source if the mission went wrong."

"I need to think on this. Everyone get back on schedule. We'll talk soon." She cut off communications to the Gulfstream. Something more was on her mind.

To Max and Darlene who were still with her, "Let's look at what we have." She turned to Max. "The Italians have an arrest warrant out on you, an unknown person provides you with a heads up to get out of the country, two Serbs attempt to murder you, the gun they possess is Russian made and re-tooled to take a silencer that can only be accomplished by an expert gunsmith and the mileage on their car does not coincide with a straight line from Boston to Maine. Khalid, a Yemen, wants you dead and Carlton Richardson takes a day off from screwing his mistress to meet with a person associated with the Italian embassy. You kill the two Serbs, leaving one on the mountain and by now the FBI is all over Baxter State Park. All this is in addition to the small matter of Khalid and his buddies plotting to create something worse than 9/11." She hesitated and neither Max nor Darlene spoke.

She continued, "Max, what are you not telling me?"

"What is that supposed to mean? You know as much as I do and I don't like the implication that I am withholding information."

"Max, listen up. When dealing with agency business you know we cut through the peripheral bullshit to get to the core. We do that so as to not be distracted. The bullshit in this case is you're asking me to believe that Khalid sent two Serbs to assassinate you. The distraction is that we are being diverted from what is essential. Everything you know about Khalid indicates that he would never contract with anyone to kill you, especially two Serbian thugs. He wants nothing better than to split your throat and watch you die. And, that is the optimistic edition of his kill."

Darlene asked, "Elizabeth, maybe I should leave you two alone. This is above my pay grade."

"Stay. If you are teaming with Max you need to know everything. So, Max, why are the Russians out to kill you?"

"I have no idea what you are talking about. The fact the Serbs had a Yargin pistol doesn't mean the Russians were involved. Elizabeth, after I was extracted from Italy, you put me on ice in Maine where I maintained a low profile. The climb was a last minute decision. Even I did not know I was going to climb the next day. The safe house in Waterville was just that, a safe house, nothing suspicious about it or the neighborhood. Who these thugs were and how they found me is a mystery. The fact remains that Khalid is the only person who wants me dead and would not hesitate to use assassins if that got results."

"Max, other than the pilot who has been debriefed, no one knew you were in Maine from my end. The flight out of Europe was secure and the route was scrambled on radar for the entire trip. I personally saw to that. You were the only one who could have revealed where you were when you arrived in Maine. Who did you call?"

"Elizabeth, what the fuck is this all about? Are you accusing me of revealing my own location so the Serbs could find me? That is crazy."

"What I am saying is that you made a call on your cell phone to a third party that was intercepted by Russian intelligence and they contracted with the two Serbs to kill you."

"Why in hell would the Russians want to kill me?"

"That, Max, is the question to which only you have the answer. Please hand over your cell phone."

"What?"

"I'll only ask once more. Give me your cell phone."

"No way, Elizabeth."

"I'm sorry it has come to this, Max, but the security of the United States is at stake." With that she touched a button on her cell phone and two of the security agents entered the room. "Max, I'm sorry but you are restricted to your cottage until further notice. Please give me your cell phone or it will be taken by force."

Darlene was struck dumb. Max Rietsema under house detention? She looked at Elizabeth and saw the sorrow in her eyes as she extended her hand for the phone. Max, looking devastated by the turn of events, removed the phone from his pocket and handed it to Elizabeth.

"You have made a terrible mistake. It is not what it looks like."

"I hope I am wrong. But in the absence of your telling me the truth, I have no other choice." With those final words, she instructed the agents to secure Max in his cottage and to cut all communications in and out of it until further notice.

When they left, Darlene asked, "Elizabeth, are you absolutely certain that Max is withholding information? My god, he is one of the good guys."

The emotional scene with Max drained Elizabeth of her energy and she sat to collect herself. "In our business, nothing is certain. There are some data that suggest Max was not totally forthcoming."

"For instance?"

"For starters, the mountain itself. Max, by his own admission, had climbed it either two or three times while he was in Maine. Compared to his European and Himalayan experiences, this was no challenge for him. It was literally a day hike. He had little reason to climb it that particular day except to draw the Serbs to a remote location to kill them. Second, I personally debriefed the pilot who flew Max to Maine. He also volunteered for a poly and passed with flying colors. There is no way he revealed Max's destination. The flight plan I filed was convoluted enough to avoid tracking by any agency, domestic or foreign. The same secure measures were used for the car we provided in Maine. The safe house was clean before he used it but only partially clean when my crew swept it after Max left. There was some evidence that Max attempted some cleaning himself which I find curious. Did he entertain someone there or have a visitor? We do not know that yet."

"Elizabeth, while there is a lot of data, none points directly to Max as being the source of the leak dealing with his location in Maine. And if he was the leak, why? "

"Darlene, while Max is a charming and sophisticated guy, he is also one tough son of a bitch. I know since I was his handler for several years. Both of us also know that because we slept with him. Two assassins would be no match for him if he had prior knowledge of them being on the hunt for him, especially if he laid the groundwork beforehand."

"Are you suggesting that he set up the assassination attempt?"

"There are pieces of the puzzle that I do not have. But, what I do have is a suspicion that Max wanted these two Serbs to attempt to kill him in a remote setting thinking that their murders would not be detected for some time, at least not until after I would have called him back to Washington for a new assignment or posting. The trouble, Darlene, is that all of us have been in Washington so long that we have lost tract of the fact that there are talented law enforcement officers outside the beltway." Just then her cell phone rang. She knew the number well. "Go ahead Ellen." She listened for a three or four minutes then, "I want you to place the Falcon on immediate standby. Within the hour a courier will bring you a set of credentials from the Washington Herald. Deliver them to the pilot and get her on the way here." She hung up with Ellen and then looked at the press release on her phone.

She was ashen. Then, speaking to Darlene, "The Bangor newspaper had an announcement in it yesterday informing the public that a body had been found on Katahdin. The article went on to note that the authorities were looking for anyone who may have been in Baxter State Park the day in question. Let me upload the article into the computer so you can read the full text with me." They read the entire text and both knew there was trouble ahead.

"As I was saying, outside the beltway there are some real cops on the ground. These men and women, especially those in rural areas, are not only good cops but they are usually great with guns and outstanding as trackers. Reading between the lines, the body is that of the other Serb and that means in addition to the local police, the state police and FBI are on the scene."

"How can they trace the body back to Max? He said he left no evidence."

"It is reverse engineering. The Serb Max shot in the parking lot will have left blood. The window he broke in the car will have left some glass crystals on the ground. Using those crystals, the FBI lab will quickly identify the model of the car and begin an investigation as to why the car is missing. The announcement is bound to get the attention of others who were in the park. Then once the interviews begin, the FBI will begin to piece it all together. An important part of the FBI routine is the ability to develop a composite picture of a suspect. The bureau has outstanding technicians. They will produce a composite of Max from the descriptions given by the other climbers. Remember, he stopped to talk to all of them. Once the composite hits the media, anyone in Waterville who believes they saw him there will contact the FBI. They will refine the composite and put out a 'person of interest' bulletin. It is only a matter of time before they have Max in their sights."

"Why the Falcon?"

"I need you in Maine as soon as possible to learn where the investigation is going. I will call Milt Houston at the Washington Herald now and arrange for you to be placed on his payroll immediately as a correspondent. Credentials will be created by him and a courier will pick them up and deliver them to Ellen who will get them to the pilot of the Falcon. When you board the plane here in two hours the pilot will have the credentials for you. As such you will have legitimate access to the crime scene and those involved. Darlene, do not underestimate the local law enforcement officers. They could teach us a thing or two about investigations. You have a couple of hours to frame a cover for yourself. As per the manual, keep it close to the truth. Ellen will arrange for a rental car to be waiting for you in Bangor. Call Ellen once you are underway. She will have booked a room for tonight in Bangor. After that, go where the evidence leads you."

"What about Max?"

"He is my problem. Right now, you should get back to the cottage and pack. Security will come for you once the Falcon is cleared for landing. I hate to have daylight activity at the airstrip, but this is an emergency. We'll talk once you are in the air."

CHAPTER 50

A TERRORIST'S THREAT

It was close to one o'clock when Khalid and Ibraham arrived at Abua Karsam's house. Suleiman Amir, Abdul jazzier, Aba Najdi, Ghani Mohammed, and Hafs Karzai were seated at the table as Khalid strode into the room, clearly the person in charge. It was the last thing he should have done given the contentious ending to the meeting the day before. The other six had enough of his posturing. They were in no mood to listen to his delusional ranting but knew that their time would come. Ibraham, sensitive to the mood of the others, stayed a stride behind his friend and quietly took his place at the opposite end of the table. He feared, and rightly so, that the day would have a cataclysmic ending. Khalid was his boyhood and lifetime friend, but Ibraham could see that his passion for suicide bombings was so strong that he would not yield to the concerns of the others.

Abua Karsam was the most reasoned and westernized of the other six. He was born in Yemen and was a true believer in the ultimate Muslim dominance of the planet and a major player in the attack on the USS Cole. He rejoiced in the damage and death it inflicted on the American crew. Like Ibraham, he was educated abroad, mostly in France. He understood western culture and viewed it to be corrupt. Like the others in the room, he also believed that the word of God was literally given to Mohammed through Gabriel. What set him aside from Khalid was his understanding of the American culture and how the population would react to suicide bombings. He agreed with Khalid that 9/11 was a mistake for the reasons he articulated to the group the day before and which ultimately led to the killing of Osama Bin Laden. Since 9/11, his followers had not had a successful major event in the United States as a result of the vigilance of the American public and its intelligence services. Khalid's complimentary comments about the CIA were accurate from the perspective of al-Qaeda.

Following yesterday's meeting, Abua Karsam had counseled with his five compatriots and all were of a mind that a national suicide bombing plot would destroy the long range goal of subduing America through an explosion in the birth rate of Muslims in America. Liberal immigration policies made it relatively easy for the best educated Muslims to become citizens of the United States and to take positions of influence in business, industry and politics. The six business men thought that Khalid was a terrorist who was still thinking like Osama Bin Laden and was out of touch with the realities of post 9/11. While he was a killer, he was not a strategist. He had the ability to rally the uneducated to his call, but lacked the vision to develop and to carry out a comprehensive plan of fear and destruction. He was willing to die, but only as a martyr. Khalid was viewed by the body of six as dangerous and a threat to the ultimate goal of Muslim world domination.

"May Allah guide us in accepting my bold plan for massive suicide bombings across the country, Khalid began. Some, perhaps all of you, not only questioned the wisdom of the plan but also doubted that we would be able to recruit those willing to give their lives in the name of Allah.

Abua Karsam spoke for the group of six. "Khalid, we have counseled and have agreed that we cannot support your plan, nor will we participate in it in any way. Not to be disrespectful, we wish to share with you the two primary reasons why, in our minds, the plan has failings. First, even if we believed in the value of the plan, there is no way you will be able to recruit sufficient bombers since we have no infrastructure in the United States. To import bombers would be impossible given the current security measures. Bombers in the Middle East are recruited from the uneducated and women and children. That will not work in the United States. Second, once your plan is activated, every Muslim in the country will be persecuted and many will be driven from the United States, thereby compromising our long range plan to subdue America through population growth."

Khalid had spent the previous evening planning how he would respond to what he knew would be the cowardly position taken by the six. Prior to their very first meeting, he believed them to be committed to bringing death and destruction to schools, theaters, malls, subways, busses, trains and literally every place where Americans congregated. After the last meeting he knew that their resolve had weakened. They had been in the Unites States too long and had become westernized. They enjoyed the benefits of wealth that stemmed from businesses that were given to them and paid for with Saudi money. They had forgotten that these particular businesses had been chosen because they employed thousands of Muslims across the nation. Did they not comprehend that those employees were part of his infrastructure? Were the six so preoccupied with their mistresses that they have lost the ability to think clearly? It was time to hit them in their soft underbelly. It was time to take command.

"Thank you Abua Karsam for reporting on the position taken by the six of you. Having listened to your collective thoughts these past few days, I anticipated your response and, therefore, am not surprised. Now, I am about to tell you how we are going to proceed. I will accept no opposition. You will have no choice in the matter. Refusal will have serious consequences, so think carefully before you make a final decision for it could be your last decision."

"I object to you making threats to us, Khalid!" It was Abdul Jazier, the CEO of the Texas based company that manufactured complex valves used in natural gas pipelines used in thirty five countries. The company business allowed Jazzier to travel to playgrounds around the world with both his wife and mistress. Strategically, it provided Khalid with thousands of Muslim employees across the nation and the ability to communicate with al-Qaeda in the thirty five countries where the company's products were used.

"I, too, find your words insulting and inappropriate. In spite of your threats, I still disagree with you and I will not be intimidated." Hafs Karzai ran a company that produced, under license, the Italian Silver Eagle X650, an advanced business jet. Like Jazier, he earned well, lived high and traveled the globe on combined business and pleasure trips. Like the others, he had the money to support a mistress. For Khalid, it also provided transportation to any country where the Silver Eagle was sold or leased. The planes could carry weapons in and out of the country without going through security checks. Their flight plans were blocked from public and government view.

Aba Najdi, quiet until now, spoke forcefully. "Khalid, it is best that you remember that we are six and you are one. For every threat you make, you could receive six in return. We are not to be bullied. Our directions come from Bin Laden's successor, not you." Najdi ran a wine and liquor import business and was in a position in import small and medium sized weapons in his containers.

There was little need for the others to speak. The group had responded forcefully and negatively to Khalid's threat. Ibraham looked bewildered and wondered where Khalid was taking this. Although Khalid's friend, he had no idea what he was up to. Of the six, Ghani Mohammed was the one person who was fearful of being assassinated. If need be, he would go along with Khalid, but not willingly. He knew that his international construction company provided Khalid with a secure means of transporting weapons and bomb making materials into the United States.

Khalid spoke. "You have had your say. Now allow me to lay down my plan and the corresponding conditions. Before I do so let me speak to the consequences of refusal. Each of you has been given a gift from Allah, by way of the Saudis. You operate six profitable businesses. Your salaries and benefits, including mistresses and prostitutes, are among the highest for companies of your size. I know that each of you have several off shore bank accounts worth millions while those that die for our cause live in poverty. You are no better than American imperialists. In addition to your travels around the globe, your families enjoy a standard of living beyond the wildest dreams of our countrymen in our native Yemen. Each of you own more than one home, some of you have several. Since coming to America shortly after 9/11 you have not been required to make a single sacrifice and our legal counsel has made certain that you are not on any watch list. You are among the most privileged in this country. Am I correct so far?"

"I take your silence to mean you agree. To continue, what has been given you can easily and quickly be taken from you. One word leaked to the CIA regarding your off shore accounts and they will be confiscated. You will join the poor in Yemen. Those who are second in command in each of your businesses are more than capable of replacing you. Surely, you knew this when you were given no choice but to accept subordinates who were named by the Saudis. They were chosen as potential replacements. They would like nothing better than to work with me and enjoy what you now possess. Your residences can easily and quickly be changed from Palm Springs, Palo Alto or wherever you live, to hovels in our native Yemen. It would take but the stroke of a pen. Overnight, you will be penniless. Do you fully comprehend what I am saying?"

Again silence, but this time it was accompanied by an atmosphere of pure fear, so intense that not one of them had the strength to speak. The threat created emotional destruction and psychological chaos. In a few words, Khalid had completely turned the tables on all of them. He had the power to destroy them and, given their prior objection to his plan, would do so without a second thought. Ibraham could only smile and admire his friend. Truly, this was the cataclysmic ending he had anticipated. But, more was coming.

Khalid continued, "I can see by your silence that we understand each other. In the event you have any idea of killing me to save your asses, be advised that Ibraham has full knowledge of our proceedings and I have put into place all of the actions required to terminate each of you and your families. While you counted your gold and enjoyed the pleasures of the flesh, Ibraham and I built a network of agents who will kill on command."

Abua Karsam spoke for his stunned colleagues. While they had not had the opportunity to confer following Khalid's ultimatum, Karsam knew what they were thinking. If they did not agree to the terms put forth, their world would cease to exist and their lives and those of their families would forever be lost. Their new lives would be ones of horror and deprivation. They had relegated to a distant memory the fact that they were sent to America ten years prior to become sleepers for al-Qaeda, ready to lay down their lives to achieve domination. For that promise of total commitment to al-Qaeda, they were given wealth, social position and a lifestyle of consumption and pleasure. Now was the moment when the bill came due. Failure to pay the price had consequences. Abdu Khalid was a killer first and a terrorist second.

Karsam spoke for all. "Khalid, I believe I speak for the others when I say we are prepared to follow you wherever you choose to go. You are correct that we have failed to remember the journey we promised to take when we were sent to the United States after 9/11. We are grateful to be reminded and appreciate the opportunity to work with you to fulfill your mission."

"I am pleased that you are willing participants to the plan. In the event you should change your mind or decide to leave the country, my operatives know where you live, where your children attend school, where your wives shop and in some instances who their lovers are. All of these precautions are, hopefully, not necessary. Yes, it is true that all your wives have lovers. This is America."

Five broken men, whittled to slave status, feared for what was to come. Khalid was correct that they owed al-Qaeda their lives if that is what it would take to create a Muslim world. As Yemeni, they were by birth committed to the destruction of western imperialism. They had been selected by Bin Laden to become sleepers in the Unites States because he determined that they could resist the pleasures of the west and remain true to the cause. They had failed the first test. To fail another meant death to them and to their families.

The sixth man was not easily cowed. While he enjoyed the pleasures of the west, he was steadfast in his commitment to the subjugation of the United States to Muslim rule and the implementation of Sharia law. He believed the way to the goal was through population growth, leading to the eventual control of the Congress. It may take fifty years or more, but it would eventually happen. His strategy was for a strategic shift in demographics, one that was hardly noticeable in an overall liberal population shift, yet overwhelming in the long run. Time was on the side of Muslims. To him and the others, Khalid was more than reckless; he was mad and he had to be dealt with and soon. The other five were too weak to fight him. There was only one person who could understand what had to be done. Abua Karsam had work to do this night. In the meantime he would listen to the ranting of a mad man.

"Now that I have your attention, let me share the basics of my strategy. It will be implemented in three waves and when completed we will have accomplished three goals. The first goal will be to spread fear across the country, demonstrating to every citizen that there is no where to hide from our attacks; the second goal is to kill as many Americans as possible; the third is to create confusion and uncertainty within the military establishment and intelligence agencies.

The first wave will consist of eighty four assassinations and bombings across the country and will conclude with the destruction of America's most important symbol of liberty and power. All actions will occur in the suburbs and rural areas surrounding seven major cities. Personnel and equipment to carry out this wave of destruction are now in place. The second wave of terror will consist of massive, widespread suicide attacks. The planning for this wave is in an advanced stage. The third wave of terror, far more complex than the first and second waves, is still in the early planning stage."

Karsam, careful to cloak his anger with Khalid, asked, "It is time you explained exactly how you will accomplish your goals."

"Together you employ, throughout your six businesses and their forty four branches, approximately forty two hundred employees. In keeping with the original business plan developed by the Saudis, a minimum of fifty percent of the employees had to be Muslim, true believing Muslims, not Americanized Muslims. I have no doubt that you have adhered to the plan.

If not, you will pay a price for your negligence. Your hand picked vendors and suppliers employ another four thousand employees, fifty percent of whom are Muslim. Therefore, you control, directly or indirectly, eighty two hundred employees throughout the United States. Four thousand one hundred are Muslims. Each is a potential bomber or true Muslim willing to assist or if need be, to die in our efforts to kill Americans."

Everyone, including Ibraham, could not believe what Khalid was suggesting. As startled as they were at what he had said, they were unprepared for the shock of what was to come. He continued, "There are more than three thousand mosques in the United States where more than four million children of Allah come to prayers. If each mosque provided only one bomber, we would have over three thousand bombers. You asked earlier how I would find bombers. Now you know. When the time comes, you will recruit them through your companies and their vendors and I will recruit them through the three thousand mosques. Together with the Imams, you and I will bring a firestorm of death and destruction to America."

There was no response for they knew the die had been cast by Khalid. He continued. "If any have doubts about the direction we are to take to destroy America, let me remind you that our brother, Aba Najdi, spoke the truth when he stated that you will follow the Imam who succeeds Osama Bin Laden. Our new leader is Ayman al-Zawahiri. Unlike Bin Laden, who had become soft, unfocused, reclusive, distant, and interested in sex and pornography, al Zawahiri brings ideological fire to our cause. He is a tactical genius who is willing to attack the United States at home. In a treatise published in 2001, he articulated for the world that the long range strategy for our movement, the jihad movement, is to inflict as many casualties as possible on the Americans and the Jews. He is also driven by personal revenge because the Americans killed his wife and two children in an airstrike in Afghanistan. The American intelligence community is trying to convince the public that al-Zawahiri lacks the personality to inspire Muslims and al-Qaeda to commit greater devastation on the Americans. All the while the CIA is on high alert to kill him because it, of all the agencies, understands that for the last five years it was he and not Bin Laden who controlled our efforts."

"Al-Zawahiri's new plans to kidnap, kill, or terrorize leading civilian, government, and military leaders on a limited, targeted basis can only help to give strength to our more widespread efforts of death and destruction. He has praise for the attack on the American embassy in Benghazi and encourages still more. You said you wanted to follow Bin Laden's successor. Now is the time to act."

Moving back and forth in his chair, Khalid chanted, "Widespread death and destruction. May Allah help us to bring it thundering down on all of America."

The five businessmen came to the same realization as Karsam: Abdu Khalid was mad. Not only had he threatened the six with death if they did not cooperate, now he was prepared to kill those Imams who resisted his demands. If what he had said earlier was true, and they had no reason to doubt him, he had al-Qaeda agents in place to carry out his assassination of them and uncooperative Imams. They all knew what had to be done.

The wild card for them was Ibraham. Was he committed to Khalid's mission or to Khalid's friendship?

Does he believe that Muslim domination of America is best achieved through population growth or by destroying its fabric through fear and death? Does he think that Khalid is adhering to the new strategy of al-Zawahiri or is Khalid massaging his own mission to make it appear to fit into al-Zawahiri's plan? What does Ibraham gain by supporting Khalid's plan and what does he have to lose by defying him? Those were the questions the answers to which were very much on Karsam's mind. The five looked to him for guidance.

Having been silent for a moment or two, Khalid brought the meeting to a close."I shall be moving to a new location tonight. You must immediately return to your homes and continue with your normal pattern of behavior. It is possible we will not meet again until victory is achieved. When the time is right for you to act, you will receive orders from me or Ibraham. No one else has any authority. Is that clear?"

As he looked around the table each of the men nodded. "We are Jihadists trusted with the work of Allah. Let us go forth as one." With that, he rose from his seat and left the room followed by Ibraham. Yousuf was waiting and escorted them to the garage. Without a word to his host, Khalid and Ibraham left the estate.

The six men were momentarily silent. Karsam spoke. "There is little to be done until I can have a conversation. When concluded, I will contact all of you. Be aware that it is possible that all of our communications may be monitored. May Allah look kindly on us."

By the time they had all left, Yousuf had returned from the garage. Karsam turned to him. "It is best if you arrange for more security for the next few days. Be alert."

CHAPTER 51

SECOND BODY

Stuart McDonald was in Bangor when he received the call from the chief forensics supervisor. "Stuart, we have something for you. The Caucasian male died from a single bullet to the head. There is an exit wound indicating a high caliber weapon. Other than that, the autopsy did not turn up anything unusual other than the fact that the stomach cavity held what appeared to be meat residue. He had eaten early on the day he was shot. Now, here's the important information for your investigation. We walked four abreast the length and width of the parking lot looking for anything remotely of interest. There was blood on the asphalt in the western third of the parking lot in the direction of the trailhead. At the opposite side of the parking lot, where cars would normally be parked, we found glass crystals and a small amount of blood. The two blood samples were the same type, but they did not match the blood type of the victim. The bottom line is there is a second body somewhere or an injured person who left or was taken from the scene."

Stuart thought about the significance of the information and asked, "What did you learn from the glass crystals?"

"Good news and bad news. The good news is that the crystals came from a Ford sedan. The bad news is that the vendor that Ford purchases its windows from used the same glass formula in all Ford sedans manufactured from 2004 through the 2011 model years. That is the best we can do. If we had either the bullet or the casing, we could identify the type of gun and caliber."

"Thanks." Stuart hung up. He knew that the chance of retrieving the bullet or casing was next to impossible. A search by agents after the discovery of the body yielded nothing. The only possibility of identifying the shooter was the composite. Having met the two families, he was optimistic that they would be accurate in their descriptions and pleased at the prospect of identifying his man. What he didn't know was that a thousand miles to the south Elizabeth English, the Deputy Director of the CIA, had a difference perspective. She was worried that the man would be identified. After moments that seemed like an eternity, she knew that like Stuart McDonald she had important calls to make.

McDonald dialed a number and on the fourth ring it was picked up by Chief McCorry. "Agent McDonald, good to hear from you."

"Hello Chief. I wanted to keep you in the loop. Our forensic team found small traces of blood, one in the middle of the parking lot and another where cars are normally parked. Both samples were identical. However, neither matched that of the victim. Bottom line is that we have a second body or victim involved. Glass crystals near the second blood sample came from a Ford but there is no way to know the year."

"It now appears that the composite is our best chance of identifying our mystery man who is involved in some way." The Chief was careful not to ask directly what the status of the composite effort was. If Agent McDonald wanted him to know, he would tell him.

"You are correct. I hope to have it in my hands within a few hours."

"Don't want to overstep my place, but what do you plan on doing with it?"

"The decision will be made by my boss but the chances are he will want my recommendation. That's usually the way it works. As for the process of distribution, I cannot help but think about the comment the teenage girl made when she said the lone climber looked and acted like the Matt Damon character. I feel a bit foolish even considering it but it makes me wonder if our guy is involved in some form of law enforcement."

"It reminds me of something Winston Churchill said or was said to have said; that important events often swing on small hinges. It might just be that the young woman was on to something. If you make your next move with the idea that our man may be in law enforcement, what does that mean for the distribution of the composite?"

"I'd recommend a distribution only within the bureau in the hope that one or more of the tens of thousands of agents and support staff will recognize him. Internal also includes all of our agents and staff working outside of the country. It will also be compared against our no fly list of all known terrorists or persons categorized as hostile to the United States. If that doesn't work, the next step is a dangerous one. It means going out to other agencies such as the NSA, CIA, Treasury and so forth. Once we do that, we run the risk of exposing what could be an ongoing project by one of them in which our man has a legitimate role."

"What about local and state agencies?"

"Other than you and Captain King of the State Police, I want to restrict its distribution until we have some internal feedback. The next step is up to my director. I'll share whatever I am able to with you and Captain King. Keep me informed from your end."

"I'll do that. Before I forget, did you find anything of interest on Mr. Robertson?"

"He served as an infantry captain in Viet Nam but had nothing to do with army intelligence. At least that is what we were told. Frankly, I do not believe it. In any event, I don't think he is a player in this matter other than his observations."

"I believe you're correct. Thanks again for the update. Talk to you soon." With that the call was terminated.

CHAPTER 52

IT HAPPENED ONE NIGHT

Vinnie and Gretchen arrived at JFK with a little more than an hour to spare. They took the airport transportation to the Alitalia terminal where they joined two agents from the regional CIA office. Jose Castillo, the older of the two, was the lead agent. The younger agent was Dave Spalding. Castillo was small for a field Agent but his physique was that of a weight lifter. His handshake was crushing. His pleasant smile and mild manner disguised a no nonsense agent. Dave Spalding, on the other hand, was younger by at least ten years and had the build of a tennis player, tall and lanky. Whereas Castillo had the complexion of a Cuban, Spalding looked every part the WASP.

After introductions, they went to a Starbuck's located in the terminal and ordered coffee. Spalding and Castillo had arrived in two cars that were being watched over by New York State Police outside the transportation area in order to be available for the upcoming surveillance. Both agents had been selected for this duty in part because they had worked in the city for several years and knew their way around. It was decided that Gretchen would ride with Castillo and Vinnie with Spalding. They exchanged cell phone numbers to stay in touch during the surveillance.

Castillo explained that his car was equipped with a transponder receiver and outlined the preparations he had arranged. Whether the suspect is being met or if she is taking a limo or taxi, it was vital that the driver be distracted long enough for Gretchen to place a transponder under the car near the trunk. Being at the rear of the car, she minimized the risk of being seen. He told them that he had arranged for the state police at curbside to play a role in distracting the driver. The transponder would guarantee that they would not lose Bettina Falaguerra. Gretchen and Vinnie agreed with the plan.

Vinnie and Gretchen gave Castillo and Spalding a color photograph of Falaguerra that had been produced on the Gulfstream. Gretchen then described what Falaguerra was wearing according to Yolanda. Both of the New York agents looked at the picture and then at each other. It was Castillo who said, "I wouldn't be surprised if every male on the aircraft is following her. We may have competition." With that, there were smiles and subdued laughter, but not from Gretchen.

The two car surveillance was a precaution because of the traffic in the city and the risk of getting cut off by other vehicles or getting stopped at a red light. There was no concern about being detected. They were good at surveillance work. All four agents assumed that Falaguerra would either go directly to the Italian embassy or to her home. They were not worried about her going to the embassy since one of their cars could easily detour to arrive there before her. There was a greater risk of losing her if she decided to go home since they did not know where that was. They did not rule out her going to a third destination for an assignation.

The arrival board for Alitalia indicated that her flight was due in 15 minutes. They took up positions and waited. It was not long before passengers began arriving at the gate. Falaguerra was one of the first to disembark indicating that she had traveled first class. She was approximately five seven, a trim figure in all the correct proportions, shoulder-length black hair swaying as she walked. The cut of her designer suit highlighted her voluptuous figure. Her eyes were deep brown and glistening. The pale blue blouse contrasted against her olive colored skin. Umberto was correct in that she was stunning. Her sculpted features were those of a patrician, a woman born of money and one who knew and enjoyed the admiration of both men and women. Gretchen knew a beautiful woman when she saw one and wondered what the unusually silent Vinnie Pagano was thinking as he observed the confident looking Bettina Falaguerra walking to her limo.

As expected, Falaguerra was on her cell phone as she rode the escalator down to the transportation area. Spalding was the closest to her but she was speaking in Italian. If he had understood Italian, he would have heard her tell the driver of her limo that she was headed for the pick-up area and for him to look for her. The other three agents were in a position to exchange places with Spalding if and when the need arose.

Falaguerra headed for the exit and, still on her phone, looked up and down until she spotted the limo which was parked a short distance to her right and just behind the location of the State Police. She put the phone in her bag and walked towards the car. Gretchen and Castillo exchanged positions with

Spalding and were less than ten feet behind Falaguerra. Castillo nodded to the state trooper who waited until Falaguerra was in the passenger seat of the limo and then walked back and approached the driver who lowered his window. "Something wrong officer?"

As previously arranged with Castillo, the officer partially stuck his head in the window and looked beyond the driver to see if someone was in the passenger seat. "Just making certain you had a pick up ready to go and not holding up traffic." Falaguerra gave the officer an annoyed look and then focused straight ahead. As the officer was speaking and had the attention of the driver, Castillo walked slowly past the passenger side and then crossed directly in front of the limo to draw the attention of Falaguerra away from the rear view mirror on her side. Meanwhile, Gretchen quickly, quietly and undetected, placed the transponder under the car directly beneath the trunk.

The limo driver was pissed at the holdup. "I do a lot of pickups here. I know the fucking rules. My passengers always alert me by cell phone when they arrive and we waste no time."

"Have a pleasant day."

As the limo pulled way the driver gave the state trooper the finger.

All four agents went to their cars and the surveillance was under way. As Castillo passed the trooper, he lowered his window and gave him a thumbs up.

The late afternoon traffic was heavy out of JFK and into the city. The four agents knew that the Consolato Generale d' Italia was located at six hundred ninety Park Avenue. If it looked as though the driver was headed in that direction, Spalding and Vinnie were to leave the surveillance and go directly to the Consolato and wait there for Falaguerra's arrival. Castillo and Gretchen would remain behind the limo. When the limo crossed Park Avenue and continued to head for the west side, both cars remained with the limo. Ms. Falaguerra was not going to her office.

Although riding in separate cars, Vinnie and Gretchen's cell phones rang at the same time. Castillo and Spalding were not in on the call. This was still a need to know situation and the New York agents were not fully in the loop. The call was from Elizabeth. "Where are you?"

Gretchen responded first. "We picked up our passenger and have a two-car surveillance underway. She is traveling west in the city and is not aware that she is being followed. Nothing else to report at this time."

"Good work, the four of you. We tapped into the state department's file on her. She is the Director of the Italian Consulate's office for Economic and Commercial Development. Her role is to assist American businessmen in opening operations in Italy and to help Italian businessmen open offices in the states. More than likely her work is a cover for something else. I don't have time to run it down now but her job gives her wide latitude to travel freely within the United States and to and from Italy. Her undergraduate degree is from a prestigious university in Italy. She took her graduate work at the London School of Economics. She comes from a wealthy and influential family in Rome which accounted for her getting the position of Vice Director for her department in New York at such a young age. The Director of her division was promoted to a position back in Italy and she advanced to her present job. Unless she has recently moved, her last address is in a sought after, high priced co-op on the upper west side. I'll give that to you in a minute."

"So far nothing seems out of the ordinary. A rich, beautiful woman from an influential family moves up the ladder quickly and buys or rents on the west side. Sounds like America. Sounds like any number of influential New York families."

"Vinnie, that may be, but on the forms she completed for the state department when she first entered the country as a diplomat, it was noted that she was fluent in both written and spoken English. According to the documents, she stated that her family had an English tutor for her since she was first able to talk. She is bi-lingual. It appears that the family was looking ahead. Then, there was a break of two years between leaving the London School of Economics and her job with the consulate. Her bio simply states, 'Additional language training.' We have to assume that she attended an advanced language school operated either by the Italian diplomatic corps or the Italian military. There may be more here than we thought. Now, for her address."

She gave them the address and added, "Instruct Jose and Dave to put Falaguerra to bed at midnight. If she doesn't leave her condo building by then, she is in for the night. Have them back at six a.m. and see where she goes. If she goes to the consulate, no need for any further surveillance until we know more. You two have had a long day. Jose and Dave can take it from here until tomorrow. I'll call you later tonight if there is something important to share. If not, I'll call in the morning." The phone went dead.

Gretchen relayed Elizabeth's instruction to Jose. Then she and Dave changed places after she took her overnight bag from his car and joined Vinnie. "I'll drive since I know the way to the hotel. It is on 54th street. You'll like it, lots of night life and excellent restaurants. We follow Elizabeth's instructions and take the night off."

"That sounds perfect. However, I have the feeling that after a long happy hour and a good meal, I will opt for a night's rest. I don't mind admitting that I am tired. The night life can wait until another day."

"I had expected more from a country boy let loose in the Big Apple!"

"So much for expectations."

They were silent for a few minutes after which Gretchen drove under the portico to the hotel. Her door was quickly opened and she was greeted by the valet. She handed him the keys and joined Vinnie at the door to the hotel. Once inside, she went to the front desk where they were expected.

"Good evening, Ms. Iverson. Welcome back to the St. Martin Arms. Your rooms are ready. As requested, they are adjoining. You should find everything to your satisfaction. The bell captain will have your bags delivered to your rooms shortly. There is a welcome basket in each room. Should you need anything, please call my number directly. I am on duty until seven a.m." He then handed her his personal business card along with magnetic door keys to two rooms.

"Thank you for your thoughtfulness. We will take our own bags since we are traveling light. I'm sure that everything else will be satisfactory." With that she motioned Vinnie to follow her to the elevator. He could not help but note that she must have been a frequent guest and wondered if the New York office of the CIA had rooms reserved on a continuing basis.

They entered their separate rooms and settled in. Within minutes Gretchen heard a knock on the adjoining door to Vinnie's room and slid back the bolt and opened it. She was greeted by Vinnie, "Hi, just checking to make certain they had not adjoined me with a stranger." A hesitation, then, "Actually I'm inviting you to be my guest at happy hour in the lounge."

"Sounds great but first I want to shower and freshen up. I'll meet you there in half an hour."

"See you then."

After his shower, Vinnie dressed in casual pants, loafers, a button down shirt open at the collar and a blazer. The lounge was partly full when he arrived. But, it was still early. He sat at the bar, saved a seat for Gretchen and then had the bartender pour him a Knob Creek on the rocks while he waited. Like most women, she was appropriately late and he didn't have to turn to know she had arrived. The action of the bartender said it all. He simply stared and whistled to himself and to Vinnie, "Your friend has arrived." As soon as she saw Vinnie, she headed for the bar.

Vinnie turned, stunned. She had on a chic black dress, modest at the cleavage that outlined her trim and well proportioned body. Its length was just above the knee and drew his eyes to her long beautifully shaped legs. Spiked heels accentuated her height. Short brown hair, stylishly cut, glistened under the overhead lights and a small pendant on a simple gold chain rested on her bosom. Her makeup was subdued and natural colored. Bettina Falaguerra may be stunning but Gretchen Iverson was quite beautiful in an understated way.

He stood as she approached the bar and knew that all eyes were on her. He took both her hands in his, "You look lovely." She gave him a quick peck on his cheek and, as she did so, he could smell the light touch of Chanel.

"Thanks you, sir. And, you look quite handsome. Now, if you are drinking what I think you are, I will have one." With that, he ordered her a drink. When it arrived, they clinked glasses, looked at each other for a moment or two and processed their private thoughts.

"I didn't know if you wanted to eat here or somewhere else, so I didn't make reservations."

"Not to worry. I have stayed here several times in the past year or so and I know of a great restaurant that has both atmosphere and wonderful food and it's only a block away. I took the liberty of having the concierge make reservations for us. Hope you don't mind."

"Not only do I not mind, I thank you for taking the pressure off me to find a restaurant."

"I sort of figured that. Now, I suggest that if we are going to talk business, we do it now and get it out of the way so we can enjoy the rest of the evening. We have a few minutes before we have to leave. By the way, we are walking."

"If you can walk in those heels, who am I to complain?"

"Well, a woman always figures that her man for the evening would carry her if it came to that."

He smiled, "It would be my pleasure. Maybe we should try it anyway."

"Let's not get ahead of ourselves. Now, business."

He took a sip of his drink. "Business. For starters, I believe I need to personally get to know Ms. Falaguerra. I have thought about two ways to do so. The first is official by showing interest in developing a business in Italy. My concern is that we have not developed any kind of a cover story for me to use. This event developed too fast."

"And, the second way?"

"Socially."

Gretchen thought about that for a minute and decided not to pursue the idea of a ruggedly handsome, Italian speaking agent meeting a beautiful Italian woman in a social setting. She stuck with business.

"That is unlikely to work since we have no connection with the Italian consulate here. Besides, what makes you think a social contact will work?"

"She is Italian, I am American; she speaks fluent English and I speak fluent Italian. We have a lot in common."

"And she is a stunning looking woman and you are a handsome guy and so forth."

He chose to ignore the comment. "You and I may not have the social contacts, but Elizabeth knows a sufficient number of influential diplomats to make it happen. I'm thinking that she can arrange an event that brings together high ranking embassy representatives, by specific name, from the Italian, British, French, Australian and German consulates to meet with our trade commission to explore opportunities. You and I would attend as ad hoc members of the commission."

"Why those countries?"

"They are the countries that provided troops and supported our Iraq and Afghanistan military efforts and this is a way to acknowledge our appreciations for their sacrifices. What better way than to open our markets to them? And, selecting those countries quells any complaints from countries that stayed on the sidelines. The idea may need massaging but I leave that up to you and Elizabeth."

She couldn't help but smile at the proposal. "May I ask when you came up with this brilliant idea?"

"An hour ago while showering."

"On that note, let me take you to dinner."

She took his arm as they walked to the restaurant. He could feel her breast pressing against his arm and was pleasantly aroused, certain that she knew what he was experiencing. He couldn't help but believe that she must know how lovely she is and how a man could be easily excited by the most casual physical contact. As they walked the ease of their relationship brought a smile to his face. He was a happy man and wondered what life with Gretchen would be like.

When they arrived at the restaurant, the dining room hostess checked their reservation and seated them immediately. They had another Knob Creek while checking the menu. They both ordered veal francaise. Vinnie ordered a French wine.

Throughout dinner they chatted easily about world events, politics, movies and current events, taking care not to discuss business or their personal backgrounds. They had come to like each other after a rocky start and were enjoying being together and alone. They lingered over coffee. Gretchen paid the bill with an agency card and they walked the one block back to the hotel. They walked slowly, enjoying the lovely evening. When they arrived at the hotel they went directly to the bank of elevators, agreeing silently that they would forego after dinner drinks. Once inside in the elevator, Gretchen selected the fourth floor. They were quiet, each reflecting on a perfect evening and apprehensive about what may be ahead.

When they reached their adjoining doors, Gretchen was the first to speak. "You were a great date, Vinnie Pagano. Thank you for a lovely evening." She then kissed him lightly on the cheek,

"And you, Ms. Iverson, made it easy to be a great date. It was a wonderful evening."

She turned and inserted her magnetic key in the door. Vinnie called good night to her as she entered her room. It was an awkward ending to a wonderful evening, not what each had anticipated.

A few minutes after they were in their rooms, Gretchen opened her door and knocked gently on Vinnie's. When he opened it, she asked, "Do you think it might be a good idea to leave our doors unlocked in case Elizabeth should call? She said she might do that. It would make it easier for us to get together on a conference call."

"Maybe we should leave the doors open. It would be that much easier."

"I like that idea. Sleep well, Vinnie."

"Buona notte, bella donna."

"Buona notte, bell' uomo."

They retreated to their rooms with the doors open.

Ten minutes later she was standing in the doorway in her terry robe with little under it. With a mischievous smile, she asked, "Have you made a monogamous commitment to Sharon Rizzo?"

He thought for a moment about the question. "No. Why do you ask?"

"Well, the way I see it, you're uncommitted, I'm uncommitted, we are partners whose lives may be in the hands of each other and, best of all, I think we like each other in spite of a difficult beginning. Am I correct so far?"

Standing there in his hotel supplied terry robe, he was for the moment less aroused than he was amused. This was a very special lady. He responded to her question, "The uncommitted part is correct. It is true that as partners we are committed to helping each other. And, the bumpy start is right on the money. Let's see, that leaves the question as to whether we like each other. Can I think on that and get back to you in the morning?" All the while he moved towards her door.

When he reached her door she moved close, grabbed him by the belt on his robe and pulled him to her. He placed one arm under her legs and the other behind her back, lifted her and carried her to the side of her bed where he gently stood her up, untied her robe, slid it off and let it drop to the floor. She untied his belt and pushed the robe off his shoulders. It fell to the floor. For a moment they stood naked looking at each other until she pulled him to her. He could feel her warm breasts and hardened nipples pressing against his chest. His hands slid down to her buttocks and, as he drew her to him, his penis expanded and nestled between her legs where he could feel moisture already forming. She dropped her hands to his buttocks and pulled him in tighter, aroused by the throbbing of his penis between her legs and his fingers exploring her anus.

Anticipating this moment, Gretchen had pulled down the comforter when she first entered the room. She nudged Vinnie to the bed where she rolled on top of him, first drawing her hands across his face, exploring his mouth with her fingers, then with her tongue, and finally pulling and stroking his penis. She slid down his chest, kissing his nipples, then his stomach and finally taking him in her mouth, all the while holding his penis. When she sensed he was close to coming, she released his penis, slid up his body and brought him inside her. He raised his body so that his penis was erect, giving her a perfect angle to rise and fall on it. The size of his penis allowed him to feel every fiber inside her as she attacked his body with hers. Her arousal of him powered his body to lift itself up to meet her as she plunged down onto him, again and again. Then a final burst of energy and orgasms. She collapsed on to his body and he held her tight, their bodies trembling from pleasure, their breathing deep and their bodies moist from sweat, semen and vaginal moisture. Vinnie reached down and pulled the sheet up and covered them both. Snuggled in his arms, Gretchen soon fell asleep, exhilarated from her passionate lovemaking. Sleep did not come quickly to Vinnie. He lay quietly feeling guilty knowing that Sharon was waiting to hear from him the next day when he was scheduled to return to West Hartford. He loved Sharon, but then there was Gretchen and Elizabeth. Sleep finally claimed him.

CHAPTER 53

ALEXEI DMITROV

Immediately after ending the call to Gretchen and Vinnie, Elizabeth wondered if she made a mistake in telling them she might call tonight. She couldn't help but wonder how they would spend the night although in her heart she believed they would spend it together in bed. Her concern would have to wait. Right now she had to check the status of her facial recognition effort. Locating Khalid was of paramount importance and she had to do it soon. Vinnie's logic that he was in the country gave greater urgency to finding him.

She made the first of two calls. It was a secure call directed to a black operation she co-managed with covert funds. The physical operation was located in the Turks and Caicos in the British West Indies. It was a joint effort with her counterpart in MI-6. The British used it to compare images of persons of interest who attempted to use false identities to enter or leave Great Britain or board and disembark any airline operating in the country. While the FBI had a similar system in place, the British program code named TWINS, was viewed by Elizabeth as being superior to the American model. She readily accepted the offer of a joint effort when the British first proposed the partnership.

TWINS had never disappointed her. In keeping with her agreement with the Brits, it was a well kept secret.

The call was answered in London by Anthony Cambridge, her counterpart and co-manager of TWINS. "Even the ring tone sounded anxious."

"Anthony. I am anxious. After considerable internal debate, we concluded that our man is in the United States and plotting his next move. We desperately need a lead on this. Has TWIN come up with anything?"

"TWIN has processed approximately thirteen million images in the last eighteen hours. We have nothing so far but the chief technician estimates that we are about sixty-five percent through the total number of images that were taken in the time frame you defined. The odds are still with us that we will have favorable results. The technicians need another eight to ten hours to complete the process. However, my optimistic personality tells me that by early morning we will have results. You need to get a good night's rest."

"Anthony, if anything comes up during the night you must call me. Do not wait until morning. Every hour counts."

"We Brits have never failed our friends across the pond."

"I know that and thank God we have you as friends. Good night."

"Good night."

It was time for the second call. This would be a sensitive one, but one that had to be made before she met with Max. She and Alexei Dmitrov were friendly enemies who prevented, through their work as intelligence chiefs, chaos from erupting between the two nuclear super powers. They helped to keep their respective countries at arm's length. Both were relentless in their pursuit of sensitive information from each other, but they also knew that there were times when some level of cooperation was necessary to keep common enemies at bay or to promote policy issues that assisted both countries. And then, there were those rare times when they helped each other on a more personal basis. This was one of those times. Because of the possibility of their call being monitored by their own agencies, the calls were routed through the secure system of the German Federal Intelligence Service, or, Bundesnachrichtendienst. In turn, the Germans had access to secure systems with either the Russians or Americans when the communications were of common interest.

She dialed the secure number and waited for a pickup. When the pickup occurred, she entered a code and waited. A male voice came on line. "As usual, it is good to hear from you, Elizabeth. I only hope I can be of service."

"And, greetings to you, Alexei. I trust you are in good health."

"As good as one can expect given the turmoil around the world. Our resources are stretched too thin to be totally effective. If only I had your budget."

"If only I had your network. Perhaps one day we can merge and save time and money. Our common enemies grow larger in number each day."

After a good laugh, he asked, "How may I help you?'

"Alexei, in spite of your financial restraints, you still maintain a world class intelligence operation. I need your help in running down a problem. You are familiar with the abduction of Abdu Khalid from Rome and his delivery to Egypt for enhanced interrogation. Khalid was subsequently released by Egyptian authorities and left the country. We extricated our station chief from Italy in order that he could avoid being arrested because of his role in the abduction. I had him in a safe house in Maine where two Serb assassins were taken down while attempting to kill him. They were carrying Russian Yargin PY, a semi automatic weapons that had been retooled by experts to take suppressors. We believe the retooling was done in a Russian ghetto in New York. I hate to ask this, Alexei, but did your agency have anything to do with the attempted assassination?"

"You disappoint me Elizabeth. If it was my agency, Max Rietsema would be dead and the Serbs killed at our hands to keep them quiet. What you experienced was the work of amateurs. Now, let me tell you what I know and save time. When Khalid was set free by the Egyptians, he vowed to kill your station chief. He was in possession of great amounts of cash and a warehouse filled with opium. He arranged a contract with FAPSI, one of our divisions charged with electronic surveillance abroad, to eavesdrop on Rietsema in order to monitor his whereabouts. Khalid then employed FAPSI to hire assassins to find and kill your man. Unfortunately, FAPSI contracted with incompetent Serbs. They should have hired ex KGB agents to do the job. In return for the killing, money and drugs were transferred to members of FAPSI. It is no surprise that Rietsema killed both of the Serbs. More than likely, they were thugs who knew nothing about the dangers of confronting a CIA agent. As for finding Rietsema, FAPSI must have monitored all his phone calls, anyone he contacted. What is surprising to me is that Rietsema was not more careful. As station chief, he had to know that Khalid could purchase any service he wanted, especially from cash poor Russians. "

"Anything else?"

"Just one thought, proven to be accurate over a lifetime of working with agents. I'm certain you have had the same experience, Elizabeth. When competent agents become careless, they usually are occupied with sex and not always with the opposite gender. Rietsema had to have been talking with someone on the phone and FAPSI caught it and shared it with Khalid."

"Did you learn who Rietsema was talking to?"

"No, but since he was station chief in Rome and was known to have an eye for women, I would look for an Italian woman. They can distract any man."

"Alexei, I'm here if you need me."

"Until then."

When she hung up, she thought about the "an eye for women" comment. Even when they were lovers, Max always had an eye for other women. She knew Alexei had it right. Max compromised himself with Bettina Falaguerra in Rome. That compromise led to his killing two Serbs which, in turn, drew the FBI into the picture. Elizabeth knew, unequivocally, that once the composite profile was complete, it would first be circulated among bureau employees in the hope that someone would identify the person. If that effort yielded nothing of value, the composite would be circulated among all of the civilian agencies including the Central Intelligence Agency. In excess of one hundred and twenty thousand employees would have the opportunity to identify the suspect. The next circulation, if necessary, would be expanded to all military intelligence agencies. Someone was bound to recognize Max Rietsema.

Elizabeth also knew that all hell will break loose if Max was identified by someone in the intelligence community. Both she and the Director would be under enormous pressure to resign. It was time to talk to Max. What else did he share with Bettina Falaguerra? While FAPSI was electronically eavesdropping for Khalid, what else did it learn about American operations that it then shared with its KGB successor, the FSB? In addition to careers being at risk, the agency would be the laughing stock of the intelligence community and adversaries in Congress would move for its extinction. All because of sex. If Max had kept his pants on none of this would have happened. Damn him and damn Falaguerra.

Elizabeth decided she had enough of the Virginia countryside for the time being and left for Washington and her own bed in Georgetown. Before she departed by helicopter, she left word with security that Max was to be allowed to roam the grounds as long as he did not have access to any communication equipment and that he was to report to Langley at four p.m. the next day. He was to use one of the cars assigned to the security detail.

CHAPTER 54

PUTTING IT TOGETHER

Elizabeth had a restless night for several reasons. Having learned what she did from Alexei Dmitrov, she had to settle matters with Max. She was not looking forward to the meeting. While this was a breach of security and an employment matter, there was the underlying issue of she and Max having been lovers at the same time she was his case officer. While that relationship took place several years ago, the bond between them remained. The line between personal and agency business was blurred. Being his superior, she knew she was ultimately responsible for his conduct. She was not certain how she would handle Max and what sanctions she would impose on him for a major security breach. While the breach was in itself a major problem, how could he have stood by and listened to Elizabeth assign Vinnie and Gretchen to meet and follow Bettina Falaguerra when she arrived from Italy, knowing that sooner or later it would blow up in his face? What was he thinking? What was he hiding?

Elizabeth knew that Max and Falaguerra had a sexual relationship. At some point she would learn just how it evolved, although she was certain that it resulted from a social affair at which they both were present. Max was a social animal and beautiful women always presented a challenge to him. Having been his lover at one time, Elizabeth knew how he operated. The odds were he was the aggressor. More than likely, the relationship was no secret to embassy personnel as sexual liaisons were viewed as standard operating procedure for agents away from home. Especially among the men it was "Wheels up, rings off."

Falaguerra's position within the Italian intelligence community gave her access to the magistrate's office. She learned of the arrest warrants being issued for Max and his team members and alerted him. He contacted Langley and the Director assigned Elizabeth the task of extracting the entire team from Italy. Until the extraction was executed, Gus and the others were locked down in several safe houses in Rome, out of reach of the magistrate. Max was locked down alone.

Once Khalid's Agents learned of the extraction through their own informant in the magistrate's office, they went on the hunt for Max. They were unsuccessful since by then he was locked down and out of reach. Khalid also learned of Max's sexual relationship with Falaguerra. It was then that he contracted with the Russians to electronically eavesdrop on Max and Falaguerra. The Russians monitored their phones, personal and business, land lines and cell. There was a period of two days between the time Falaguerra alerted Max and when he was flown out of Italy. In those two days, there were multiple phone calls between them. Only one of the calls was significant. He told her he was being flown out of Italy that night. He was careful not to give her more details, especially his location in Italy and promised to call her once he was settled. The Russians shared this information with Khalid who requested that the monitoring effort be continued.

Max kept his promise and called Falaguerra from Maine. He never removed the call from his phone. The damaging call remained in the "calls made" log. Elizabeth, who had taken his phone with her back to Washington, examined it before going to bed. Thinking about it kept her awake. If, as she suspected, Max learned through Falaguerra that FAPSI had been electronically eavesdropping on both of them, then it was possible that Max knew his call to Falaguerra from Maine was monitored. If so, it stood to reason that Khalid would learn of his whereabouts and send someone to kill him. Elizabeth knew it was pure conjecture, but her experience as an agent and her understanding of Max and agents like him led her to initially believe that Max set the stage to entrap any assassin. She knew that her agents were trained to kill. She was one of them and understood their motivations. Max killed two foreign assassins by design. He set them up. He did what he was trained to do. He did it without approval from Elizabeth, his boss. The question in her mind was whether it was murder.

There was still another reason for Elizabeth's restless night. With the FBI on the scene in Maine, it was only a matter of time before they would find the second body and follow the evidence. The bureau was outstanding at following leads. They had the manpower and the technology. They had experience. She was also certain that by now the witnesses who had seen and talked to Max in Baxter State Park would have provided sufficient information for the bureau to construct a composite of Max. She knew the routine; distribute it internally to all bureau personnel and if no recognition was made, expand the distribution to other agencies. From her point of view the best scenario among several bad ones was for the FBI to make a match internally. They would automatically contact the CIA and Elizabeth would have an opportunity, however futile it may be, to initiate damage control. The FBI would hold the upper hand. It would be an opportunity to take the CIA down a peg or two. And that was the best scenario.

A worse scenario would be if no one in the bureau recognized the composite and it was distributed to other agencies and then appeared on the computer screens at Langley. Her own agency would be asked to identify one of their own, someone who had murdered two Serbs. The thought of it sent shivers up her back. The shame of being fired was unsettling but she could handle that. She had no such confidence that she could handle a ruined career or be responsible for providing adversaries in Congress with the ammunition to cripple, perhaps destroy, the agency. She needed to talk to Darlene, Vinnie and Gretchen in the early afternoon. Not in the mood to talk to them now, she sent a secure text message to them to meet her the next day at noon. She would meet with Max in the late afternoon. She noted in the message that no reply was necessary.

Another reason for her unrest was Vinnie and Gretchen. Elizabeth had no illusions about them. They were now lovers. And, she had made it possible. What a fool she had been to pair them. She wanted Vinnie for herself. Being the boss, sooner or later she would have him.

Finally, and of greater importance, was the fact that Khalid was in the United States. The only person up to the job of finding and killing him was Vinnie with Gretchen's help. If Elizabeth knew of Vinnie's destruction of the two thugs in the parking garage at Global Insurance, she would realize just how perceptive Darlene and Gretchen were in bringing Vinnie to her. If only it was to her and not the agency.

She desperately needed sleep. Tomorrow would prove to be a trying day. She had ignored Max, but the time was at hand for a debriefing. Then TWIN would call with the results of the image screening. Darlene would call in and Elizabeth dreaded what she would have to report from Bangor. Now that she knew who Max's informant was, there was no need for Vinnie and Gretchen to remain in New York. It was time to bring her team together and find Khalid. She felt very much alone. Finally, she closed her eyes, dreamed of making love to Vinnie and eventually fell into a deep sleep.

CHAPTER 55

ELIZABETH'S AGENDA

Her phone rang at four twelve a.m. Dog tired, she did not want to answer. She desperately needed rest. She looked at the source of the incoming call. Reluctance gave way to reason and she picked up. "You have a match?" It was both a question and an answer.

"We have a match. TWIN worked beautifully and exceeded our expectations. Here is what we have, love. Abdu Khalid entered the United States by way of Los Angeles as Hamil Zahid, a lesser known Saudi prince but, nevertheless, a member of the royal family. Approximately two hours later, he boarded a flight for West Palm Beach, Florida as Jonathon Drew. While TWIN compared millions of images, the match was relatively easy since Khalid did not change his appearance, only his documents. Clearly, he did not know of TWIN and its capabilities. The bottom line is that Abdu Khalid, a.k.a Hamil Zahid, then a.k.a Jonathan Drew is in the United States. I wish we could do more, but this is now in your court. My sense is he has already discarded the Jonathon Drew cover and taken on another alias. He came well prepared with perfect documents. Elizabeth, he had help from a country that has the expertise to generate them."

"Anthony that was great work by the TWIN team. Please extend my thanks. You're right, it is our problem. At some point I will bring you up to date. One question. What day did he enter the United States?"

"It was Friday last."

"I doubt he will use the airlines to make a move to another location but we need to continue with a facial imagery comparison from West Palm Beach."

"Already working on it. I'll stay in touch."

"Thanks again." With that Elizabeth terminated the call.

She sat on the edge of her bed in her panties and tee shirt processing what Anthony had shared. If Khalid had taken the identity of a Saudi Prince, it means that he had to move quickly after the murder in order to leave the country before the body was discovered. It also means that he had serious and talented help in manufacturing several sets of documents so quickly. Vinnie had sized that up perfectly. Khalid has been in the United States for five days, not enough time to initiate chaos, but long enough to set his scheme in motion.

She called her security detail and asked that her car be brought around at five thirty a.m. She wanted to be at the office by six fifteen. It was time to begin the hunt for Khalid.

At that very moment, Max was lying awake in his cottage in the woods in Virginia, worried about his meeting with Elizabeth and debating with himself as to just how much he could or would tell her. Darlene was sound asleep at a Hampton Inn in Bangor, Maine. She had pried as much as she could from Agent Stuart McDonald and had bad news to report. In a warm bed in an upscale hotel in New York City, Gretchen was snuggled in Vinnie's arms, wide awake and aware that a woman in West Hartford was waiting to have Vinnie in her arms.

Elizabeth headed for the shower and on the way stopped and looked in the full length mirror that was attached to the sliding door of the walk-in closet. She thought her body looked damn good for forty. In fact, she thought it looked fabulous. All she needed was a man, a younger man to share it with. She had someone in mind.

Ellen was at her desk when Elizabeth arrived. The security detail had alerted her soon after they had been called. "Ellen thanks for getting here early. We will be on overload for a day or two. Let's set the day's agenda."

"Boss, you look dead on your feet. You need some caffeine. Have you had breakfast?"

"Not yet. But you can order a muffin and coffee from the dining room. Get something for yourself. While you are at it, order sandwiches and cold drinks for noon for five of us including yourself. Then, let's get started."

Six minutes later Ellen was back. "Ready to go."

"Gretchen, Darlene and the new agent, Vinnie Pagano, will be here at noon. Make certain that no one bothers us for at least forty five minutes. I want you there so you'll need to make arrangements for incoming calls to be transferred to someone responsible."

Ellen made a note of the command. "Do you want an audio and visual recording of the meeting?"

"Not then, but at four p.m. Max Rietsema will be here. Make arrangements for that conversation to be recorded, both audio and visual. I do not want to be disturbed unless it is the President or the Director. Same goes for the noon meeting. Ellen, it is important that Max not be seen by staff entering the building. He is still in Virginia and will be driving here in one of the cars assigned to the security detail there. Call the detail in Virginia and get the number of his car phone. Then call Max as soon as we have the day's agenda set. Have him call your private number when he is close by and instruct him to enter the building by my private entrance. Then call security and make those arrangements for him. I want you to meet him at the entrance when he arrives and then escort him up in the private elevator."

"Do you want the same procedure when he leaves?"

"I'll let you know since it depends on the outcome of the meeting." Ellen was surprised at the response given that she was aware her boss and Max were former lovers.

"Then call Anthony Cambridge at TWINS. I spoke with him early this morning but forgot to ask him for the photographs of Abdu Khalid, the one taken in Los Angeles when he arrived and the one taken when he departed. We need them for the noon meeting. Do not share them with anyone other than those at the meeting."

"How about the Director?"

"As far as the world is concerned, you and the Director have no knowledge of any photo. Now, listen up. I have formed a new team comprised of Gretchen, Darlene, Vinnie and a fourth member yet to be named. I want them to have total access to me either as a team or individually, at any time, day or night and no matter where I may be."

Ellen knew better than to ask too many questions. If Elizabeth wanted her to know more she would tell her. The questioning look on Ellen's face prompted a response. "This team is on a hunt for Abdu Khalid, the world's most notorious terrorist. He is in the United States plotting al-Qaeda's next moves. We need to find him." She decided not to mention that they needed to kill him. Ellen had worked for Elizabeth long enough to understand that it was a given.

"How can I help besides my regular work?"

"Sooner or later other personnel here and at other agencies will get wind of something related to Khalid and will press you for more details. You know what to do. We may need help, but for the time being we need to go it alone. Just let me know if you hear anything. One other thing, Ellen. Max is currently on the inactive list so you are not to share anything whatsoever with him unless I give the word. You will learn more at the noon meeting."

"I'll be especially alert to any inquiries from anyone. Are you ready for the prioritized list of calls to be returned?"

"I am ready. First, are there any calls on the list that have any relationship to the matter I just shared with you or that referenced Rome, Italy or Bangor, Maine? Anyone pissed at me?"

"When you retire you could get a job as a fortune teller. Carlton Richardson called from Rome and he was definitely pissed. Darlene called from Maine and left a message to confirm her noon meeting with you. She was her usual composed self. It must be wonderful to be both beautiful and accomplished. Speaking of beautiful and accomplished, Gretchen also called. She and Vinnie will be here on time. She didn't say where they were, but I checked the area code and the call was from New York City. Politically, you have several calls but there are two that need attention. The first was from the Department of Justice wanting information on Max's whereabouts. They are taking up where the Italian magistrate's office failed. I got the distinct feeling that while they are not about to send out bounty hunters to apprehend him, they definitely will be on the hunt for him sooner rather than later. They want Max. Let's hope they do not learn of his meeting here this afternoon. The second call was from the chairperson of the intelligence oversight committee expressing anger that the Director, meaning you, allowed Max to escape Italy without facing charges from the Italian magistrate's office for the Khalid incident. She wants an answer."

Elizabeth chose to ignore all of the calls except the one from Carlton.

"What did Carlton say?"

"You promised to call him after his last call and you didn't. He gets that tone in his voice as though you work for him. He is a pain in the ass. Granted, a damn good looking one, but still a pain in the ass." Ellen was aware that he had been the personal choice of the Director and probably has set his sights on succeeding Elizabeth.

"Sooner or later that tight little ass of his will land him in serious trouble."

That comment brought a smile to Ellen's face. It did not go unnoticed. "Alright, what do you know that I need to know?"

"According to my friend, Lisa, who works in the American embassy in Rome, Carlton has a new mistress, a gorgeous twenty-five year old, center fold material who works at the German embassy. Apparently everyone but Carlton knows she is an agent for the German intelligence service. Has lunch at her place every day according to the scuttlebutt where he probably trades information for sex."

Realizing she had said more than she had planned, she apologized. "Sorry about that. Didn't mean to waste time on matters unrelated to those at hand."

"What is her name?"

"Gisela Rudenschroder, daughter of a very, very rich German munitions manufacturer."

"Ellen, see if the American embassy in Rome has had any contact with German arms suppliers. I could use the information before I return Carlton's call later today."

"I'll get right on it."

"Good. Hold his call until later. Give me five minutes and then we'll start with the priority list." With that Ellen left for her office.

Elizabeth needed eleven minutes, three of which were used to process the DOJ call. It would not make this move unless pressure was being exerted from above. She whispered aloud, "Those bastards won't be satisfied until they shut the agency down and prosecute one of us."

She needed the other eight minutes to process what Ellen had shared about Carlton. She now wondered if he was in any way involved in exposing Max's safe house in Maine. She knew that the German federal intelligence agency, the Bundesnachrichtendienst, or, BND, depended heavily on wiretapping and electronic surveillance for the collection of information. It also depended upon covert agents such as Gisela Rudenschroder. Did Carlton learn of the

Waterville safe house and inadvertently share it with his mistress who then gave it to the BND? The question was why would they have an interest in Max? And why would they want him dead? And, how would they have learned of the safe house? None of it made sense to Elizabeth.

She sat quietly and played out another possible scenario. Did Carlton share something, anything, with his mistress that was of interest to the Germans and that prompted them to monitor his calls? As station chief for the agency in Italy, he was privy to information that required the highest level of clearance. Did the Germans learn of the safe house by intercepting his unsecured phone calls and then sell the information to Khalid? But, why? The Germans are friends and allies. She rejected that idea but began to wonder if Carlton was sleeping with his mistress to learn of her father's role in supplying arms to the Middle East, rather than her sleeping with him to gather any and all intelligence he might share. It is entirely possible, she thought, that he manipulated this sexual relationship to his advantage.

Her final scenario was that the leadership of the German intelligence service, like all undercover operations, knew the power of sex and arranged for the young center fold to seduce Carlton in the hope of learning anything of interest. It may have nothing to do with Max or with arms. Elizabeth decided that the only way to resolve the matter was to deal with Carlton directly. The question she pondered was whether or not he should be confronted on a secure phone call or if he should be recalled from Rome and meet her in person. With that her phone rang. It was Ellen. "Senator Wilkinson on line one. Friendly call in support of your budget requests. Should be a good start to the day."

She had made up her mind. "Ellen, call Carlton in Rome and arrange for him to be here tomorrow."

"He'll ask for an explanation."

"Do not give him one and under no circumstances are you to mention Gisela Rudenschroeder."

With that, Elizabeth dropped the intercom line and picked up the incoming call. "Senator, Wilkinson, good to hear from you."

CHAPTER 56

CONSPIRACY

Khalid's ordering of his colleagues to immediately leave Palm Beach set into motion a series of phone calls. The first was a conference call originated by Abua Karsam with his five colleagues. Following a short discussion, there was a unanimous voice that Abdu Khalid had to be stopped before he destroyed the Muslim community in the United States. If he were allowed to initiate widespread assassinations and bombings, the first wave of his strategy, the American public would rein its own terror on all Muslims in the country. It would make the aftermath of 9/11 look like child's play. The strategy would set back, for decades, Muslim plans for controlling local, state and national governing bodies and eventually the Congress of the United States. Unspoken, but clear in the minds of all Muslims, was the goal of breeding children far faster than any other ethnic or religious group. The Imams of the thousands of mosques would pay substantial "breeding bonuses" to families who have five or more children. The Muslim leadership would also take advantage of a liberal immigration policy to enhance their presence in the country. They were a patient people and knew that eventually America would be home to the largest Muslim population on the planet, a nation ruled by a restrictive religious and cultural society. There would be no place for Christians or Jews. Sharia law would dictate religion teachings, the Taliban would enforce cultural rules and al-Qaeda would control all law enforcement including the Pentagon. It might take four or five decades but it would eventually happen. For the first time in the history of mankind, Muslims would have a home of their own. America in its current social and cultural forms would no longer exist.

The second call was also initiated by Abua Karsam. It was agreed that he would explore with Ibraham Malik the possibility of Malik becoming the voice for Muslims in America. Malik had been given a phone number by Karsam after the second meeting with Khalid but had chosen not to use it. Nevertheless, Karsam had taken note that during the last meeting of the entire group Ibraham appeared shocked at the idea of using suicide bombers. While Ibraham and Khalid were childhood friends, the Muslim plan to dominate the United States was more important than personal friendship. It was time for Karsam to take the initiative and to do so immediately since he assumed that Khalid and his party would soon be leaving Palm Beach for another destination.

Karsam knew the hotel where Malik was staying and placed his third call. When the hotel operator answered, Karsam asked to be connected with Mr. Malik's room. Ibraham picked up on the fourth ring. No names were used. "We need to meet. Time is of the essence."

"Tomorrow at 10 a.m."

"We will meet here. Allah is with you."

"And with you"

Ibraham ended the call and stood quietly wondering what chain of events he had unleashed. He could not help but tremble at the prospect of Khalid learning of the meeting and what it meant. There were no friends when it comes to treachery. Yet, he was exhilarated at the prospect of becoming the voice of Muslim leadership and of al-Qaeda in the United States. For too long he had been in the shadows, unknown to the masses while managing the work of the organization and acting as a confidant while Khalid maintained the public face of al-Qaeda. Unlike Khalid, he was the one person who was effective in soliciting funds to keep the organization operating and he was the one person who controlled the finances and knew how to access them. Yet, it was Khalid who had villas in Paris and London. Life was unfair.

He poured himself a Jack Daniels, opened the slider to the balcony, went out and leaned against the railing. Looking out at the vast wealth that surrounded the hotel, he reminded himself that far too many Muslims had bought into the American dream. Would they now be willing to sacrifice it all in order to create a Muslim nation? Had they become soft and westernized as Khalid believed? While Ibraham could never accept suicide bombings as an acceptable means to the end, he could accept the short term mission of creating widespread death and destruction in America as long as there remained the long range goal of overwhelming the country with new births and immigration. The question remained; how committed was the group of six to his cause? They were placed here as sleepers to fight for the cause when called upon. While handpicked by Bin Laden, Ibraham was not convinced by what he had seen so far that they would be willing to sacrifice their lives if called upon.

Experiencing some unease at what was about to occur, he knew in his heart that he was more capable than his friend, had a clearer understanding of the American culture and was more committed to a long range strategy. Unknown to Khalid, Ibraham had quietly and carefully built a small network of agents in the United States who had sworn allegiance to him. They were ready to act.

When Ibraham set his meeting with Karsam and his associates for ten a.m. the following day, he knew that Khalid and Marta were to spend their last day together. Ibraham had chartered a plane and arranged for them to fly to Key West for the day. They would not be returning until early evening. The next day Khalid and Ibraham would be moving together to a new location and Marta would be returning to the villa in Paris.

When Ibraham arrived at the home of Abua Karsam the next morning, he was greeted by Yousuf who escorted him to the meeting room. There ahead of him were Karsam, Amir, Jazier, Najdi, and Karzai. He looked around the table and asked. "Where is Mohammed?"

"We do not know. After I spoke with you, I called his cell and confirmed our meeting. Although I sensed some hesitation, he assured me he would be here. I suggest we have coffee and refreshments and wait a few minutes. It is best that all of us be present."

"I agree with you, Abua. Let us wait fifteen minutes. Then, I suggest you call his cell once again."

With that they recessed for coffee. When the time was up and Mohammed had not arrived, Karsam called his cell. The phone rang four times and then went on voice mail. "I am unavailable. Please leave a message."

"He does not answer. I am concerned."

Ibraham looked at Karsam and then turned to the other four. And spoke. "You are all staying at the same hotel. I assume you talk to each other. Did you see Mohammed this morning when you left?"

Aba Najdi spoke up. "It is true that we are staying at the same hotel but we are colleagues, not friends. Some of us met for the first time at the initial meeting with Khalid. Some of us have rental cars and others used a taxi to come here. I, personally, did not think it strange that Mohammed was not in the lobby when we left this morning."

"Karsam, I suggest you call the hotel and see what you can learn." It was Ibraham.

Karsam called the hotel. When the receptionist answered, he asked to be connected with Mohammed's room. "One moment sir while I call that number." After a short delay, the receptionist returned to the phone. "I am sorry sir, but Mr. Mohammed checked out last evening."

"That is impossible. Please try again."

Another delay and she returned to the phone. "I am sorry but he checked out at eight fifty six p.m."

Clearly in panic mode, Karsam asked, "Did he leave a forwarding address?"

"No sir. There is no forwarding address."

Karsam shut his cell phone and looked around the table. There was little need to say anything but he did anyway. "Mohammed has left and there is no forwarding address. He checked out at eight fifty six last night."

Suleiman Amir jumped into the conversation. “It is possible he has already left for Seattle. Khalid was adamant that we return home quickly.”

“That is not likely. He was clear in his comments to me that he would be here this morning.”

Karsam had no sooner made that statement, than a chill swept over everyone. They all believed they knew what was happening and were too frightened to speak up. That is, all except Ibraham. “It is Khalid’s doing. Of that I am certain. We must fear the worse for Mohammed.”

Abdul Jazier, in a panicked voice asked, “But why? What was to be gained by his killing Mohammed?”

“To keep all of you in line. Khalid knew, as did you, that Mohammed was the weak link in the chain. Not only would he be the first to yield to Khalid’s demands, he would also have been the first to reveal everything to the authorities under enhanced interrogation if he had been apprehended. His death eliminated a potential leak and also stands as a warning and threat to all of you.”

Karsam spoke. “Ibraham, you are the closest to Khalid. Did you have a hand in Mohammed’s death? And, if you did not, who did? I cannot believe that Khalid would have run the risk of personally killing him.”

“I had nothing to do with his death. In fact, I am only suggesting his death since none of us know exactly what has happened to Mohammed. You are correct in that Khalid would not have personally killed him.”

“If not you and not Khalid, then who? We have been led to believe that you are the only person with him other than a mistress.”

“Karsam, Khalid is a resourceful man. That is why he has avoided being killed and why he is able to move freely around the world. Remember, he negotiated his way out of Egyptian hands at the expense of the CIA, convinced the Iranians to provide multiple sets of documents along with substantial traveling funds and then entered the United States with no difficulty. He is a force to be reckoned with. None of us should underestimate his ability. Be aware that he has no soul when it comes to eliminating those he believes to be his enemies. Believe me when I tell you he can be a butcher. There are times when I believe he knows exactly what I am thinking. He creates a sense of unease within me. To all of you I say, be careful what you say and to whom you say it."

Aba Najdi asked, "Who then could have killed Mohammed if that is what happened?"

"Unknown to you, Khalid is being protected in Palm Beach by three senior al-Qaeda operatives who have been living in the United States for several years. One of them is acting as Khalid's driver. I have no idea where they live and have no idea who they are or from what country they came. Those are not questions I would ask Khalid. We are friends but not friendly. Like you, the three operatives are sleepers with a different mission. Your mission is to mobilize resources, both human and material, when the order is given. Theirs, we must assume, is to eliminate anyone who is a threat to al-Qaeda leadership and Khalid. Simply stated, they are professional assassins. Mohammed was seen as one who could not endure enhanced interrogation. Let this be a lesson to all of you. Show no weakness to his cause or demonstrate any hesitation in dealing with Khalid or you will be next."

With those words the chill in the air deepened and the five men were frozen in place, unable to speak and fearful of what lay in store for them. Ibraham, knowing why he had been called to this meeting, chose to remain quiet and let them take the next step. With the assumed assassination of Ghani Mohammed, the group needed both his protection and his willingness to stop Khalid. The minutes passed slowly and quietly until Hafs Karzai spoke up. Being the CEO of the company distributing the Italian Silver Eagle X650, he traveled the globe making sales pitches to both private and military customers. While Karsam was the most proficient at coordinating the actions of the group, Hafs was the intellectual who moved easily with the rich and powerful and had the more commanding presence. "If I may," he began in his understated way, "Now is not the time to be fearful of what lies ahead. Rather, it is the moment when we choose the path that Muslims around the world demand we take. For eleven years we have, with the blessing of Allah, lived comfortable lives, typical of those enjoyed by the highly successful American captains of industry. The same is true of our families. We have become degenerate consumers of everything wealth can buy. When we were given our appointments as heads of major corporations, it was with the understanding that the day would come when once again we would become what we once were, al-Qaeda warriors, committed to the destruction of America and supplanting it with a Muslim country. Is this not true?"

The others stirred in their chairs and took note of what was being said by Hafs. Ibraham, too, was curious as to where the group was being taken. Hafs Karzai continued. "I know you all worry about your families given the threats made by Khalid. Once he is eliminated…

Before he could finish the sentence, Abdul Jazzier interrupted, "Eliminate who? Kill Khalid? Are you mad? Defying him or circumventing him is one thing, but murder!"

In a quiet voice, Hafs responded. "Was it not made clear by Karsam when he called this meeting with our approval that Khalid had to be stopped and that we would look to Ibraham for leadership? Are you so naïve as to think you could stop Khalid without killing him? To answer your question, Abdul, we must kill Khalid and soon. Before you object allow me to give you the two most practical reasons for doing so. First, our families will be safe. If Khalid remains in charge our families will always be held hostage to the demands he makes of us. When he is eliminated, and if Ibraham agrees to be our leader, I strongly suggest that we all move our families to Switzerland while we carry out our business. There they will continue to live the good life, away from the reach of American law enforcement agencies."

"And, what is the second reason for eliminating him." It was Karsam.

Hafs responded. "We must assume that the full force of the CIA is currently engaged in the hunt for Khalid. By now they would have determined how he entered the country and are in the process of tracking his movements. It will not be long before agents will swarm over Palm Beach. That is why he plans to move out of here soon and why he wants us gone. If he is dead, the CIA will waste valuable time and resources chasing a dead man. As long as his body is not found, they will continue with their endless search. In the meantime, we will have time to work with Ibraham in setting a course for Muslim domination of America."

"That is brilliant." It was Ibraham. "Now, let us talk about our next moves."

CHAPTER 57

THE COMPOSITE

Agent Stuart McDonald placed a call to Chief McCorey. "Hello, Agent McDonald."

"You have one of those smart phones with caller I.D."

"Even in Maine we are on the curve, even if not ahead of it."

"From what I have seen, you are well ahead of the curve in law enforcement. You have great instincts."

"Down here, we call it experience. What can I do for you?"

"Good news. Between the Robertson and Wilcox families our lab completed work on the composite. There were many similarities between the observations of the two families which means we are certain it is an outstanding composite. We are hopeful it will produce results."

"What is the next step?"

"The usual route is to show it to law enforcement officials and potential witnesses in the area of the crime. If that does not produce results, we would make a circulation within the bureau to determine if any of our units had contact with the subject in other crime investigations. To get the process started, I am faxing it to you and Captain King at State Police headquarters. Since he covers the entire state, I will request that he make a state wide distribution. If we get inquiries, it is important that we not provide any information other than the composite itself."

"How much time do we have before you make an internal circulation?"

"Forty eight hours. If we do not get any leads, then we will go ahead with our internal circulation. I'll hang up now and get the composite on the fax."

Chief McCorey stood by the fax machine. When the composite was received, he took it from the incoming bin and examined it. He had not seen this person at any time. He dialed Captain King at state police headquarters in Bangor. When the receptionist answered, he identified himself and asked to be connected to King.

"Hello chief. I assume you are calling about the composite. How do you suggest we proceed?"

"If our suspect was climbing in Baxter State Park, the odds are he drove there in the morning; therefore, it stands to reason that he had to have housing somewhere in Maine. If you put out a statewide request for identification of the composite, someone, somewhere, will recognize our suspect."

"Why are you so sure?"

"If you had met the two families who created the composite, you would have the same level of confidence level as I have. They met and talked to our suspect and all of them described common traits attributed to him. How soon can you get the composite distributed?"

"Actually, Chief, I sent the composite out statewide to all law enforcement agencies before you called. I had the feeling that you would recommend doing so. If and when we hear anything, I will get back to you and Agent McDonald."

"I'll wait to hear."

In exactly twenty three minutes Captain King called Chief McCorey. "Chief, we have a solid lead. I just called Agent McDonald with the information. The Chief of Police in Waterville believes he had breakfast with our suspect. There is a diner in town that is frequented by the locals and by serious climbers who shy away from the fancy coffee shops and hotel restaurants. Seems our guy frequented the diner for two or three weeks. One day, the only seat available to him was next to the chief at the counter. The Chief was wearing civvies so there no reason for our boy not to sit down. By the way, the Chief is John Hudson. Says he knows you from statewide meetings. Anyway, the Chief and the suspect struck up a conversation or should I say the chief struck up the conversation. According to Hudson, our suspect was a quiet type of guy who came across as pleasant, experienced as a climber and tough. The type of guy you would want as a friend and not as an enemy. Physically, the Chief described him as good looking, well built and someone who carried himself with confidence. Here's the weird part of the story. I recall that you mentioned to me that the teenage girl, Alex Robertson, said our suspect reminded her of Matt Damon. Damn if the Chief didn't say the same thing. He couldn't remember Matt Damon's name but he remembered the Bourne movie series and the hero. More and more, Chief, I have the gut feeling that our guy is something more than a murderer, if he is a murderer at all."

"I share your opinion. The question is who is he and why was he at Baxter State Park?"

"We'll have to leave that to McDonald. He and his men are on their way to Waterville. If our guy was staying there for two or three weeks, they will find that out and locate where he stayed. When I hear more, I'll call."

"Before you go, I have a question. Did our suspect mention his name to the chief?"

"No, but I see where you are going with this. Given the time he was in Waterville, he must have used his name somewhere. And, how about a credit or debit card? If we don't know his name, then a check of credit card companies is worthless."

"Not entirely. Almost everyone who eats at the diner is local. The FBI can look at all of the charges at the diner, run the names by the owners and determine which names they do not recognize. This assumes he used a credit or debit card. Let's assume he did at one time or another. Where else is someone most likely to use a card?"

"Gas station."

"Correct. So the FBI goes through the same process at the local gas stations. Compare the names and see which show up at both places. The list will be small and easily followed up on. If he didn't use a card, then showing the composite around town is bound to yield something. The guy may be tough, but he has to sleep somewhere."

"Do we assume Agent McDonald will be thinking along the same lines or do we mention what we would do if the investigation was ours?"

"I think we should sit on it for a day or two and see what turns up. He strikes me as a competent investigator."

"I agree, but he is not from down east. Lacks the insight that comes from being humble."

Laughing, the chief ended the conversation. "I'll stay in touch."

CHAPTER 58

IBRAHAM

It was settled. Khalid would die and Ibraham would make it happen. But first the group had to accept Ibraham's conditions if he was to assume leadership. The five men were warriors in name only. It had been eleven years since they wore the tunics and head dress of al-Qaeda terrorists in their native Yemen. During the eleven years they lived in America they had not touched a Kalashnikov assault rifle or manufactured an IED. They had never witnessed the destruction caused by a suicide bomber. Their stomachs never ached for food, their backs were never bowed from carrying heavy loads into the mountains to reach their comrades and their wounds had never gone unattended. They had forgotten the horror of seeing comrades blown to pieces and body parts clinging to anything and anyone close by. They had forgotten how it was to be without warm clothes in the depth of winter and without ammunition for their weapons. None had to seek shelter behind rocks to avoid the unrelenting firepower spewing out of the bellies of American helicopters or fear the constant nighttime raids conducted by the Seals and Special Forces. They were now captains of industry living lives they may not be willing to relinquish, even for Allah. Ibraham knew the dilemma he faced.

"Before we proceed let me caution you that moving your families to Switzerland in no way provides them with the security you wish for them. Al-Qaeda operatives have a long reach and neither women nor children will be spared if you fail to do what you promised Allah you would do when you came to the United States. Are we clear on this point?" He waited and hearing no objection, continued.

He had their attention. "The reason we are conspiring this morning is because we are fearful of Khalid's strategy, believing that if it were to be implemented we would sacrifice our long term goals of creating a Muslim nation in America. He will stop at nothing. Ghani Mohammed was a warning to you. If you do not support Khalid, I guarantee that he has already chosen the next one of you for assassination"

"You cannot be serious, Ibraham. Without us he has nowhere to go. We control thousands of Muslims who are important to his strategy." It was Jazier.

"Have you already forgotten his words? You were chosen for your positions by the Saudis. They also chose the number two man in your company and they are equally qualified to lead, perhaps more so since they have not been pampered as have you. They would like nothing better than to prove their ability to the Saudis."

Hafs Karzai, the one person who knew or thought he knew what had to be done, spoke. "Ibraham, it is time for serious words. I believe you know what steps need to be taken by you and by us. We are of one mind that we object to the use of suicide bombers. Our reasons are many. That being the case, what do you have in mind?"

"Before we discuss that let us concentrate on the number one issue, that of eliminating Abdu Khalid. He and his mistress are now in Key West. They flew there on a plane I chartered for them. They plan on staying overnight and returning here by noon tomorrow. Shortly thereafter the three of us will leave Florida. Khalid and I will travel together and Marta will return to Paris. I have no idea where Khalid and I will be moving to or what means of transportation we will use. He has not shared that information with me. Khalid's three al-Qaeda operatives will fade into the background. Given that schedule, we have approximately twenty four hours to accomplish our mission."

Aba Najdi, "It does not seem possible to accomplish our mission since he is in Key West and will not return until tomorrow. We have but a few hours, not twenty four."

"Hafs, you have the most experience with aircraft having flown the Silver Eagle around the world. Khalid's chartered plane is a Cessna Citation Mustang. If you wanted to destroy it in the air and bring it down over water, how would you do it?"

The others were fascinated at the question and could not believe that Ibraham could kill Khalid in the short time remaining.

Without hesitation, Hafs responded. "There is only one effective way to bring down the aircraft and it is with an explosive charge. There are two ways to accomplish the detonation. The first is by placing a bomb with a timer on board the plane and the second is to detonate a bomb remotely. Both methods have limitations not the least of which is being able to acquire an explosive device. There is also the problem of locating either a timer or a remote and deciding which method of detonation works best for us.

Suleiman Amir turned to Ibraham and asked, "Is it possible to get such a device on such short notice?"

"Let me worry about the device. Right now we need to know where on the aircraft to plant the explosive for maximum effect. It is vital that the aircraft goes down over water so that there is no evidence for the FAA to examine."

"Ibraham, believe me when I say that given the small size of the Mustang any explosive will bring down the aircraft. Much of the flight from Key West to West Palm Beach airport will be over water so any debris from the wreckage will be buried at sea along with the passengers and pilot."

"Thank you Hafs. Now, I assume you flew yourself from Chicago on the Silver Eagle. Did you have a co-pilot?"

"No."

"Excellent. Therefore, there is no one to whom you would have to explain a sudden trip to Key West. Have your plane fueled and ready to fly to Key West at six p.m. tonight. You and I are going to take a trip to the southernmost point of land in the United States. File a flight plan that provides for a return trip to West Palm Beach airport tomorrow at approximately the same time as Khalid's return flight."

"What is expected of the rest of us in the meantime?"

"Abdul, you and the others will follow Khalid's orders and return to your homes today if flights are available, otherwise you are to leave tomorrow. Do nothing different. As soon as Hafs and I have completed our business, I will be in contact with you."

"What of Ghani Mohammed?"

"It is out of our hands. If a body is found, the police will take over the investigation. If there is no body, he will be declared missing when he does not show up to run his company. We are not to trouble ourselves with it unless Khalid lives, which is not likely."

Hafs remained after the others left. "Ibraham, is it your intention that we fly to Key West, gain access to Khalid's charter plane and plant an explosive?"

"That is exactly what we are going to do and the Silver Eagle will play a major role. Khalid does not know you arrived on a company plane and therefore would have no idea when he departs Key West that we will be right behind him. Even if we get delayed from the tower, the Silver Eagle has a cruising speed of four hundred and thirty knots whereas the Citation has a cruising speed of three hundred and forty knots. You would easily approach Khalid's plane and I will trigger the explosive charge from the air when we are over water. Then, we will continue our trip to West Palm Beach."

"How did you know the cruising speeds of the two aircraft?"

"When I conceived of the idea last night, I simply went to the two company web sites for specifications."

CHAPTER 59

TEAM PLAY

Elizabeth had just completed a phone conversation with the chairman of the intelligence committee when Ellen buzzed. “Everyone is here. Shall I send them in?

“Yes, please.”

Unlike the casual clothes worn at the Virginia facility, today they were dressed for business. Both women wore suits, Gretchen in dark blue and Darlene in a grey pin stripe. Both were Armani creations. Gretchen wore an off white blouse while Darlene chose to eliminate the blouse and show a little flesh. Vinnie wore a dark blue, double breasted suit, light blue shirt and a cream colored tie. Standing together with a statuesque and beautifully poised Elizabeth, they looked like corporate CEO'S and bore little resemblance to four former and present covert agents who were authorized to kill and who had killed.

After Elizabeth's cordial welcome they sat in expensive dark brown leather chairs positioned around an equally expensive conference table. They no sooner had made themselves comfortable when Ellen and a cafeteria worked arrived with a cart that carried coffee, tea and pastries. When the dining room attendant left, Ellen took a seat off to the side and Elizabeth began. “First, I want to thank the three of you for your work the past two days. It has been admirable. In addition to your accomplishments there were outstanding efforts by our contract lab technicians in processing the evidence left at Baxter State Park. And, before you ask, I am meeting with Max this afternoon. Until then it is best you ask no questions."

"Being his colleague for so long, we hope that the meeting ends on a positive note." It was Gretchen. It was more of a plea than a statement.

"I know that you and Darlene, being co-workers with Max, are deeply concerned for him. Let's wait and see what happens. Now, for the good news and bad news. Darlene has been in Maine posing as a reporter. I want her to share what she learned."

"Elizabeth arranged for me to work as a reporter in order to gain access to the bureau's investigation. I flew into Bangor late at night. In the very early morning I drove directly to Baxter State Park. Incidentally, Maine in the early morning is quite beautiful. It will be my next vacation spot. But to continue, I didn't expect to find anyone at the park since the crime scene was several days old but I needed to get some idea as to the setting when and if I got to speak with the FBI agent in charge. As luck would have it, the park Ranger was there. His name is Amos Trumbull. Apparently these guys start work early since the day climbers begin to arrive around dawn and the Ranger likes to meet as many of them as possible. Most of them are repeat climbers so he knows many of them. I introduced myself and he was willing to share what he knew and what was already public information. He led one of the search parties that found the body. More importantly he was the one who, early in the morning of the day the body was discovered in the woods, spotted the glass crystals and what looked like blood stains and scuff marks on the pavement. He may be a country cop but, in talking with him, I knew I had met a savvy law enforcement officer. According to him, one shot to the head was all it took to take down the guy. There was no gun to be found, nor was there any identification on the body."

"It was early in the morning, so what made him think, since the body in the woods had yet to be discovered, that a crime had been committed?"

"Good question, Gretchen. According to him, it was no single piece of evidence; rather, he was concerned with the combination of evidence, especially the scuff marks across half the width of the parking lot and ending where he found the crystals. He knew they were not made by an animal. Not being certain of his next step he wisely called an old friend of his father who used to be the Chief of Police. His name is Horace Browning. Horace listened, believed that there was something of police interest and advised him to call the local Chief of Police, a guy named McCorey, then the state police and in that order. Even in Maine, protocol was important."

"Did you get to meet any of them?" It was Vinnie.

"I did. I called Chief McCorey and he gladly met with me. Rather than my repeating what he told me, which was pretty much what the park ranger had said, I'll share the most important piece of news. He and the state police were able to contact two other climbing parties who had been on the mountain the day Max was climbing. A total of six climbers actually met and talked to Max however briefly. McCorey interviewed all of them and came away convinced that the FBI could easily create a composite picture of Max based on the descriptions provided by the climbers. The bureau was working on the composite when I was in Maine."

Elizabeth asked, "What did the climbers have to say about Max? Did McCorey share any comments?"

"He did. According to the climbers, they all were convinced that there was more to Max than met the eye. They thought him to be a skilled climber, pleasant to talk to, handsome as hell, gentle on one hand but a man you would not want to tangle with. A sixteen year old teenage girl who was climbing with her family insisted Max was just like Matt Damon in the Bourne Trilogy movies. She also was convinced that the two guys who were after him never stood a chance. At first the family kidded her but the Chief had the distinct feeling they knew she was close to the truth."

Darlene, "How credible is the girl?"

"If the Chief thinks she is credible, then she is. He is not easily impressed. After the conversation with the Chief, I called the Bangor office of the bureau and spoke with the agent in charge, a Stuart McDonald. I decided it was too risky to meet him in the off chance we had been at some law enforcement event at the same time. Besides, it was not necessary. I learned what we needed to know. The composite was completed and they were about to begin circulating it with law enforcement agencies in Maine. Chief McCorey is certain that there will be a positive identification based on his interviews with the six climbers. That is the bad news."

There was silence for a moment or two as Elizabeth looked around the table. Then she spoke. "More bad news in that we know for certain that Abdu Khalid has entered the United States."

The comment caused all three to stare at Elizabeth knowing that Khalid would be plotting another 9/11 and beginning his hunt for Max.

Elizabeth continued, "The good news is that we have learned where and when he entered. Additionally, we know that within two hours of entering the states via Los Angeles, he boarded another flight to Palm Beach International Airport in West Palm Beach, Florida. We need to determine why he went to that particular location. That was last Friday. It is reasonable to assume that he may have left for another destination although we have no evidence of that. By now he must know that we know he is here so he will be on the move. Tracking his movement will be a challenge but we must find him. However, before we get to that we need to discuss the New York City adventure." She glanced first at Gretchen and then Vinnie.

Not certain how to take the "adventure" comment, Gretchen decided the best approach was to ignore it and move on to the adventure. "Your agent in Rome described Bettina Falaguerra accurately and we had no problem identifying her when she arrived at JFK. The surveillance went as planned. She went directly to her west side apartment and did not leave while Vinnie and I were on surveillance. I assume the night shift had the same experience. We would have learned more if we stayed in New York and visited the Italian Consulate this morning."

"Thanks Gretchen." She continued, "I asked for the three of you to be here today because we now have to concentrate on finding Abdu Khalid."

"Why are we not continuing with Falaguerra? I thought she was the key to the situation in Rome."

“She is, Gretchen, but not only in the way had we originally thought. We will learn of her true role in all of this once I speak with Max. In the meantime she is not going to disappear on us. If she is not in New York, the chances are she will be in Rome. Just to be certain that she doesn’t travel to a country other than Italy, I have placed her on a watch list. Before she is allowed to board any commercial aircraft we will be alerted and I will make a determination if she is to be retained. If she was the person who alerted Max about the arrest order, then she is a potential asset to us within the Italian embassy. I still plan on having Vinnie work that angle.” Gretchen and Elizabeth exchanged glances and then they both looked at Vinnie who, head bowed, was discretely looking at his hands.

“Elizabeth, I’m certain you did not recall us to relate what we could have discussed by phone.”

“You are correct, Darlene. Let’s recap. Within hours, Max will be identified in Maine if he has not already been identified. They will trace him back to the safe house which is now closed. It will be turned upside down but our housekeeping crew sanitized it after Max alerted us. The bureau will run down the ownership and eventually they will penetrate our cover and learn that it belongs to us and therefore to Max. Once that connection is made, the bureau’s Deputy Director will be involved and he will call me at which time I will have to deal with it. Our only hope is that the bureau, in spite of their ambivalent feeling towards us, will understand what any intelligence organization has to go through to protect one of its agents. The local Chief of Police and the state police could issue an arrest warrant charging Max with murder. The bureau could stop that action if it is viewed as advantageous to them. There remains the Congress. If they get wind of this, Director Mallory is then involved which will escalate this to the highest level. This would not be good. Are you with me so far?"

Not receiving any response, she continues. "I have reason to believe that Khalid learned of Max's whereabouts in Maine through an intercepted call he made to Bettina Falaguerra from Maine." The group was shocked at Max's indiscretion.

"How the hell could Khalid pull that off? He doesn't possess the technology to do an intercept, nor do the countries he is associated with, namely, the Saudis or Iranians."

"You are correct, Vinnie, as far as you went. Unfortunately for us, Khalid has access to large amounts of dollars and a huge stockpile of opium. He traded some of both to FAPSI who monitored all of Max's incoming and outgoing calls both in Italy and in Maine."

It was Darlene who asked, "Who and what is FAPSI and why was Max calling Falaguerra from Maine?"

"FAPSI is a branch of the old KGB, now the FBS, and is charged with all out of country electronic surveillance. As to your second question, I believe that Falaguerra, in addition to being an informant, was also having an affair with Max. It is more than likely that she was a lover first and an informant second. Whatever the arrangement, it was discrete until the phone calls."

Silence, then, "I still do not understand why we are trying to save his ass. He broke the law in Italy, sent Khalid to a brutal regime for torturing, compromised the work of the embassy, undermined the work of the agency, broke communication silence and kills two thugs who never stood a chance against a skilled agent. And then he stood here while you sent me and Gretchen on a wild goose chase knowing all the while it was futile. I don't give a damn who he screws, but if his indiscretion ever compromises me, he will never get to do it a second time."

"Vinnie, why are you so unwilling to accept the reality of our agency having to send some suspects to other countries for enhanced interrogation? Its either that or we lose an opportunity to gather valuable information. You certainly used advanced interrogation techniques in Afghanistan."

"Darlene, I often needed the truth when in a fight and did what I needed to do. But, for the record, there is no such thing as enhanced interrogation. That is the politically correct terminology for torture. Am I against the concept of torture? Not at all, but if it has to be done, then let it be done by us. If we don't have the stomach for it or for its political cost, then don't engage in it. Max had no trouble killing two outclassed Serbs but couldn't bring himself to deal with Khalid. He exported him to Egypt. That is pure and simple cowardice."

"Enough. This is not helping." Elizabeth knew Vinnie was right. Max screwed up big time.

"If you expect me to pursue Khalid in order to stop him from killing Max then I am out of here. I signed the secrecy agreement and will never mention what has occurred to date. If you want me to find and kill Khalid because he is a direct threat to the United States, I will stay. It is your call."

"Nothing has changed since we brought you on board. You and Gretchen are assigned the task of killing Khalid. Once he is dead, there will be an interruption in any attempted repeat of 9/11 until his successor is chosen."

"Elizabeth, does that mean you do not want us to interrogate him?"

"Gretchen, that is exactly what I mean. Whatever there was to learn from him, we learned in Rome. Since enhanced interrogation is illegal, the justice department will be watching our every move. There is nothing more we will extract from him. He will die before he talks to us. Killing him is the best solution and it will make it clear to al-Qaeda that we are taking no prisoners."

Vinnie asked, "Where do we go from here?"

"Darlene is to return to Simsbury and take charge of the facility." Turning to Darlene, "You need to increase electronic surveillance now that we know Khalid is here. While we can assume he will use alternative means to communicate with al-Qaeda operatives in the United States, we must nevertheless be alert to all electronic communications."

"I'll call ahead and have the change made immediately. I'll leave as soon as you wish."

"The three of you will leave together. Gretchen and Vinnie will be heading to Florida but not before they have time in Connecticut to deal with personal matters. They may be on the road for some time. A car is waiting to take you to the plane. You'll be hitching a ride back to Bradley on a Bombardier Challenger 850, new to the fleet." Turning to Gretchen and Vinnie, "Call me in the morning and we will arrange transportation to Florida and discuss available assets. You get two days in Connecticut. That's it. Get a move on."

CHAPTER 60

THE BOMB

Ibraham arrived at the private plane area at the Palm Beach International Airport at five thirty in the evening as planned. Hafs Karzai was waiting. The Silver Eagle X650 had been fueled and ground checks completed. A flight plan was filed earlier with a Key West destination.

"Are we prepared to leave?"

"Once I complete the on-board check list, I will contact the tower for instructions. There is light traffic so we will be airborne within minutes. May I help you with the bag?"

Ibraham was carrying an over the shoulder bag. The way the shoulder strap pulled against his jacket indicated that the bag had some weight to it. "I can handle it."

"Then, let us get on board." With that, they climbed the stairs and Hafs activated the control that quietly lifted the stairs and placed the unit snugly into the fuselage. "Ibraham, you get to be a co-pilot today. Once you secure your bag come join me."

Once both were seated, Hafs instructed Ibraham on how to connect the seat belt system. Once done, he looked at the check list and began the process of completing each step. He worked carefully and thoroughly since his co-pilot was one in name only. Once he completed his work he contacted the tower, gave the tail number and was given instructions to proceed to runway fifteen.

The Silver Eagle X650 was second in line for take-off. Once the lead plane had released its brakes and hurled itself down the runway, Hafs moved ahead and made a left turn on to the runway. He engaged the brakes, steadily moved the throttle ahead and when he had sufficient power and the plane was vibrating from being held in check, he released the brakes and the two powerful engines propelled the Silver Eagle down the runway. Ibraham, who had never been in a flight cabin, was thrust back into his seat as nose of the plane lifted abruptly to the sky. The experience of flight from the pilot's seat was one of exhilaration. The expression on his face was one of wonder at the beauty of flight and grudging admiration for the capitalists who built this incredible machine. For a moment or two he caught himself wondering if capitalism was all bad. He quickly ripped the thought out of his mind but it lingered subliminally.

The Silver Eagle reached cruising speed within minutes and Hafs set a course for Key West. The aircraft performed perfectly, easily exceeding the published specifications. He knew that once the company gained a foothold within the private and corporate jet community, the Silver Eagle would outperform all competitors. It was a dream to fly and its advanced and creative avionics provided pilots with a great sense of security.

The flight would be uneventful and relatively short. Ibraham was enthralled by the aircraft and hardly spoke. Hafs knew from prior experience with those new to corporate aircraft that they were almost always quiet, thinking they would one day fly such a plane. His passenger may be a terrorist but in some ways no different than other men. Yes, he thought, Ibraham would like to own such a plane.

"How much does this aircraft cost?"

"This model is in the vicinity of five million five."

"Only for the rich."

"No, Ibraham, it is for the successful. Rich follows. Most men who can afford this aircraft have worked hard, made sacrifices, taken risks and made a lot of money for themselves and others. They are also very smart men who knew how to read market trends and play tough in a global market."

"You sound like you are one of them."

"Ibraham, I am one of them as are the others who have committed themselves to your goals. We are rich men running successful companies and who have been called to action. But, I would lie if I told you I will not miss the rewards of capitalism."

"Tonight you are called, but I worry that you and the others have adopted American values."

"Do not worry Ibraham. In our hearts we are Yemeni."

The Silver Eagle entered Key West airspace and Hafs was given landing instructions. The touchdown was smooth. He taxied toward the private plane area and, as he did so, Ibraham pointed out the plane that belonged to the charter service that flew Khalid and Marta earlier in the day. He had Hafs taxi the Silver Eagle to a tie down six or seven planes away. He wanted to be close enough to be able to approach Khalid's plane without raising a suspicion but not so close that Khalid could see them. After moving into the tie down spot the engines were silenced.

"It is still light. I suggest we find a rental car and go into town for dinner. We will return later this evening."

Ibraham was quiet during the drive. He was a worldly man, one who traveled the globe with Khalid and who enjoyed the best that Saudi money could buy. He was a terrorist by training but an ordinary man by birth. His conversation with Hafs about the aircraft, its cost and his comments about the rewards of hard work and risk taking created ambivalence in him. On one hand he was going to be witness to the birth of a Muslim country in America and, on the other hand, he knew that he was most often the smartest man in the room and could prosper as a capitalist. What did he have to show for his intelligence and commitment to Allah? Whether he was with Khalid as his chief of staff or succeeded him, Ibraham was a man with a price on his head. He was well known to American intelligence agencies, especially the CIA and its Deputy Director. Elizabeth English knew that it was Ibraham who negotiated with the Egyptians for Khalid's release. As Khalid's friend and chief of staff, it was he who arranged with the Russians for the electronic surveillance of Max Rietsema. Elizabeth knew a great deal about Ibraham. He is and would be a hunted man until the CIA eventually killed him. Once he murders his friend and shows his hand, Elizabeth English would then know he was in charge of al-Qaeda in the United States. The hunt for him would begin. He and Khalid had foiled her efforts in Egypt but she was not one to take a loss lightly. So beautiful and yet so committed to killing Khalid and Ibraham.

Following dinner, Ibraham and Hafs returned to the airport at nine fifteen. The airport, located in a remote end of the key, was mostly dark with only a few dim outdoor lights near the small terminal building. There were no lights in the area of the private planes. The tower was closed and incoming planes activated the landing lights. They parked the car in the small lot next to the planes. Ibraham decided that they would go first to their plane, openly use a flashlight and make a little noise to test whether or not there was a security person on duty.

A few minutes later, certain that there was no security, they approached Khalid's chartered plane. Hafs, assuming that they would have to get into the exterior baggage compartment, brought a set of small tools with which to pick the lock. Having been around aircraft for many years, he knew that aircraft storage locks were only a deterrent to entry and not designed to keep anyone out. Within minutes the door to the baggage compartment was opened. With only two passengers with overnight bags only, the pilot would store their bags in the cabin and not in the external baggage hole. That meant extra work.

Once the door was opened Ibraham unzipped his bag and removed what looked like a large cloth pouch. He opened the pouch and removed a metal container that measured six inches wide, ten inches long and four inches deep. From the way he handled the container, it appeared to weight between fifteen or twenty pounds. There was also a smaller device, the size of a TV remote control. That he placed in his pocket. He put the container on the ground, opened a small cover on the top and set a switch to the on position and then closed the cover.

Hafs had never seen such a device before but he knew that it was a remote controlled explosive. Ibraham took a coin out of his pocket and held it close to the bottom of the container. The coin was immediately was drawn to the container. He was pleased that the magnet was effective. The door to the compartment was small but Ibraham was able to crawl in. He then reached far into the compartment just behind the back wall of the cabin and held the container to the metal surface which immediately drew the device to it. Khalid then pulled on it to make certain it was secure. He smiled at his success. Even if the pilot used this compartment he would not see the device.

"Now, Hafs, let's get out of here and into town where we will spend the night."

"That was not the plan. You asked that I change the flight plan for a late night flight."

"A new plan was necessary. I originally thought I could acquire a device that we could set to detonate at a given time. I was not able to do so. Even if I had located such a device, I worried that Khalid would change his time of departure and the device would detonate while still on the ground. Instead, I planted a remote controlled device that is more accurate for our purpose. Khalid is scheduled to leave at ten a.m. He is always on time. When we get to the hotel, you can use the internet to file a revised departure time of ten fifteen a.m. We will be in the air within minutes of Khalid. Given the greater speed of the Silver Eagle you will quickly be within detonation range of his plane. Then I will do what we planned to do."

"The FAA has my tail number and will know we were in the air at the same time as Khalid. How do we explain our presence in Key West?"

"It is unlikely that anyone took note of the fact that there were two of us on the plane. You remained on board working the shut down checklist while I rented the car. There is no connection between you and me, none whatsoever. As far as the FAA is concerned, you are a private pilot accumulating air time. Once we return to town we will register at different hotels for the night. Given the crowds on the street earlier in the evening there is nothing to link the two of us. In the morning, I will get to the airport early and drop off the car, reducing the risk of bumping into Khalid. I'll take a cab back into town, have breakfast at the hotel alone and then take a cab and return to the airport. In the meantime, you will take a cab to the airport and go directly to the plane. You must avoid having Khalid see you."

"We are playing this very close. It is risky."

"Didn't you tell me earlier that those who take risks reap the rewards?"

"That was about business, not about murder."

"Whether you kill a person, an idea or a business venture, it is all the same. To the victors go the spoils. Now, let's get out of here."

CHAPTER 61

SILVER EAGLE DOWN

Khalid and Marta arrived by cab at nine forty five a.m. They were dropped off at the small parking lot and walked directly to the plane where the charter pilot was waiting. He had completed his check-list and was ready to contact the tower for instructions. When they approached, he met them and took the two overnight bags and walked up the stairs and into the plane. He placed the bags into the overhead bin. Khalid and Marta followed him into the plane and took seats opposite each other. The pilot raised the stairs and walked forward to the cabin, put on his head phones and contacted the tower. Within a minute he started the engines and began to taxi to runway fifteen. He was the only plane in line and was given permission to take off. The Cessna Citation roared down the runway and lifted its nose to the sky. The bright morning sun reflected off the white fuselage. Soon, they were out of sight of the airport.

Khalid's assassins watched the departure from the cockpit of their plane. They had arrived early to limit the risk of being seen. They were partially hunched down in the cabin when Khalid and Marta arrived. Hafs could listen to the charter pilot's conversation with the tower. Once the charter had been given clear-ance and took off, Hafs contacted the tower for his instructions. He was also directed to runway fifteen. With Ibraham in the right seat, Hafs powered the Silver Eagle X650 into the morning sky and set a course that would position him directly behind the chartered flight.

"Does the company own this plane?" It was Ibraham and his continued fascination with the aircraft.

"The Italian manufacturer owns the plane and as the North American distributor, we use it to demonstrate its capabilities to potential buyers. It is one of several models we maintain in Chicago. As CEO, I have authority to use this one for personal trips. It also gives me the opportunity to improve my own competencies with the plane. It helps when I demo it to a CEO. If I can fly it, they believe they can. The truth is they can fly a Silver Eagle if they have a good instructor and many hours in the air."

"Could I learn to fly this plane?"

"Of course. If you are willing to spend time in Chicago, I have two outstanding instructors who work with customers. If you are in a hurry to fly, you could learn on a single engine plane."

"I like this plane."

"You need to be a capitalist to be able to afford this aircraft."

"Al-Qaeda has money."

Afraid of where the conversation was going, Hafs changed the subject. "It is time to look for the charter. It is within ten miles or so given the departure times and our relative speeds."

They were quiet until Hafs spoke again. "If you look to our left at eleven o'clock you will see the charter. We will soon be within range for your remote to work."

"Let me know when we are within a half mile of them. I need to be within three thousand feet for the remote to be effective."

"Any closer and we could be hit with some of the debris. I will use caution and pray that Allah is watching over us."

At that very moment the charter with Khalid and Marta aboard initiated a sharp 180 degree turn and established a heading that brought it around to a heading directly back and parallel to the Silver Eagle, less than a half mile off its port side, and on a heading back to Key West.

It was Ibraham in the right seat who first saw the charter make its turn. "Hafs, what is happening? They have turned around."

"I have no idea. We are in no danger. They are well off our port side but we will be opposite each other in less than a minute."

Ibraham, stunned at the turn of events, was no longer thinking about the remote in his pocket. His immediate concern was Khalid's plane heading back towards Key West. He turned to Hafs. "What is happening? Why are they returning to Key West? Something is wrong." When he regained his composure and realized that if he didn't act now, Khalid would be out of his reach, he dug into his pocket and removed the remote. When the charter was directly opposite the Silver Eagle, Ibraham screamed, "Allah is great, Allah is great" and pressed the activate button on the remote.

No sooner had he uttered what were to be his last words on this planet but that his plane, the Silver Eagle X650, erupted in a ball of fire. It disintegrated as an explosive charge in its baggage compartment detonated and ripped the aircraft into hundreds of pieces of molten metal. The engines were torn from the fuselage and burning white hot as they fell into the sea. The wings were wrenched from the frame and dropped to the ocean where, when they made contact with the cold surface, sent up a cloud of white steam. The fuselage, separated from its body parts, was nothing more than a charred tube that twisted and turned as it fell from the heavens. Ibraham and Hafs were no longer of this life. Their bodies were incinerated.

"Hold on!" The pilot of the Citation called out to Khalid. The shock waves from the blast hit the charter like a hurricane. Both men were shaken in their seats and they heard Marta cry out from the main cabin. Then it was over as quickly as it began. The pilot, seeing the ball of fire, made a tight turn and watched the remnants of the Silver Eagle drop to the ocean. The pilot yelled, "Holy mother of God. What was that?" He immediately contacted the tower at Key West, reported what he saw, gave his location and volunteered to maintain surveillance of the area in the event there were any survivors. In his heart he knew there would be none. Khalid, sitting in the copilot seat of the Citation, expressed faked dismay at the explosion. "May Allah be kind to the survivors. I have never seen such an explosion. How did it happen?"

"Mr. Drew, I have never seen such an explosion myself. I have no idea what happened. The FAA will take over now. It is clear to me there are no survivors, but we will maintain our position until the Coast Guard in on the scene and then I will return you to Key West. We may be here an hour or more. It is good you decided to extend your holiday and return to Key

West otherwise we would never have witnessed the disaster."

"The poor pilot. We can only hope there were no passengers. What a terrible way to die."

The charter pilot spoke. "Whatever make of aircraft that was, all of the remaining ones in service will be grounded and subject to a thorough inspection until the FAA knows what caused the explosion. Given its heading it must have taken off from Key West."

"By the time we return to Key West, there will be some answers. If you do not mind, I will join Marta." Khalid then returned to the main cabin with a smile on his face. With the murder of Kafs and Ibraham, the other four men will do whatever is asked of them. The death of Kafs and Ghani now required that Khalid meet with the next in line at both companies.

Unknown to Ibraham and Hafs, Khalid was suspicious of his intended assassins when his driver, an al-Qaeda operative, saw Ibraham leave the hotel at mid-morning when he had been given specific instructions by Khalid to remain there in his absence in the event any emergency came up. When Ibraham hailed a cab, Khalid's driver called him while he was in the air headed for his short vacation in Key West with Marta. When the driver related what he had seen he was instructed to follow Ibraham and then call back. When Khalid learned that Ibraham had gone to the home of Abdu Karsam, he ordered the driver to follow Ibraham every minute and to assign a second operative if necessary. It was essential to know what he was up to.

Ibraham returned to the hotel and was not heard from or seen for two hours. All the while the driver remained in the lobby and the second operative watched the room. The driver observed with interest when a Muslim looking man approached the desk and asked to be connected with Ibraham Malik. Shortly thereafter Ibraham left his room. The operative used his cell phone to call the driver in the lobby. The driver stood where he could not be seen. In the meantime, the Muslim looking man went to the lounge. He was carrying an over the shoulder bag that had considerable weight. When Ibraham left the elevator he went to the lounge and joined the man. The driver ordered the second operative to enter the lounge and observe the two men since he was not known to Ibraham.

Khalid and the Muslim man ordered drinks and looked the part of two men conducting business. When the drinks arrived, the men clinked their glasses. Then in unison and quietly, "Thanks be to Allah."

They chatted briefly and then the Muslim got up, shook hands and left. Ibraham remained for another minute or two, finished his drink, picked up the bag that was left behind and walked to the elevator. The driver reported the incident to Khalid who immediately knew what was in the bag. He had carried many of them himself.

The surveillance continued all day but Ibraham did not leave his room until five o'clock. He took a cab to the airport and met Hafs. They boarded the Silver Eagle X650 and flew south to Key West. When Khalid received this message he finally understood what was happening. A betrayal was in the making.

Ibraham and Hafs were wrong in thinking that no one had seen them approach Khalid's plane in Key West. When they returned to the airport after having dinner on Duval Street, they were certain that it was safe to approach Khalid's chartered plane and to plant the explosive. Unknown to them Khalid was already there, deep in the shadows watching their every move. Once he understood what was in the bag, all the pieces fell into place. Ibraham was planning to betray him and assume leadership of al-Qaeda in American.

After Ibrahan and Hafs had placed the explosive in Khalid's plane they left the airport and returned to their hotels. They underestimated their target. Khalid waited until it was safe to move and then went to his plane, opened the baggage compartment and removed the device. He then went to Ibraham's silver Eagle and placed the device in the exterior baggage compartment. Little did Ibraham suspect that when he depressed the button on the remote he would be committing suicide, not murder.

While Khalid's charter plane was flying a slow continuous circle over the area of the explosion awaiting the Coast Guard, it was Marta in the main cabin who spoke to Khalid. "I am surprised that you want to spend another day in Key West. We had planned on leaving Florida tomorrow."

"With your leaving for Paris I wanted another day to play with you. It will be too long until we are together again."

"Then we will play all day and night. Perhaps you will allow me time for dinner. When a girl works hard she needs nourishment." With that she rested her head on his shoulder and day dreamed about Paris and who she might risk playing with there. Khalid, on the other hand, reviewed his brilliant move in transferring the remote explosive from one plane to another and having Ibraham blow himself up along with his co-conspirator. Looking out of the cabin window and down on the ocean strewn with debris from the explosion, he suddenly had a feeling of despondency when he thought about a friend from childhood betraying him and he, in turn, having to kill him. There was silence for the remainder of the return trip to Key West.

CHAPTER 62

TIME OUT

The backlog of phone calls to be returned was numerous enough to occupy Elizabeth until early afternoon. With Max arriving at four, she needed what time remained to review what she knew about the relationship between Max and Bettina Falaguerra and the relationship between Carlton and Gisela Rudenschroeder. Max couldn't have done more to compromise himself if he had established it as a priority. The question for Elizabeth was whether Carlton inadvertently played a role in revealing damaging information about Max that led to the German intelligence apparatus taking an interest in him. While she was reluctant to admit it, Elizabeth believed that Bettina Falaguerra was actually a friend of the CIA as witnessed by her alerting Max of the impending arrest warrant to be issued by the magistrate's office in Rome. Gisela Rudenschroeder, on the other hand, was a covert agent working for the Bundesnachrichdienst. Falaguerra provided information while Rudenschroeder acquired information. One a friend, one a spy. Both beautiful and both able to entice men into their arms and draw then into their bodies. Two men, one who is currently in charge of a major intelligence operation in Italy and one who previously had been in charge. Both men had violated their trust; Max with

Elizabeth and Carlton with the Director. Changes had to be made.

She walked to one of the many windows in her office that looked out onto the countryside. Rarely did she stop to enjoy the beauty that unfolded outside the building, outside her windows. The pace of her job and the time it required to stay on top of intelligence issues around the world provided her with little opportunities to enjoy life. The many covert operations underway at any one time and for which she was responsible often drained her of physical and emotional energy as she worried about the safe return of her agents, many of whom she knew personally. Her days blended into night and professional time washed over personal time like a tsunami.

The pressures were constant with the drum beat of Congress and its anti CIA bias always present. While the Director fielded the political criticism Elizabeth, as operations officer, was held accountable for failed or botched operations. Every day of the year she mounted covert operations around the world in places both friendly and hostile. Out of the public eye and beyond the reach of the media, her covert agents risked their lives so the general population could sleep soundly at night. The agency, while vilified for conducting enhanced interrogations, has witnessed its own agents captured, tortured and killed in ways that made enhanced interrogation the equivalent of fraternity paddling. And still the constant criticism.

She checked her watch and realized that Max would soon be with her. It was important to maintain her composure with him. She alerted herself to the fact she was feeling depressed and must not signal that to Max. He had the right to state his case in a fair environment. She knew him as a co-worker and as a lover. There were moments years ago when she thought of marriage but she forfeited that dream for promotions within the agency, eventually being named Deputy Director for Operations. The love she felt for him now was that which you carry for a friend of many years. She whispered every so quietly to herself, "Christ, Max, why, why, why?"

Giving up Max was not easy and she tried to fill the void with other men who admired her for her beauty and for her position as Deputy Director which could open many doors for ambitious lovers. Now, as she waited for Max, she mentally sorted through her many casual liaisons and the three serious ones. She concluded that none fulfilled her. Sexually, most were adequate playmates but none stirred her to passion. They all worked from the same playbook with nothing new or exciting offered to her. As she reflected on those who worked hard at pleasing her it was obvious during their initial engagement that they would not be adequate mates over the long run. Each temporarily filled a void in her life. The man she believes is able to satisfy her innermost sexual desires is a man she is about to send on a life threatening mission. One day Vinnie would be hers.

She was interrupted by the intercom. "Boss, Max is here. Is now a good time?"

"Send him in."

She rose from her chair, straightened the creases in her suit and adjusted the jacket. With her hands she fluffed her short hairdo and walked to the door to offer a cordial welcome to Max. The door opened and he entered. Max looked stunning to Elizabeth. His complexion was that of a physically fit man and his expensive, tailor made, blue pin striped, single breasted suit showed off his beautiful athletic body. It was complimented with a white silk shirt and dark blue silk tie. His shoes were black and Italian made. His hair was rakishly long but neatly trimmed.

Each had given thought as to how they would greet each other. Would they reach for a little hug and a peck? Or, would they shake hands as befitting a business meeting? Perhaps a nod, a smile and no physical contact? What takes precedent, love or business? Max made it easy by extending his hand which Elizabeth graciously took.

"Hello, Elizabeth."

"Max. Come and take a seat." With that they sat in lounge chairs away from the desk and facing each other. "I want you to know that this conversation is being audio and video recorded. If you have an objection, please say so now in which case we will defer the meeting until you can get counsel."

"Why the recordings? I'm an employee not a suspect in a crime."

"It is true you are an employee. However, you have breached your confidentiality contract with the agency, have withheld valuable information and may have committed a double murder. While there are other issues, those will suffice. If you fail to be truthful I want it on record. Now, let's begin."

Although clearly shaken by her comments, Max took the initiative by asking, "What exactly do you want to know?"

"Everything you failed to tell me or the others at the mansion. So why don't you begin with Bettina Falaguerra?"

"What does she have to do with this?"

"That is what you are going to tell me, Max."

"If anything we, or I, owe her a debt of gratitude. She is the informant who alerted me to the arrest warrants issued for me and my team. If it wasn't for her we would all be in Italian custody. As it were I was able to contact the agency. In turn you made our extraction possible."

"She is your lover." It was a statement not a question.

He did not hesitate to respond. "Yes, she is my lover. I met her two years ago and one thing led to another."

"Would you like to respond to the damaging call to her that you carelessly failed to remove from your cell phone?"

"It was stupid of me. I had no idea that I was under electronic surveillance. I felt I owed her an explanation. I would never have made it to Maine without her help in Italy. She put herself in a compromising situation with her embassy and would have been demoted if it learned she had warned me about the magistrate's arrest warrant. I owed her something. Elizabeth, to this day I have no idea who was tracking my calls. While Khalid wants me dead, he does not have the capability to monitor my calls in a foreign country."

"That is true but he does have an ample supply of money and drugs to buy such a service."

With surprise, "Is that what he did?"

She did not answer. Instead, "Tell me about your stay at the safe house. You were there three weeks. What was a typical day?"

"I would rise early, exercise vigorously for an hour or more, take a shower, walk to town, have breakfast at a local diner, buy the Bangor paper and the New

York Times and walk back to the condo. I'd bring a fresh cup of coffee with me, read the papers and then take a long walk in the hills or climb one of the minor mountains in the area. On three different occasions, I climbed Mt. Katahdin."

"How about the rest of the day and night?"

"Often my hikes and climbs were long. As a result I wouldn't return until late afternoon or early evening. For dinner I would drive to one of the neighboring towns to find a restaurant. It's a recreation area so there was no problem with locating them. In the evening I would watch TV. It was a boring existence waiting for a call from the agency."

She let the last comment pass since he really meant a call from her. "Who did you talk to or meet while there?"

"I would occasionally chat with someone in a restaurant when eating out. There was no one person in particular."

"How about waitresses or waiters?"

"There were only waitresses at the diner and not many waiters in the restaurants. I had no continuing contact with any of them."

"Did you meet any women, especially foreign women, who showed an interest in you and who may have been connected to the Serbs?"

"In fact I did. On two occasions, I met four American women all of whom were vacationing together. All worked as traders on Wall Street with the same firm. Hard to believe they would be connected to the Serbs."

"And?"

"And nothing.

"By choice or lack of opportunity?"

"Not for lack of opportunity."

"What about on your hikes and climbs? Did you meet anyone?"

"I spoke with a number of hikers and climbers. They are generally friendly folks. It is especially true of those who climb the big ones like Katahdin where you run the risk of bad weather or accidents. There is a camaraderie you don't experience in most other recreational endeavors."

"On the day you had the encounter with the Serbs did you meet and talk to a family with a teenage daughter?"

"Yes. Why do you ask?"

"Tell me about it."

"Mother, father, son and daughter. They looked like Barbie and Ken and two offspring. Nice folks. Had the best of gear, looked wealthy, friendly and turned out to be good climbers. Saw them briefly at the outset and then passed them on the way down. They were still moving up to the summit. When I left they had not yet returned to the trail head. Nothing more."

"Anyone else?"

"Yes. There was a husband and wife team. Excellent climbers, very strong and very experienced. Spoke briefly with them. I also met them at the outset while everyone was getting their gear ready."

"Do you know Gisela Rudenschroeder?"

"Never heard of her."

"Did you have any contact with Carlton Richardson either before or during your extraction?"

"None whatsoever. Where are you going with this, Elizabeth?"

"Later. The two Serbs followed you to Katahdin. Did you know they were going to be there or that they were tracking you?"

"So that is why you mentioned murder. You think that I knew they were after me and that I lured them to Katahdin to kill them. If that is where you are coming from you are wrong."

He hesitated and then continued. "I knew nothing about them until they showed up at the trail head. From that moment on, it was me or them. Let's get serious. It was not going to be a school yard tussle. This was an attempted assassination. You would have done the same as I did. The only difference would have been a different choice of weapon."

"Perhaps so."

"Elizabeth, how did the Serbs find me?"

"Khalid paid an arm of the Russian FSB to monitor all of your calls and those of Bettina Falaguerra. Once you made the call from Maine, they began tracking you."

"What happens now? How serious is this?"

"The climbers you met, the family and the couple, gave descriptions of you to the FBI. The agency has completed a composite and it is to be distributed throughout Maine as early as today. The local Chief of Police and the Captain of the state police are convinced that you will easily be identified. The six climbers on Katahdin all gave comparable descriptions. The bureau is very good at detective work. In short order they will put a name to the composite and then our troubles mount. I plan on talking to the Director tomorrow following a meeting that may have some bearing on the situation. Following that, if he approves, I will call the Deputy Director of the bureau and admit the composite is of you and explain exactly what happened at Baxter State Park. One major goal is to keep the Congress from finding out. You are on their hit list and this could kill your career."

"Jesus, I made one phone call, one mistake."

"No, Max. You made two mistakes that led to many problems. Without authority, you sent Khalid to Egypt. In addition to wanting to kill you, he is now in the United States preparing another 9/11."

"I can find him. You know I can."

"Too late for that. Don't be surprised if the Director asks for your resignation tomorrow. I will do my best to protect you but this could be out of my hands. In the meantime I want you out of Washington. Until I have a better understanding of how this will play out you are going to join Darlene at the Simsbury facility."

"Please, Elizabeth, let me loose to go after Khalid. I know him, I know how he thinks."

"Gretchen and Vinnie have been given authority to kill Khalid. You are out of it. I want you in Simsbury tomorrow. No excuses."

With anger in his voice, "So the new guy gets the assignment and the girl. That is bullshit. This assignment is mine."

"Your new guy is a battle hardened hero. You are making a mistake seeing him as competition. Right now he is the only person in the agency who can save your ass. Please remember that it was you who sent Khalid to Egypt and it was you who failed to send competent agents with him to see to it that the Egyptians played it straight. Instead, you were too engaged fucking Falaguerra. Khalid buys his way out and you initiated a call from Maine that has created multiple problems for the agency. Your unprofessional conduct may cost me and the Director our jobs and give Khalid an open field to rain more horror down on the country. My suggestion to you is to quietly leave this office now and head for Simsbury before I decide to fire you myself."

Without another word Max stood and left the office closing the door softly as he left. Elizabeth rose from her chair and went to the window. Her eyes were moist with sorrow for a man she once loved and still cared about.

CHAPTER 63

GOING ROGUE

The Bombardier Challenger 850 made a final turn on its approach to Bradley International in Windsor Locks, Connecticut. It dropped altitude slowly over the Farmington Valley, applied flaps, made a final adjustment over Suffield and glided smoothly into its final approach. There was a small jolt and squeal as the tires made contact with the runway. The pilot applied brakes, reversed the engine thrust, and as the aircraft slowed, he turned off the runway and taxied to the private plane parking area. While it seemed like weeks since the three passengers had left for Virginia, it had been only a matter of days.

The three passengers harbored different thoughts as the plane came to a halt. Vinnie was juggling his relationship with Sharon, his distaste for Max and the mission ahead. Gretchen was worried for Max, anxious to work with Vinnie to kill Khalid and wondered how Darlene was taking her being assigned to Simsbury rather than joining forces with Vinnie and Gretchen. Darlene worried about Max and was upset that Vinnie had little use for him. They all knew that it was early in the game and things could change. They did not anticipate just how soon and dramatically it would happen.

Darlene's phone rang and she picked it up, listened to the caller for exactly two minutes and fifteen seconds and then the caller hung up. She held the phone in her hand and stared straight ahead. Gretchen asked, "What is it Darlene. What's wrong?"

"The meeting with Max did not go well. He has been assigned to Simsbury until Elizabeth speaks with the Director tomorrow following a conversation with Carlton Richardson who has been ordered to be on the first available flight from Rome tonight. "

"What does Richardson have to do with Max's situation?"

"I have no idea, Gretchen. Rest assured that Elizabeth would not recall Carlton if it was not important. Max's job is in jeopardy."

"He won't report to Simsbury."

They both stared at him. "Vinnie, what are you talking about?"

"Max will go rogue. He screwed up and now he is going to do what he should have done in the first place. He is going to prove his worth by pursuing Khalid by himself. Finally, he is making sense."

"I can't believe he would do this to Elizabeth. This could compromise her."

"Darlene. She doesn't realize it yet but his going rogue allows her to deny access to him by any Congressman or any other of his enemies, including the Italians. All she has to do is tell everyone he is on a special assignment and not available."

Gretchen spoke up. "You're certain he's gone rogue because that is exactly what you would have done, isn't it?"

"Not just me. Most guys in Max's position with something to prove would do it. "

"Damn macho men."

"No need for us to get angry with one another, Gretchen. I can picture you and Darlene doing the same thing. In addition to our being a team of two at the moment, very shortly we are going to be a team of four."

"What the hell are you talking about?"

"Darlene, if you were Max and given the current circumstances who would you turn to for help?"

Without hesitation, "Me and Gretchen. The three of us have worked together on covert operations. "

"And I make four."

"I thought you could not stand him."

"That was before. Now, he is doing the right thing and we need to support him, but only if he works with us. Whatever we do, we must protect Elizabeth. She has to have deniability if pressed by the Director."

"And what about me? I have the facility to run."

"Darlene, for the record, you will run the facility but in fact you can assign it to Louise Wilson. She is ready and capable. Make up some story for your absences and make certain she does not tell Elizabeth what is going on. The fact is we both need to get back into the field. We have done all we can do in setting up the facility."

"It's Monday. Gretchen, we are expected to be back at Langley no later than Wednesday. Can you arrange a flight?"

"I'll make arrangements. Plan on a noon flight on Wednesday. By then you will have to notify Elizabeth that Max is a no show. My guess is that he made contingency plans as soon as he was extracted from Italy."

"Knowing Max, he made plans long before that. I have no doubt he has a safe house and has stashed both cash and weapons. If Vinnie is correct he will contact you or me." It was Darlene.

She continued, "When he does it may not seem at first that it is him. We need to stay alert since I doubt he will use a phone or e-mail. Whatever he does will be risky since he cannot use a third person. If I were Elizabeth I would put a watch on me and Gretchen since she knows how close we have been to Max over the years. Since we have no evidence that he is going rogue, there is no reason to say anything to Elizabeth just yet. I will call her if he does not meet me at the facility by Wednesday morning. That gives him ample time to go deep until he needs to surface. If I had to guess I say that he contacts us before I report him missing. "

Vinnie suggested that they arrange for a ride home. All three lived in West Hartford. "It is time to deal with personal business."

With that, Gretchen looked at him in a questioning way, then at Darlene and asked, "Shouldn't we meet before Wednesday?" She wanted Vinnie before then.

"If you are leaving at noon why not get here around eleven and we can do some planning before you depart."

Vinnie did not want to meet with Gretchen before Wednesday. "That sounds good to me. How about you, Gretchen?"

In a disappointed voice, "Fine. Wednesday at eleven it is."

Vinnie was the first to be dropped off. With the hectic pace of the past few days the condo was a welcome haven. He dropped his overnight and went to the liquor cabinet and poured a healthy portion of bourbon, then went to the refrigerator and reached into the freezer compartment for ice. It was late afternoon and he just had time to call Sharon before she left work.

"Global Insurance, Sharon Speaking. Hello stranger."

"Hi. I see you have caller I.D."

"Just in case I am harassed by big strong men who want to torture me."

"I know just the guy. He is available for dinner if you are."

"Pick me up at seven thirty."

"Great. Any special place?"

"It is a week night and foot traffic will be light. We can get into any restaurant. Why don't we walk around LaSalle Street and Blue Back Square and then make a decision?"

"Sounds perfect. See you later."

"Casual dress."

He was at her door at seven thirty five and anxious to see her although apprehensive. She opened the door, he stepped in and they embraced. When they released each other, they kissed lightly and looked lovingly at each other. "I am happy to see you safe and sound, Vinnie."

"And I am still awed by you. You are lovely."

"Before you have a chance to retract that statement, let's go. I am starved."

They spent the better part of an hour walking in Blue Back Square, window shopping, looking at pedestrians, holding hands, occasionally locked arm in arm. "Time for a decision. Where do we eat?"

"Where we had our first date. Back to LaSalle Street and Leon's."

She did not press him for information as much as she wanted to. When he was ready to tell her what he had been up to, he would. Same as the first time they had dinner at Leon's, they were the two most beautiful people in the restaurant. Other customers stared. They passed on dessert, he paid the check and they walked back to the car and he drove her home.

Once in the condo he poured them after dinner drinks and then settled on the couch. They touched glasses and sipped their drinks. "I am going to submit my letter of resignation tomorrow. I wanted you to be the first to know. I'll give the company a two week notice but will do that by using vacation time. I need to be in Washington on Wednesday of this week."

"I knew you would be leaving and I know you are not able to tell me what you will be doing. Vinnie, I know you well enough to understand that whatever it is you will be engaged in will be important to the country. I admire you for that. Throughout your life you will always be a hero to someone or some cause. You are a very capable man who can take care of himself and demonstrated that in Iraq and Afghanistan and in the parking garage. Yet, why do I have the feeling that what you are about to do is far more dangerous?"

"It is not more dangerous, just different."

"Will you be alone?"

"Occasionally, but most of the time with a partner. There is the possibility two others will be joining us. What you need to know is that it will require travel for an undefined period. I'll know more Wednesday, but I believe I will be working out of the Washington area which means I will not be back in West Hartford until the project is completed."

Tears swelled in her eyes but she did not cry. "Vinnie, I want you with me until Wednesday. I'll call in and take two vacation days. Before I lose you I would like you to take me to bed. I need you around me, on me and in me. I want as much love as you can give."

Meanwhile Darlene, charged now with running the Simsbury facility, went to her office after she left her things at the condo. She had work to do and assignments to give. On one hand she wanted Max to be there in the morning but on the other hand she wanted him to find Khalid and restore his credibility with Elizabeth.

Gretchen believed that Vinnie was in Sharon's bed and resented it. Their lovemaking was fabulous in New York and she wanted more, as much as he could give. She was more experienced than Vinnie and could offer more than Sharon. There was much she could teach him. Tonight was lost on that account. She opened her bedroom closet and located against the back wall was a gun cabinet. She unlocked it and took out the Glock 22, a .40 caliber weapon with a 15 round cartridge. It felt good in her hand being the correct weight and balance. It was her first choice of a weapon. Then she reached in and took out a Sig 226. It was a 9 x 19 mm with a parabellum load. It was her back-up choice. She reached in and removed a pistol gun case and placed both weapons inside, adding several boxes of ammunition. She closed the lid and headed for her car. If she wasn't going to fuck Vinnie tonight, she decided to take out her frustration on the firing range. For the past year she frequented a private range in Bristol. It was a modern facility and there was always the chance that a surrogate Vinnie might be playing with his gun and looking to shoot someone. She might be an easy target tonight.

Sharon was tucked into the folds of Vinnie's naked body. He was sound asleep, exhausted from a night of lovemaking. She was in and out of sleep, needing the rest but wanting to enjoy looking at him, praying he would be safe in his secret mission. Theirs had been a whirlwind affair with her being swept off her feet by him. The thought of losing him was more than she could bear.

The quiet of the early morning dawn was broken by the sound of the doorbell. She quickly rose from bed unable at first to recognize the sound or where it was coming from. A quick second later Vinnie was out of bed and pulling on his pants. "It's the doorbell. Stay here. I'll be back." With that he made his way down the stairs. The first light of day could be seen through the small window panels at the top of the door but they were too high to see who was at the door. Having no weapon, he went to the kitchen and grabbed a six inch chef's knife and returned to the door. It wasn't a USMC KABAR that he used as a Seal, but it would do. The bell rang again. He looked through the security peep hole, opened the door and the man stepped inside.

"Didn't expect you until later this morning. How did you get to Connecticut and how did you know to look here? And, why here and not at my place?"

"As soon as Elizabeth threw me out of her office, I rented a car and drove through the night. I knew it would be safer and I could easily shake off a tail. As to why here and not at your place, I figured that this would be the fourth place they would look for me after checking in with Gretchen, Darlene and then you. How did I find you here with Ms. Rizzo? Let's just say it is the wonder of technology and the ease by which one can infiltrate phone company records."

"The three of us decided that you are not to be reported as missing by Darlene until tomorrow noon. Once that report is made a full press will be initiated by Elizabeth to find you and bring you in."

"There is no way they will bring me in until I am ready. I won't be ready until Khalid is dead."

"We figured you made plans many years ago to have your private safe house, maybe two and that you have cash and weapons stashed. I assume you have at least one other identity available."

"Correct on all counts. The safe houses are not close by and I need to be near Darlene since she will be my contact with you and Gretchen."

"Vinnie, is everything all right? I hear voices." Sharon was standing at the top of the stairs wrapped in a salmon colored, knee length silk robe. She wore nothing underneath.

"Sharon, come on down and meet a colleague."

As she walked down the stairs, Vinnie wondered how she could look so beautiful this early in the morning. Max, who had been without a woman since he fled Italy weeks ago, could only stare at this lovely person. Back at the mansion in Virginia he overheard Gretchen and Darlene discussing her by name. They wondered if she would complicate their recruiting of Vinnie. He could understand the difficult choice Vinnie had in leaving her to work for Elizabeth. "Sharon, I want you to meet Max." She extended her hand and he took it gently in his, held it longer than necessary and smiled. "Hello. Sorry to bust in like this."

"Not a problem. I'll let you two talk while I make us breakfast, that is if Vinnie lets me have my knife back." She took the knife and left for the kitchen.

"She is stunning. I hope you know what you are doing giving her up for the agency."

"I'm hoping to have both."

"Not likely, but the best of luck."

"You started to say you needed to be near Darlene. Given how professionally close the three of you are, Elizabeth is bound to put a watch on all of you. She'll also include me and Sharon."

"Vinnie, what you need to know about the boss is that she really is the smartest person in the room. She never shows her full hand. While our covert operation is a layer that even the Director does not know about, the fact is she has many layers of covert operations that are known only to her. She is a genius. Sooner or later she will find me. I need to move quickly and will need a place to hole up in when I need it. Any ideas?"

"I do. On the northern border near the Massachusetts line near the small rural town of Holland, I have a winterized cottage on a lake. It is less than an hour's drive from Simsbury, even closer to West Hartford where Darlene lives. I purchased it with accumulated combat pay when I retired a year ago. Not fancy, but it will do. Unfortunately, it is in my name so sooner or later it will be discovered. In the meantime it is yours to use. It is sufficiently secluded so your coming and going will not be noticed."

"Sounds perfect. Give me directions and I will be on my way."

"First, Breakfast."

They ate but did not discuss the agency or what Vinnie and Max were up to. It was best that Sharon not be party to this affair. She frequently looked inquisitively at Max and he often looked at her longingly. Vinnie wrote the directions to the cottage and Max was ready to leave but not without first thanking Sharon. "Thanks for breakfast and sorry for the interruption."

"It was nice to meet you Max." Then, looking directly into his eyes, she smiled and added with a sense of concern, "Be safe."

Looking at her and leaving the comfort of this home made him realize how shallow his life was without a woman like Sharon to share it. He told Vinnie he would see him soon and left.

Once he was out of the house, Sharon looked at Vinnie. "I won't ask what you are up to but I just met a mirror image of you."

"Meaning?"

"He is adorable, sexy, dangerous and has the moves of what I think of as a special forces guy like someone I know. He is an absolute hunk. Together, you will spell trouble for someone."

"That is the idea. Now, I need to shower and get to Global and submit my letter of resignation."

"Why the rush?"

"True, why the rush?" They climbed the stairs to Sharon's bedroom.

CHAPTER 64

CENTRAL CASTING

The Director of the Central Intelligence Agency did not come from central casting. He was five foot eight inches tall and weighed in at one hundred eighty five pounds. To suggest he was stocky would be kind. His body had the shape of a block. He was overweight, drank heavily and smoked frequently. His clothes were off the rack and hung limply on his frame. Both his hands and head were oversized for his height. While eastern European by birth, his complexion was pale, giving the impression he was not well. His hair, what little there was of it, was black and combed straight back. His thick bushy eyebrows and deep set eyes served to make you uneasy in his presence. When he spoke, the deep baritone of his voice, delivered in an almost inaudible level, caused his visitors to be unusually quiet and to listen carefully to what he had to say. If Elizabeth was the smartest woman in the room, the Director was the smartest person in the room.

Anthony Mallory graduated from a lighthouse public high school in Massachusetts. It was then that he knew he was unlike most high school students. He breezed through his courses, especially languages, literature, music and mathematics. Already showing indications of being overweight, he used his physical strength to excel at wrestling and football. He was the class valedictorian and had offers from many ivy leagues colleges and universities.

Both of his parents were college professors. His mother came from a wealthy family. Money was not a problem. Being an only child, dinner table conversation was adult and stimulating. They opened his eyes to the many changes taking place around the world, politically, economically and militarily. At age seventeen he chose, with his parent's support and encouragement, to defer college and travel to as many foreign countries as was possible in two years. He promised his parents he would accept a delayed admission offer from Yale when he returned.

He left home following his high school graduation and did the usual youthful grand tour of Europe and after several months realized that he had seen enough of art, cathedrals and museums. Thinking about the conversations he had with his parents and their interest in the Middle East, he decided to experience for himself the changes taking place. For the next eighteen months he traveled to Israel, Jordan, Lebanon, Syria, Libya, Iran, Iraq, Saudi Arabia, Pakistan and Afghanistan. The seventeen year old boy returned home a nineteen year old wise man. He entered Yale and majored in Middle East Studies. It was while at Yale, a school with historical ties to the CIA, that he was recruited. Between his brilliant mind and his strong body he excelled at everything during the training cycle. It was exactly twenty six years from the month he graduated from high school to the month he was confirmed as Director of the Central Intelligence Agency. At age forty three, he was the youngest Director ever confirmed for the position and surely the most brilliant. No Director looked less the part.

No other Director ever had a wife as beautiful as Randy Mallory, also a Yale graduate.

Anthony Mallory's secretary told Elizabeth to go right in. The Director was ready for her. She entered. "Hello Elizabeth. Make yourself comfortable."

"I know how busy you are so I'll get right to the point. This concerns Max Rietsema." For the next twenty minutes she touched on the highlights of the case and ended her comments with her meeting with Max the day before.

"Do you believe Max was an assassination target?"

"Initially I had doubts. After my conversation with Alexei Dmitri, I am convinced that Khalid hired the Serbs to kill Max. He did what he was trained to do when in a life threatening situation. If we believe Khalid is focused on killing Max it is nothing compared to Max's need to hunt down and kill Khalid. He is further upset because I have not assigned him that task."

"Who did you assign?"

"Gretchen and the new hire, a former recruit of ours, a decorated Seal and a hero from Iraq and Afghanistan. He is about the best recruit I have seen in years, maybe ever. If anyone can find Khalid, he will."

"What about Max?"

"I need to keep him out of the way a bit longer. He has been assigned to work with Darlene on routine matters. He is to report to her tomorrow. Between the two of us, I have my doubts about his reporting. Max is one of the best agents the agency has ever had. His skill set is hard to match. If he were to leave or be dismissed, it would be a great loss. He sees Vinnie Pagano as competition, not just for finding Khalid, but also with the women. Given what has happened to his career as a result of the Rome affair, Max believes he has to find Khalid to redeem himself to me."

She waited to see if Anthony Mallory had some words of wisdom. "Would you like a second opinion?"

"Not only would I like your opinion, I need it"

"Max did to Khalid what he should not have done but what he believed had to be done. Most of us would have done likewise although we would not say that publicly. All of us have done something in this business that calls for redemption. So it is with Max. He's a proud man, Elizabeth, and I believe he will go rogue rather than be chained to a desk job at the monitoring facility in Simsbury. If that occurs, I suggest you make but a modest effort to bring him in. Let him and the others believe you want him when in fact it is best if we let him attempt to locate Khalid and kill him."

"What about Gretchen and Pagano?"

"Gretchen has proven that she is one of the best trackers we have. If the new guy is as good as you believe, together they will get to Khalid first. In the meantime Max will more than likely team up with Darlene and, behind our backs, go on the hunt for Khalid. Elizabeth, we will have two teams, four top agents on the hunt. Damn, but it sounds like a move script." He was pleased with himself.

"I'll buy that, Anthony. Now, I have to deal with Jordan Rich. I need to convince him to abort the bureau investigation before Max's composite is distributed to all agencies. If it gets out that the bureau is about to apprehend an agency agent the Congress will be all over us. There will be one kangaroo hearing after another."

"Do you want me involved?"

"Only if Rich insists on going forward."

"What is your rationale going to be?"

"Simple. Neither the bureau nor the agency can stand by and allow assassination attempts on our agents. Regardless of our inter-agency rivalry we need to protect our men and women in the field. I will owe him big if he agrees but I can live with that."

"Call if you need me."

"One other thing before I leave. Ellen got a call from the Department of Justice. They were making inquiries about Max. As she put it, they were looking for an update on him and left the impression that, sooner or later, they will go on the hunt for him. I'll stay on top of this one."

"They would like nothing better than to have a public hanging. Let me know if you need any resources."

"Thanks, Anthony. Give Randy my best."

She returned to her office and asked Ellen to get Jordan Rich on the phone. Five minutes later he returned the call. "Hello Elizabeth, nice to hear from you. It has been a long time."

"Hello Jordan. Thanks for getting back to me. I need to talk to you."

"I'm listening."

"I need to see you in person."

He did not press her. "I'm free from five to seven today if that works for you. How about meeting in the lounge at the Dickenson House?"

"I'll be there at five thirty." She hung up and dialed Ellen. "Have we heard anything from Max?"

"Nothing."

"Make a note to call Darlene tomorrow and see if Max has reported. I need a car at five fifteen." She hung up.

Jordan was waiting for her when she arrived. The lounge had several patrons so they took a booth in a far corner away from the bar. She ordered a dry martini and he ordered a scotch on the rocks. "This must be important, Elizabeth, for you to meet off campus."

"Jordan, it is important. I am going to share information related to an incident your Bangor, Maine field office is working on. In fact, I'm going to ask your help in protecting one of my agents who was the target of an assassination attempt in Baxter State Park in Maine. Your Bangor field office was called into action when a park ranger found what he thought was evidence of a crime. The ranger talked to the current Chief of Police and one thing led to another and resulted in a search of the woods near the parking lot where a body was discovered. The body was one of two that our agent killed when his life was threatened." She hesitated to think how she would proceed.

"I'm listening. Please go on."

"You're aware of the incident in Rome when Abdu Khalid was apprehended by our agents and sent to Egypt for enhanced interrogation?"

"It would be difficult not to know about it given the publicity. As I recall, the Italians still have arrest warrants out for your agents with emphasis on finding your former chief of station, Max Rietsema."

"You remembered his name. How so?"

"His notoriety is world-wide within the intelligence community, especially in the Middle East. I'm sure that Khalid is not the only terrorist who wants your guy dead."

"Jordan, Khalid contracted with the Russians to have Rietsema assassinated by two Serbs. Through electronic eavesdropping they learned of his location in Maine where I had him secured in a safe house. Again, it was accomplished through the Russians."

"How do you know it was the Russians?"

"From a high level contact I maintain from my time in Russia."

"Are you telling me that it is Max Rietsema my men are looking for in connection with the Baxter State Park incident?"

"I am. Your team, led by Stuart McDonald, managed to create an accurate composite of Max and it is being distributed to law enforcement agencies in Maine. If that doesn't yield what they need, I believe the standard procedure at the bureau is to distribute it internally in your organization. If that doesn't work it goes to all other agencies including mine. I cannot let that happen."

"Elizabeth, do you understand what you are asking? You want me to shut down an investigation? What aren't you telling me?"

"I'm telling you what I know. Max killed both assassins. He had no option if he wanted to live. The local police found one body. There was a second one that I had removed along with the car used by the assassins. The body and the car have been disposed of. I had no choice."

"You want me to shut down an investigation in which two men were killed, evidence removed and destroyed and the killer is wanted by the Italian authorities?"

"Jordan, you are in charge of hundreds of covert agents in the field. You were out there at one time. Put yourself in the role of one of your agents who makes an operational decision he or she believes is correct and does so because administrators like you and I gave them the authority to make field decisions in the best interest of the mission. The decision leads to a contract being put on his life and two assassins are dispatched by an enemy of yours to kill the agent. Your agent knows that running away from his assailants is futile since they will only continue the chase. It will never end until he is dead or he deals with them. The choices are either running or doing what they have been trained to do. You and I have the luxury of second guessing our agents who make decisions on the run or during a firefight. We are experienced field agents and know that if we do not protect agents who do the right thing, then there is no way we can depend upon each other for our lives. Both of us take a lot of crap from the Congress and our agents are vilified by many who think we should not be in the intelligence business. If we cannot protect our own we have no right leading men and women into danger."

He thought for a while, and then looked at Elizabeth. "Max Rietsema was engaged in an illegal act in ordering enhanced interrogation by the Egyptians."

"Let's not start with recriminations. The bureau has been involved in some nasty high profile stuff over the years, not all of it within the law. You do what you have to do and you make decisions that sometimes backfire. I'll tell you this, Jordan, if one my agents ever did anything to compromise one of yours, there is no outpost far enough away from civilization for my man to be assigned to. Let's be realistic and acknowledge that we have few, if any, friends in power. We do what we do because we believe in preserving our way of life. Max Rietsema deserves better, all agents deserve better. I'm willing to be taken down on this case but I do not want either the field agent or the agency to be a target. If the Congress can destroy one of my agents it can do likewise to one of yours. I need your help."

"Who besides me knows of this discussion?"

"Director Mallory. I had to give him a heads up in the event you decide to make the distribution of the composite to other agencies."

"What exactly do you want me to do?"

"Call Stuart McDonald and inform him that what occurred at the park is a matter of national security and that the investigation is being assigned to the Washington office. Nothing more. You're the boss and he'll not question the decision. If he is talented enough to run a field operation, he understands and appreciates protocol. He must be good in that the local chief of police spoke highly of him to one of my agents. It isn't often that local cops appreciate our work. Maybe you should find a high visibility assignment for McDonald in Boston or New York. Reward him for a good investigation in Maine. Same goes for his subordinates. They will appreciate you for recognizing the work of agents in the field."

After a brief hesitation, "Elizabeth, I will do it for you and for our field agents. I don't like it but I understand what the situation is. I don't know you or the Director very well but the word in the bureau is that both of you would fall on your swords to bring home your covert agents. That's good enough for me. I'll call Stuart when I leave here."

"I owe you Jordan."

"Someday you will have the opportunity to repay me. And, one last thing."

"Yes."

"You pay for the drinks."

"Gladly."

As soon as she returned to the office, she called Anthony Mallory. "Jordan Rich has agreed to drop the investigation in Maine. What won the day was the fact that within the bureau, the word is that you and I would sacrifice most anything to bring home our agents. It helped that Jordan spent time in covert operations and could sympathize with Max's situation and the dilemma we face. With this behind us, we can get on with finding Khalid."

"Well done, Elizabeth. Call if you need anything."

Before he ended the call, she said, "I am meeting with Carlton Richardson in a few minutes. He may have compromised his position in Rome. I may have to ask you to consider a reassignment for him. I'll know better after we meet."

There was an unusually long silence as he thought carefully about his response. Carlton was his selection but Elizabeth English was the best thing that ever happened to the agency. "No need to seek authorization from me. Do what is necessary for the agency."

"Thank you, Anthony." The conversation ended. Anthony Mallory was indeed the smartest person in the room.

She looked at her watch. It was a little after six. She remembered she had asked Ellen to move Carlton's appointment back to five. By now he must be pacing in the outer office. With Ellen gone for the day, Elizabeth went out to greet Carlton.

"Carlton, I am pleased that you arrived safely." She had learned from Anthony Mallory never to apologize to subordinates for being late.

"It was an uneventful flight."

"Please come in and let's get started" She was known throughout the agency for never wasting time on formalities. With Elizabeth, it was all business. It mattered little to her that he had flown from Europe for this meeting. They seated themselves at a large table, one at each end. This was not going to be a lounge chair conversation.

In her quiet, level and neutral voice she asked, "Who is Gisela Rudenschroeder?" Carlton, a man who usually intimidates others was momentarily taken back with the directness of the question at the outset of the meeting. He was immediately put on the defensive with one simple question. Earlier, in thinking about the meeting, he had determined that Gisela would eventually be brought into the conversation but never considered that she would be the focal point. In the few seconds he had to respond, he processed the question and considered how much Elizabeth knew. He was already on her shit list for letting the two Serbs slip through his hands at Fiumicino. Now this. Whatever Elizabeth did not know she could find out in short order. To tell the truth will finish him in Rome; to tell a lie will both finish him in Rome and disgrace him within the intelligence community. He staked out what he believed was neutral ground. He wasn't going to let this bitch get the better of him. Or so he thought.

"She is a member of the German Embassy in Rome."

"And?"

While she had a pleasant smile on her face he could feel the laser like coldness of her green eyes jamming his nerve center. She was forcing him into a corner, forcing him to admit to his dereliction of duties. One more try without telling a lie.

"We are social friends." Still no lie.

"Apparently the long flight has exhausted you to the point where you are unable to remember who she is or the circumstances of your relationship. So I will help you although it would have been more to your credit if your memory was not on hold."

"It's not..."

Before he could finish the sentence she interrupted, "You had your opportunity Carlton, now it is my time. Gisela Rudenschroeder is a centerfold whore who works for the Bundesnachrichtendienst, better known as the German Federal Intelligence Agency. She is a spy, a twenty five year old beauty, who you fuck every noon. Her father, Carl Rudenshcroeder, is the CEO of the largest munitions manufacturer in Europe whose sideline is selling weapons to every terrorist organization in the Middle East. They are the weapons that kill American soldiers."

Carlton, while trying to appear in control of his emotions, was reeling from Elizabeth's attack. She continued, "The American Embassy in Rome was kept apprised of all negotiations between American weapons manufacturers and the Italian government, in particular the Italian Military Procurement Office. Carl Rudenschroeder would find that information valuable since he bids against American companies for those contracts. You are privy to classified information regarding types of weapons being sought and bids being prepared by the American companies. Is it just possible, Carlton, that while your centerfold was stroking you, feeding you her breast or spreading her legs that you may just have had some weapons pillow talk?"

Ashen, he spoke, "I had no idea she worked for German intelligence."

"You are one arrogant son of a bitch. You are the station chief, the number one American spy in Italy and you don't know you're sleeping with another spy? Just how did you ever pass muster with the agency? Someone screwed up along the way and just passed you along like a social promotion in school. No more. Your incompetence stops here. As of this moment you are suspended. Before you are allowed to leave the building you will surrender to security all documents, weapons, cell phone, computer, electronic devices and passports that you have with you. Security will also accompany you to your hotel and confiscate any material or equipment there. It will notify security at the American Embassy in Rome that all personal effects are to be confiscated and you are not to have any contact with the embassy. Finally, security is authorized to search your apartment and car in Rome for any other materials."

"You cannot do this. The Director will never approve."

"He has already approved. The only thing that remains is for legal counsel to determine if you should be tried for treason."

"Treason! Elizabeth, whatever I gave her didn't amount to shit. It was low level stuff. Besides, the Italians don't have a real army."

"The Italian economy is the third largest in Europe and the number one trading partner with the prospering African countries. It is an important customer to American exporters who do not need you to create an uneven bidding field."

"You are blowing this out of proportion. I made a mistake or two but they can be fixed."

"Too late. You are relieved of your duties and placed on paid administrative leave until further notice. Under no circumstances are you to leave the country. I will today place you on the watch list. Now, Carlton, I will walk with you to security."

When she returned to the office she sat quietly for a moment or two reflecting on the day. She had a very good day. The Falaguerra issue was cleared up and the agency may have a new prospect for a double agent. Vinnie and Gretchen arrive tomorrow for a final briefing before taking on Khalid. Darlene will team up with Max who is theoretically out but, in practice, very much in the game. The bureau and Jordan Rich came to the rescue. The Director gave her great discretion in dealing with Carlton. He is no longer station chief.

There was a knock on her door. It was head of security. "Ms. English, everything is done or being done including Rome. We will secure the documents and passports until you tell us otherwise."

"Thank you." He left.

Finally, she thought, the hunt is on for Khalid. Four of the best agents are on the case and she had no doubt that he would be found and killed. It was a matter of when and where.

She packed her briefcase with documents for bedtime reading. One of these nights Vinnie will distract her reading, of that she was confident. As she walked the corridors on her way out of the building she was surrounded by the comforting sound of second shift analysts dissecting information that continuously flowed into the agency day and night from around the world. There will be no such comforting sounds at home.

CHAPTER 65

THE HUNT

Vinnie arrived at Global and looked for his boss who was not in. He left a message in Evan's voice mail explaining his resignation and the use of vacation time to satisfy the two week notice. He took the elevator up to the personnel department and left his letter with a clerk and requested that it be given to the Director. Then he drove to Simsbury, but not to Metro Plaza.

When he arrived at the town hall he went directly to the office of the town clerk. A young woman was at the front desk. He approached and asked, "Is Rachel Blackstone in?"

"She is. May I give her your name?"

"Vinnie Pagano."

She left and shortly thereafter Rachel came out to greet him.

"Hello Vinnie. Let's go to my office."

Once seated, she asked, "What brings you back?"

"I wanted to set the record straight. I owe you that much. You were very helpful and the information you provided eventually helped me to make an important decision. When I first spoke with you I was considering a change of employment but I needed to engage in a serious background check before I made a commitment. That is how I came to ask the questions of you that I did. As it happens, I have taken a new job."

"I assume that you will not tell me what it is."

"Let's say that the job is designed to make the country a safer place."

"I would expect nothing less from you. Now, I have a question for you that I hope you will answer. What do you have to report on the two women, Ms. Iverson and Ms. Hunt?"

"You were right on all counts. It was a wonderful experience to meet them and learn more about them. They are talented, committed to their jobs, lovely to be with and, if I had to guess, are destined for more responsible positions within their company. They are very special people. The more you get to know them, the more you like them."

"I'm sure they will also help make the country safer." She smiled at Vinnie but he changed the subject.

"I haven't forgotten my lunch promise. I'll be away for a time but when I return I will call. And, thanks again."

"Ciao."

"Ciao."

As she watched him walk out of the office she couldn't help think what a lovely man he was. She would look forward to their lunch and whatever it was he could share with her.

Vinnie spent the remainder of the day with Sharon and they made love in the late afternoon. He made cocktails and together they prepared dinner. It was a happy time and both avoided dealing with what lay ahead. Sharon made the best of what she knew was to be a long period without him and Vinnie, not used to an enduring relationship, wondered what the future would be with Sharon. When dinner ended they walked to the door where they embraced for a long time. He could feel her trembling body and the moisture on her cheeks.

"Sharon, I will be back. It may be a while but it will happen."

"I want you to return for yourself, not for me. I love you but know you have things you must do. When you leave, I know you will be engaged in dangerous work. You have not said as much but I know it in my heart. Now, I wish I had never left the ad on your desk. If anything happens to you I could never forgive myself."

"Nothing will happen to me. I will be back." They kissed softly and parted.

When the door closed she put her head against it and sobbed and the tears ran down her face. Sharon knew he would be back but she was not at all certain it would be her to whom he would return. Her heart ached with the pain of separation. She turned off the lights, climbed the stairs to her bedroom rolled herself onto the bed and cried. Then she whispered, "Please God, keep him safe and bring him home whole. I love him so." Then, fatigue that was borne of parting overwhelmed her and the darkness of sleep enveloped her.

He met Gretchen and Darlene at eleven a.m. at World Wide Jet Services at Bradley International Airport. Once they were seated in a small conference room Vinnie related the events of the previous morning when Max arrived at Sharon's condo. They were not surprised that he made contact but a little taken back that he would arrive at Sharon's doorsteps.

"Where is he now?" asked Darlene.

"It is best you don't know. There is little good to come from your being complicit in this. He'll take the initiative in contacting you. Once that occurs you both will be on the hunt for Khalid."

"That is, if Elizabeth doesn't rein me in knowing that Max is bound to contact all of us sooner or later. I'm the logical one since he knows where I am."

Gretchen chimed in. "Given that he found Vinnie at Sharon's condo tells me that Max will find any of us when needed. Vinnie, you and I need to get started. Our plane is here. Khalid has a head start. The two of us have a lot of work to do in Florida to pick up his trail."

"Actually, Gretchen, there may be four of us on the hunt. I cannot imagine Elizabeth expending resources to find Max. If she really wanted him on the sidelines, security could have picked him up at Langley. I think she expected that Max might go rogue and decided to do nothing about it."

"At the moment it is not our concern. We need to go. Darlene, stay in touch."

Vinnie and Gretchen boarded the Challenger 850 and within minutes they were airborne. The plane banked, turned to the south and began its climb to cruising altitude. Looking out the starboard side Gretchen could make out the Heublein Tower perched on Talcott Mountain and below it the Metro Plaza building. On the port side, Vinnie could make out the cities of Hartford and West Hartford and knew that somewhere down there was a woman in love with him. Without turning he could sense Gretchen looking at him. She was not pleased that Max had drawn Sharon into the picture. Vinnie continued to stare out the window.

It was a little past two when they arrived at Palm Beach International Airport in West Palm Beach. When they entered the terminal building they were met by a CIA Agent. Elizabeth had arranged for the Miami office to work with Vinnie and Gretchen to determine where Khalid had stayed while there. They needed a starting point. The agent, Carlos Hernandez, had established a work station in the Holiday Inn in Juno Beach, thirty minutes north of the airport. Hernandez was a Florida native, born of Cuban parents. He knew Florida like the back of his hand. Five other agents from the Miami office were with him. While the entire team was working this phase of the investigation they would stay at the hotel and operate out of there. Hernandez reserved eight rooms for the agents and two adjoining rooms to serve as an office equipped with a secure phone line, computers, printer, fax machine and scanner.

Agent Hernandez spotted Vinnie and Gretchen from the descriptions provided by Elizabeth. He walked up to Gretchen and introduced himself. "Agent Iverson, I'm Agent Carlos Hernandez of the Miami office." He extended his hand.

"Agent Hernandez, this is Agent Vinnie Pagano." Vinnie and Carlos shook hands. Hernandez had a strong hand grip and the solid hard build of someone who worked out regularly. He was short for a field agent, no taller than five seven or eight. His complexion was not unlike that of Vinnie but his face was rounder. Two piercing black eyes matched the color of his wavy hair. Women would think him cute, even cuddly. Vinnie quickly classified him as dangerous, especially if he could get close in to your body. He was someone most men would want to stay clear of. The positive side was that he was on Gretchen's team.

Once they retrieved their bags Hernandez escorted them to a waiting car driven by one of his five colleagues. He introduced the driver as Paul Williams. Although hard to tell since he was seated, Vinnie nevertheless pegged Paul as considerably taller than his boss. He was blond and young.

"We have thirty minutes before we get to the hotel. I will use the time to bring you up to date. Deputy Director English spoke with my boss late last night. She requested that he assign me and five other Agents to assist you in locating the subject. In addition, she asked that we establish a base of operations. I made three assumptions that you may disagree with and, if so, I can readily make the necessary adjustments."

Gretchen, "What assumptions did you make Agent Hernandez?" There was an edge to her question"

"Given that Abdu Khalid flew into Palm Beach International Airport, the first assumption was that he stayed within driving distance of the airport. The second assumption was that, given his status in the al-Qaeda hierarchy and having substantial funds available to him, he is staying in a high end hotel or resort. The third is that he is using an assumed name."

"I agree with all of your assumptions. I assume you made a fourth assumption regarding how we should go about locating him?" It was a friendly question from Vinnie. Gretchen began to worry about male bonding.

"Correct, Agent Pagano. We can change direction at any time. I booked us into a hotel that is located approximately half way between the two ends of a shore line region that has the most upscale hotels and resorts. It is approximately twenty miles in length. Initially we need to contact all hotels and resorts in that stretch. If that doesn't produce results, we can extend the north-south borders and go inland a bit. But, from what I know of the area, there is nothing inland beyond a mile or two of the shore line."

Not willing to let the boys take charge, Gretchen moved into the conversation. "Tell us about the operations center at the hotel."

"Yes, certainly." He said it politely and meant it. "Basically we have established the center to serve as a communications point so that all of us can keep in contact while we attend to our individual assignments once you approve a course of action." He knew that Gretchen was to be the head of the operation and wanted to establish a cordial working relationship with her. "I believe you will be satisfied with the arrangements. Once we get to the hotel and settle in I will show you a map of the area and make suggestions for allocating the work among the other agents."

As they drove north Agent Hernandez gave them a running commentary about the area and points of interest. Once they arrived at the hotel, he gave them keys and suggested they drop their bags and go directly to the two-room operations center.

Once all eight agents were assembled in the operations center, Hernandez introduced the other four agents to Vinnie and Gretchen. "From what Deputy Director English shared with my boss, I understand that you must locate the subject, Abdu Khalid, as quickly as possible He is considered a dangerous person and is in the United States to duplicate the terror and loss of life of 9/11. We are to assist you in any way you request. With that I will turn the meeting over to you, Agent Iverson."

"Thank you Carlos. I think things will run more smoothly if we use first names if that is alright with you. Vinnie and I are pleased with what you have done so far and would like to hear your ideas for locating Abdu Khalid."

"The number of luxury hotels and resorts in the twenty mile stretch is substantial, approximately one hundred and fifty seven of them. It would be too time consuming for us to send an agent to every site. Our suggestion is that we fax to all hotels and resorts the photograph of Khalid that was obtained when he entered the Palm Beach International Airport. I understand that it is the same photograph that was obtained when he entered Los Angeles International Airport. Of the hundred-fifty seven units we need to check, I have identified thirty six of the most luxurious ones. They are also the most expensive. There may be reluctance on the part of management to acknowledge that our man stayed with them if they suspect he is a person of interest. I recommend that my five agents make personal visits to those sites and speak directly with senior management. If you approve, I have worked out a grid with the units listed and have developed a tentative assignment for each agent."

"I like the plan and appreciate the work you have done to develop it. Vinnie, what is your reaction to it?"

"I like it and suggest that you give Carlos and his men the authority to move on it. There is one recommendation I would make. If anyone gets a positive hit when questioning senior management you need to inquire as to who may have been with him. It is unlikely he is traveling alone." It was Vinnie.

Carlos responded. "When we get a positive, either through the visits or the fax approach, we will definitely pursue our questioning. The fax communication and picture will request acknowledgement within twenty four hours of the time it was received. If we do not get a confirmation we will make a personal visit. More importantly, if we get a positive hit, I will contact Gretchen so you can meet with us if you wish. Clearly we need his name and those of his companions. There is one other thing. It is most likely that these high end hotels and resorts video tape everyone who enters them for security purposes whether they register or not. It is not widely advertised. If they do video we will ask for the surveillance tapes."

"You have done a good job, Carlos. Gretchen and I have time to help out this afternoon. If you give us some of the units to be visited we will get started."

"Thanks, Vinnie. As for the list, I anticipated that you would want to make a few visits." With that he handed Gretchen a list with four hotels on it including addresses and phone numbers."

"Now if there is nothing else at this time we should get moving. Since senior management generally works the daytime shift in these luxury places, we only have an hour or two in which to work today. We will cover a few of the closest units now and tomorrow we will complete the list. Paul will remain behind and manage the fax distribution. I wouldn't be surprised if we receive some responses tonight. Before we leave I would like to exchange cell phone numbers."

By six o'clock all seven of the agents had checked back in at the operations center. Together they had visited a total of twelve of the thirty six hotels and resorts on the priority list. They came up dry on all of them. Of the hundred and twenty one faxes sent to the other hotels and resorts, sixteen responded.

There was no positive identification at any of units. So far, nothing positive to report.

Vinnie and Gretchen ate at a steak house across the street from the hotel. Following dinner they took a walk. The restaurant was one block off the water. The road along the beach had no commercial businesses. The entire mile stretch was a sea of luxury high rise condominiums with unobstructed views of the ocean. The road was heavily patrolled by the local police. They walked in silence, happy to be together. When they reached the point where Ocean Drive intersected with the highway they reversed their route and returned to the hotel. Gretchen, the leader of the effort to locate Khalid, set the tone to end the evening.

"Good night, Vinnie, see you at breakfast at eight." She raised herself on her toes, gave him a kiss on the cheek and then walked up the path to her room.

"Good night."

Gretchen had set a morning meeting for nine a.m. and everyone was on time. Carlos Hernandez, who organized the search, recapped the situation. "We have twenty four luxury hotels and resorts on the list for visits. With four teams of two, each team will have six units to check. I have a schedule worked out for each team. This phase should be completed by the end of the day. By then we will have received more responses to the fax requests. We are waiting to hear from one hundred and five of them. Tomorrow we will visit those units that do not respond to the fax request unless we get a positive hit during our visits today. Any questions?" There were none. The teams left the operations center. Gretchen and Vinnie were a team.

By noon there was no progress with the visits. Carlos checked the fax returns at that time. Sixty five more units responded with no positive identification. The teams went back to work after lunch. Vinnie and Gretchen were on their fifth visit when Carlos called. "We have a positive identification. Paul Williams and his partner are at the Remy Plaza talking to the day manager who believes Khalid was there. I'm on my way and will meet you there."

"Good work. See you there as soon as we can."

"Gretchen, we need to be sure to let the Director of the Miami office knows what an asset he has in Carlos. Maybe they would put him on temporary assignment to us. He is good."

"I won't forget."

When they arrived at the Remy Plaza Carlos and Paul deferred to Gretchen. She wasted no time. "Mr. Josephsen, please take another look at the photo and tell us why you think this is the gentlemen who registered as Jonathon Drew."

"There is literally no difference between the photograph and the man listed as Drew. The eyes, the nose, color of hair, build, everything fits."

"You mentioned to Agent Williams that he was accompanied by two others. Please tell us about them."

"There was a well spoken man who pretty much kept to himself. If I had to guess I would say he was a bodyguard or a security person assigned to Drew. Except for the times when Drew was with the woman, the second man was always with him and clearly his subordinate. Both men were about the same height and weight. Both looked in excellent condition."

"Tell us about the woman."

"Gorgeous. No other way to describe her. European, either German or Austrian. Had a distinct accent. Her clothes were those from a fashion house. We have many beautifully dressed women as guests and she would keep up with the very best. Again, if I had to guess, I would say she was dressed in Paris. I heard Mr. Drew address her as Marta. Never heard him address the other man."

"Do you have a security video recording of everyone who enters the hotel?"

"We do and I would be pleased to let you review the recordings. There is no doubt that all three will be on them."

"Mr. Josephsen, I need a minute with my partner." With that she and Vinnie stepped out of the office. They were joined by Carlos and Paul. When they were in the lobby Gretchen addressed Vinnie. "We need to know the identity of the other man. Elizabeth, who has been on the Khalid case for some time, will know if he has a confidante, a second in command, someone who travels with Khalid. While I continue to question Josephsen, why don't you call Elizabeth and see what you can find out. If she is tied up tell Ellen it is vital that you speak to her. If there is someone, see if Elizabeth can fax a picture of the guy directly here. Carlos has the fax number. Come in as soon as you hear." She returned to the office along with Paul.

"Mr. Josephson, we are expecting a fax to be sent here shortly. It may be a picture of the second man. Back to Mr. Drew and his guests. Please tell me when they left, if together, where they went, what the means of transportation was and whatever else you know."

"It would be best if we called in the bell captain. He will remember any details."

He asked the bell captain in and Gretchen repeated what she had asked of Josephsen. The bell captain had a register in his hand and opened it and quickly reviewed some of the data.

"Mr. Drew and the woman left around ten a.m. That was a week ago yesterday. They used the resort limo and were taken to the private aircraft area at Palm Beach International Airport. We did not know of their plans from there. According to our records, the other gentleman took the limo to the airport late in the afternoon that same day and was left off at the private plane area. The register notes that Mr. Drew was to return the next day. The limo record shows he returned the day after that. There is no record of the other man using our limo to return here."

Gretchen turned to Carlos who had returned to the room. "As soon as we receive a fax from Langley with a photo of the second man, you need to get to the airport and talk to every charter service and see if they recognize Khalid or the second man." At that moment, Vinnie stuck his head in the room and beckoned Gretchen to come out.

"I spoke with Elizabeth and she is certain that the other man is Ibraham Malik. He and Khalid grew up together in Yemen and are close friends. Malik is a terrorist of the first order, handles all funds for al-Qaeda operations in Europe and the United States and is Khalid's confidante. His picture should be on the fax by now."

"Excellent. Let's go back in."

When they returned, Josephsen was holding a picture of Ibraham Malik. "This is definitely the second man."

"Please make us four copies." They waited while Josephsen did so. Gretchen handed two copies to Carlos who, together with Paul, left the room.

Gretchen turned to Josephsen. "We would like to look at those surveillance tapes."

They reviewed the tapes from the day all three departed to go to the airport. There was no doubt that the two men were the same men in the photographs. Marta was a gorgeous as Josephsen had said.

"Mr. Josephsen, I want to thank you for your assistance. Any of the agents you met today may be back to work with you again. In the meantime, please except our appreciation for your assistance. Also, be assured that what went on here today is confidential. We in no way wish to upset your operation. There is also no need to worry since it is with certainty that we can say that the three persons will not be returning to your resort. Your guests are quite safe. Again, our thanks."

"I am pleased that I could help. Whatever it is you are doing, best of luck."

Gretchen and Vinnie returned to their hotel which was near the Remy Plaza. Vinnie parked the car and turned to Gretchen. "Until we hear from Carlos, there is little we can do. How about if we step across the street to that little outdoor café and have a drink? It is happy hour, if not here, somewhere."

"I like the idea. If Carlos has something to share, he will call. Let's go."

They sat outdoors in the quiet of late afternoon. Happy hour had not begun and there were few customers sitting outside. It was perfect setting for recapping the day. They both ordered Knob Creek on the rocks. When the drinks arrived they clinked glasses and toasted a rewarding day. Khalid was on the move and they were not far behind. The question was if they would get to him before it was too late to stop him from creating chaos.

"Do you intend to share what we know with Max and Darlene?"

"Once we hear from Carlos, we report what we know to Elizabeth. Then we update Darlene. Max is her responsibility. I have worked with Darlene in the field and she always used good judgment. We go with her call, whatever it is."

While they were working on their second drink, Carlos called. Gretchen listened and then asked him to hold on until she and Vinnie could walk to the parking lot. Vinnie dropped two twenty dollar bills on the table. Once in the parking lot, she put the call on speaker phone. "We have information on Khalid and Malik. The photographs were valuable. Khalid and the woman were easily recognized, especially Marta as you might have guessed. They chartered a Cessna Citation to take them to Key West. They left in mid-morning. The charter service filed a plan for a return flight late the same day. It turns out that they did not return until the following day. Malik is a different story. He did not charter a flight. One of the mechanics at the charter service used by Khalid recognized Malik from the photo. It was late in the afternoon and the mechanic observed Malik meet the pilot of another plane for which a flight plan to Key West had also been filed. The mechanic did not recognize the make or model of the plane. I spoke with the controller in the tower who had the tail number of the plane. The plane was of Italian manufacture. I called the FAA in Washington and learned that the aircraft was registered to a company in Chicago that is the North

American distributor for an Italian aircraft manufacturing company. I punched up the company on my lap top and learned that the CEO is a guy named Hafs Karzai who, according to the PR on the company web site, is certified to fly twin engine jets. It is not specific as to what class of aircraft. For what it is worth, he is a Muslim. The aircraft that Malik flew into Key West is a Silver Eagle X650, a luxury private jet that is distributed by Karzai's company. The plane did not return to Palm Beach International Airport."

Still on speaker phone, "That is great work Carlos. Look, we don't have an agency plane readily available. You and Paul are to charter a flight to Key West as soon as possible and learn whatever you can. There are several questions that need answers. First, why did Khalid delay his return? Second, why did Malik fly to Key West on a plane owned by a company run by a Muslim? Third, if Malik was going to Key West, why didn't he hitch a ride with his buddy, Khalid? Fourth, where are Malik and the Silver Eagle? Fifth, did Karzai fly the plane that Malik flew in to Key West in and, if so, what was their connection?"

"No problem, Gretchen. Paul and I will take a charter to Key West. Anything else?"

"Check with the FAA for any missing aircraft that departed Key West on the day in question. If the Silver Eagle is not in Palm Beach or Key West, where the hell is it?"

"Will call when I know more." Carlos hung up.

Vinnie spoke up. "We are getting close. But I have a gut feeling that Ibraham Malik is not of this world." They returned to the café and had an early dinner.

Following dinner, they returned to the hotel at seven. They no sooner entered the lobby when Carlos called from Key West. She put him on speaker phone. "Gretchen, I have some answers. Both the Cessna Citation and the Silver Eagle left Key West heading north within minutes of each other on the same day; first the Citation, followed shortly by the Silver Eagle. Exactly twenty nine minutes later, the Citation reported to the tower at Key West that it was reversing course and returning to Key West. It gave no explanation. Four minutes later the Citation again contacted the Key West tower and reported that a plane a half mile off its starboard side and heading north exploded and fell into the sea. The Citation gave its position and remained in the area looking for survivors but there were none. We located the charter pilot of the Citation and showed him the pictures of Khalid and Malik. We have a positive identification on Khalid. According to the pilot, Khalid was accompanied by a beautiful woman. The pilot did not recognize Malik. Oh, one other thing. The charter pilot did not recognize the model of plane that exploded. If I may be allowed to make a couple of reasonable assumptions on which to proceed, I would say that Malik and Karzai were on the plane, it was destroyed while in the air and Khalid had something to do with it."

"Both you and Vinnie are of the same mind believing that Malik is dead. The question is why would Khalid murder his childhood friend and confidante?"

"The first thing that comes to mind is betrayal. If we can figure out what Karzai was doing in Florida in the first place, we may have the link we need. Look, it is late, the charter company is closed and we are tired and hungry. If you don't have a problem, we would like to stay over and catch a charter flight early in the morning unless you have an agency plane to pick us up now."

"Carlos, I'm good but not that good. See you tomorrow."

Turning to Vinnie, "Well, what do you think?"

"Think about it. Khalid, Malik and Karzai are all in Florida at the same time. Karzai is a successful business man who teams up with Malik and both are murdered by Khalid. Karzai is also a Muslim. At least that is my current thinking. It would be a good idea if you ask Elizabeth to assign agents to quietly pull Karzai's company apart. We may learn more about the operation. There is or was a definite link between a known terrorist and a successful business man. We need to know what it is. There is one other matter that intrigues me. Carlos told us that Karzai's main facility is in Chicago and that he had a second distribution center in Denver. For what it is worth, both are in middle American."

"And?"

"And, I don't know."

"Can we go to bed now?"

CHAPTER 66

DETECTIVE WORK

With Carlos and Paul in Key West and not returning until noon, Gretchen and Vinnie met with his four Agents. Gretchen gave the assignment. "We need to know the movements of both Khalid and Ibraham while they were at the Remy Plaza. They had a rental car, but they also made use of the resort's limousine. We also have reason to believe that a man named Hafs Karzai stayed in the area at the same time. It is likely that he used his own name. Your job, until Carlos arrives, is to revisit the thirty six luxury hotels and resorts and check the guest registers. Hafs Karzai may well be the key to our finding Khalid. Once you learn of his movements, you need to determine who he may have visited. If he did visit anyone else, get the address and check out the location, but do it without drawing attention. Call me immediately with what you find. There is no need to double up on these visits. It is important that you move quickly on this assignment." With that, the four agents left.

Gretchen and Vinnie were having a second cup of coffee when Darlene called. "Max is with me. How can we help? We are on speaker phone."

Vinnie briefed them on everything to date right up to the briefing of the four agents a few minutes before Darlene called. Max responded. "Look, Darlene and

I will do what we can via the internet to dig into this Hafs Karzai guy. What is the name of the company?"

"The aircraft is of Italian manufacture. Karzai's distribution company, an American corporation, is Silver Eagle Aircraft Industries, Inc."

"We will leave for Chicago this afternoon. We'll have something for you tomorrow morning."

Carlos and Paul returned from Key West just before noon. Gretchen briefed them on the assignments she had given to his agents. "Carlos and Paul, we need to find out where this man stayed and to track his movements. He is a key link to whatever it is that Khalid was doing in Florida."

"Gretchen, we don't deal with many terrorists in the Miami office, but we are the best trackers in the business, just ask some of the cartel boys who are behind bars. If Hafs Karzai stayed anywhere in Florida we will find him or a record of him. Not to worry."

"I love your attitude, Carlos, and that of your men. I'll leave you to your work and wait to hear something."

Carlos called the most senior of his men, Donald Bell, and got an update. Nothing so far but the day was young and they had fifteen or sixteen more units to check out. Carlos made arrangements to join Bell. In the meantime, Gretchen and Vinnie reviewed what they had to date. Khalid travels to Florida with his mistress and his second in command, Ibraham Malik. The men are friends since childhood and they are the number one and two terrorists in North America. Malik has some connection to Hafs Karzai, a Muslim, whom he meets with and dies with when the plane Karzai is piloting explodes a short way out of Key West while headed north.

Vinnie, used to working with battlefield maps, lays out a map of the United States and circles four cities that have emerged so far in the investigation: Key West, Palm Beach Gardens, Chicago and Denver.

It was ten past three in the afternoon when Carlos called. “Gretchen, Donald Bell got a hit. I am with him and the others at Royal Palms Spa and Resort located on Military Boulevard, less than fifteen minutes from you. It is an upscale facility and Hafs Karzai was a guest here. You may want to be in on our interviews.”

Fifteen minutes later, Gretchen and Vinnie joined Carlos and agent Bell. They were with the day manager. “Gretchen, this is Howard Kelly the day manager of the Royal Palms. I’ll let him tell you what he knows.”

“Mr.Karzai was a guest here for several days. On the registration form he listed Chicago as his business address, but listed no home address. He is still a guest in that he has not checked out as of this morning. There was nothing unusual about him. He made no special requests, used our dining room for most of his meals, and when he left the hotel he either used the resort limo or a cab. There is no record of his having a rental car. Agent Hernandez asked if we have surveillance cameras and we do. If you wish, I can make the tapes of the relevant dates available to you. I only ask that they be returned in a timely manner.”

Vinnie asked, “Do you recall seeing Mr. Karzai with any other guests?”

“It is interesting that you ask. Given the nature of our resort business, which is primarily a destination for wealthy guests who book extended stays in order to use our world class spa and physical conditioning facilities, we mostly attract couples. The majority are foreigners. However, in a two or three day period around the time that Mr. Karzai registered, we also had several other single men register. All of them had addresses in the United States, but all were foreign. If I had to venture a guess, I would say they were from the Middle East."

About now, Gretchen, Vinnie and Carlos believed they had discovered the mother lode. Vinnie continued, "Do you keep a record of where the resort limo takes guests?"

"We keep accurate records in the event there is an emergency and the guest has to be contacted, although we try not to interrupt them for obvious reasons. They are not always where their partners believe they would be. Let me look at the records and check Mr. Karzai's travel record." He left to fetch the records.

"We are on to something. Gretchen, if it is alright with you, I suggest that agent Bell and the others stay here and examine the tapes and get a photograph of Karzai. They also need to look for the other single men who registered a day or two around the time Karzai registered."

Howard Kelly returned. "On two different occasions, Mr. Karzai took the limo to Presidential Estates. The address is one of the premier locations in all of Florida. According to the records, he visited twenty nine Blue Heron Drive. The record also shows that another guest visited the same location. His name is Ghani Mohammed. When my assistant manager saw me talking to you about the single men, he informed me that Mr. Mohammed, while still registered, has not used his room for at least two nights. Housekeeping thought it unusual enough to report it to management."

"Mr. Kelly, do you think you and your staff could identify the single men on the tape who registered around the time that Mr. Karzai registered?"

"Not a problem. It may take a couple of hours."

"Agent Bell and four other agents will remain here and work with you. If necessary, I may call on your services again. I also want you to know that whatever has taken place here today will remain confidential. In no way will your resort be identified." It was Gretchen speaking.

"I appreciate that. As outstanding as we are at what we do, there is a great deal of competition in the area. Negative publicity is not what we need."

"Thanks again. We'll be on our way." Gretchen, Vinnie and Carlos, using Carlos as a driver who knew his way around, headed for Presidential Estates. The entry protocol was not what one usually finds at a gated community in Florida. There was the standard resident line and a separate guest line, but it ended there. If you entered the guest line, you were first met by a cordial, attractive Florida blond in her late twenties or early thirties with a Dallas Cowboy cheerleader body and dressed professionally in an attractive uniform. This is what greeted Carlos when he lowered his window. Before she could say anything, he showed her his credential and spoke. "We are here to visit twenty nine Blue Heron Drive."

With a beautiful smile, she requested, "May I please have your entry code number."

With his very best Latino smile, "As I said, we are here on government business. Please lift the gate."

Friendly, but firmly, she answered, "I'm sorry sir, but without an entry code provided you by the resident at twenty nine Blue Heron Drive, you are denied access. If you wish to pursue entry, please move ahead to the security building on the right." Carlos accepted her rebuff and drove to the security building.

"I'll take care of this. You guys wait here."

"Vinnie, what makes you think it takes a male to handle this?"

"Sorry, but it's a guy thing" He got a stare from Gretchen that could kill.

Vinnie entered the security building and was greeted by a tall, well conditioned, strong looking, tanned, perfectly uniformed and well spoken "receptionist/guard" who gave the appearance of taking his security job seriously. As they say, it takes one to know one. Vinnie decided to test his intuition. "Good afternoon, sir." The emphasis was on "sir." The guard automatically responded with a "Good afternoon, sir." So, he was ex-military. These were perfect early retirement jobs. Vinnie played the odds believing that an address like Presidential Estates would not have hired a rent-a-copy for security duty. Looking at the guard, he was certain his intuition was accurate.

"What rank and outfit if I may ask?"

A slight hesitation, then, "Colonel, battalion level, infantry, Iraq. You?"

"Captain, APET, Iraq and Afghanistan."

"Advance Penetration and Extraction Team. You earned your combat pay the hard way. You ran the Ranger extraction in Wardak a year or so ago?"

"That was us."

The colonel hesitated only a moment and then asked, "What can I do for you?"

Vinnie talked while he showed his credential. "I'll tell you as much as I can and let you fill in the blanks."

Vinnie then provided more information for him than he would have shared with a regular gate guard. "The bottom line is that something serious is in the planning stage and twenty nine Blue Heron Drive may have been the staging area. We know that at least two of the men we are interested in were here, arriving by limo. Whomever they visited is of interest to the agency."

"If this is as serious as you say it is, then let me take a look at the records." He opened a file cabinet, looked first at one record and then a second one. "There is more to the story. The first list I just examined shows the residence as being owned by a company in Atlanta, Georgia. The name is Imperial Import/Export Company. The resident is Abua Karsam. The second record was a list of entry codes that were given out by Mr. Karsam. If you have a code, you are allowed entry. You didn't have one so you were directed to this building. The record indicates that Karsam recently gave out seven codes, so he had seven visitors. Actually, there was an eighth one, but it was given out some time ago to a guy who had all the moves of a bodyguard. I didn't give it much thought when I met the guy, but now it makes senses. None of the codes have names attached to them. One last thing. I work days so I have observed all seven of the visitors. All seven are Muslims. The eighth guy, the bodyguard type, is also Muslim."

"I noticed there is a security camera at the first gate. Is everyone who stops at the gate photographed?"

"Yes. The tapes are kept here for six months. They are controlled by the Presidential Estates Association Board but kept here."

"What if a government agency asked to review them?"

"In the interests of national security, they would be released. Best if done quietly." The colonel went to a storage cabinet, reached in and took out a disc and handed it to Vinnie. "Need it back by tomorrow morning. That should give you time to compare the photographs with those at the resort."

"Can't thank you enough for your help."

"Consider it a commendation for saving the Rangers."

Not to get sentimental, Vinnie nodded his head in appreciation, turned and joined Gretchen and Carlos. On the ride back, he told them about the colonel and the information and tapes he provided. They were dumbfounded that he knew the guard was ex-military and a combat veteran at that. The information he provided was the breakthrough they needed. Carlos raced back to the Royal Palm eager to compare the tapes. Gretchen, often pissed at the male bonding thing, smiled when she thought about Vinnie and his instincts. All along he believed there was a pattern although not certain what it was. By tonight, the pattern would reveal itself. She was thinking; no wonder this guy is so loveable.

When they arrived at the resort, it was decided that Carlos would remain with his team and go through both sets of tapes and determine who visited Karsam at Presidential Estates. Once that was determined, they would have an address for the business of each of the seven men. The eighth man was the resident of 29 Blue Heron Drive.

Vinnie and Gretchen decided to return to the hotel and wait for Carlos to call in with information. They also had to plan the next moves. On the way back to the hotel, it dawned on Vinnie that the tapes at Royal Palm would probably only give them the names of five of the seven men since two of them had to be Khalid and Malik who were not staying at the Royal Palm. Vinnie called Carlos and alerted him to this fact so they would be looking for five men rather than seven.

Back at the hotel, Vinnie went to the map of the United States he had placed on the table earlier. He circled another city: Atlanta, Georgia, home of Abua Karsam. If his thinking was correct, he would circle four more cities before the end of the night.

CHAPTER 67

A PATTERN

It was late afternoon when Carlos returned to the hotel. He told his men to take the remainder of the day off. They had been doing yeoman's work for several days running and deserved some down time. Gretchen and Vinnie were still in the operations room when he arrived. They looked at him with apprehension, anxious to hear what he had for them.

Once they were seated, he began. "First, you really need to thank the Colonel at Presidential Estates. His information was critical to our work today. We matched four more men at the Royal Palm to the tapes we received from the colonel. While there were a total of seven visitors, one was Khalid, one was Malik and one was Hafs Karzai. All of this we already knew. This is what we learned about the other four men." As he was about to begin, Vinnie walked over to his map.

"The first man is Suleiman Amir. He is from San Francisco. The company he listed on the guest register is International Deep Water Exploration and Salvage Operations. The second man is from Dallas and his company is Malavi Industries-Manufacturer of Natural Gas Pipeline Valves. His name is Abdul Jazier. The third man is Aba Najdi from Boston. He operates World Wide Wine and Spirits Distributors. The fourth guy is Ghani Mohammed. As you may recall, Howard

Kelly told us that his room has not been occupied for a couple of days, but he has not checked out. He operates Global Construction, Inc. out of Seattle. Their companies are spread out all over the country.

Vinnie spoke. "Seven cities that cover the perimeter and belly of the country. That is the pattern we have been looking for and that may be the key to finding Khalid. These are his staging areas. We don't know how and we don't know when, but I am certain that, not one, but all of these cities are the locations for his disaster strikes. While the country worries about a repeat performance in New York and Washington, he has chosen, with the exception of Chicago, cities we would not consider prime targets. We need to call Elizabeth now and alert her. We cannot keep her or the Director in the dark with impending disasters threatening us. She needs to acquire background information on the men, especially their country of origin. Given that Khalid and Malik are from Yemen, chances are that all of them are from there. Yemen is now the number one site in the world for the training of terrorists."

Gretchen, still in charge, "Vinnie, you call Elizabeth. You worked out this pattern and no one is better qualified to explain it. Do it now."

He spent the next twenty minutes briefing Elizabeth. She did not interrupt him until he was finished. She wanted to know if he had more information on the suspected murders of Malik and Karzai and did he have any thoughts on Mohammed being missing. His responses were negative on both counts but assured her he would keep working on both matters.

"Elizabeth, we need to know country of origin, when they entered the Unites States, any record of foreign travel, data about the companies they operate, if they have possession of corporate aircraft and any affiliation with terrorists groups. Because of the nature of their businesses, they can easily move around the world without any hassle and can avoid security if they have private planes and ships. Given what little we know about their businesses, they are in a position to move cargo in and out of the country easily and avoid custom inspections. I mean cargo like weapons, explosives, chemicals and biological material. Sorry to lay so much on you."

"Great work down there. I'll put all regional offices on alert as soon as we end our call. I'll have something by tomorrow, if not later tonight. Unfortunately, there is also a bigger issue here. I need to inform the Director. He'll ask if we believe the threat is serious enough and timely enough to inform Homeland knowing that the minute they are notified they will alert every other agency and attempt to push Langley aside."

"For what it is worth, I would inform them if only to avoid being the fall guy when disaster strikes. As for being pushed aside, that will never happen. Khalid is ours. This is our mission and I plan on killing that butcher myself. I am not sharing him with anyone. By the time Homeland gets out of its parking lot, this could be over. Once the other agencies are involved, there will be territorial wars that will stall any meaningful action. We've seen it before. All of the agency heads will fight for time on the Sunday morning network shows, each with a different twist to the story to be shared with the public and each playing to a different political base. While they perform their theater, we will be at work."

"Whatever you do, be safe. I need you here for a celebration when this is over." She meant it, a celebration for two. From the tone of her voice, Vinnie thought he detected another pattern developing.

When he ended the call, Gretchen and Carlos were engaged in a debate as to how Khalid left the area. She was convinced that he had flown out of West Palm Beach International Airport on a charter and was headed for one of the seven cities. Carlos was of the opinion that Khalid drove out of the area with one or more of his operatives and would then fly out of Jacksonville or Savannah, Georgia.

"What operatives?" It was Gretchen.

"The operatives he used to conduct surveillance on Malik, eliminate Ghani Mohammed and maintain surveillance on the five men who stayed at the Royal Palm." He turned to Vinnie, "What do you think?"

"Let's keep in mind that until now we did not have an alert out on him. In fact, we still don't. I think he left the same way he arrived and that is by a commercial airline. He has a new identity and is out of here. As for operatives, we have to believe that for years he has been creating a sleeper network of terrorists in the country, some homegrown, most from Yemen and all brought here by one or more of the six companies that travel worldwide with ease. Think about it; his operatives traveled here first class on private planes or company ships. They never had to clear security!"

"Do you think he is headed for one of the seven cities?"

"I don't think so, Carlos. If I were in his situation, I would want to keep you off balance and confused as to where I was headed. I would take a flight to Montreal or Quebec, and then return to the states via Detroit or

Buffalo. I would have you looking in the wrong places. I hate to say it, but he has us on the run. As fast as we try locating him through facial recognition, he will be off to another destination."

"If that's the case, we have no chance of locating him. I can't believe, after all we have discovered, that he is out of our reach."

"Carlos, we will locate him, but I'm afraid we may pay a price. Soon, very soon, there will be a terrorist event in or, close by one of the seven cities. There will be deaths and Khalid will be responsible. Then there will be terrorist attacks involving all seven cities. There will be a pattern and we will need to decipher it if we have any chance of finding him. Sooner or later he will make a mistake."

"How does Homeland fit into this now that Langley will inform them of what we learned?"

"Once Homeland and the other forty or more intelligence agencies in the country get involved each of the seven cities will be crawling with agents, mostly getting in each other's way. Add to that mix, state and local responders and you have the makings of political chaos. If any one of the agencies, in addition to us, is capable of figuring it all out, it will be the bureau. They are the best trackers in the world, but at the moment they lack the information we possess."

Gretchen, again. "Then let's give it to them. We need all the help we can get."

"That's the Director's call. Remember, we have the resources of seven field offices to work on this. You and I should be discussing how we use the services of our sidekick from Miami."

They both looked at him. "Carlos, you have been an incredible help to Vinnie and me and to the entire effort. The pattern that has developed, and which was suggested earlier by Vinnie, would not have been evident without your work and that of your colleagues. I know I speak for both of us when I say we wish we could take you along for the journey. You are as good at tracking as anyone at the bureau. Unfortunately, you do not belong to us."

"It has been a pleasure to work with both of you. What I admire the most are your instincts. It is clear that you have been where the action is and bring great experience to the agency. When you need a spare, I'm available."

Vinnie had a question for Carlos."Before you go, I would like your opinion on Khalid's next move. When you look at the seven cities and the type of work performed by each of the companies, where would you strike if you were Khalid and why?"

Carlos hesitated only for a moment or two. He had given prior thought to the matter. The answer seemed so simple. "There are two possibilities. They are where he has an easy target, the manpower and the equipment to make it happen."

Before he could continue, he was interrupted.

"Chicago and San Diego."

"On the money, Gretchen. Vinnie, you look surprised."

"Only at Gretchen's rapid response. It seems you two have given thought to this. But, I see where you are going. International Deep Water Exploration and Salvage Operations has the experience, the manpower, the equipment and hundreds of targets in the same harbor where they conduct their business. His choices in San Diego range from aircraft carriers to the largest cruise ships in the world. Khalid is betting there are no underwater detection systems in place for pleasure craft and cruise ships. They are sitting ducks."

"Since the Navy may have security systems, it means private and commercial ships would be the logical targets."

"Carlos is correct in terms of one city, Vinnie. While San Diego is certainly one of the possibilities, I believe Chicago and Denver present more likely sites. Unlike 9/11, when al-Qaeda had to hijack aircraft, they now have planes available through Silver Eagle Aircraft Industries with locations in Chicago and Denver. There is no way to stop a private jet from attacking our population centers. By the time our air defenses have jet interceptors in the air, the damage will have been done."

Carlos again, "What you and Gretchen have to decide is which of the three cities is the immediate target. It may not be a single target and they may not be large targets."

"I believe it will be San Diego for several reasons. First, al-Qaeda has proven, with the attack on the USS Cole, that it knows how to cripple a ship. Second, if they can pull of a successful attack on a cruise ship, it will force Homeland Security to deploy more manpower to our major harbors at a time when federal budgets cannot sustain more hiring and additional training. Third, such an attack will panic the cruise industry and cause widespread cancellations and possibly bring about another economic meltdown. Finally, it will lay bare the government's ineptness and wrong-headed approach to national security."

"Gretchen, that is a good analysis of San Diego. I make the case for Denver. Unlike the other cities, it is not considered a major population center. I agree with you about the wrong-headed approach to national security. While the money and manpower have gone into securing our largest cities, I believe al-Qaeda will turn the tables on us and attach a second level city, thus making it impossible for Homeland Security to provide protection for every city. While there is no symbolic target in Denver, like the Twin Towers or the Pentagon, there are any number of high profile facilities that could be destroyed. What about you, Vinnie? Which city?"

"Khalid is going through exactly the same exercise we are. He's running all of the possibilities so his first attack will have the most psychological impact in addition to loss of life and loss of confidence in our government's ability to protect us. By now, Director Mallory will have contacted Homeland Security and their experts are engaged in the same process. As creative as we think we are, all of us are mentally sterilized by our group think culture. In Khalid's shoes, I would avoid all three cities in spite of the fact that they appear to be the most logical targets."

"Carlos and I are waiting."

"Boston. The historic city and its suburbs is the birthplace of the American Revolution with truly symbolic targets. You have the North Bridge in Concord, Bunker Hill and the Old North Church in the North End of the city. At the Charlestown Navy Yard, you have the frigate USS Constitution, better known as Old Ironsides. It is a symbol of power. And, of course, Boston harbor, site of the Tea Party. Politically there is Quincy, the homestead of John Adams. Khalid is a bright man, an educated man, who will see the symbolism in inflicting pain on the very city that led to the creation of a united country fashioned out of thirteen independent states. Had there been no Boston, no John Adams, no tea party and no defeating the British in Concord, there would be no United States of American, the country Khalid hates with a passion. There are additional symbolic targets along the Freedom Trail in Boston from which to choose. But, if I were he, I would choose the one that would have the same impact as if we sank a carrier or battleship in San Diego Harbor but one that carries far less risk for him. I would sink the USS Constitution, a fully commissioned naval vessel. As for symbolism, its location at the Charleston Navy Yard is at one end of the Freedom Trail. The Constitution fought in forty two battles and won every one of them. You sink her and you thrust a knife into the spirit of freedom and liberty. I have walked its deck many times while growing up in Massachusetts. It remains a symbol of American naval might. He is going to sink Old Ironsides."

Gretchen and Carlos did not know how to respond. On one hand, Vinnie made a credible case for Boston. On the other hand, for Khalid to select it as his major symbolic target assumed he understood early American history. He graduated from Stanford where history, unless it is revisionist, was not given a high priority.

"By tomorrow morning, agents from multiple intelligence agencies will be swarming across the country. Seven of our regional offices will be on full alert. We need to make a decision and move on, first to alert Elizabeth as to what we decide and then to call Darlene and Max. What is it going to be?"

"Gretchen, we need Elizabeth's thinking."

Two minutes later the three agents were on a conference call with Elizabeth. Vinnie brought her up to date on their thinking. As committed as they were to their choice of symbolic targets, they reminded her of the other three cities; Atlanta, Dallas and Seattle. She listened to their arguments for each city, understood that targets could be large or small, the need for symbolism, the vast array of targets including road bombings, assassinations of public officials, derailing trains and contaminating foodstuffs being among the options. And there were many more possibilities including bombing subways, busses, churches, schools, senior centers, convalescent homes and hospitals. Khalid had to do nothing more than research the French underground activities against the Germans in World War II to discover still more creative targets of opportunity. Homeland Security had recently stated that the country had to be alert to the fact that homegrown terrorism was an emerging threat to the security of the nation. Langley, along with other agencies, was well aware of plots that had been disrupted by law enforcement agencies. There was no doubt in Elizabeth's mind that Khalid had been building a network in the United States long before he was abducted in Rome. Each of the seven men with him in Florida was from Yemen, the newest and most dangerous breeding ground for terrorists. The unanswered question was how many operatives he had in the United States and in what locations. What she did believe was that there were active cells in at least seven cities. She hesitated in responding.

"Elizabeth, are you still there?"

"Yes, I was processing your data. They are complex and somewhat confusing. Nevertheless, let me share my thoughts." She wondered if her future agenda with Vinnie was clouding her thinking because, once again, she had to agree with his thinking about Khalid's first target."First, the other three cities do not have symbolic targets. Nothing matches the Twin Towers, the Pentagon or the White House. Seattle has the Space Needle, Atlanta has the Coca Cola Building and Dallas has the Bank of America Building. That's it. None of them match Boston for pure symbolism. I see the priority as Boston. Destroying the USS Constitution would be a blow to the Navy and a blow to the country given that the ship was named the Constitution to honor the written document. In one blow, he takes down a commissioned naval vessel and a symbol of individual freedoms."

There was silence as the three agents thought about her analysis and were impressed with her logic and the speed with which she developed it. She was quick to pick up on what little the three other cities had in the way of symbolisms. Everything about Boston made perfect sense. Gretchen asked, "What then?"

"After Boston, I think he would be less interested in symbolism and more interested in keeping Homeland Security off balance. In other words, he will move around the country and force Homeland to move its assets after the fact. He will want to stay ahead of them. If I were he, I would select San Diego as number two, Dallas as number three, Chicago as number four, Atlanta as number five and Denver last. After that, it is anyone's guess."

"Of course, there is always the possibility that Khalid has set this seven city strategy into motion to mislead us and his targets are elsewhere."

"That is always a possibility, Gretchen, but I don't believe it. Too many factors are in favor of the strategy we just discussed. Before I forget, Carlos, you are to report back to the Miami office. I will write a letter of commendation to your direct supervisor. I will also place you on my short list of agents who are to be considered for a regional Director position as soon as an appropriate one becomes available. Gretchen, you and Vinnie are to stop here on your way to New England."

"Something is not right."

"You have a problem, Vinnie?"

"Not a problem, Elizabeth, just a serious question as to the sequence of events. I have confidence that the pattern is as we have identified it, but the more I think about the larger picture, I am now doubting how it will unfold."

"Get to the point."

"If Boston is the primary target for symbolism, why wouldn't you save it for the finale? Why waste it up front when you can lay it on the country after it has been attacked on many fronts in many cities? Think of Khalid's entire scheme as a huge fireworks display where, after a fabulous performance, you send an aerial bombardment into the sky that is spectacular, filling the heavens with fire and color and ear piercing explosives. That is what the audience remembers. And that is what Khalid wants America to remember; fire, explosions and death."

Elizabeth was silent for a moment or two, processing yet another of Vinnie's out of the box ideas. "What do you think, Gretchen?"

"If any city is hit before Boston, then Vinnie will have made his point. Personally, I think he may be on to something."

"I'll sleep on it. I'll see you tomorrow on your way east. Goodnight." She was gone.

CHAPTER 68

WHEEL OF TERROR

Ibraham's attempt on Khalid's life altered the planned sequence of events. Khalid was to finalize plans for his strategy while in Florida but had to flee to avoid being apprehended. Fortunately for him, it took Vinnie and Gretchen three additional days to learn the identities of the seven other men who met at Karsam's residence. With time running out, Khalid took the bold and risky step of meeting with five of them in Denver. Since his final destination was Boston, he arranged to meet there with Aba Najdi, CEO of World Wide Wine & Spirits Distributors since the company was headquartered in Boston. It was a decision Khalid would regret.

What Ibrahim Mali did not know was that when Khalid made his frequent visits to Marta at their Paris and London villas, he also met with high level al-Qaeda agents who operated in the United States. In the ten years since 9/11 he and his operatives had developed a loyal network of cells in the seven American cities. The network was funded with Yemen money funneled to Khalid through Middle East drug cartels operating in the United States. At least twice a year, while on trips to Europe, he would travel to the United States to review the operation. He entered the United States posing as an executive with one of the six companies that had operations world-wide and that used private jets to avoid customs and immigration. He knew, based on his own pleasures in Paris and Rome, that the six CEO's could be compromised by the American culture and would need to be under the thumb of Khalid's operatives. The CEO's were a perfect front for his operations and they provided a secure means of bringing Khalid's operatives into the Unites States on private planes and ships owned by the six companies. They had been doing so for eleven years under the nose of Homeland Security.

The second thing that Ibraham did not know was that Khalid, while in Paris, had been certified to fly the French Falcon jet. The third thing Ibraham did not know was that while he was the chief financier and custodian of funds provided by the Saudis, Khalid had substantial financial resources provided him by Iran, including the purchase and upkeep of the Falcon. Among his al-Qaeda operatives, Khalid spoke like a terrorist but lived the life of a mogul. Khalid stored his plane at the Charles deGaulle Airport with a company that ferried aircraft anywhere in the world. The plane was registered to a French software company that existed only as a post office address. When Khalid discovered Ibraham's treachery, he knew that his time in Florida was limited. He placed a call to the aircraft storage company in France and had the Falcon ferried overnight to Jacksonville, Florida. Believing that his phones were being monitored, he used pre-paid card phones to contact the five co-conspirators and arranged to meet them in Denver. Two of the men had recently been promoted to take the places of Karzai and Mohammed, both of whom died at the hands of Khalid.

While Vinnie and Gretchen were in the midst of identifying all of the men in Florida, Khalid had flown himself from Jacksonville to Denver in the Falcon. The five men and Khalid, all dressed as American corporate chiefs, met at the Silver Eagle Aircraft Industries corporate offices. Ayman Kashmir was the new head of the company, replacing Karzai. Khalid immediately took charge and introduced the new chief of Global Construction, Inc., Nasir Al Awalki. The two new CEO's were completely loyal to Khalid and willing to follow his orders without question. The other three, believing that two of their lot had been murdered, were now compliant. Khalid was in complete control. He unfolded his strategy, new to the recently appointed chiefs and a review for the others. While his first choice of terrorism in the United States remained suicide bombing, he explained that until he could negotiate with the powerful Imams of the major mosques to help in recruiting the bombers, he would initially use other methods of terrorizing the public. Since Homeland Security had publically stated that terrorists would be employing simpler but effective means to intimidate the public, Khalid and al-Qaeda decided to make it a self-fulfilling prophesy. He then handed each of the five men a single sheet of paper that listed twelve different events or attacks for his wheel of terror. Six cities formed the geographic rim of the wheel with Denver as the hub.

He waited until each man read the list knowing that none would question or challenge him on the content. It was implicit that they were expected to participate in implementing the wheel of terror or face elimination. With both Karzai and Mohammed dead, they understood the price of defection, betrayal and failure. When it was clear that they knew what was expected of them, he went on to explain that the wheel of terror would begin with an event in Massachusetts. Once that event took place, it would be the signal for the six men to build the twelve spokes of the wheel of terror in their region.

"It is your responsibilities to utilize devout Muslims from within your companies and have them ready to act. They are to assist my operatives when called upon. Each attack will be conducted by experienced operatives I will assign to you. There will be many of them over the course of implementing twelve events. Each will have a specialty. They are to be brought into the firm as employees so they can have effective cover from the prying eyes of American intelligence agencies. When their work is completed, they will leave and you will never hear from them again. Understood?"

The first question came. "What is the event in Massachusetts and how will we know it has taken place?"

"For security reasons, the event will be known only to me and those who will make it happen. On the outside chance you are taken into custody by American intelligence agencies and tortured, you will have nothing to give and the interrogators will soon discover this. As for the second part of your question, you must trust me when I say that you will know when it happens. Other questions?" Being none, he continued.

"The operatives assigned to you are battled tested fighters who have killed in the name of Allah. You must listen to their advice and orders and take them to heart. They will have operational control over the events, both in timing and selection."

"How soon must these events take place?"

"Once the Massachusetts event takes place, you will have sixty days to implement twelve events. Each event in your area must cover a different point on the compass so that the widest geographical area is covered in order that the greatest number of Americans are impacted."

"Is death to the greatest number the goal?"

"Death is important but creating fear of the unknown is the number one priority. By the time the eighty four events are completed, I will be prepared to implement the next and more deadly second wave of terror."

"What of those who carry out our plans? What if they are apprehended?"

"That is none of your concern. Your primary task is to provide manpower and assistance to the operatives. All must be prepared to die for Allah."

"When will we meet the operatives?"

"Each of you is to expect the first operatives at your office on Thursday morning, two days from now. You are to inform your receptionists to expect them and not to keep them waiting. They will identify themselves by telling your receptionists they are computer specialists on a special assignment."

The meeting continued for another hour with most of the time used to discuss the acquisition of raw materials to be used and how they would be obtained. When the meeting ended and the men left, Ayman Kashmir, the host remained. "Abdu Khalid, you have outlined a masterful plan for terrorizing the American public."

"Thank you Ayman. Now, if you would excuse me, I wish to be alone for a few minutes."

When Ayman left, Khalid sat quietly and read the list of terrorist events to himself.

Car bombing of a high profile official
Poisoning of high school cafeteria food
Derailment of a commuter train while in transit
Destruction of a commuter bus while occupied
Murder of a chief of police
Destruction of a convalescent home by arson
Downing of a military aircraft
Explosive destruction of a fire station
Fire-bombing of a fire station
Release of poison gas in an anchor store in a major mall
Bombing of a local television station
Murder of a chief operating officer of a major metropolitan paper
Destruction of a place of worship

Each event met his goal of creating fear while killing Americans. His next wave of terror, suicide bombings, would create even greater havoc. He whispered quietly, "Abdu Khalid, you have begun to spin the wheel of terror. The CIA will regret it sent me to Egypt to be tortured and sooner or later, I will kill Max Rietsema."

Unknown to Khalid, outside the headquarters of Silver Eagle Aircraft Industries, two CIA agents were keeping surveillance on everyone who entered or left the building. One of those agents was the very man Khalid planned on killing. Shortly after Max Rietsema and Darlene Hunt learned that Hafs Karzai was the CEO of the company, they left for the Chicago headquarters of the company. Pretending to be owners of World Wide Jet Services interested in acquiring new aircraft and insisting on meeting with Karzai, they were told that he was on extended leave and that Ayman Kashmir was acting CEO. Persistent in wanting to speak only with the new CEO, they were told that he was out of the state and would not return until the following Monday. Taking that to mean he was at the Denver facility, they flew to Denver and met with Kashmir. Sticking with their cover, they made arrangement to return the following day to tour the facility and take a test flight in the Silver Eagle X650. They left the building and as they were approaching their car in the lot, a limo pulled up to the entrance of the building. They turned to see who the VIP was. Max could hardly believe his eyes when he saw Khalid exit the car and enter the building. "Holy shit!"

"What is it, Max?"

"Khalid. That was Abdu Khalid who just entered the building. If he is here, then something significant is in the works."

"The question is what?"

"Listen, Darlene, we know that Kashmir is the replacement for Karzai who, in turn, was one of the men who met with Khalid in Florida. We must assume that Khalid, Ibraham and the six men hatched something in Florida that is being played out here. Vinnie and Gretchen have photographs of three of the men taken from the surveillance tapes at the Royal Palms. We need to get those. It is entirely possible that if Khalid is here, so are the other men. For now, we need to stay put and photograph every male who exits the building, especially those who may leave in a group."

"Max, I'll call Elizabeth and see if Kashmir is in our archives. I'll also ask her to get the name of the

CEO at Global Construction in Seattle and to check him in the archives. By tonight, we should know if any of the six men met with Khalid today."

"That's good. Let's think about Khalid for a minute. We could easily pick him up, but we know from experience that we will learn nothing of importance from him. If we try enhanced interrogation again, the Justice Department will throw away the key to our prison block. For now, I say we remain where we are, take our photographs, try putting a tail on Khalid and learn the identities of the others."

"Then what?"

"One of these men may have to disappear."

"What does that mean?"

"It means we may have to abduct one of the six and ask a few questions."

"Not a good idea. Once we do that, Khalid and the others will go to ground and we will have little chance of learning what the alternative 9/11 is. We need to be patient. As anxious as you are to take Khalid down, this is not the time."

While they discussed the matter more fully, two men entered the building together. They had the bearing, confidence, walk and grooming of bureau agents. Even from a distance it was obvious they were carrying.

"Are you thinking what I am?"

"I'm thinking that two bureau agents are entering the building. But why? Do you think it is a coincidence?"

"Max, there is no way the bureau knows that Khalid is in the building. They have to be here on other business. Either that or they are not bureau."

"Nothing we can do but wait."

The two men approached the receptionist, had a few words with her and were ushered into the conference room where Khalid was still mentally plotting his next act. When they entered, Khalid stood. The taller of the two men spoke. "I am Ilyas and this is Anwar."

"I have been expecting you. Be seated." When the men had taken seats, Khalid continued. "Are the other operatives in position?"

"As planned, each of the five men will have visitors on Thursday. The sixth will have visitors once you have met with him in Boston. All of the operatives have been briefed as to their responsibilities. There will be no trouble in executing the twelve events. All have the technical knowledge to implement your strategies. Once they have completed each mission, they will fade into the Muslim community in the city and remain there until it is safe to leave the country. As agreed, they will leave on ships or planes owned by the six companies. Each event will have a new group of operatives and none will know of the existence of other events or the operatives who will carry them out. We have planned well so there is little to worry about."

"I always worry so do not fail me."

"There is a small matter of concern, Abdu Khalid. It appears that you have two observers maintaining a surveillance of the building. One is male and the other female."

Clearly unhappy at the turn of events, Khalid asked, "How do you know they are keeping watch on the building?"

"Exercising our usual caution, we arrived an hour early to keep watch on who may be interested in you and your visitors. Before you arrived, they entered the building and were gone for thirty minutes. They then returned to their car. It is a rental car. It was easy to notice them because they made a handsome pair. The woman is quite attractive. They had started their engine but did not move once you exited the limo. We could just make out the man's expression and it was one of surprise. They had a discussion and then stopped the engine and waited."

"Are they still there?"

Without being asked by Ilyas, who was in charge, Anwar left the room. The two men remained quiet until Anwar returned. "They are still there."

The room was quiet as the two men respected Khalid's desire to think. He picked up the inter-office phone and got the receptionist. He asked to be connected directly to Mr. Kashmir. When the latter came on the line, Khalid asked, "Ayman, did you have any business visitors today, a man and a women? Both American, the woman attractive."

"I did. They operate a private charter service and are interested in the Silver Eagle for their fleet. They are returning tomorrow afternoon for a test flight. Is something wrong?"

"Nothing to be concerned with. Go ahead with the test flight. Did they mention where they are staying?"

No."

"Thank you Ayman." If Khalid knew that it was Max Rietsema who was in the car, he would have him killed in the parking lot. Since he did not know, he returned the phone to its cradle and turned to Ilyas and Anwar."Kill them somewhere other than here."

Gretchen and Max saw the two men come out of the building and quickly took their photographs. "They look like bureau but the timing is all wrong.

Max, what is it about them that doesn't fit the bureau model?"

"Their haircuts. Their hair is too long for bureau agents. They look foreign, not from the Middle East. Maybe European. We need to be careful with them. Let's wait and see what they do next."

In the meantime, Ilyas and Anwar were waiting in their car for Max and Darlene to make a move. "Why are they not moving, Ilyas?"

"They saw us enter the building after Khalid entered and then observed us leaving shortly after that. We are on their radar screen. By now, our pictures have been transmitted to some agency they work for. We need to move quickly. If Khalid wants them dead we must assume they work for a government agency. We need to set them up for a kill. But first, we must know if we are of interest. If they follow us, we know we are under surveillance."

Ilyas started the car and left the parking lot. He turned left on to Sullivan Boulevard and headed toward the center of the city. In his rear view mirror, he saw the other car make the same moves. For the trip into the city, they drove in tandem. Ilyas turned right on to Hemlock, a commercial road with wall to wall strip malls, gas stations, convenience stores and fast food restaurants. Max and Darlene followed. To prove to himself that he was being followed, Ilyas pulled into a strip mall and parked the car. Max entered the lot and parked leaving a good distance between the cars and parked. Both cars idled and none of the passengers moved outside. Ten minutes later, the first car left the lot and turned right on to Hemlock and drove two blocks and pulled into another small strip mall. Max did the same.

"Max, they just verified they are being followed which means they spotted us at Silver Eagle Headquarters. They must have arrived before us and set up protective surveillance of the building for Khalid. Why?"

"They work for Khalid and did what we do when we are running protective cover for a VIP, which is to arrive early and set up a watch. They were there when we arrived, we looked suspicious in that we remained in our car after we left the building and after we saw Khalid arrive and enter the building. They reported what they saw to Khalid and probably have orders to take us down. Because this surveillance is upside down with us following them, and not the reverse, the only way they can eliminate us is to lure us to a spot where a killing would go unnoticed."

"If we drop the surveillance of them, they will learn where we are staying and make a move there. What are our options?"

"We need to turn this around and have them follow us to where we have the upper hand. We must assume they are armed, probably automatic weapons. I have a small caliber ankle pistol and a KABAR on the other ankle. Both are close in weapons. How about you?"

"A small caliber pistol in my shoulder bag. We are not especially well armed."

"We didn't expect that we would be in this position. Here is what I suggest. Call Elizabeth and bring her up-to-date. This is what we need her to do." He gave Darlene the particulars. Then, he pulled up closer to Ilyas and Anwar and when he was certain they had him in view, he took a left turn and slowly drove down Arlington Street. Ilyas did a quick turn and followed which was exactly what Max and Darlene hoped they would do. They drove around Denver for forty-five minutes being careful not to lose Ilysas and Anwar.

They had booked two adjoining rooms at the Hilton Hotel using their own names. When they arrived at the hotel, Max pulled into the valet parking line, took a receipt for the car and handed the valet captain a twenty dollar bill. He opened the trunk, took out a briefcase and then he and Darlene walked into the lobby and headed for the lounge. They sat at a table and ordered two drinks. Four minutes later, the two men entered, sat at the bar and ordered two beers. Ten minutes later Max signed the bar check and he and Darlene left the lounge and headed for the elevators. Ilyas left a ten dollar bill on the table and he and Anwar followed them to the elevators. Max and Darlene entered the elevator and Darlene hit the button for the twelfth floor just as the two men followed them in. Max and Darlene had positioned themselves on one side of the elevator with Darlene closest to the door and Max next to her in the corner. Ilyas stood facing Darlene and Anwar opposite Max. Once the door closed, the two men would attempt to kill Max and Darlene.

Just as the door was about to close, a man reached in and held it open with his hand as he stepped into the elevator. He was six two or three, lean, blond, blue eyed and smiling. His clothes were casual-khaki pants, turtle neck sweater, Denver Broncos jacket, Nike sneakers and he held a pint bottle of Jack Daniels in his other hand. He held the door while his friend stepped in. She was five nine or ten, Indian or Pakistani heritage, wearing tight jeans, ankle height boots and an expensive leather jacket over a beige cotton sweater. She carried an over the shoulder bag. "Damn near missed it, Lucy." She rushed in and both she and her companion stood on the opposite side of the elevator from Max and Darlene, facing the backs of Ilyas and Anwar.

Talking to the other four in the elevator, Sam said, "My woman hates to wait for elevators so we're always rushing like hell to squeeze in whenever we can. But, hell, there is plenty of room" Looking at the buttons, he continued, "Looks like we are all headed for the same floor. We can call up two of Lucy's friends and have a party, plenty of girls to go around." Looking at Darlene lustfully, "You sure have the makings of a party girl. How about a drink?" He tried to hand her the bottle which she pushed aside.

"Keep your lecherous thoughts and your booze to yourself or you and I will have a party you wish didn't happen."

"Forget it folks. He's had one too many. He's harmless. I know. Sam, shut up."

Ilyas and Anwar turned to get a look at the couple. What they saw were two degenerate Americans who were morally corrupt. Ilyas looked at Anwar and his body language and head motion signaled that it was time to take out the newcomers and then kill Max and Darlene. They knew there would be a short window of opportunity when the doors opened. The elevator stopped at the twelfth floor and the door opened. No one was waiting for it. Ilyas nodded to Max and Darlene that they should exit first. "Thanks, but after you." It was Max speaking. Ilyas looked at Anwar and motioned that they would go first. As they stepped out of the elevator and into the hallway, they turned and at the same time reached into their jackets for their automatic pistols prepared to kill all four of the occupants and send the elevator on it way. As they completed the turn and before they could fully extract their weapons, they faced the two degenerate Americans, both with .45 caliber silenced pistols pointed at them. The fear of death lasted only until silenced bullets ripped into their chests. As the two men fell, Sam and Lucy reached out and pulled them into the elevator. Before the elevator door closed, four agents who had blocked off and secured the twelfth floor entered.

Lucy spoke to Darlene and Max. "We'll take it from here. There is an agent in each of your rooms as back-up. Please tell them to meet us in the basement. And, good luck." The door closed and the elevator headed for the basement with six agents and two dead al-Qaeda operatives.

Darlene turned to Max. "Your instructions to Elizabeth were perfect as was her orchestrating a successful ending. Some woman." Max thought so.

CHAPTER 69

BOSTON

By the time Ilyas and Anwar left the meeting with Khalid in Denver, Darlene had photographed everyone who had left the building before them including the men who were at the meeting. She then transmitted the photographs to Elizabeth. When the two CIA agents left for the basement to meet their colleagues, she and Max were alone. Darlene then received a response from Langley. The photographs confirmed that present at the meeting with Khalid were Abdu Karsam from Atlanta, Suleiman Amir from San Diego, Abdul Jazier from Dallas, and the new man from Seattle, Nasir Al-Awlaki. The host for the meeting was the new man from Chicago/Denver, Ayman Kashmir.

"Boston is missing. This means that Khalid is heading there as we speak. It also suggests that whatever he plans on doing, he is kicking it off in the Boston area. Elizabeth needs to put a twenty four hour surveillance on the five men who were here today the minute they arrive home. We need to know who they meet and where they go."

"Darlene, what about Najdi in Boston? Why wasn't he here?"

"My guess, Max, is that Khalid did not want the others to know too much about Boston for fear they would break under interrogation by our people. In any event, he's ours. Also Vinnie and Gretchen. The four of us can handle the surveillance of Khalid and Najdi at the outset. You call Elizabeth and explain what happened today and have her move on the surveillance of the other five men immediately. I will call Gretchen and Vinnie and bring them up to speed and arrange for us to meet them in Boston in the morning. We can catch a flight late this afternoon."

They arrived at Logan International Airport in East Boston at nine forty five p.m. They rented a car and drove to the Four Seasons on Boylston Street where they had booked two rooms. Once they had checked in, they went to the Bristol Lounge where they were greeted by Vinnie and Gretchen. The place was jumping with the rich and beautiful having a great time dining and drinking. There was the usual kissing and hugging as the four agents greeted one another. Once they were seated and had ordered drinks, Vinnie began the conversation. "You two did great work in Denver, especially matching the photographs of those at the meeting with the pictures taken in Florida. Speaking of Florida, I really miss Carlos. Great guy and a great agent. I hope Langley moves him up."

"Actually, what we accomplished in Denver could not have happened without the work done in Florida. I understand that Carlos and his team were great trackers, but your laying out the pattern was the key. We know who they are and where they are. What we don't know is what they are up to."

Gretchen added, "We do know with some degree of certainty that Massachusetts will be the first area to be hit. Personally, I don't believe it will be in Boston at the outset. That is too obvious."

"Gretchen, you make it sound as though there will be more than one event. Why is that?" It was Darlene.

"It is difficult to mount a duplicate 9/11. The logistics would be difficult to arrange. Even Homeland Security acknowledges that the new terrorist attacks will more than likely be derailments, food contamination, abductions and individual killings. Khalid is about to surprise us in ways we are not prepared for and he will do it where security is lax. It won't be long before it begins."

"I agree with Gretchen. Once we put the pattern together and identified the seven cities, it became obvious that we would waste valuable resources if we think in terms of Twin Towers, the Pentagon or the White House. We need to think of small but multi ple targets. While symbolism is important to Khalid, I believe that creating fear and uncertainty are his primary objectives. The general public quickly forgot about 9/11 because it directly impacted a small percentage of the population and was restricted to three sites, one of which caused no deaths except to those on the plane. All these years later, we reflect on 9/11 each September and then go about our business. If Khalid has his way, the impact of his new efforts will be long lasting."

"Darlene and I need nourishment. What say we order dinner and then continue our strategy session at breakfast?"

"Thank you Max for watching out for me. And before you two ask, Elizabeth knows that Max is with us. Actually, what she said was Max is on his own and she did not want to know any details as to his whereabouts, even if we knew of them. We are now officially a threesome and unofficially a foursome. Khalid does not stand a chance." That brought smiles to everyone and another round of drinks was ordered. They all believed Khalid to be close by and scheming.

For the first time in what seemed weeks, the four agents relaxed and had a pleasant evening. When dinner was over, and as tired as they were, it seemed fitting to walk in the Public Gardens. They walked out of the hotel, turned left and then right on to Arlington. Rather than enter the Gardens, they walked along the perimeter of it and then decided to stop in at the old Ritz Carlton, now the Boston Taj, for a nightcap.

While the four agents were enjoying their after dinner drinks, a quarter of a mile away Khalid was using a public pay phone in the Copley Square subway station to place five phone calls. The response to the first call he made to Ayman Kashmir, who was still at the Denver facility, was cause for alarm for there was no word from Ilyas and Anwar. The other four calls yielded the correct responses. Once he had heard from Kashmir, his first call of the five, he ordered the other four CEO's to move ahead within forty eight hours to initiate an action and not to wait for a major event in Massachusetts as he had instructed them to do while in Denver. Conditions had changed dramatically and his strategy had to change. Other attacks should follow as soon as possible. Once the operatives made contact with the CEO's, action plans would be implemented.

In Khalid's mind, the fact that the two operatives he had met with in Kashmir's office had not made contact as required could only mean they had been apprehended or killed by the two individuals who had Kashmir's building under surveillance. The consequence of that failure was that the CIA was closing in and Khalid had to move up his timetable. It also required reordering the events. Rather than attack the USS Constitution, he would order Aba Najdi to implement one of the twelve events in the Boston region within twenty four hours or as soon as the operatives contacted him. Khalid needed to draw attention away from the city of Boston proper. To meet the timetable, Najdi's operatives would need to select an event that required little planning and low level skills.

What Khalid needed was fresh air and exercise to clear his head. When he exited the subway station, he walked two blocks to Newbury Street. He then turned left and was quickly immersed in capitalism at its best. The street was crowded with people of all ages; residents, visitors, and business men and women, most of whom had finished dinner and were window shopping on one of Boston's upscale business destinations. He walked the length of the crowded street until it intersected with Massachusetts Avenue, where he turned, crossed over and walked down the opposite side of Newbury Street from the way he came. Little did he know that his hunters were were so close. Little did the hunters know that the hunted was within their grasp. But, it was too soon to apprehend him. First, they needed to unravel his plan.

Khalid was staying at the Richmond Plaza Hotel on St. James Street, just blocks from the Four Seasons and the hunters. Upon returning to the hotel, he decided to have a night cap. The Oak Bar was vibrant with guests and he was pleased to be among the rich and beautiful. He missed Marta, her warm and sensuous body and the excitement she could have provided him tonight.

Though angered that the two operative in Denver had failed in their mission, he decided not to let it interfere with his precious moments of relaxation in the Oak Bar. It had been an exhausting three weeks since he entered the United States. He arrived as Prince Hamil Azhid, transformed himself into Jonathon Drew while in Florida and now was Thomas Gilbane, British business man. When his work was done he would exit the country with still a fourth name. He couldn't help but reflect on how easy it was for the Iran intelligence agency to forge four sets of identity documents and how lax Homeland Security had been in tracking al-Qaeda operatives as they entered and exited the United States on ships and planes that belonged to the six companies. With all of its electronic sophistication and tens of thousands of agents and employees, the intelligence community was unable to stem the flow of terrorists into the country. Khalid's operatives moved easily. The multiple American intelligence agencies spent more time monitoring each other than they did pursuing terrorists. He was the perfect example. In spite of a world-wide search for him, he was sitting in public view in a bar in one of America's icon hotels. Regardless of how this mission turned out, in his heart he believed that eventually America loses.

Khalid cut a dashing figure in his tailored tan slacks, light blue linen jacket, pale pink silk shirt and dark blue tie. His long hair was rakish looking, befitting a successful playboy of European origin. He drew the attention of many in the room when he entered. His first action was to make a visual sweep of the room, always on the alert for someone who may be monitoring his activities. Satisfied that he was not being observed, he asked the hostess for a small table rather than sitting at the bar, and then pressed a twenty dollar bill into her palm. She smiled invitingly, seated him in the midst of the action and took his order. Once he ordered his Absolute martini up with two olives, he sat back and enjoyed the ambience of the Oak Bar.

Khalid lived in two worlds, one in which he was expected to terrorize westerners, another in which he enjoyed the life of one born of money and position. He grew up in an educationally impoverished country, but was educated in one of America's great universities. In Yemen, women were suppressed into slavery while in America most of the wealth was owned by women. His was a world of contrasts.

He sipped his martini slowly, reflecting on what had occurred since he left Egypt and processing what was to come. Glancing around the room, he enjoyed the vibrant atmosphere and the soft jazz that filtered through the speakers. This was one of the many playgrounds where the beautiful people of Boston gathered to enjoy an evening and to make plans for the night. Everything about the room and its occupants was visually pleasing. For the first time in weeks he was relaxed and playing his new role of the debonair British businessman. He had been sitting for the better part of a half hour and was thinking of ordering a second martini when his thoughts were interrupted.

"Excuse me, but my friends and I couldn't help but notice you were sitting alone and wondered if you would like to join us? My name is William Worthington and I am here with my fiancé and her sister. It is a shame to drink alone in such a festive setting."

Khalid looked up into the face of a movie star handsome man of approximately his own age, beautifully groomed and dressed, and well spoken. He had the moves of a wealthy Bostonian.

Standing, he took the man's hand and spoke. He was equally if not more impressive looking than Worthington. "Thank you for the generous offer, but I cannot disrupt your evening."

"Nonsense. You would only add to our pleasure. Please come and we will welcome you to our city."

"You are from Boston?"

"My ancestors helped settle the city. Yes, you could say we are from Boston."

"My name is Thomas Gilbane."

Khalid left a twenty dollar bill on his table and followed William Worthington. When they approached his table, two women looked up at Khalid. "Thomas, I would like to introduce my fiancé, Lee Horton, and her sister, Kay Horton." Thomas Gilbane extended his hand to each woman who, in turn, took his and gave him their very best Boston Brahman smiles.

"You must excuse me if I appear surprised, but the friendliness of Americans is always something of a wonder to Brits. Inviting a total stranger to share a drink would never happen in England. But thank you."

Lee Horton was a year or two younger than her sister Kay. Both were ravishing beauties, with bodies that spoke of sex, physical activities and youth. They shared blond hair, blue eyes and were wearing designer cocktail dresses that exposed bosom and highlighted ass. Thomas wondered if William Worthington was fucking both of them, perhaps as a threesome. If Thomas Gilbane was off balance, it was not the invitation, but the prospect of a rewarding night. Thomas also had the fleeting thought that if he were to get close to

Kay Horton, he might just acquire himself an address unknown to his hunters.

Once seated, Lee asked, "What brings you to Boston, Thomas?"

Looking directly at her and employing his most reserved manner, "I am here on business, but intend to combine it with pleasure. This being the home of the American Revolution that we Brits would rather forget, I plan on seeing some of the actual sites of the historic conflicts including Concord, Lexington, the church where your hero, Paul Revere, held the famous 'one if by land and two if by sea' lanterns, and so on. I would also like to take a ride in the harbor and visit your USS Constitution."

"You appear to have done your homework already, Thomas." It was Kay and her smile would melt glaciers.

William asked, "What line of work are you in, Thomas?"

"I'm an international broker. I bring buyers and sellers together from around the world to complete transactions to the benefit of both parties. The business requires my traveling the globe. Most of my clients have been with me for some time and almost all have assets in multiple companies in several countries."

"What type of transactions do you facilitate?" It was William who asked.

"Hard assets of considerable value and selective intellectual property."

"It doesn't sound as though you have time for developing long-term relationships." It was Lee.

"That is true to some extent, but my bases of operation are London and Paris. I have developed some friendships in each city but nothing long term. There will be time enough for that."

"Enough talk of business. Perhaps one of you gentlemen would be kind enough to order me another cosmopolitan."

"Kay, to ensure that you get your drink in record time, I will go to the bar and fetch it for you." With that Thomas, a.k.a Khalid, went to the bar.

"What do you think, Kay? You have been complaining that Boston has only the dullest of men. London, Paris, travels the globe."

"Well, William, the night is young. Let's see if he is as sophisticated as he appears on first blush. But, yes, he is beautiful."

For the next three hours, the foursome had a pleasant time exchanging friendly talk about their respective countries and the fact that England was America's only true ally. Thomas made it a point to avoid controversial topics. William had several drinks but Thomas limited himself to two martinis in addition to the one he had when alone. He did not want to run the risk of saying anything that would give away his true motive and reason for being in Boston. He also wanted to impress Kay Horton. Lee and Kay both had three drinks. From comments made, it was clear that William and Lee were living together in Boston. Kay, at a relatively young age, was socially active but free of any binding attachment but apparently had many suitors from which to choose. She was Chief Investment Officer of one of the several funds that William Worthington managed under the umbrella of Galaxy Investments, LLC. Lee, on the other hand, was a social giant in Boston, due primarily to the Worthington name and fortune. She met William when she was managing another of his funds. Shortly thereafter, they decided to become a couple and to use Galaxy funds to mount a major social initiative. Lee was spectacular at raising money for charity and at soliciting new clients for Galaxy Investments, LLC.

Kay gave no indication during the evening that she had any continuing interest in Thomas. He displayed no visible interest in her but each time he looked at her he could feel a stirring between his legs. However, fatigue was getting the better of him. "I want to thank you all for a wonderful evening and especially you, William, for inviting me to join you. I have been traveling extensively for three weeks and am exhausted and ready for sleep. So, I must say goodnight and, unfortunately, goodbye." He stood to leave.

"Thomas, we have enjoyed your company immensely. Sorry the evening has to end. If you are here for a few days, one or all of us would love to show you the sights. Here is my card. Please call me tomorrow on the private line and we will arrange to do the town." William, always the salesman, thought perhaps he had a potential customer in Thomas Gilbane. That aside, he was great company and he sensed that Kay was interested in seeing him again.

Thomas and William shook hands. The two women stood and gave him a light, socially correct kiss on the cheek and wished him well. They both smelled delicious to Khalid who had been without a woman since Marta left for Paris. All three, along with a number of other women, watched as he strode from the room.

"With the weekend coming, Kay, this might be an opportunity to do some sight-seeing and get to know him better."

"Perhaps, William, perhaps."

When Khalid returned to his room, he placed the business card William had given him on the night stand. He was confident he would be offered a guide for a sightseeing tour of historic landmarks in Boston and the area. If only Galaxy Investments owned a yacht that would serve as a torpedo to ride into the Navy yard and the USS Constitution. On the other hand, he had the French Falcon to accomplish his mission.

At the old Ritz Carlton the four agents finished their drinks and walked back to the Four Seasons on Boylston Street. On the way, they decided to meet at breakfast and plan their work for the day. Darlene and Max had booked separate rooms. Vinnie and Gretchen also booked separate rooms but had planned on leaving one unused. Not certain what Darlene and Max knew of their relationship, they decided for this one night to utilize separate rooms.

CHAPTER 70

THE TOUR

Thomas was up early and had returned to the hotel after a vigorous hour's walk in the Public Gardens. He was opening the door to his room when the phone rang. He rushed to pick it up. "Good morning. This is Kay Horton. I hope I didn't wake you."

"Not at all. I rose early and walked in the Gardens. Nice to hear your voice."

"We begin your tour at one o'clock. I thought we would visit the North Bridge in Concord. It was the site of the battle that began the American movement for independence. Concord is also a lovely town to visit. I'll pick you up at the St. James Street entrance to the hotel. See you then." She hung up.

He looked at the receiver in his hand and then carefully put it down. In Yemen, she would have been stoned for speaking to a man in that manner. In America it was the norm for successful women. He was finding it difficult to keep his focus and remember that he was a Yemen terrorist and not a British businessman.

Not expecting to be entertained, Thomas did not have a wardrobe for casual wear. He walked across the street to the upscale mall in the Weston Hotel building where he managed to outfit himself with slacks, loafers, a Polo short-sleeve shirt and a blue hopsack blazer. Kay skidded to a stop at exactly one o'clock in a black M3 BMW. Thomas got in and she was off to connect with the turnpike extensions and then to route 2 and Concord.

"Good morning, Thomas. I love your outfit. You look like you live in Boston."

"And you, Kay, are a designer's dream. You look quite beautiful this morning. Thank you for arranging the tour of Concord. It will be interesting to visit the site where a group of farmers defeated a well trained and disciplined British Army."

"Now, don't be a poor loser. In the end, it all worked out fine. Our countries are still friends."

She reached Concord center in less than forty five minutes, then turned on to Monument Street and headed for the North Bridge.

"I must tell you that the North Bridge we are about to see is not the original. In fact, it has been rebuilt several times. But, it remains a symbol for the beginning of the conflict. As history has it, the American militia was unable to stop the British force in Lexington. The British army then regrouped and marched to Concord where it was confronted by a militia comprised of men from surrounding towns. The militia actually outnumbered the British but was untrained for combat. But, good always wins over evil and the British were stopped at the bridge and then began a retreat to Boston. On the way out of town, the army took heavy losses from still another militia force from other towns.

"Is this a story told to all schoolchildren?"

"April 19, 1775 is a date to be remembered by all Americans. It represents the day that America decided to be free from oppression. It was a day that symbolized not just freedom of speech but freedom from bondage. To this day, Americans believe that our country is a model for countries around the world that want liberty and equality for all men and women. I believe it, Thomas."

"I shall remember the story, Kay."

"I visited this site many times while growing up. I especially wanted you to experience it now that our countries are but one in the fight against terrorism. We have put our political and economic differences behind us and moved on. There are two plaques I want you to see."

She parked the car in the lot near the bridge and they walked together. He wanted to hold her hand, but shied away from doing so thinking that he would compromise his beliefs. A story of liberty and freedom was not one he particularly wanted to listen to, especially from a woman.

When they reached the bridge, she said, "The first plaque is just over here." She took him by the hand and they walked to the statue of the Minute Man by Daniel Chester French. Khalid looked intense as she quietly and slowly spoke the words inscribed at the base of the statue.

By the rude bridge that arched the flood,
Their flag to April's breeze unfurled,
Here once the embattled farmers stood
And fired the shot heard round the world.

"Thomas, the statue was cast from iron salvaged from seven cannon used in the Civil War."

"The poem is quite touching, Kay."

"Come, I want you to read another poem. It speaks for itself. The plaque was placed here in 1910 by residents of Concord. It speaks to the British soldiers who fought and died here in vain."

Before she could continue, he said, "Please, allow me." Then he read the plaque.

Grave of British Soldiers
They came three thousand miles and died,
To keep the past upon its throne:
Unheard, beyond the ocean tide,
Their English Mother made her moan.
April 19, 1775

"I'm pleased you are here, Thomas, to witness the site of a revolution that has brought hope to many millions. It is remarkable that two countries which were at war with each other so long ago are now partners in promoting democracy around the world."

"Kay, not everyone believes democracy is the appropriate form of government for all countries."

"I think it is a matter of semantics. If you substitute the word freedom for democracy, non-believers may have an easier time buying into the concept. As difficult as it is to change governments, we must continually make an effort to free people from bondage, to safeguard children around the world and to put a stop to the abuse of women."

"You captivate me first with your beauty and now with your passion."

She shifted the conversation. "I hope you are in Boston long enough for us to get to spend some time together."

"I am working on several projects so I should be here for at least a few days, perhaps longer depending upon how successful I am. I would like very much to spend some time with you and to see still more of historic Boston."

"Let's make it happen."

He looked at her and wondered why such a beautiful woman with everything at her fingertips would care about what others needed or aspired to. He had to remind himself that his goal was to destroy American for what its leaders did to countries in the Middle East when they partnered with evil monarchs. Together, they slaughtered women and children and destroyed historic cultures in order to extract oil from land that did not belong to them. Yes, he could love this delicate and kind woman, but he must first complete his wheel of terror.

Kay drove around Concord showing Thomas some of the many historic sites. It was close to four o'clock when she suggested they head back to the city.

Meanwhile, the four agents had an unproductive day. They met for breakfast and realized that there was little they could accomplish. Massachusetts was the site for Khalid's 9/11 alternative, but they knew not what it was or when it would occur. Homeland Security was now in the picture as were multiple intelligence and law enforcement agencies. Elizabeth had ordered the Boston regional office to establish a twenty-four hour surveillance of Aba Najdi's home and business. Nothing unusual had occurred. That was not a surprise to the agents since they had concluded that Khalid had already provided Najdi with whatever he needed in the way of support. All they could do was wait and attempt to discern a new pattern that would allow them to get ahead of the curve and stop the bloodshed. In the meantime, they agreed to go their separate ways for the remainder of the day and to meet for dinner at seven in the Bristol Lounge. If anything of consequence occurred, they would use cell phones to talk.

It was four thirty p.m. and Kay and Thomas were on the outskirts of the city listening to music on WBX 1050. At that moment, Vinnie was in a sports bar on Massachusetts Avenue watching baseball on a wide screen TV. Gretchen and Darlene were on Newbury Street looking at clothes in upscale shops. Max was walking in the Public Gardens thinking about Bettina Falaguerra and how much he missed her.

WBX interrupted its programming for a special announcement. "The Massachusetts State Police just announced that the body of Robert Asbury, Chief of Police in Merritt, Massachusetts, was found this morning in a rest area off Interstate 495 near Lawrence. Merritt is a small community east of Haverhill. According to the State Police report, the Chief was last seen at a health club in Haverhill around nine last night after he had finished his workout. His wife called his assistant at midnight when the Chief had not arrived home. Although not confirmed, our reporter has learned that al-Qaeda called the State Police this morning and claimed responsibility for the death. The State Police are not confirming the report nor is it revealing the cause of death. Our reporter claims that the death scene was gruesome. The Federal Bureau of Investigation is on the scene along with Homeland Security."

Kay turned off the radio, stunned at what she had heard. Thomas played along. "Is it possible, Thomas, for this to happen here?"

"Homeland Security warned all western nations that this could happen. But first, what we heard needs to be confirmed."

The baseball game was interrupted with the same announcement. Vinnie left a twenty on the bar and left. He dialed the group, copied Elizabeth. "It has started. Everyone back to the hotel ASAP."

He placed a second call to Elizabeth alone. She answered on the third ring. "You heard?"

"Call came in along with yours. I have upgraded the surveillance on the other CEO's to the maximum but I hold out little hope it will make a difference. I believe Khalid has orchestrated this to the end without his having to make any contact. The son of a bitch is good. We are in for a bad period."

"By this time tomorrow we can expect more. I agree we may be unable to stop any of it. Our only hope is if and when he goes for something large and significant here in Boston. I am certain that this is where his symbolic attach will take place. I will talk to you after I meet with the others." He hung up.

The four agents met at the hotel and went to Vinnie's room for privacy. "What we know is that Khalid orchestrated this from Denver and Florida. Intercepts will not work because every move has been planned to the bitter end. He is engaged in exactly what Homeland Security has been warning about, but has done little about for ten years. If all seven cities have similar incidents, then we know that there must be many operatives at work, both foreign and domestic. It is too late for recriminations, but when this is over, some heads have to roll. Failure to identify so many homegrown al-Qaeda members is a major disaster for Homeland Security."

"Fine, Vinnie, but what now?"

"We could ask Elizabeth to bring in all six CEO's and interrogation them, learn what they know."

It was Gretchen again. "On what basis? The fact that they were in Denver proves nothing. If anyone is guilty of something, it is us. We could have taken Khalid and chose not to. Homeland Security would love to know that."

"Let's look at what we do know."

"Then you start, Darlene."

"From what you and Gretchen told us, the only one of the six who was not in Denver was Aba Najdi. You concluded that if he was absent, it meant that Khalid would meet him personally in Boston where World Wide Wine and Spirits is located. By inference, Boston is the main target. Killing a police chief is not a major event. It is intended to frighten the public, make it insecure. The way the story will be interpreted is that if al-Qaeda can kill a law enforcement officer from a small town in Massachusetts, then no one is safe."

"Good so far, Darlene. Go on." It was Gretchen.

"We will not have a firm idea as to what Khalid's total plan is until other events play themselves out. That could take days or weeks. In the meantime, we need to determine what major targets Khalid has in mind within Boston proper or in the Boston area."

"Darlene has recapped perfectly. What is missing is Khalid's location. Even if we are successful in preventing a disaster, we still need to kill the fucker. He cannot remain on the loose. He must be taken down."

Vinnie jumped into the conversation. "That will happen, Max, but not until we figure out his pattern of terror. I made a promise to take him down and nothing will interfere with that. He is here and will remain here until his work is done. There is no way he will miss his big event. It is also possible that he intends to participate personally. Initially, I did not think that running his picture through the hotels as we did in Florida would bear fruit, but the more I think about it, the more I believe we could just get lucky. Any thoughts?"

"I'm all for getting Carlos Hernandez and Paul Williams on a plane out of Florida and having them run a repeat of the Florida process here in Boston. We wouldn't be here if it were not for them. If you agree, I will make a request of Elizabeth. They could be here by midnight if the agency has a plane in or near West Palm."

"I agree with you, Gretchen. We need Carlos and Paul." Max and Vinnie nodded approval.

"Thanks, Darlene. Once I make the call, let's have drinks and dinner. Later tonight we will work on a list of possible target in Boston and suburbs."

About the time of the meeting in Vinnie's room, Kay pulled up to the St. James Street entrance to the Richmond Plaza Hotel. "I had a lovely day, Thomas. I was planning on drinks and dinner, but if you don't mind, let's do a rain check."

"Something I said?"

"Nothing like that. You were great company. No, I am really saddened with the murder of the police chief. Reading between the lines, you know his throat was slit. The man was slaughtered. What savages would do that? What possible grievance could elicit such brutality? I need to go home, Thomas. We'll talk again."

"Yes, of course." He slipped out of the car and entered the hotel. He did not feel or think like a savage.

It was happy hour at the hotel. He sat at the bar and ordered a martini. Seated next to him were two college age women, quite lovely and dressed to attract. He invited them to join him at a table where they all drank for the better part of an hour, playing flirtatious games with each other, occasionally touching hands and rubbing bodies. It was not long before they left for Khalid's room. Tonight he would be the hunter, taking what he could from his beautiful prey.

CHAPTER 71

EVOLUTION

The four agents met for breakfast at eight o'clock. They were joined by Carlos Hernandez and Paul Williams who had arrived from Miami. It was a happy reunion. Gretchen, still the agent in charge, reviewed with the two men what the group had learned. She went on to explain that she wanted them to duplicate what they had done in Florida, explaining that the number of high-end hotels in the immediate area was significantly less than the luxury resorts and hotels in Florida and they should be able to complete their work in two or three days. They had the authority to do whatever was necessary to accomplish the mission. Carlos and Paul left immediately after breakfast.

Gretchen had just signed the check for breakfast when they heard a commotion in the main lobby. The four of them joined a crowd around a television monitor. What they saw was a reminder of what Vinnie had predicted; another Khalid directed holocaust. The screen displayed a raging fire at what looked like a single story Cape Cod style rambling building. They caught a repeat of the voiceover. "At five this morning, a fire broke out in the Sunlight Convalescent Home in South Wilson, a small town near Plymouth. According to the state fire marshal's office, the fire was too far along to save many of the elderly and sick who were residents of the home. There is no official count of the dead but we learned that the home houses one hundred and thirty five residents when at capacity. The staff numbers approximately sixty during the night shift. By any measure, this will be one of the most horrendous fires in the history of the state if not the country. When the spokesperson for the fire marshal's office was asked if the fire was arson, he deferred the question to the state fire marshal who was not available for comment. As we learn more about the tragedy, we will report it to you. Stayed tuned to Channel 12."

The screen displayed dozens of fire rescue vehicles, fire trucks and dozens of ambulances. Relatives of patients of the home were being held back by police. Helicopters from numerous media outlets were hovering above the smoldering ruins.

The scenes of the ruins were replaced by the Channel 12 anchor as the word "Alert" wormed its way across the bottom of the screen. "We have just learned that WBX 1050 received a call at seven thirty this morning from a man representing himself as an al-Qaeda operative claiming responsibility for the fire and warning every resident that they are not safe from future acts of violence. He went on to say that there is no safe haven anywhere in America. Channel 12 is attempting to reach the Governor for comments. Efforts are being made to contact the Secretary of Homeland Security. Stay tuned for more information."

The screen went back to scenes of the fire with a repeat of the earlier message and the new message received by WBX 1050. The crowd grew larger as word spread throughout the hotel. Everyone in the room was stunned into silence. The four agents knew that more devastation was to come.

Gretchen was on her phone to Elizabeth. On the third ring she answered. “The Director and I have it on our screen. We have three monitors open and on each there is a different disaster. South Wilson is but one of them. In a suburb a hundred miles south of Dallas, a non-denominational church was partially destroyed last night by an explosive device. Fortunately, it happened after the evening service was completed and the church had emptied. The church custodian was killed. The third disaster occurred this morning in a small town midway between Savannah and Charleston. Another explosive device destroyed a small fire station and two fire engines. There was one death, the fireman who had night duty in the station. Al-Qaeda has claimed responsibility for both. That makes four and counting. You must find Khalid and kill him. It will not stop what is happening, but it could abort whoever his big bang is going to be, especially if he is to be a direct party to it. Abdu Khalid’s assault on America has begun.”

“Carlos and Paul are also working with us on finding him now. I expect results soon.”

“How soon?” There was tension in her voice.

“A day or two.”

“Gretchen, when you do find him, I do not, repeat, do not want Max anywhere near him. He is too emotionally tied to this. Vinnie and you are to take over.”

“I hear you loud and clear.”

“I need to talk to Vinnie. Have him call me now on his phone.” She ended the conversation.

Anthony Mallory turned to his Deputy Director. “Elizabeth, these are going to be a hellish few days.

There will be more finger pointing than we have ever experienced. I don't want you to pay any attention to it. I want you to take down Khalid as brutally as possible. But, save his scalp for my trophy room." She smiled at Anthony as he left her alone with her thoughts.

Her phone rang and she activated it immediately. His voice came through loud and strong.

"Hello, Elizabeth. I wish I had good news. No such luck."

"It's rarely luck, Vinnie."

"You wanted to talk?"

"Tell me about the pattern and how what is currently happening fits into it."

"The basic pattern, now that we have pieced it together, is straight forward. Khalid has selected seven cities on which to unload his personal hell. When I say cities, more than likely the attacks will actually occur outside the core cities themselves and in areas where there are fewer law enforcement agencies. He met in Florida and Denver with the CEO's of the companies that are located in the cities he has chosen. For reasons we are not certain of, he killed two of the original six, most probably because they were not to be trusted. Nevertheless, they have been replaced. I have no way of being certain, but based on my experience in the Middle East, whenever a complex operation was in progress by the enemy and where their communications could be intercepted by us, they had developed plans that required no interaction between the disparate parts. In other words, an operation is worked out such that no communication is required. If something goes wrong, you chalk it up to the unexpected and play it out as best you can. Much like our own forces, al-Qaeda gives it field commanders the authority to do as they please. Ninety percent of the time it works."

"And you believe that Khalid is running this operation the same way?"

"I do. And here is the important question that will be answered in the next few days. Will the four events that have taken place in three of the seven cities or regions be repeated in the other four cities?"

"In other words, does each set of operatives in the seven cities have the same list of disasters to be completed or to choose from?"

"That is where I'm coming from. As I mentioned, we will know it, for example, if a Chief of Police is murdered in another city, if a fire station is destroyed, a convalescent home torched or a place of worship destroyed."

"Your educated guess?"

"Each event will be repeated in each of the seven areas. What we do not know is how many events are planned. I conducted a bit of internet research last night to see if there is a number that is especially important to Muslims, thinking of Khalid and symbolism. I did not find anything of value. What I did was create an eight column grid; in the first column I listed the four events that have taken place up to now. As the others occur, I will add them to the column. In the other seven columns, I listed the cities where they have taken place. I'll fill it in as we go. It will not be long before the pattern is confirmed. I'll email the grid to you when we end our conversation."

Before she responded, she thought to herself that with any luck he spent all night on the computer and not on Gretchen. "I'll have some of our people work on the number angle and get back to you if there is anything to it. Vinnie, I believed in the basic pattern when you first argued for it and I believe in the concept now. Good analysis of the data. I want to talk strategy with you as it concerns killing Khalid."

"I'm listening."

"I instructed Gretchen that Max is to be nowhere near Khalid. This is too personal. I don't have to tell you the danger in confronting an enemy when you are emotionally involved. I fear for Max's life. That leaves you and Gretchen. She is an incredible soldier, smart, tough, and experienced, but I want you to take the lead since your field work is more recent than hers. Khalid defines evil and I hate to think of what he would do to Gretchen if she is caught in his web."

"I understand. Try not to worry."

"You are new to me as an agent, but I trust your instincts and you skill. Nevertheless, be careful. I am still planning on a celebration."

"I promise you, Elizabeth, I will be at your party."

"Let's talk tomorrow." She ended the conversation.

He mustered the others and briefed them on most of his conversation with Elizabeth. When done, he shared copies of the grid with them. "The most troubling aspect is that we have no idea how many events Khalid plans for each of the seven areas." Just then his cell phone rang. He saw that it was Elizabeth.

"Vinnie, are you where you can go on speaker phone so the others can hear me?"

"Yes." He switched to speaker mode.

"Homeland Security has just ordered the FBI to take the six CEO's into custody. The secretary notified Director Mallory a few minutes ago. The DOJ advised Homeland there is sufficient cause to bring them in for interviews and has issued a warning about enhanced interrogations."

"The bureau must be pissed. They know the interviews will yield nothing of value. Khalid has appointed militants to run the show, not the CEO's. The bureau will have to release all six within twenty four hours and it will be the laughing stock of the intelligence community. The apprehension of the CEO's is nothing more than political posturing. If anything, this will encourage al-Qaeda to step things up from their end. Goddamn Washington idiots. By this time tomorrow, we will see the results of the DOJ decision. The irony is that the only way to get information from these guys is by enhanced interrogation and that is not about to happen."

"What makes you believe this will spur more activity?"

"The simplest of motives: pure retaliation. Terrorists think with their swords, not their heads which makes them dangerous."

"Keep in touch." Elizabeth's voice had a smile that Gretchen took note of and didn't care for.

Vinnie spoke to the group. "None of the four events required highly skilled operatives or sophisticated equipment to be successful. Therein is the danger. Unlike 9/11, where it took skill to operate the aircraft and truly brilliant logistical support to make it happen, the events we are experiencing can be conducted by almost anyone."

Gretchen added to the discussion. "Vinnie is right on. Anyone could have pulled off what they did. If we think about it, 9/11 ended up being an assault on New York, the Pentagon and an aborted attempt to reach the While House. Elizabeth stated it perfectly; now we are experiencing Khalid's assault on all of America. If Vinnie's pattern is accurate, there is no place to hide from Khalid's strategy. There is no way to stop what is happening. Khalid is a genius for developing terror tactics that require no specialized skills. By employing that strategy, he literally has an unlimited number of potential militants in this country."

Darlene spoke. "We never did create the list of historic and symbolic major targets in the Boston area. It should be easy enough to do. Rather than all of us conducting research, Max and I could do it while you two work with Carlos. Let's meet back here at five. I have no doubt that by then we will have more reports of terrorist activities."

They all nodded agreement.

Kay Horton spent the day in her posh condo in Louisburg Square, located at the corner of Mt. Vernon and Cedar at the foot of Beacon Hill, and only two blocks from both the Public Gardens and Boston common. She spent a restless night thinking about the murder of the Chief of Police in Merritt. Her misery was accentuated when she heard the news of the convalescent home fire and the massive loss of life. The news of the church explosion in the Dallas region and the destruction of the fire station in Atlanta had not yet made the local news. She reflected on the abruptness of her parting with Thomas the day before and decided to call him.

He picked up on the fourth ring. "I was afraid you would not be in your room at this hour."

"I just got out of the shower and was dressing. I thought I would take a walk in the Common and then retreat to the Oak Bar for a drink. Why don't you join me?"

"I would not be good company. I'm still upset over the two terrorist attacks."

"Kay, there have been two more. The news is on the national networks. A church was destroyed in a small town near Dallas and an explosion destroyed a fire station near Atlanta. Al-Qaeda has claimed responsibility for both attacks. This is no time for you to be alone. Please join me."

She was silent for a moment, the asked, "Were there any deaths?"

"The church was empty at the time, but the custodian was killed. A fireman who was in charge of the fire station that night was also killed in the explosion."

"When will this end, Thomas?"

"There is no way of telling but you can rest assured that the authorities are doing all they can to stop what is happening and to apprehend the persons responsible."

"I have another engagement at seven this evening, but I will meet you at the Oak Bar around five thirty for a drink if that works for you.

"Sounds perfect. See you then."

At exactly five minutes past five, Gretchen received a call from Elizabeth. "It will be on the news as we speak. A member of the state legislature in Denver died in a car explosion within the hour. He was leaving the state capitol when it happened. The device was set off by a simple remote. According to the first reports, the device was a relatively small explosive charge, but sufficient to kill him by trauma. Once again, al-Qaeda has claimed responsibility. The intelligence community is in chaos, not knowing how to respond. No finger pointing yet, but it will begin. In the meantime, keep pressing for an answer."

The phone went dead. Gretchen shared the news with the others. Carlos and Paul joined the group. They had waited for his report. "We are making headway and should have our man identified by tomorrow. We have used the same system employed in Florida but have a smaller number of hotels to cover. Paul and I have four agents from the Boston office working with us."

"What have you found to date?"

"Max, we have several hotels we need to follow up on, mostly high end. They were not responsive to our fax requests. We need to wait until tomorrow in order to meet with the day managers, front desk personnel, bell captain and doormen. They are the most likely to have seen Khalid. If that doesn't yield anything of value, we will repeat the process with the night staff. The hotels we have yet to contact include this one, the Weston across the street, the Sheraton down the street and the Marriott on the harbor. What we have found to date is that every hotel we have contacted has video recordings of every person who enters and leaves the hotel. They generally keep the tapes anywhere from sixty to ninety days. So, we are in luck in that regard."

"Let's have drinks and dinner." They all agreed with Gretchen.

At five thirty five, Kay walked into the Oak Bar. Thomas was waiting for her and guided her to a table. He ordered a martini and she requested a glass of cabernet sauvignon. Drawn and tired looking, she did not resemble the vivacious beauty of yesterday. "Kay, there has been another attack, this time a car bombing of a state representative in Denver. I'm sorry to give you the news."

"Thomas, you strike me as a very worldly person, a successful business man who has traveled to all parts of the globe, including the Middle East. Undoubtedly, you have conducted business with Muslims and have had conversations with individuals of different political persuasions. Can you explain to me why the United States is so hated and despised in the Middle East?"

Fearful that he may sound like Abdu Khalid and not Thomas Gilbane, he hesitated, looked at the bewilderment and despair displayed in her eyes and then spoke. "I'll try to explain as best I understand it from meeting with individuals in my travels. I don't vouch for the accuracy of my comments since I am not a historian. The events that led up to 9/11 occurred before you and I were born, as far back, at least in the modern sense, to the creation of the Israel in 1947. The breakup of what the Palestinians believed to be their land, planted the seed for instability in the Middle East. The partition occurred when the British gave up its mandate in Palestine and the United Nations sought a homeland for Jews. There is some thinking that behind the scenes the United States coerced other nations to support the creation of the Jewish state. There is no way to know if that was the case. Ever since then, the United States has been viewed as pro-Israel and anti-Palestine. And in fact, that is true to the objective observer. There may be legitimate reasons for the American position but to Palestinians, it is an unjust one."

"But, the British seem to be immune from the hatred."

"Not entirely. We have had our problems, but your country is the most hated and it is due to oil that is extracted from the desert."

"Thomas, we pay dearly to purchase oil. Middle East countries are not giving it away."

"That is now. I may not have the exact date, but I believe that OPEC was established in 1960 or 61." He knew the exact date to be September 14, 1960. "It was established by several countries with the most notable being Saudi Arabia, Iraq and Iran. Before OPEC, the United States practically stole the oil. The way they did it helped to keep despots, monarchs, dictators and cruel men and their families in power. The ruling families drowned in wealth while the average citizen was relegated to abject poverty. Billions of dollars were transferred out of these countries by their leaders to safe havens around the world. OPEC was finally created and it now controls production and sets world prices for oil"

"You seem to know a great deal about the Middle East."

"Not really. Just repeating themes I hear in my travels. My thoughts are quite simple. I'm certain there were many more complicated issues that came into play. Regardless of what you and I believe, there are millions of Muslims who hate the United States and the killing of Bin Laden will not deter terrorists. But, enough of Middle East history. Let's talk about something pleasant."

"I know I promised to show you the town, but let's put it on hold for a few days. Which reminds me, how long will you be in Boston?"

"Probably a week. That way I can wait until you are ready to become my tour guide again. Will that work for you?" All the while, he knew his time in Boston was measured. He was a hunted man with little time left to complete his work.

"The reason I asked, Thomas, was not to be inquisitive for the sake of being inquisitive. I had something in mind. William has an apartment on Beacon Street overlooking the river that is absolutely beautiful. He uses it for wealthy investors visiting Boston. I asked him about its use this week and he assured me that it would be vacant and you could use it. It is far more comfortable than a hotel room. And I will know where to find you. In the event you might worry about missing happy hour at the Oak Bar, it is a ten-minute walk to here. It is yours for the asking."

"How could I possibly refuse? The answer is yes." He wondered if she had learned of his escapade with the two college women.

"Great. Check out of here tomorrow morning and have the driver take you to this address. There will be someone there to help you get settled." She handed him a card with the address all the while thinking what a beautiful specimen of a man he was. It was almost time to take him into her bed.

"This is really wonderful of William."

"Now, I must go. She stood as did Thomas. She leaned across the table and gave him a light kiss on the cheek. She smelled young, lovely, fabulous and sensual. He wanted very much to make love to her as he watched her walk from the bar.

He remained long enough to finish his martini, after which he decided to walk to Park Square and have dinner at Nino's. He had no reservation and the bar was red hot with singles drinking heavily and looking forward to some match making. Tonight he was not in the mood for sex, except with Kay. He quickly finished his drink and returned to the hotel. Although he was the architect of the five attacks, he had no idea what his many operatives were selecting as the next targets and when. He did know that tomorrow would bring more disaster to the United States.

He called for room service and ordered a light supper and a bottle of red. Kay was on his mind. Her abhorrence of what was happening struck him as out of character for a successful woman. Surely, she understood that this was war and in any war men become savages and inflict upon each other the most horrific kinds of cruelty. Was al-Qaeda's brutality any greater than what the Germans or Japanese inflicted on American prisoners of war in World War II?"

He watched television until nine and fell asleep with not the slightest sense of guilt for what had happened or for what would continue to happen. He found it exhilarating to anticipate what the next event would be and where. Chicago, San Diego and Seattle were falling behind. While he was sleeping, one of his concerns was eliminated. A small town on Lake Michigan, just north of Grand Rapids, felt the wrath of his wheel of terror. During the night, two of his operatives broke into a local television station, overpowered a rent-a-cop and planted a remote controlled explosive in the control room. Seven minutes later they activated it as they drove out of town. By the time the local police and fire department arrived on the scene, the two men were on Interstate 196 headed for urban Chicago.

The first confirmation of Vinnie's pattern was established early the next morning in Washington State. In a community south of Seattle, the local Chief of Police, something of a local embarrassment because of his heavy drinking, was shot to death in his car in the parking lot of a local bar. According to the first reports, the killer or killers must have used a suppressor since the few patrons remaining in the bar after closing hours heard nothing. He was killed with a single shot fired into his left ear. After the shooting, it was believed that the operatives headed south on Interstate 5 to Portland, Oregon where they would disappear into the local Muslim population and make a cell phone call to take credit for the killing.

The killing of the cop in the Seattle area was the second assassination of a law enforcement officer, the first having occurred in the small town of Merritt, Massachusetts where the Chief of Police was murdered. The second killing was sufficient to confirm that each of the seven cities or areas would experience the killing of a Chief of Police or a law enforcement officer. It was also confirmation that every attack, however many there were to be, would be replicated in each of the seven cities or regions. If Khalid was successful, the country would experience eighty four attacks in what Vinnie believed to be only the first wave in a continuing program of national harassment. The plan was a masterpiece for destruction and simplistic in design.

Vinnie had heard the news while shaving. He dropped his razor and called the others. They were to meet in twenty minutes in the breakfast room. Max and Darlene arrived first and had taken a table in the far corner of the room and ordered coffee for everyone. Vinnie and Gretchen arrived five minutes later. "Sorry I'm late, but I spoke with Elizabeth to give her the news. She already had it. This murder confirms what we thought might be the case. Each of the seven areas will experience the identical types of terrorist attacks. So far, there have been six different types of them. If that is the maximum number planned by Khalid, then we can expect a minimum of forty-two attacks, six in each of the seven areas. In other words, there will be seven murders of high ranking law enforcement officials, seven convalescent homes torched, seven churches fire bombed and so forth."

"Vinnie, are you telling us that if there were, for instance, ten different events planned by Khalid, that we have the potential for seventy attacks?" It was a question from Darlene.

"That is exactly what I suggesting. Khalid doesn't want another 9/11. He knew it was almost impossible to pull one off so he decided long ago to scare the shit out of the entire population. He is signaling us that no one and no place is safe. In other words, there is no place to hide. He doesn't need sophisticated weapons; he only needs dedicated terrorists, including home grown ones, although my gut tells me that the operatives working now have been here for many years as sleepers. I believe more trouble, more serious trouble, is on the way. He has yet to use biological or chemical tools, both relatively easy to acquire and use. So far, there have been no attacks on busses or trains. Or, for that matter, the military. Then there are malls, where large numbers of people congregate. I am thinking out loud, but we are in for more hell."

Vinnie held up his grid. "We have yet to hear from San Diego. But rest assured, we will. After that we wait. Once San Diego is hit, Khalid's wheel is complete. Every city will have been the object of an attack at least once. The entire country is in play; East coast in Boston and Atlanta, the South in Dallas, the West coast in San Diego and Seattle, the North in Chicago and the belly of the country in Denver. His wheel, however lopsided, will be complete."

"Where has he recruited his domestic militants?"

"My best guess, Darlene, is from established Muslim organizations. The most radical organizations are specific mosques that are breeding grounds for terrorists. The Imams have incredible power over their congregations and are in a position to silence dissidents. I don't know how he accomplished it, but Khalid managed to identify a sufficient number of radical Imams to man his terrorist army. There are thousands of mosques in the country that are conservative and whose congregations are comprised of full-blooded Americans. Unfortunately, there are other mosques that have a different agenda. Just how he identified the radical mosques is a question the answer to which we must learn. Any attempt by the intelligence community to dig into mosques activities will be met with strong resistance and the threat of prosecution by the DOJ. Whatever information we acquire on a specific mosque will be that produced by local cops. Without them, we would have nothing to go on. They are the indispensable force. They have boots on the ground and know how to collect vital information. But let's remember that these attacks are more than likely the work of militants who have been here for years. If domestic people are used, they work for the militants."

Khalid rose early, showered, shaved and dressed. He packed his clothes, left the luggage in the room and went down to breakfast. He was looking forward to William Worthington's apartment and the possibility that Kay would be a frequent visitor. He had to remind himself that he was not long for Boston. The time was near for his symbolic masterpiece after which he would disappear. He finished breakfast and was greeted by a large group of guests surrounding the television in the lobby. The channel 12 reporter was breathlessly explaining the killing in the Seattle region of another Chief of Police. She went on to explain that al-Qaeda had taken credit for the killing and that it followed on the heels of a similar murder in Merritt, Massachusetts.

He went to the lobby and checked out. As he was walking away from the front desk, he overheard Carlos introducing himself to the manager as a CIA agent. Carlos then introduced Paul. Khalid turned away from the desk so as not to expose his face to the agents who may have had his picture in their possession. He was momentarily taken off guard but knew that he had to think clearly. He had to get to the apartment. While a sense of panic was still with him, he begrudgingly admired the ability of the CIA agent in charge to have learned of his being in Boston.

CHAPTER 72

JOINT OPERATION

Khalid returned quickly to his room, made a check to remove any evidence that could be used to locate him, picked up his luggage and returned to the St. James Street entrance. He entered a cab and was on his way to Logan Airport or so the bell captain was led to believe. As soon as the cabbie made his first turn out of St. James Street, Khalid spoke to him. "I have changed my mind. Take me to South Station." The cabbie was clearly pissed because he was looking forward to the long haul fare to the airport. Khalid read his expression. "I will pay you the full fare to the airport. I'd appreciate it if you did not mention my change of plans to anyone. My wife's divorce lawyer would love to get his greedy hands on me. He's already sucked up most of what I own."

"Nothing to worry about. Those stinking guys get rich on everyone else."

"Thanks."

Ten minutes later Khalid was let off at South Station. The cabbie removed the bags from the trunk and Khalid handed him two twenties and a ten. He thanked Khalid and took off. Khalid waited until the cab was well out of sight, walked to the nearest cab stand and asked to be taken to North Station. Once there, he would take a third cab to the apartment on Beacon Street.

Back at the Richmond Plaza Hotel, Carlos had received the permission of the manager to show Khalid's picture to members of the staff. He went first to one of the front desk clerks. She thought she recognized him, but was not certain. He went to the second clerk who looked at the photograph and quietly said, "He checked out ten minutes ago. You should talk to the bell captain."

"What name was he registered under?"

She looked at her computer for recent check outs. "Thomas Gilbane."

Carlos turned to Paul. "Have the manager get you into Khalid's room and see what you can find. I'm sure it is clean, but we need to look. I'll meet you back here."

Carlos showed the picture to the bell captain. "He left here less than ten minutes ago and asked to be taken to Logan Airport. It was a Yellow cab, but we don't record the registration number of cabs. I assume the driver checked in with his central dispatcher. However, we have a surveillance camera under the canopy that films everyone who enters and leaves. It may have caught the cab number. The manager controls the tapes."

Carlos asked the bell captain to stay for a moment while he made a call to Gretchen. "We have a hit at the Richmond Plaza Hotel. Two positive identifications, both high value recognitions. Registered under the name of Thomas Gilbane. Our man took a cab to Logan Airport although I doubt if he would leave such an obvious trail for us. I think the team needs to start from here."

"We're on our way."

Turning back to the bell captain, "Had you seen this man before he asked for the cab today?"

"While you were on the phone, I thought back on when I had last seen him. A couple of days ago a young woman picked him up. She was driving a BMW convertible. I don't know who she is, but I have seen her here several times with a couple who frequent the Oak Bar."

"Do you know the name of the couple?"

"Not the woman, but the man is William Worthington. I remember him because management trains us to recognize our wealthy guests. He runs a hedge fund or something. He isn't married, but always has the same gorgeous woman with him. The woman who picked up your man is also a beauty."

Just then Paul returned. "He left a cell phone. It's a throw away with nothing on it. Other than that, the room was clean. Nothing for us to use."

Carlos explained the surveillance tapes. "Talk to the manager and see if you can confirm it was Khalid. We also need to have the name of the company that a William Worthington operates, an address and a phone number. I'll wait here for the other members of the team." While waiting he searched the phone number of the Yellow Cab dispatcher on his iPhone and made the call. He introduced himself and asked for information on a cab pickup ten minutes earlier at the hotel that was destined for Logan Airport. The dispatcher said she had no authority to give out that information.

"Where are you located?"

"Why do you want to know?"

"Because, if you do not give me the information, you will have a team of federal agents swarming all over you for interfering with a federal investigation. Do you understand?"

"Yes."

"Good. Now while I hold on, you are to call the cab and find out exactly where the fare was dropped off. Do it now and be certain to tell him that anything but the truth will land him in a federal penitentiary."

While he waited, Gretchen and Vinnie arrived by cab. Carlos motioned that he was on the phone. The dispatcher came back on. "The driver said the passenger got off at South Station and paid him the fare to Logan to keep his mouth shut. Something about a divorce lawyer looking for him."

"Good work."

Turning to his colleagues, "Here is what we have." He proceeded to give them all of the information he and Paul had obtained.

"Excellent work, both of you. Vinnie and I will deal with Worthington. Carlos, you and Paul are to continue to follow Khalid's trail. I don't know what you will learn at South Station, but it is the starting point. It is entirely possible Khalid was in the lobby and overheard the conversation you were having with the manager. If so, he knows we are hot on his trail and will make several diversionary moves to stay well ahead of us. Sooner or later he needs to settle somewhere if he intends to pull off a major attack. We need to find him before that happens."

"Gretchen, before we chase our tails, we need to first talk to Worthington. I suggest we make the call to him now and let Carlos and Paul move on to South Station. So far, Khalid has used transportation destinations to convince us he is leaving Boston. I suggest we have Darlene and Max check out North Station.

I don't believe it will yield anything of value, but we need to be certain. Once they do that, have them meet us at the apartment."

"You call Worthington and I'll call Darlene."

Using the information Carlos had received from the manager, Vinnie called Worthington's office. He identified himself as Agent Pagano of the Central Intelligence Agency and asked to speak to William Worthington informing the receptionist it was government business. She put him on hold and when she returned, "Mr. Worthington wants to know what kind of business?"

"Tell Mr. Worthington it is a national security matter and that it is imperative I speak with him immediately. Either that or we will come to his office with several officers."

Moments later, William Worthington came on the line. "Agent Pagano, this is Bill Worthington. What is it that you wish to talk about?"

"Thank you for your time, Mr. Worthington. The agency is interested in talking to a man who may be friendly with a person with whom you are acquainted. A young woman driving a BMW convertible picked up a man at the Richmond Plaza Hotel two days ago. We have since learned that the woman has been seen with you and another woman at the hotel many times. Do you know the woman I am referring to?"

After a slight hesitation, "Yes, her name is Kay Horton, the sister of the other woman who is my fiancée. Kay Horton is a fund manager for my firm."

"When we have concluded our conversation, I may want to be transferred to her office. Are you familiar with the man Kay Horton picked up? He would have been someone who arrived on the scene recently; a somewhat sophisticated and worldly man, quite handsome and well groomed."

A longer hesitation. "We met a British man in the bar a few days ago. Kay took a liking to him, but did not display her interest overtly. His name is Thomas Gilbane and he said he was here on business."

"What type of business?"

"He said he was a deal maker, worldwide in scope, significant assets and funds involved. Big time operation. I had the feeling he works both sides of the street and profits handsomely. A very charming man. I work with some of the most sophisticated men in America and Thomas Gilbane would fit right in."

"Did he mention where he was going next?"

"Actually, yes. I own an apartment on Beacon Street and use it for out of town investors. It is currently vacant and Kay asked me to allow Gilbane to use it for a few days while he was wrapping up business in Boston. He is probably there. Look, I've answered all of your questions. How about answering one for me. Why do you have an interest in Thomas Gilbane?"

"I need the address of your apartment." Worthington gave it to Vinnie.

"Again, what about Gilbane?"

"You have been most helpful. The agency appreciates that. However, this is a matter of national security and we have a need to talk to Gilbane. I can tell you nothing more at this time."

"Is Kay in any kind of danger?"

"It is in her best interest not to meet with or talk to Gilbane under any circumstances. The same goes for you. Now, does your apartment have live-in help who may be there now?"

"I asked my cleaning service to be there to open the apartment for Gilbane."

"Do you know if the service arrived?"

"No, but I can find out. Please hold while I make the call." It was three minutes before he came back on.

"I contacted the lead service personnel on her cell phone. She is no longer in the apartment. She said that two men arrived about an hour ago representing Gilbane. They were still there when she and her helper left. The men spoke only a few short sentences, but she said they spoke a language she did not recognize. Since she is Romanian, she knew the accent was not European."

Vinnie processed what he heard. "Mr. Worthington, I want you to be certain that Ms. Horton does not leave her office and go to the apartment. She could be in danger. This is critical. Can you do this?"

"Yes, of course."

"Good. Also, make certain that the service personnel do not return to the apartment today. I will arrange to meet with Ms. Horton later this afternoon. I need your help on one matter. Your office is very close to the Richmond Plaza Hotel. We need a key to your apartment. How quickly can you get it to us?"

"I'll have my assistant run it over. She'll be there in five or six minutes."

"Thanks for your help. And, forget about transferring my call to Ms. Horton."

"I look forward to seeing you later this afternoon."

"I want to mention one last thing. It is possible that there may be some damage to the apartment. If so, the Central Intelligence Agency will pay for any restoration."

"Thanks for the heads up."

The four agents were outside the hotel waiting for a key. Vinnie brought everyone up to date regarding the conversation with Worthington, the role of Kay Horton, the apartment and the two men who are or were there. "Look, we know that Khalid is not going to the apartment. With us in pursuit, he is trying his damndest to stay out of our line of fire. We are fairly certain that he has not communicated with the two men in the apartment who have to be his operatives since he would not risk the call being monitored. We can safely assume he was planning a strategy meeting with them there. Conditions have changed and his operatives are on their own."

"What are you suggesting?"

"What I'm suggesting, Carlos, is that once the key arrives we pay a visit to the apartment. I want those operatives."

Just then a cab pulled up and a young woman got out. She looked around, but before she could move, Carlos went up to her, introduced himself and asked for the key which she willingly handed over along with a beautiful smile for a very handsome young man. Then she was back in the cab and gone. "Why do I always meet lovely young women while I'm on duty?"

"Come on, Carlos, your country calls."

"Duty first. I know, Gretchen."

Gretchen turned to Vinnie, "I want you to take the lead on this next move."

"Happy to oblige. We'll use the car Carlos rented. Once we arrive on Beacon Street, we will exit the cab a full block from the apartment building. Many of the buildings, as expensive as they are, have alleys behind them that are used for parking and for dumpsters.

Carlos and Paul, since you have worked together as a team, it makes sense for you to remain as such and cover the back entrance to the apartment. We'll communicate by cell phones. Gretchen and I will take the front door. If at all possible, we should try to take them alive, but not if it threatens our own safety. Once in place, make certain your weapons are loaded, safety off, and backup magazines easily accessible. Assume the operatives have more firepower than we do. There may also be more than two operatives. Speaking of weapons, what are you and Paul carrying?"

They discussed the weapons each was packing. Carlos and Paul carried Heckler-Hock MK23 handguns, powerful 45 caliber weapons with a laser aiming module. Each man carried two extra magazines. The MK23 was designed for special operations and the magazines carried 12 rounds.

Gretchen and Vinnie carried the SIG P28, the most popular weapon with federal law enforcement officers and most intelligence agencies. It is a smaller caliber 9 mm weapon with a magazine that holds 13 rounds. It also has a laser aiming module.

"Vinnie, this being an old building, the doors will be heavy and thick and we have no way to ram them. If his operatives are inside, they know the layout of the building and we don't."

"Carlos is right, Vinnie. Get Worthington back on the phone and have him describe the first floor layout. Put him on speaker so we can all hear."

Vinnie made the call and Worthington described the floor plan. "The front door swings left when opened. There is a large front foyer with a grand circular staircase to the second floor. To the right of the foyer is a library with two doors, one from the foyer, and one leading to a large dining room behind it that opens to a kitchen that extends to the back wall of the apartment. To the left of the foyer is a small sitting room with a door that enters into a large parlor. A door at the rear of the parlor leads into a combination laundry room and back hall that has a door leading to the outside. The rear door, reinforced with metal sheathing, opens to the top of a platform that measures approximately six feet by six feet. There are four steps that lead from the platform to ground level and the alley."

He continued. "The grand staircase in the foyer leads to the second floor. At the top of the stairs, a hallway extends back on both sides of the open foyer towards the rear of the house. Each of the four bedrooms is entered from the hallway and each bedroom has its own bathroom. The master bedroom is in the front and on the left side. The first floor is without any large closets where someone could hide, but the bedrooms all have large walk in closets and there are multiple doors in each room. Between the two bedrooms on the left side of the apartment, there is a large sitting room/library. The right side has the same configuration. Each of the two rooms has a complete wet bar, fully stocked. The apartment has a cellar, but it does not have a hatchway to the outside. It is entered from a doorway in the back hall."

Once Worthington had completed his description of the apartment's layout, Vinnie thanked him, ended the call and spoke to his partners. "We cannot wait for reinforcements or we risk losing the chance to apprehend the men. Gretchen and I will use the key to enter the front door. If there is no resistance, one of us will go through the apartment and open the rear door while the other remains in the foyer in the event there is gunfire from upstairs. Should you hear gunfire, you will have to shoot out the lock to the rear door. Use standard entry procedures once you force the door. I'll call when we are about to place the key in the lock. Any questions?"

It was Gretchen. "We need to call Elizabeth and bring her up to speed."

"You can do that as we drive. Now, let's do what we do best." Gretchen made the call. Elizabeth was on another line so Gretchen left a brief message as to the current status.

The apartment was at seven fifty five Beacon Street. They drove past the address and determined that it was roughly in the middle of the block which would make it difficult to find the rear door if there was no number on it. "Carlos, drive around the block once more. I want to count the chimneys from the end of the block to Worthington's apartment. These are classic apartments and each will have a large colonial type fireplace with a traditional chimney."

Carlos made another loop around the block and Vinnie was convinced that the chimney for the apartment was the third from the end. Using it as a landmark, the rear door to the apartment could be identified. The decision was made to let Vinnie and Gretchen off at the end of the block and they would walk to number seven fifty five. Carlos and Paul would park the car at the end of the block and take a position at the rear of the apartment until Gretchen gave the word to move. Before Vinnie and Gretchen got out of the car, Elizabeth was on the line.

"I hate to spoil the party, but we have no authority to storm the apartment. At the moment, this is a domestic issue and the bureau, by agreement with Homeland Security and us, must take over any invasion of the apartment. After Gretchen called, I contacted Jordan Rich, Deputy Director of the bureau. By now a 7/24 assault team from the bureau's Boston office is on the way and will be there in minutes. Your job is to maintain a surveillance of the apartment. The bureau's team will have more firepower, body armor and the equipment to ram the doors."

The four agents were stunned by the decision that they were to play a supporting role after all they had accomplished to get to this point. Sensing their disappointment, Elizabeth put the issue into perspective. "Jordan Rich saved the agency from a Congressional hearing by ignoring two assassinations in Maine. He personally saved Max's reputation. All of us owe him big time and this is one way to repay an interagency debt. This action in no way hinders your work in finding Khalid. There is one plus for us. The feds have a close working relationship with the locals who will help to downplay public concern when all hell breaks out in a residential district, especially this street. The locals also have a good relationship with the media and together they will manage the news. One final note. The bureau's lead agent is one Stuart McDonald. He was the agent in charge of the investigation in Maine and who dropped the investigation on advice of the Deputy Director. He'll know Max by photographs that were circulated in Maine and he will probably recognize Darlene's voice from her phone conversation with him when she posed as a reporter. The bureau's regional office was so impressed with his work in Maine that they transferred him to a high profile position in Boston. It should be an interesting homecoming for some of you. That's it. Take care and keep me up to date." That was the end of the call. There was to be no further discussion regarding the assault on the apartment.

In less than five minutes, two Cadillac ESU Escalades arrived and four Agents wearing body armor and carrying Colt M4A1 assault rifles exited each vehicle. The first man out was Stuart McDonald and he headed for the group. Gretchen, as the lead agency agent, went up to him and introduced herself. While they were talking, a third Escalade arrived. It was an EXT with an eight foot open bed that contained a two-man battering ram. "How many men are in the apartment?" McDonald asked Gretchen.

"Our only report from the cleaning crew is that two men arrived while they were there. There could be more. I have two agents watching the rear door in the alley so we know no one has left since we arrived. Let me detail the floor plan for you as given to us by the owner." When she was finished, he spoke. "Without body armor and heavier firepower, you and your people are at risk. I ask that you and your agents move off a bit. We will force the front door, use stun grenades and then make an assault. I will use five men and myself for the assault, with two in the alley to cover that exit. You could be a great help in backing us up if things do not go according to plan. Now, I need to deploy my men."

He spoke to his men and briefed them on the floor plan. Shortly thereafter two men removed the ram from the EXT and placed it on the ground in front of the steps leading to the door. Two other men drove the vehicle into the alley and waited for Stuart's orders. Carlos and Paul moved back and became spectators. A Boston Police Department cruiser arrived and a captain stepped out. He met with Agent McDonald and informed him that Beacon Street had been closed off at each end and at all intersections. The operation could proceed.

At that moment Max and Darlene arrived to join the others who briefed them on Elizabeth's call. They had found no evidence at North Station that would help in locating Khalid.

In the front, the six FBI agents lined up in three rows, two abreast at the bottom of the steps. The first two climbed the four steps to the front door and with two powerful blows of the ram, sent the door reeling on it hinges. They quickly stepped back on the outside and put the ram to one side. The second set of two agents stepped forward and lobbed two flashbang grenades inside and stepped back. Once the light and the blast subsided, McDonald and the sixth agent stepped into the foyer and took positions on each side of it. The agents who used the ram followed them in, and close behind them were the two agents who lobbed the flashbang grenades. McDonald and one agent moved to the right into the study and then the dining room. Two agents moved left into the sitting room and then into the parlor. One agent remained in the foyer watching for any movement at the top of the stairs while the sixth agent moved through the foyer into the kitchen, and then he opened the rear door. Two more agents entered bringing to eight the number of agents in the house. There was no resistance on the first floor.

McDonald opened the cellar door and threw in a flashbang grenade and closed the door. He waited for the light and blast to diminish and, not hearing any noise or movement, motioned for two agents to descend into the cellar. They found no one. The most dangerous stage of the assault was about to take place as they attempted to clear the second floor. They no longer had an element of surprise working for them.

Two of McDonald's agents had started up the stairs, moving slowly, when two operatives appeared in the doorway of the bedrooms, one on each side of the landing and fired at the two agents before they could return fire. The operatives then kneeled and two more operatives appeared and began to fire over the shoulders of the first two operatives. The two FBI Agents were staggered when the first rounds hit their Kevlar vests and then fell backwards down the stairs as both took bullets to their exposed thighs and legs. The four operatives then retreated back in to the bedrooms, unharmed. Two agents then carefully approached the stairs and pulled their buddies into the study on the right.

McDonald knew his team was in trouble when he heard glass braking and automatic pistols being fired in the rear of the house. The operatives on the second floor were firing at Carlos and Paul in the alley. McDonald was uncertain if the firing was being done by the two operatives who had fired on his men from the top of the stairs or if there were more operatives in the house. Another agent was taken down in the alley with a bullet to the shoulder. All the while Carlos and Paul had followed orders and pulled back out of the line of fire. Carlos called Vinnie on his cell. "We have one bureau agent down here. What the hell is going on out front?"

Vinnie, who by now had disobeyed both McDonald's and Elizabeth's instructions, was at the front door to the house. "There are two agents down in the house. It appears the operatives have the upper hand at the moment. There is no way to get to the second floor without being exposed on the stairs. It could be a shooting gallery. What about the rear?"

Carlos said, "If Gretchen gives the OK, I can reach the second floor windows without being seen. There is a strong looking down spout, a small overhang and iron work that would make it easy for me to gain height. The iron work is located in the middle of the back wall and leads to the side of the window that must open to the upstairs hall. Paul could give me cover all the way. Without the weight of body armor, I can move easily. Once there, I could target some of the operatives through the window and it would give an opening to the agents out front."

"Hold on."

Vinnie then spoke to Gretchen. He got back to Carlos. "As far as she is concerned, you are on your own, but do it."

Carlos stripped off his jacket, checked his weapon, secured it in its holster and began the climb. Both Paul and the other FBI Agent gave him cover. He reached the second floor window in less than two minutes. By then Gretchen and Darlene were in the alley to give support. Carlos had a plan in mind. The final length of rain gutter was on the left side of the window. When he was just below the window, he reached up and smashed the glass in the lower sash with the barrel of his pistol and then pulled himself up and to the left of the window so he could look in. An operative, who was in one of the rear bedrooms, stuck his head out of the door to see what the noise was about and took three of Carlos's MK23 slugs in the neck and face and then fell backward into the bedroom. A second operative in the opposite bedroom looked through the door and saw his dead partner and quickly determined that the bullets came from the outside. He ran to the window in his bedroom, smashed the glass and took aim. Carlos was hanging on to the down spout and could not see the operative leaning out of the window behind him. He was totally exposed. As though prearranged, Paul, Gretchen, and Darlene fired a fuselage of bullets into the window. The operative, half hanging out to see Carlos, fell across the sill and remained there.

Gretchen, always the field agent, called Vinnie and gave him a brief report and urged him to tell McDonald to storm the stairs while the four agents in the alley fired at the windows and rear wall as a distraction.

Vinnie, inside the lobby, yelled to McDonald, "Go, go now!" Based only on the trust of a fellow agent, McDonald was first up the stairs, firing all the while, followed by three other agents, all of whom were firing at the two doorways of the two rear bedrooms. Vinnie and Max were both on the stairs looking over their shoulders at the doors to the two front bedrooms and protecting the backs of McDonald and his three agents who were ahead of them. A man stepped out of the front right bedroom and raised his machine pistol at the agents higher up on the stairs. He never got off a round as Vinnie shot him in the neck and face with his P28 handgun. Another operative appeared from the other front doorway, but before Vinnie could react, McDonald and Max, simultaneously, had turned and shot him in the chest and shoulder. The four agents, Vinnie and Max stormed through the bedrooms, covering each other as walk-in closet doors were opened.

Finally, they determined that there were no other operatives in the house.

Ambulances arrived and three agents, wounded but alive, were taken to Massachusetts General Hospital. Carlos was treated on site for cuts and slashes to his hands from the sharp edges of the metal work and downspout. Within minutes, an FBI forensics team was on the scene. Twenty minutes after the arrival of the team, four of Khalid's dead operatives were taken to a secret location. Two of McDonald's agents loaded the ram on to the bed of the EXT and left. Although Beacon Street had been closed, a substantial crowd had gathered, made up of residents of the street, tourists who happened to be there, merchants and their customers and many first responders. Deep within the crowd, but hidden from view, Khalid witnessed the attack on the apartment. He had arrived on Beacon Street by cab just after the team had gotten there. Once he saw the team outside of the apartment, he had the cabbie drop him off a block away. He decided to stay out of sight and watch the proceedings since he had no place to go. A chill went up his back as he saw Max Rietsema standing outside the front door and then enter the apartment with another man who looked every inch an assassin. It was then that Khalid knew that time was running out. He had to make his move soon.

McDonald had his two remaining agents wait in the Escalade. He then asked Gretchen if she would mind assembling her team in the parlor. Once they were all in the room, he spoke. "Two of the agents took hits to the thigh or leg, and the third agent took one in the shoulder. None of the wounds are serious. They will all be back in service after a recuperation period. If not for all of you, we would have sustained more injuries and perhaps deaths. Your teamwork was impressive." Turning to Carlos, "If you were one of us, a formal commendation would be in order. That was professional level work. Again, all of you played it as though you had just completed a training mission on this exact operation." Turning to Max, "You look exactly like your picture. You're a good shot." Max wasn't sure whether he was referring to the operative he shot a few minutes ago or the two Serbs in Maine. He remained quiet. The others smiled. Looking at the two women, he asked, "Which of you is the 'reporter' who called me in Maine?" He said it with humor in his voice. Darlene sheepishly raised her hand and threw a beautiful smile to a very handsome and heroic federal agent. She wondered if they would meet again. He wondered the same. "If you write as well as you shoot, you must be good." He got an even bigger smile.

"Time to go. I suggest you not linger or speak with anyone." He left and the team followed. Thirty minutes later they were in the Bristol Lounge at the hotel having lunch.

CHAPTER 73

ASSAULTS

Gretchen, Vinnie, Darlene, and Max were congratulating Carlos and Paul for their work in the alley. They had become favorites of the team ever since they had accomplished so much in Florida "When this is over, we are going to ask Elizabeth to recognize your outstanding work, perhaps assign you to work with us as a team."

"Thank you, Gretchen, but as much as we enjoy working with you, we are more comfortable working in Florida. Both Paul and I grew up there and we have made contacts with those who work both sides of the street. However, we would not turn down the opportunity to work with you on special projects. Paul and I have discussed this and we want to say that all of you are the best we have worked with."

Gretchen's phone rang. It was Elizabeth. "Are you where you can go on speaker phone?"

"No."

"I'll plug Vinnie in and you can share the information with the others." Vinnie's phone rang and he picked up. "First, I received a call from Jordan Rich five minutes ago. Congratulations on your non-authorized escapade. Special thanks to Agents Hernandez and Williams. That's the good news. The bad news is that within the past five hours there have been reports of six additional attacks. In the Dallas area, a high school cafeteria came close to a disaster. There was an attempt to poison the lunch for fifteen hundred students. One of the cafeteria workers observed a day worker pouring a liquid into a soup kettle. When the day worker was confronted, she took a ladle of soup and threw it into the worker's face. The police were called along with the community health director. The additive to the soup was deadly. Fortunately, the students never knew how close they came to death. The day worker is in custody, but we hold out little hope of gaining information using the conditions outlined in the field manual. If Khalid is operating as usual, the woman belongs to a cell that has no communication with other cells. "

"My God, Elizabeth, does this never end?"

"According to Vinnie, the answer is not until Khalid has finished his work. The second incident was in the San Diego area. The editor of a major paper was murdered. He was killed by a shotgun blast as he drove from his office in broad daylight. The third attack took place in Atlanta. A commuter train was derailed. The operatives chose a stretch of track where the train ran at high speed, at the end of which was a substantial curve. The operatives placed a length of actual rail across the track on the curve. There was insufficient time for the train to stop. The engine and seven cars derailed. The operator and assistant were killed."

Vinnie spoke up. "If I'm counting correctly, this makes nine different attacks in seven cities. At this rate, we can expect a total of sixty three attacks, and counting."

"Actually, Vinnie, there have been twelve different types of attacks. Let me share the other three. A commuter bus that was traveling from the suburbs into the city of Denver experienced a drive by shooting. The attacking vehicle was an SUV carrying at least three men who were firing assault weapons of some kind. Five passengers were killed and thirteen passengers were wounded. The driver lost control and the bus ran over a guard rail and flipped on its side. The SUV was found abandoned."

"Have any of the men been apprehended?"

"I'll get to that in a minute. Fortunately, the next attack was unsuccessful. A canister of what later was identified as poisonous gas was left in an anchor store in a major mall in a Dallas suburb. It failed to detonate. There is no report as to why it failed but our best guess, until the lab report is completed, is faulty software programming of the timing device. An FBI bomb squad has it. Earlier in the day, a woman entered a store carrying a large, expensive looking shoulder bag. The management of the store caught her on surveillance tape which is now being examined by the FBI. Finally, and clearly the most significant of the six attacks, was the shooting down of a military helicopter in East Windsor, CT. There is a service road on the northwest side of the international airport that has a clear view of the runways. According to first reports, the road is not heavily used. A stinger missile was fired. Using Vinnie's accounting, there have now been twelve different types of attacks. If each city or region experiences all twelve of the different types of attacks, the total could reach eighty four. And, that does not include whatever major event Khalid has planned. None of the attacks required highly technical skills or equipment. While the Stinger is difficult to acquire, it is relatively easy to use. You may recall its effectiveness in Afghanistan against Russian aircraft."

"This is his idea of an alternative 9/11. Rather than mount a major disaster, he is telling us that no one, at any time, in any place is safe. There is no place to hide. He is warning us that al-Qaeda is alive and well."

"You are absolutely correct, Gretchen. That is why I do not believe he has a final event of a major proportion planned. That would be inconsistent with what he has done to date. I believe he is planning a symbolic attack somewhere in the Boston region. It is more important than ever that you determine what it is and kill him before it happens. Vinnie, you asked if any of the operatives have been apprehended. Jordan Rich shared with me that, except for the day worker at the cafeteria, there have been no arrests. What he believes has happened, and I concur, is that once the operatives complete their work, they move quickly into a Muslim community in an adjoining city with a mosque. They simply disappear among the masses. They are used only once. Every attack has taken place within a short distance of a city. Once they feel safe, they will leave the country and others will take their place. There are literally thousands of federal, state and local law enforcement officers at work around the country. Unless the DOJ is willing to allow enhanced interrogation of the six CEO's, the intelligence community will have little to go on. Once the operatives seek safe haven in a mosque, we are helpless. I have work to do. Call me when you have something." The phone went silent.

Gretchen and Vinnie briefed the others. All were stunned, struggling to comprehend what Khalid had accomplished. For all of their efforts and successes in tracking him from Los Angeles to Florida, then on to

Denver, and now to Boston, and coming within minutes of apprehending him at the hotel, he was still not in their grasp. Abdu Khalid was no ordinary terrorist. He was a genius at planning. He is of the new order wherein he and his followers will keep the American population awake at night worrying about living through the next day. No one, no place, no event would ever again be safe from al-Qaeda. This was terror at its best.

Vinnie, having been in tight spots before, was not about to let the team spend time commiserating about the past. It was time to move on. He quickly reviewed what the team knew. Elizabeth had faith that the team would accomplish its mission and he was not about to fail. That was not an option. Khalid was here, close by and plotting his next step. Kay Horton may know something of value as to his whereabouts. He remembered that William Worthington had mentioned that she was taken with Khalid or Thomas Gilbane. He knew from experience that women with the hots for a guy will do most anything for them. Yesterday, the team was to develop a list of symbolic targets in the Boston region that could be Khalid's target. That list needed to be completed. Because Khalid had demonstrated his ability to pull a rabbit out of the hat many times, Vinnie made an intuitive leap and decided that Khalid was licensed to fly dual engine aircraft. He based that leap of faith on the fact that Silver Eagle Aircraft Industries, distributor of the Silver Eagle X650, was operated by one of the six men working with him. Then, there was the incident in Key West that may have indicated that Khalid flew the charter plane. He was less certain of that and more certain of the Silver Eagle connection.

That being the case, he wondered how Khalid could use his flying ability to bring off his last event. Or, is that what he wanted Vinnie and the team to think? He wondered where Khalid would stay while he made and executed his plans now that the apartment was compromised. Finally, had Khalid flown himself here from Denver and, if he did, where is the plane and was it a Silver Eagle?

"Vinnie, you look lost in thought."

"I was thinking about our next steps. Here is what I suggest for consideration. Gretchen and I will talk to Kay Horton as soon as possible. We need to know what she knows about Khalid. Darlene, you and Max need to complete the list of possible targets in the Boston area with emphasis on symbolic ones. I'm with Elizabeth in thinking that Khalid needs a symbolic victory to top off what has been an incredibly successful series of attacks with many more to come."

"I assume that Paul and I are done and that we should head back to Miami." It was Carlos.

"Unless you can come up with an idea for locating Khalid."

"If he is in a hotel, it is not a high end one. He knows we would look there first. There are literally hundreds of middle class and low end hotels. By the time we surveyed all of them, he would be long gone. That is a dead end activity. If I were in his position, I would look for a condo, pay a month's lease and look as though I am staying for a while."

"That means he has to use a realtor."

"I don't know if that is how it works, Vinnie, but it is where I would begin. If you want, Paul and I will get to work on it now."

"Keep in touch."

With that Carlos and Paul left and Darlene and Max said they would use the business center at the hotel to research symbolic targets. Vinnie and Gretchen left for Worthington's company and an interview with Kay Horton.

She was expecting them. William Worthington had informed her that the CIA agents wished to speak with her. Before Worthington escorted them to her office, he spoke to them in a tone that reflected his anger at the destruction of his apartment. "Was it necessary to shoot the place up like it was a bunker in Afghanistan?"

"It was either that or risk death to agents. I assure you that the danger to the agents was real. Whenever you have to storm a second floor without the element of surprise, you place law enforcement agents in serious jeopardy. Under those conditions, Mr. Worthington, it is very much like storming a secure building in Afghanistan. As it is, we have three agents who were injured. Both agencies appreciate your help and I assure you that you will be fairly compensated."

"It's not the money. I just want the apartment to be restored to its original beauty."

"I will make that clear to my boss and she will make the FBI aware of your concern."

"Thank you, Agent Pagano. Now, let me take you to Kay.

Kay Horton's office was befitting a chief executive officer of a Fortune 500 company. Not only was it expensive, it was exquisite and beautifully appointed. It was on the thirty third floor and looked out on to the Charles River. When she looked across the river she could see the Harvard Campus to the left, and the Massachusetts Institute of Technology to her right.

When William Worthington entered, she stood to greet Vinnie and Gretchen. Worthington made the introductions and left.

"Please have a seat. May I get you something to drink?"

Both Gretchen and Vinnie declined. They wanted to get down to business. Vinnie took the lead. "Ms. Horton, we understand that earlier in the week you met a Thomas Gilbane at the Richmond Plaza Hotel and had cocktails with him."

"The statement is correct as far as it went. My sister Lee and Bill Worthington were also present. In fact, it was Bill who invited Thomas to join us."

"Why was that?"

"Thomas Gilbane was drinking alone and Bill thought it would be a friendly gesture to ask him to join us. It was a good decision."

"The next day you arrived at the hotel in your BMW and picked up Mr. Gilbane who was waiting at the St. James Street Entrance."

"That is true. May I ask how you learned of our meeting?"

"The bell captain recalled your meeting him and the surveillance camera at the entrance verified it."

"My god. They have surveillance cameras at the Richmond?"

Gretchen answered. "There are cameras at most upscale hotels as a security measure for guests."

"It may be a security measure, but it also takes away a bit of our liberty, doesn't it?"

Neither Vinnie nor Gretchen responded. Vinnie continued. "It would be helpful if you shared with us any information about Mr. Gilbane that you possess, such as the type of work he is engaged in, where he was going once he leaves Boston and so forth. We would also like to know where you went when you drove off from the hotel."

"Why all the questions about Thomas Gilbane?"

"Mr. Gilbane is a person of interest."

"What kind of interest?" There was a distinct edge to her voice.

Vinnie looked at Gretchen and concluded they were interviewing a hostile witness, someone who is not used to being asked questions; rather, someone who raises them. Gretchen entered the conversation. "We are not at liberty to offer more in the way of explanation. We need to speak with Mr. Gilbane and soon. You may have information that would speed the process."

"And, what if I do not wish to talk about Thomas Gilbane?"

Again, Gretchen. "In that case, you would become a person of interest."

"What the hell does that mean?" There was anger in her voice.

"It means that we will recommend to our supervisor that a formal investigation be launched into your relationship with Mr. Gilbane."

"I have no relationship with Thomas Gilbane, as you put it. We had cocktails a couple of times and we took a ride to Concord to experience a part of his British history. I resent your attitude and implication."

Not one to get flustered, Gretchen continued. "Perhaps, then, you will answer Agent Pagano's first question; what does Mr. Gilbane do for a living?"

Although angry at being questioned, she responded. "He told us that he brings international buyers and sellers together to make deals that require substantial capital. The deals can include both material assets and intellectual properties. He did not mention who he did business with either by name or company. If you met Thomas you would appreciate why he might be successful. He is urbane, smart, handsome, well groomed and articulate. On one hand he has the common touch and, on the other, he is quite sophisticated."

And, he is ready to share her bed which she is keeping warm, thought both Gretchen and Vinnie.

Vinnie took over. "Please share with us the details of your trip to Concord." She explained in detail what she had shown Thomas Gilman in Concord and the conversation about the British defeat at North Bridge. She shared her dismay at hearing of the murder of the Chief of Police in Merritt. They heard it on the radio as they were driving home.

"What was his reaction to the attack?"

"He didn't have much of a chance to say anything since I asked him why America is so hated by those in the Middle East."

"What did he say?"

"That it all began with the partition of Palestine and the greed of the United States government in supporting dictators who kept their people in poverty while they enriched themselves with American dollars received from the sale of oil."

Gretchen continued with the interview."Do you know where Mr. Gilbane is now?"

Angrily, "I do not."

"Have you spoken with Thomas Gilbane today?"

Angrier still, "I have not."

Vinnie, the good cop entered the conversation. "I want to thank you for your assistance. Should Mr. Gilbane call you, please let us know. We want to impress upon you that it is in your best interest not to meet with or contact Mr. Gilbane. It could be dangerous. Now, we'll let you get back to your work." They all stood and Vinnie handed her a card with his cell phone number. She walked them to the door. Once outside, Gretchen was the first to speak. "She is one arrogant bitch. We need to get a judge to authorize phone taps, now!"

"I agree. You call Elizabeth and ask her to contact the Boston office and for it to move fast to get approval. Even at that, we may be too late. We need Carlos and Paul to set up a surveillance on her as fast as possible. While you call Langley, I'll call Carlos. I'll also get the registration number on her BMW. Since Carlos has not met her, the only way for him to make a connection is through the car."

"I think we should remain outside the company's garage on the chance she might leave before Carlos arrives. We know she drives a convertible BMW. There can't be many of those leaving at this hour. Vinnie, I do not trust the woman and we must stay on her. The distressing thing is her not understanding the dangerous situation she is in."

"I agree." After they made their calls, they established a position on the street where they could observe cars leaving Worthington's parking garage.

Once they were out of the office, Kay Horton turned, went to a cabinet, took out a bottle of vodka and poured herself a drink. She stood looking out at the river, her whole body shaking. "Who the hell are you, Thomas Gilbane, or, whatever your real name is? Why did they warn me not to contact you?" Then, she picked up her cell and dialed. When it was answered, "Where are you?"

"I'm looking for a hotel with some privacy. The apartment is now out of the question."

"You'll find that no hotel is secure with federal agents looking for you. They have a long reach. What is going on, Thomas?"

"They are interested in me because of a dispute between two of my clients. Let's meet and I will explain." She wanted very much to believe him. Thomas Gilbane was a magnet and she was drawn to him in spite of the warning from Gretchen and Vinnie. He was not a man to be ignored by women.

"I have a boat. It is moored at Constitution Marina in Charlestown. It is easily reached by taxi. I will be there to meet you. The name of the boat is 'Money Talks.' Again, it is Constitution Marina in Charlestown. See you there." She told her secretary she had an appointment and not to expect her until morning and quickly left the building. As Vinnie had feared, Kay Horton called Thomas Gilbane before a tap could be placed on her phones and she left the parking garage before Carlos could establish surveillance. Kat Horton had outwitted her pursuers and was on her way to rendezvous with one of the world's most evil men, a man she wanted to bed.

As soon as she left the garage, Vinnie and Gretchen followed. She left Government Center and entered on to Hanover and headed toward Commercial Street. She took a left on Parmenter, and then a right on to Salem, a quick left on to Cooper, a right on to Margin and then they lost her. "Vinnie, she knew we were following her. I knew she was trouble. She's gone."

"On the plus side we know she will not be going to her apartment. If she is meeting Khalid, it is someplace that is private. Call Worthington, see if she has a summer place or another apartment or condo that she has available for her clients. And, there is her sister. Get her number from Worthington. Kay Horton is on the run and we need to find her and when we do, we have Khalid."

Vinnie cruised the area, but he knew that Kay Horton was not to be found. She was on her way to a designated location. In fact, Kay had made her way to the John F. Fitzgerald Surface Road, then to Joe Tecce Way, and to the Charlestown Bridge, also known as the Freedom Trail. In minutes, she would be with Thomas Gilbane.

Gretchen finally got off of the phone with Worthington. "She has a home on the North Shore in Manchester-by-the Sea, an up-market community. Apparently, Kay Horton is one hell of a fund manager to afford a second home in Manchester-by-the-Sea. The only other property he knows of is the apartment where she lives. He will call back after he has spoken to her sister, Lee, to see if Kay has other properties. He doubts she has any others. Most of her substantial wealth is invested in the fund she manages for Worthington. I have her address and I suggest we head to the North Shore."

"It sounds too easy and too obvious. Anyone this young with the success she has enjoyed has to be damn smart. She lost us once and if we are not careful, she will send us on a wild goose chase."

"We have no choice, Vinnie. Until and unless we have additional information, we need to go to Manchester-by-the-Sea. It's only twenty miles from here. Even with the traffic, we'll be there in less than an hour. We can be back here in time to continue our search."

"It's against my better judgment, but let's get it over with."

"I don't sense a great deal of confidence in that comment."

"It wasn't meant to be. Why would anyone hide out in a house that can be easily found? I think we are being jerked around by Worthington. As for her sister, remember that blood is thicker than water."

Vinnie decided that the fastest way to Manchester-by-the-Sea was to take Interstate 93 north to Interstate 95. Then they would continue on route 128 north to exit 16, Pine Street. It was four miles from the exit into the center of town. The sea coast town was a picture postcard, upscale community. The harbor just sits there in the middle of town, crowded with expensive yachts and day sailors. The shops were small but exclusive, and everything about the community was pristine.

They stopped at the only gas station in town and asked directions to Kay Horton's address. They did not mention her name. As expected, she lived in a grand house situated on a secluded section of the oceanfront. As far as they could determine, the only house within sight was a quarter mile or so to the north. They pulled into the driveway, parked, and went to the front door. They rang, but there was no answer. They tried a second time without any response. They walked around the house checking other points of entry. Still no response. Next, they began to look into windows to determine if there was any sign of life. Finally, they went to the side of the house where there was a three stall garage. None of the overhead doors could be opened by hand. A side door was locked, but had a window. Looking inside, they could make out a Jeep Cherokee. The other stalls were empty. There was no BMW to be found. About then, they heard the crunching of the gravel driveway. They returned to the front of the house to be confronted by two local cops leaning against the rental car.

"I'm sergeant Ritter of the Manchester Police Department. This is Officer Mayo. What you are doing here?" There was nothing cordial about his introductions.

"I'm Agent Pagano of the Central Intelligence Agency and this is my partner, Agent Iverson. If you allow me to reach into my jacket, I will show you my credentials."

"Please do so slowly."

Vinnie withdrew his credentials and displayed them to the sergeant.

"And you, miss," looking at Gretchen.

She reached in her bag and took out her credentials. She, too, showed them to Ritter.

"What is the CIA doing here?"

"Sorry, but that is confidential, other than to say that we would like to speak with the owner of this house."

"Ms. Horton rarely uses this house. When she does, it is mostly on weekends in the summer."

"How did you know we were here?"

"Small town. You bought gas, asked for directions, aren't local and we got a call. This is a quiet town and we intend to keep it that way."

"Quiet is good." He nodded at Gretchen and without another word, they got in the car and left.

"So, where is she?"

While Vinnie and Gretchen were wondering about Kay Horton, she was arriving at "Money Talks."

She was a few minutes ahead of Thomas Gilbane. By the time he arrived, she had changed into loose fitting white pants, no panties, an oversized light beige cotton pullover without a bra, no socks and grey deck sneakers. Her long blond hair was pulled back into a single pony tail and she wore only a faint hint of expensive perfume. Her makeup was neutral and subdued. She was every man's summer love aboard a world class 110 foot yacht. The boat belonged to her fund and employed a fulltime captain and first mate. When she had overnight guests on board, like tonight, she employed a steward to handle drinks, dinner and night time duties. The moment Thomas Gilbane boarded, the first mate released the lines, fore and aft, and the captain gently nudged 'Money Talks' from its mooring and out into the inner harbor on what was to be the first leg of its voyage.

William Worthington and Lee Horton had failed to make known to Vinnie and Gretchen that Kay Horton owned 'Money Talks' and that its home port was the harbor at Manchester-by-the Sea. They rationalized, for Kay's benefit, that a boat did not fit the description of "property" as used by Vinnie and Gretchen. Kay did not live aboard the boat. The cops in Manchester were not about to share anything with federal agents of any stripe. Silence was a valuable commodity for local law enforcement officers and they were not about to squander it on out-of-towners, especially the feds. William Worthington and Lee Horton would eventually be exposed to the wrath of Vinnie and Gretchen.

"Welcome aboard, Thomas. The sooner you get out of those business clothes and into something comfortable, we can have cocktails. I have many business guests aboard 'Money Talks' so we keep a good selection of clothes for both men and women. Your stateroom is the second door on the left."

"If someone is mixing, I'll have a vodka martini, two olives." With that he was gone, carrying his suitcase, a carry-on with a loaded Heckler & Hock MK23 with three magazines, a flight map of the United States, a AAA map of Connecticut, Massachusetts and Rhode Island, and a lap top.

When he returned topside, the boat was passing over the tunnels buried under the inner harbor that connected Boston to East Boston and Logan Airport. Kay was waiting with two cocktails in her hand. She handed one to Thomas and delivered a light kiss on his cheek. The smell of her perfume and the touch of her lips aroused him. He returned her kiss with one of his own. She shivered ever so slightly at his touch. They clinked glasses and took sips of their drinks. "You look quite beautiful this afternoon, Kay."

"And you look quite dashing. The fit could not have been better." He was wearing white cotton pants, a soft yellow short sleeved shirt open at the neck, deck shoes and no socks. Thomas Gilbane could easily pass for a wealthy Bostonian playing on his yacht with his girlfriend.

"This boat is magnificent, Kay. Is it yours?"

"In a manner of speaking. It is registered to my fund and is used primarily to entertain wealthy clients, potential clients, influential politicians, friends and local Manchester residents or officials who look out for my home and the boat when it is in harbor there. Once or twice a year I hold a party on board for my middle managers and their wives or significant others who rarely, if ever, have the opportunity to cruise on a luxury boat. I also lease it at a tidy profit to other fund managers at the firm as a way to assist in underwriting both its capital cost and operating expenses. I maintain mooring space at Constitution Marina for the convenience of my clients, but Manchester is my home port. There are certain weeks of the year that I reserve it for my own personal pleasure."

"Is this one of those weeks you reserved the boat for personal pleasure?"

"That depends on what you have to tell me about the visitors to my office this morning."

"I was hoping that I could finish my martini and enjoy your company. I have missed seeing you since our trip to view the North Bridge where my countrymen were defeated. We never did meet for dinner."

"You will get your wish. Tonight we have the option of dining on board under the stars or on the waterfront in the community we are headed for. "

"Is it inappropriate to ask the skipper where we are headed?"

"Not at all. We are headed to Provincetown and will spend the night there. In the morning, we will discuss new plans."

"Are private boats like aircraft wherein you have to file a flight plan?" Khalid wanted to know, without asking straight out, if the government could trace his whereabouts.

"Technically yes, but we have more freedom from regulations. On the other hand, we need to reserve space at a harbor for a boat this size if it is to be moored overnight. Our captain has done that. Those records are public if anyone wanted to know where we have been. With the new high tech global positioning systems, we can pinpoint our location within meters if we need assistance. If we notify the Coast Guard of our destination, they keep constant track of our movements. For the moment, we are essentially at sea and headed to a place unknown except to those on board. So, relax Thomas and enjoy the ride."

He was hoping there was another meaning to her comment.

"Would you prefer to have our drinks in the lounge or go topside and visit with the captain?"

"I prefer to be with you, wherever you choose to be."

"While it is still light, let's go topside so I can point out famous landmarks."

"While I think of it, Kay, is your marina named after the United States Constitution?"

"It is. Equally important is the fact that the frigate, USS Constitution, is moored less than a hundred yards to the north in the same naval shipyard that I use for 'Money Talks.' It is the oldest commissioned vessel in the Navy and was named after our Constitution. It has historic significance of major proportions. It is a symbol of our independence, our fighting spirit and our desire never to be conquered by foreign powers. In over forty encounters, it never lost a battle. Of the hundreds of famous landmarks in Massachusetts, including the North Bridge, none are as symbolic as the USS Constitution."

"I would like to see the ship before I leave for London. In the meantime, please point out the Boston landmarks." Khalid made his way to the top deck with Kay, all the while thinking about his incredible stroke of luck in meeting a woman with a powerful boat that is anchored next to his main target, and where its movement in and out of the harbor at all times of day and night raises no concern with the port authorities or the Coast Guard. Allah was exceptionally kind for creating this turn of fortune. Between his pleasures this night, he would be plotting how to gain control of 'Money Talks.' To pull off what he has in mind and survive to continue his terrorist activities, he will need to depend upon his operatives. He has men in place, but the challenge is to get them operational at the right time. Time was running short and he had to act in the next day or so.

He also thought about the need to kill the crew and Kay Horton.

CHAPTER 74

SYMBOLISM

While Khalid and Kay Horton were having drinks aboard 'Money Talks,' Vinnie, Gretchen, Darlene, Max, Carlos and Paul were having their own happy hour in the Bristol Lounge. They had asked for and received a table in one of the corners of the lounge along the windows facing Boylston Street. They had just ordered drinks when Vinnie's phone rang. "Are you able to speak?"

"No, hold on a minute." He excused himself by letting the others know it was Elizabeth. Gretchen was not happy that Elizabeth was calling Vinnie and not her when she was the senior agent. On the other hand, he was the one who articulated the pattern.

Once outside on Boylston Street, he continued with the call. "Vinnie, we have some great news and some devastating bad news. The good news is that one of our agency drones killed Anwar Al-Awlaki this morning along with another American who was working with al-Qaeda. There is some minor collateral damage in that a few politicians are stating outright that it was an assassination of an American citizen who had not yet been officially charged with a crime. The accusation has no traction. It was a great day for our men and women who control the drones. The bad news is that there have been five more attacks, all of which are following your pattern. Two were in the Atlanta area; a church was destroyed with loss of life and a local television station was bombed, also with loss of life. In Chicago there were two attacks, an alderman was shot arriving at a meeting and a commuter bus was attacked in the same manner as the one in Denver. The fifth attack was in the San Diego area where a commuter train was derailed."

There was silence while Vinnie thought about the five attacks. "Elizabeth, there is no doubt in my mind that we are faced with a total of eighty four attacks, twelve in each city or area. Unless Khalid's operatives make a mistake, we have no way to stop the attacks from occurring or in apprehending the operatives."

"I know all that Vinnie. The reason for my call is to urge the team to move quickly to find Khalid. His death may not stop what is already planned, but it may slow up or stop the next round so we can do a better job of locating his operatives."

"I'm with the team now and by morning we should have more to go on."

"Call me early. I'll be waiting." End of the call.

Vinnie returned to the table and quietly informed everyone of the content of Elizabeth's call. They were pleased with the drone attack and killing of Al-Awlaki, and not the least bit surprised with the attacks. "We have our work cut out for us. First thing in the morning, we lean on William Worthington and Lee Horton. They must know where Kay is."

Carlos spoke. "We know that Worthington and Lee Horton frequent the Oak Bar at the Richmond Plaza Hotel. In the off chance they are there now for happy hour, why don't Paul and I pay them a visit? We haven't met them, but I believe Paul and I will have no trouble identifying them." He looked to Gretchen for advice.

"No confrontation. It will suffice to inform both of them that withholding information in a national security matter is a federal offense and given the mood of the courts, it will go hard on them if they do not cooperate. Inform them you will call early in the morning. They can sit on the matter overnight. No longer."

Vinnie agreed. "Good strategy, Gretchen."

Carlos and Paul left.

Gretchen asked. "Darlene, what do you and Max have for us? You were going to compile a list of symbolic historic sites as possible targets for Khalid."

She pulled out six copies of a list. "The list is untitled for security reasons. Max and I reviewed many sites dealing with historic landmarks and these are what we decided upon as being symbolic." She handed each a list. It read:

Paul Revere House
Bunker Hill Monument
Old North Church
Freedom Trail
John Hancock Tower
JFK Library and Museum
Isabella Gardner Museum
Museum of Fine Arts
Old State House
Trinity Church
Boston Public Library
USS Constitution
Massachusetts State House
Faneuil Hall
Symphony Hall

"I suggest we have dinner after which you can raise questions about our suggestions."

The lounge was busy and there was a vibrant feeling to the atmosphere. Most of the patrons were young professionals with a sprinkling of older, well heeled Bostonians. Although Vinnie was new to the team and a potential competitor to Max, a strong friendship had developed. Along with Gretchen and Darlene, they were among America's best intelligence agents and they were determined to find and kill Khalid before he could spread more devastation. In the lull between dinner and dessert, Vinnie brought up the assassination of Al-Awlaki. "I'm curious as to whether or not Al-Awalki's assassination works to our advantage or if it will serve to encourage others to take his place? And, what about the fact that he was killed based on what we believe he did, but for which we never issued an arrest warrant? Is the assassination of an American citizen justified morally if the subject was never charged with a crime?"

Max offered an opinion. "The moment we begin to act like our enemies, the faster we will lose the moral fiber that has been the underpinnings of our democracy. To be blunt, the Director should never have authorized the drone attack."

Darlene responded. "How do we know he did? It could have been Elizabeth or the President. The fact is, whoever authorized it put the death of an alleged terrorist ahead of justice and politics ahead of policy. I agree with Max that it was morally wrong and undermines our philosophy of promoting freedom around the world. How about you, Vinnie? You raised the question, how about an answer?"

"I believe this to have been a serious lack of judgment. We kill Bin Laden and then dump his body into the sea. Since when did we, by executive order, make a decision to purposely destroy the bodies of our enemies? Al-Awalki was the target of a drone even before he was charged with a crime. Suddenly, we have become the 'death by drone' nation. He was a United States citizen and he was assassinated before he had a trial. Khalid is a known killer and deserves to die, but we cannot give license to anyone, even the president, to kill someone without charging them and finding them guilty of a crime for which the death penalty is appropriate. I pray that neither Mallory nor Elizabeth gave the go-ahead with Al-Awalki."

Gretchen intervened. "I am the odd person out on this matter. Given what we know about al-Qaeda and its philosophy of killing American and Israeli citizens, and their efforts to take over western civilization, I believe that killing Al-Awalki was the right thing to do."

The discussion continue for another half hour and just as it was beginning to heat up, but before it could come to a boil, Carlos and Paul walked in and took seats. "Mission accomplished. Paul and I showed our credentials to the bell captain and were assured that Mr. Worthington had arrived with a woman who turned out to be Lee Horton. We took seats in the bar, ordered drinks and observed them for a few minutes. Once they appeared happy and content, we took our drinks to Worthington's table, sat down and introduced ourselves. Although displeased with our visit, he was not surprised. We asked if he had heard from Kay Horton today, to which he answered in the negative. Then, we posed the same question to Lee Horton and she answered in the negative. We then asked both of them if they had attempted to contact Kay Horton on her cell phone. Again, two negatives. Finally, we asked if they had heard from or attempted to contact Thomas Gilbane. As we expected, they did not hear from him, nor did they try to contact him."

Carlos nodded to Paul who took over. "I asked them if they had any additional information as to properties Kay Horton owned other than the apartment she lived in and her house in Manchester. When they had nothing more to offer, I asked the question in a slightly different way. I wanted to know if they were aware of any property that she may rent or lease, or otherwise have access to even if it belonged to others such as Lee Horton or William Worthington. Once again, negative responses. With the preliminaries out of the way, I briefed them on the Patriot Act, Homeland Security policies and federal law in general regarding the withholding of information in a matter of national security."

Carlos got back into the discussion. "I reminded them that federal prisons are very threatening places for those, especially women, who have lived luxurious and fulfilled lives and I certainly would not want them to be incarcerated. Then, I told them they would be contacted by us at ten in the morning in the event they remembered anything of value. Paul then informed them that they would have amnesty if they told us what they knew but, that after ten in the morning, they were to be considered accomplices in a crime of national security. Then we left. And, now we need dinner. Hope we didn't interrupt anything important?"

"I hope we all realize that there is no reason why Worthington and Horton are compelled to talk to us. The fact that Kay Horton may be with Khalid means nothing since she is unaware, as far as we know, that

Thomas Gilbane is Abdu Khalid. We have not charged her and, therefore, I doubt if we have a case that would allow us to employ any federal statue. It's a bluff we hope works. We'll know in the morning when we contact them."

"Darlene is correct. We have nothing." Gretchen then briefed them on Elizabeth's call and the list prepared by Darlene and Max. When she had completed her briefing, Vinnie asked if anyone was interested in a walk in the Boston Gardens after dessert, to which all answered in the affirmative.

CHAPTER 75

LOVE BOAT

In contrast to the quiet purring of the diesel engines on "Money Talks," the noises from Logan International Airport were deafening as large jets roared down the runways and their powerful engines thrust them into the sky over Boston's inner harbor. As dusk was settling on the city the lights from populated areas along the harbor began to accentuate the skyline. As Khalid watched the jets flying overhead, he was cognizant of the advantage he had over his pursuers now that he possessed or would possess a large, powerful boat. The boat was in addition to the Dassault Falcon that was tied down at Hanscom Field in Bedford along with a pilot willing to give his life for Allah. When Khalid had flown out of Denver, he required an airport sufficiently close to Boston so the city could be easily reached, yet not so close that the CIA might stumble upon it. Hanscom Field was perfect, only 30 minutes from downtown Boston. It was located in one of America's technology regions on the 128/95 and 495/3 corridor. The Falcon was just another beautiful corporate jet among the most popular private aircraft in the world sitting on the tarmac. No one paid it much attention. With "Money Talks" and the Falcon, he had two powerful weapons with which to sink the USS Constitution. While he would command "Money

Talks", the Falcon would be flown by one of his operatives. It was a matter of timing and choice of weapon.

On the down side was the fact that the USCG station was located on Atlantic Avenue, across the inner harbor from where the USS Constitution was moored. He would have to plan carefully by determining the location of the Coast Guard cutters at any given time. Watching the jets overhead reminded him that the air defenses for Boston were provided by the 104th Fighter Wing located at Barnes Air National Guard Base in Westover, Massachusetts. Working under the protocols of Operation Noble Eagle, the F-15's, once alerted, would be in the air in a matter of minutes and screaming towards Boston harbor at their low altitude speed of mach 1.2, or 900 mph. Khalid, whether by boat or air, would not have a second chance to sink the USS Constitution.

"You look far away, Thomas. Where are you?"

"Kay, I haven't been this relaxes for ages. The salt air, the humming of the engines, the fabulous skyline and you are enough to make a man intoxicated. As for where I am, I am more interested in where I would like to be."

"And, that is?"

"In your arms, making love."

She walked over to him, took him by the hand and guided him below to her stateroom that was secure from the rest of the boat. Once inside, she closed and locked the door. When she turned, he held her tight, moved her so her back was leaning against the door, kissed her gently on the lips, pulled up her sweater and put his hands on her warm and ample breasts. She removed her sweater, kicked off her sneakers and unbuttoned her baggy pants letting them drop to the flour. She then started to unbutton his pants. He helped by removing his shirt, and shorts and then kicking his sneakers and pants aside. Both naked, they fell onto the bed. She pushed him down and got on top of him. Her body was burning with desire and his penis had rapidly expanded. Their bodies were toned like those of athletes and they were going for the gold. As she grabbed his penis, he pulled her to him and took one of her breasts in his mouth and sucked. Moments later, he took her other breast in his mouth and ran his tongue over her nipple which was erect and her breast firm. He then placed his hands on her shoulders and gently pushed her down his body until her mouth was over his penis. She took it in her mouth and with one hand pumped it. She knew it was not long before he would ejaculate, so she placed her hands on the bed on each side of him and pushed herself up, and then dropped herself onto his penis and pushed down hard so he was fully inside her. Then, she rose and pushed down hard on him, then rose and pushed down hard on him, over and over, until they both reached orgasm. She rolled over on her back and he turned on top of her, still aflame with passion. He kissed her mouth, her neck, and then her breasts, her stomach and finally found his treasure. Wet from intercourse, she lifted her legs and pulled his head between them, placed her hands on his face and guided his mouth to her vagina. His tongue found its target and she rolled slightly from side to side as his tongue discovered her very special place and his mouth absorbed the moisture between her legs. When finally he lifted his head, she put her hands on his buttocks, and pulled him up to her. They rolled over so she was on top and guided him into her again.

Kay Horton lay quietly while Thomas dozed from fatigue and realized that she had never had a sexual experience like that gifted to her by Thomas Gilbane. Never had she so openly and quickly offered herself to someone. She remembered telling her sister Lee that Thomas Gilbane was a magnet and, when in his sphere, there was no escaping his charm, attraction and control. She reached over and fondled his penis, but her lover was not yet ready to give his body to her. Looking at him, she ran her fingers over his face, his mouth, his chest, over his stomach to his penis. He stirred from her touch, reached over and pulled her on top of him so her warm breasts settled on to his chest. He ran his hands to her buttocks and gently pulled her closer and then a surge of passion rose in him and once again they made love.

CHAPTER 76

MEDIA FRENZY

The eighteen attacks, spread over seven regions of the country, had the public in a panic mode and the intelligence community rattled. There was no place where the public felt safe from Khalid's terrorists. Investigative reporters working for major cable news outlets pieced together the geographic positioning of the attacks and, in so doing, played into the hands of the terrorists by emphasizing that convalescent homes, trains, busses, schools, and places of worship were not safe. Local police forces throughout out the country were providing additional security for their chiefs. The killing of the state legislator in Michigan had politicians hesitant to attend legislative sessions. CEO's of media outlets were apprehensive to go to work for fear of being assassinated.

Two television stations had been bombed and the head of a metropolitan newspaper was murdered. A fire station was destroyed and a high school cafeteria was the target of a poisoning attempt. Shopping malls were experiencing a drop in sales after the attempted explosion in the Dallas area mall. And, if that was not sufficient to frighten the public, the downing of a military helicopter confirmed that even the military was helpless. The final blow to public confidence was the fact that, with a single exception, no al-Qaeda operatives had been apprehended, and the one exception was a woman who only had knowledge of her assignment and did not understand how the cell operated. Khalid's "wheel of terror" was so simplistic in its design that law enforcement agencies were unprepared to deal with it. At the heart of the problem was the failure of the intelligence community to keep track of terrorists who had entered the country shortly after 9/11 and well before border safeguards were put into place.

The media figured out the pattern that Vinnie had identified earlier; twelve different types of attacks over seven regions. Using the same logic as Vinnie, the public also worked the math. Twelve attacks in each of seven regions. Thirteen down and seventy one to go! Little wonder there was widespread panic. The media went wild with the concept, playing up the fact that local, state and federal law enforcement agencies were impotent in stopping the attacks. The public began its own assault on law enforcement agencies accusing them of ineptness and demanding protection. Conservative political groups accused the current administration of lacking the courage to confront American Muslims, while Progressives fingered the Republicans as the cause of the attacks.

The finger pointing that Elizabeth predicted would begin, began in earnest with the federal intelligence agencies finding fault with one another and questioning the effectiveness of local and state law enforcement agencies. Homeland Security, being the centerpiece of the intelligence community, was taking the biggest hit with politicians of all stripes demanding that the agency become proactive in apprehending the militants before there were more attacks. POTUS went on national television asking for the public's patience and assuring it that everything that could be done was being done. He spoke the truth, but the efforts were too late and not effective. The public, often depicted as the dumb unwashed by the Washington elite, knew in this case that the hunt for al-Qaeda in the United States should have started in earnest ten years earlier.

When the team returned to the hotel, the bad news continued. Elisabeth was on the secure line to Vinnie. "I was hoping that there would be a lull, giving us time to work on the problem, but the attacks are continuing. It is now obvious that each area has its own set of cells and they are at liberty to move at their own speed. There has been no contact between any of the regions and Khalid and no communication among the cells. If there had been contact, we would have picked it up either at the monitoring station in Simsbury or here at Langley. You warned us earlier that his strategy would resemble that used in Iraq and Afghanistan where the Taliban and al-Qaeda empowered its field commanders with great latitude in selecting the timing and location of targets. That is what we have going on now. Even if Khalid wanted to slow down the attacks, there is no way he can contact the cells without compromising himself and his location. Unless he is desperate, that will not happen."

"How bad is it, Elizabeth?"

"An admiral in San Diego, dining out with his wife, was killed in a drive by shooting when they left the restaurant and were walking to their car. His wife is in critical condition. The terrorist car careened over a curb and struck a utility pole. The driver was killed, but the shooter who was in the back seat was apprehended. Naval Intelligence has him in custody. What we need to learn is if it was a random shooting or if the admiral had been specifically targeted. We have one of our agents observing the interrogation. I don't anticipate any valuable information being gained through soft interrogation."

"What else?"

"Denver. Another place of worship. This time Catholic. An attack during a late afternoon service. The explosive had been placed in the sacristy. It is a room usually located behind the alter where sacred vessels and vestments are kept. It is also where priests attire themselves. No one was in the room, but the explosion blew out the wall behind the alter and killed a deacon assisting in the service. The priest was injured, but nothing life threatening."

"You have more, don't you?"

"One more. A long distance bus traveling in a rural part of Washington State near the Oregon border was shot up by a passing pick-up truck. The bus veered off the road into a ditch. Luckily, no one was injured, just shook up. Two teenage eye witnesses said the truck looked like one you see in films of Afghanistan where the shooter is in the truck bed. It was found several miles from the shooting. No mention of its occupants. The best guess is that they are headed for Portland, Oregon."

"That makes twenty one attacks."

"Where are you with Worthington and Horton?"

"They know where she is and are not talking. However, I know we are close so bear with us."

"Whatever you need in the way of transportation and weapons, just ask. The Boston office is well equipped and there are several military installations within minutes of the city, including air bases on the

Cape and in the western part of the state. There is also a coast guard station in Boston harbor. You'll have approval within minutes. Need to go."

It was a dejected group of agents after Vinnie finished briefing them.

CHAPTER 77

PROVINCETOWN

While they were putting their clothes on, they heard the engines revving down as the captain slowed the boat to enter the channel to Providence harbor. Fifteen minutes later he was easing the boat to the designated mooring in the marina. It was evening and the marina was alive with cocktail parties on many of the boats, especially those of a similar luxury class as "Money Talks." Kay's boat was among the smallest of the luxury class in spite of a seven million dollar price tag when her firm purchased the boat from Atkins and Wilkinson, boat brokers in Fort Lauderdale. It was on the market as a result of a developer going belly up in the Miami real estate market. When he purchased it two years earlier from the Italian boat yard in Genoa, he paid twelve million delivered to Fort Lauderdale. It fit nicely into Khalid's life style and he regretted it would be destroyed.

Kay came topside first and talked to the steward and confirmed that he had made reservations at a waterfront restaurant that Kay frequented when she was in Provincetown. She had changed into form fitting denim jeans, a white tank top and a pale blue cashmere cardigan hanging loosely over her shoulders. She exchanged her sneakers for designer flats. Her hair hung loose around her face. She had transformed herself from a summer love to a successful fund manager and the indirect owner of a luxury yacht. When Khalid came out of the hatchway, she was standing at the rail with her back to him. He walked over, put his arms around her waist and hugged her gently. She could feel his penis on her buttocks. She turned, smiled and gave him a kiss on each cheek.

"You must stop looking so beautiful or I will never be able to leave."

"Why do I suspect that your time is running out in Boston and shortly I shall be back on the hunt for eligible dates?"

"It is true that I must soon take care of my business interests elsewhere. As for eligible men, you will be pursued your entire life, Kay. You are a very special woman."

"Considering our afternoon, you are a very special man, Thomas. I shall miss you a great deal. However, I have not forgotten that you owe me an explanation about the apartment."

"Let me clear that up now so we do not spoil dinner and our evening. The nature of my business is such that I occasionally deal with a client who may be involved in a dangerous activity but I do not deal with those with a criminal record. I have refused to broker deals that involve any type of hand held weapons, but I do arrange for sales and purchases of large assets such as aircraft, power boats, anti-aircraft guns, heavy weapons, land vehicles of all kinds and other military hardware. It is mostly sold to governments, but could end up anywhere. I have no way of knowing. The inventory is mostly of American, Russian or French manufacture and is stored at several facilities I maintain in Switzerland where I can be assured of tight security while the assets await shipment.

Kay, being a successful hedge fund manager asked, "Who owns the inventory?"

"I do. It required major funding at the outset of my business. Initially, I was deep in debt, barely surviving. Once I proved myself with a few clients, my fortunes took a decided turn for the better. I have a long list of satisfied clients, my inventory is fully paid for and I replenish it as needed with cash at deep discounts. Substantial amounts of money change hands. I take a percentage from both the seller and buyer. Unfortunately, money makes for greed and greed makes for problems. The men in the apartment represented a sovereign nation that is geographically centered between two countries that recently consummated a sale and purchase of superbly reconditioned fighter aircraft, fifteen to be exact. I initially brokered the deal. The country that made the purchase is seen as a threat to the sovereign nation represented by the men in the apartment. The solution was an attempt to assassinate me rather than the country that made the purchase. I know that is irrational behavior, but that is what occurs when one acts out of anger. I must have been under surveillance since I left London."

"Thomas, is what you do illegal?"

"Not illegal, but highly dangerous at times."

"You could have been killed."

"It is not over yet. There will be more attempts on my life unless a new bargain is struck. It is for this reason that I must leave Boston soon and return to Europe."

"What does the CIA want with you?"

"They want to know who the buyers and sellers were and where the aircraft are located. I cannot help them. If I identify my clients, they would soon find another broker to work with. All my clients will drop me as a source if they learn that I cooperated with the CIA. British intelligence is also pressuring me for information that I refuse to give them. I have worked too hard to lose my business because of government interference."

"What are you going to do now?"

"I don't know. Between the assassins who were waiting for me today and the intelligence community, all of the hotels will be covered. I need to remain low profile until I can return to England and fix the problem. Until then I will be on the run. Since I have not broken any American law, I am able to leave the country. The CIA and British M16 can harass me, but they have no authority to detain me. However, I must first evade the assassins then I must find a way to leave the country without being detected."

"I have an idea. When we return to Constitution Marina, you should stay aboard the boat. It will give us time to figure out how to get you out of the country. You will be quite comfortable for a few days. There are restaurants close by and I can visit whenever I want to. They would have no reason to look for you in the boat. Consider it done."

"You are wonderful beyond words." He kissed her gently on the lips.

"Now, let's have dinner." With that they left the boat and walked to the restaurant.

It was eleven thirty when they returned from dinner. They sat on the aft deck looking out on the marina and the lights reflecting on the water. Most of the boats were quiet and darkened as owners and guests began retiring for the night. Kay was silent, wondering what lay ahead. Khalid knew what was ahead for him, but after the attack the CIA would step up its efforts to find him. He had the documents to leave the country; the question was if he could do so given what is now a heightened state of alert. Kay, on the other hand, sensed that Thomas would soon be on his way out of her life. She would have but a short time to love him. She also believed that Thomas Gilbane was not who he was claiming to be. She did not have any specific idea, but knew that his tale of being a broker was a cover story for something far more dangerous. There was more to the apartment fire fight than he explained. The involvement of the CIA indicated that the United States government has an interest in the matter and that meant Thomas was involved in some serious business of a national security nature. But she did not care about any of that as long as she had Thomas in her bed. His sexual offerings were beyond anything she had experienced or had heard her girlfriends or sister talk about. Kay Horton had the feeling that her time with Thomas Gilbane was limited and she was to make the most of it. She was not going to help the CIA find him. There was a danger about Thomas that excited her.

She turned towards Thomas who was looking at her. "What is it Kay?"

"Take me to bed, now."

Thomas Gilbane lived up to the expectations that Kay harbored. She gave of herself as though it was the last night she would spend with Abdu Khalid, aka, Thomas Gilbane.

Kay was on the bridge with her captain when Khalid came topside in the morning. Not knowing how much the captain knew of the relationship, he merely greeted her. The captain, no older than thirty five or six, introduced himself to Thomas who immediately showed an interest in the boat. The captain, used to guests wanting to know about the boat, was more than happy to describe some of the specifications.

"Mr. Gilbane, 'Money Talks' is powered by twin diesels and has a cruising speed of twenty knots and a maximum speed of twenty four knots, fast for a boat of one hundred and seventeen feet in length. It carries ninety seven hundred gallons of fuel and has a range of 2800 nautical miles. It is registered in the Turks and Caicos in the British West Indies."

"I couldn't help but admire the way you eased the boat to its mooring last evening. That takes great skill."

"To be honest, sir, it is a lot easier than it looks. The key to success is to move the boat slowly, pay attention to the angle of approach, have good hand and eye coordination and steady hands on the throttles. When we return to Constitution Marina, you should plan on joining me on the bridge as we approach the mooring to see exactly how it is done. In the meantime, you can remain here and observe how I ease her away from the dock."

"Thanks, I will."

CHAPTER 78

WORTHINGTON

It was Sunday morning and the team did not meet for breakfast having decided the night before they would make it a leisurely morning and meet for lunch. Carlos, however, rose early and attempted to reach William Worthington on his cell phone at nine am. There was no answer. He tried Lee Horton and got the same results. He and Paul had to return to Miami today. When he reported his findings to Gretchen around nine fifteen, she informed him she and Vinnie would take over. She thanked Carlos and Paul and wished them a safe journey. She then rolled over in bed and shared the news with Vinnie. "Let's pay them a home visit after breakfast."

"I doubt they are at home. The rich are always on the move. Hell, they could be in Palm Springs this morning."

"Nevertheless, we will conduct a home visit. Please respect the fact that I am the agent in charge. And I have other weapons to use if you do not straighten out."

"I am straightened out."

"I'm out of here." With that she went to the shower.

In addition to the apartment on Beacon Street, Worthington maintained his personal residence on Beacon Street. From the street, it looked much like the other up-market real estate that surrounded it. On the inside it was magnificent, a world class apartment, created by the best architect and designer that money could buy. It was the envy of every wannabee. William Worthington was a genius at making money for himself and his hedge fund clients. He was high up in the one percent that the Occupy Wall Street crowd was complaining about. There was nothing he could not buy and he was not about to share his reward with those on the street who bitched about the wealthy, but who wished they were one of them. He viewed those on the street as being either hypocrites or anarchists.

Gretchen rang the door chime. It was eleven in the morning. A servant answered. He was Caucasian, in his forties, outfitted in an appropriate uniform and quite formal. "May I help you?"

Gretchen had her credential out and displayed them to the servant. "I am Agent Iverson of the Central Intelligence Agency and this is Agent Pagano. We would like to see Mr. Worthington."

"He is not at home. Did you have an appointment?"

"No appointment. Do you know where we can find Mr. Worthington?"

"I'm sorry but I am not at liberty to tell you that."

"Is he with Lee Horton?"

"I do not know and if I did, I am not at liberty to tell you."

"When do you expect him back?"

"I will not know that until such time as he calls and informs me."

"Thank you for your time." They left knowing that they were not about to get any information from the servant.

"Until tomorrow, we have time on our hands Vinnie."

"Before we relax for the day, I think you should call Elizabeth and have her assign local agents to maintain low visibility surveillance at the list of possible targets that Darlene and Max prepared. A single agent at each site will do. It is only to determine if we can spot one of Khalid's operatives. I'd love to have a few minutes with just one of them."

"I'll do it now."

The four agents met for lunch but nothing much took place. They decided to go their own ways until the morning when Gretchen and Vinnie would confront Lee Horton and William Worthington. After that, they would find Kay Horton and raise hell with her.

The following morning, Vinnie and Gretchen were up early, took a walk in the Gardens, returned to shower and dress and were having breakfast when Darlene and then Max arrived. Gretchen outlined the work for the day. She and Vinnie were to pursue the questioning of Lee Horton and William Worthington. Once that was completed, they were hell bent on finding Kay Horton and Thomas Gilbane, aka, Abdu Khalid. Up to now, they had not mentioned Khalid's' name or who he was and why they wanted him to either Worthington or Horton. Given the lack of cooperation by the two, Vinnie and Gretchen did not intend to release that information now. They would deal with them as hostile witnesses. They decided Gretchen would interview Horton and Vinnie would interview Worthington and they would do so at the same time thereby eliminating the possibility of them working on similar stories. Gretchen would return to

Worthington's residence where they knew Lee was living and Vinnie would go to Worthington's office. They synchronized their watches and set eleven as the time they would show up to interview them.

Gretchen's interview yielded nothing but hostility from Lee Horton who didn't, in her own words, give one damn about what the CIA wanted. The sophisticated socialite spewed invectives at a federal agent and everyone in law enforcement, especially the Securities and Exchange Commission that had too many regulations for Worthington's hedge funds. Gretchen had all she could do to restrain herself from smacking Lee Horton. In the end, she left with one objective in mind; to see that Lee Horton spent time in federal custody for failing to provide information vital to national security.

Vinnie ran into a similar refrain with Worthington who was demeaning in his attitude. He stated emphatically that the CIA was intruding on privacy matters and that he would no longer talk to any CIA agents on this matter unless he was forewarned so he could have his lawyers present.

Gretchen and Vinnie met for lunch. "Why are they putting up such a barrier to our finding Kay Horton and Thomas Gilbane? Does she have something on them and has threatened exposure if they talk to us? Does she have some leverage related to Worthington's hedge fund operations? Has he been cooking the books and Kay knows about it?"

"I don't think so, Gretchen. It's a good thought, but I think it comes down to us against them. We are basically cops, at the bottom of the food chain, and they are Boston Brahmans, at the top of the food chain. With all of their money, they spit on the 99% who work to make an honest living. Whether the market goes up or down, these folks profit because they still get their commissions. That is why Boston Common is filled today with Occupy Wall Street supporters. When I think about it, the site of the Boston Tea party is not far from here."

"What now?"

"Did you ever get to ask Lee Horton if she talked to Kay yesterday or where she was?"

"Never had a chance. She was on the attack the moment I arrived. I assume the servant had warned her we were there yesterday. Why do you ask?"

"Worthington was a bit more forthcoming when I asked him if he had seen Kay yesterday and where he was if not with her. He said that he and Lee were sailing in Newburyport on the north shore. I have no idea if it is true or not."

"Let's find out. I'll call the harbormaster in Newburyport now and ask if Worthington was there. Harbormasters are always local men and women and they know if a fish is missing." She dialed information, made the call and talked to the assistant harbormaster after identifying herself as a federal agent. The assistant confirmed that Worthington was there. She said it would be hard to miss his boat; huge, luxurious, impressive under sail and worth a fortune. Almost always has several guests on board."

"Let's go to Louisburg Square and see if Kay Horton is home."

"Why not her office?"

"Later. I want her to be upset that her neighbors are seeing two individuals at her door who are clearly cops. That will start the rumor mill."

Kay Horton was not at her office and her administrative assistant did not know when to expect her.

Vinnie and Gretchen sat outside the condo in their rental car. "Do you think that Kay Horton owns a boat? If Worthington does, perhaps she does. It seems that the wealthy who live on the coast all have impressive yachts. Why not Kay"

"If she owns a boat, why did they not tell us?"

"Because, Gretchen, she owns a boat. They are screwing with us."

"Are you saying that they purposely withheld that information?"

"I am. These two Brahmins are going to jail."

"Where is the boat, assuming you are right?"

"Manchester by the Sea. Since she has a home there, my guess it's the home port for her boat and those two cops didn't tell us that. On the other hand, we were not very forthcoming as to why we wanted to know about Kay Horton. I'll cut them some slack."

"We find the boat and we find Kay Horton and Abdu Khalid."

"Easier said than done. First, we need to confirm she owns a boat. If so, it could be in any one of hundreds of marinas on the east coast. We need a lead of some kind."

"How about the Coast Guard?"

"Not unless we have credible information to give them. Have Elizabeth call the Massachusetts State Police and request that they bring Lee Horton in for questioning. Then we will call on Mr. Worthington and use her as leverage to find to locate Kay Horton."

"Can we do this?"

"Until someone tells us we can't. Make the call and then we'll go back to the hotel and wait."

Forty five minutes later, Elizabeth called. "The state police agree there is sufficient information to justify bringing Lee Horton in for an interview. They'll take her in around two o'clock. After that you may call Worthington."

At two fifteen, Vinnie called Worthington who was not pleased about the call. "Mr. Worthington, Lee Horton is being taken into custody by the state police as we speak. She will be charged with withholding information from federal authorities. Call your lawyer if you wish, but once I hang up this phone without the information I need, you will also be taken into custody. Now, where the fuck is Kay Horton's boat?"

There was dead silence as Worthington caught his breath. For the first time in many years he was not in charge. If he was arrested and it became public, his hedge fund would go belly up. He also assumed, wrongly, that agent Pagano knew that Kay owned a boat and answered accordingly. "She moors it in Manchester-by-the Sea and also uses Constitution Marina in Charlestown where she picks up guests. As to where it is now, that is anyone's guess. If she is trying to avoid you and your partner, she could be tucked away in some small town marina or be at sea. Her boat has a range close to three thousand miles. Hell, she could be headed for South America. Boats move in an out of harbors all the time without being noticed."

"What other ports does she regularly use when entertaining guests or when on vacation?"

"The usual, Nantucket, Martha's Vineyard, Provincetown, a number of Rhode Island harbors.

"How about Newburyport?"

"No. with my boat there, she has no reason to use hers."

"What is the name of her boat?"

" Money Talks."

"Do not leave town, Mr. Worthington." He did not leave town, rather, he walked out of his office to the nearest subway station and found a pay phone. He dialed a cell number.

"William, what is it?"

"I don't know where you are and do not want to know. They have taken Lee into custody for questioning and pressured me to tell them about your boat. Do not return to either Manchester or Constitution Marina."

"Where, then?"

"If Thomas needs time, transit the canal and head for Narragansett Bay. You may need a layover since it is getting late. Depends how comfortable your skipper is in bringing the boat in after dark. You might consider Fairhaven. That will allow you to get to Beavertail Lighthouse during daylight tomorrow and drop anchor at the small town of Pomfret Landing. It has many large boats so 'Money Talks' will not be noticed, and the town is small enough not to be considered if someone is looking for you. It is either that or you call the Coast Guard and turn Gilbane in."

"No chance of that happening. The CIA can go to hell."

William placed the phone back on the hook and returned to his office. He knew the CIA was not bluffing about Gilbane being dangerous. He also knew Kay should call the Coast Guard.

CHAPTER 79

ON THE MOVE

When Vinnie ended his call to Worthington, he briefed Gretchen. "I think we have a lead. Worthington may have given us information he had not intended to. I'm certain he talked to Kay on a phone that could not be monitored. When I asked about ports that Kay would typically use, he mentioned some specifically by name, but when it came to Rhode Island his comments were general. She is headed for Rhode Island, of that I am certain. It may not have been part of her initial plan, but with us now on top of Horton and Worthington, she will make for a port of safety to give Khalid the opportunity to disappear. She certainly will not return to Manchester or Boston."

"Where then?"

"I'm from this state and if my geography is correct, you need to use the Cape Cod Canal to get to Rhode Island unless you want to spend a lot of time traveling around the cape. I am betting she is headed for the canal. All we need to do is contact the United States Army Corp. of Engineers and have them look for 'Money Talks' when it enters the canal.'"

"Vinnie, I loved the way your mind worked the minute I met you which, by the way, seems like years ago."

"And now, you love more than my mind?"

"I'm certain that I am not the only one who loves more than your mind."

He chose not to respond to that; instead, "We have several matters to deal with. First, I will contact the Corp. of Engineers and request that they assist. You are to contact the Coast Guard and request that they monitor 'Money Talks' when it enters Buzzard's Bay. For those of you who are not from these parts, that is the body of water at the other end of the canal. The Coast Guard needs to stay far enough away from the boat so as not to alert Horton and Khalid. Sooner or later, 'Money Talks' is going to go into hibernation and we need to know where. This is the opportunity we have been waiting for."

"Can a Coast Guard boat keep up with Kay's boat?"

"Easily. Some of the newer boats can run in excess of thirty knots when need be. Kay's boat will be no match for the speed of the new Coast Guard Sentinel Class boat."

"Vinnie, I have the feeling that with Khalid's plans now in turmoil, he may not try a symbolic attack at all. He has inflicted sufficient damage as it is. More attacks will continue without him. I think he will scrap any plans he has and make a run to get out of the country. Kay and her crew are in danger."

"Kay is in mortal danger as is the crew. As for a symbolic attack, I would not dismiss it so quickly. Remember, he has operatives, at least one of whom will be willing to die for the cause."

"Again, you are probably right. But first we must deal with Khalid."

"Once they transit the canal, they have a couple of options. One is to head for either Nantucket or Martha's Vineyard which is unlikely. She knows they are the first places we would look."

"What is the second option?"

"The second option is to continue along the Rhode Island coast and find what they believe is safe harbor in one of the many coastal towns thereby giving Khalid shelter while he plans his escape. The Coast Guard should have no problem following them once 'Money Talks' enters Buzzard Bay. If Kay travels as far as Narragansett Bay, it is more complicated. There is both the bay and the river. Fortunately, the Coast Guard knows where all of the marinas are located. They could request several strategically located harbor masters to keep a watch for Kay Horton and report when her boat passes. As for Thomas Gilbane, the nearest major airport is in Providence. He would have little trouble getting there. It is not international, but it could connect him to any number of international airports with flights to Europe."

"How should we play it now?"

"When you talk to the Coast Guard, ask for a restricted frequency we can use to communicate with them on. We don't want Kay listening in. We have the agency Gulfstream at Logan. I suggest we alert the pilots and fly to Providence as quickly as possible. Having it close by gives us flexibility in pursuing Khalid if need be. Once we arrive in Providence, we stay in contact with the Coast Guard. Max and Darlene remain here in Boston for any developments. I suggest we each bring the SIG P228's with the thirteen round magazine and the MK23's with the twelve round magazines. I'll pack extra magazines for both of us. Let's get moving."

"And the KABAR?"

"That, too."

On the way to Logan they made their calls to the Army Corp. of Engineers and the Coast Guard. An hour later they exited the Gulfstream in Providence and rented a car. The pilots rented rooms at an airport hotel.

Gretchen drove the rental car while Vinnie studied the AAA map of Connecticut, Massachusetts and Rhode Island. They decided to take 195 southeast to Fairhaven placing them close to where Kay would exit the canal. It would be late in the afternoon and she might find a port somewhere in the area. Vinnie also knew that the longer she remained at sea, the greater the possibility of their losing her and Khalid. She could head for open ocean and South America.

They were approaching Fairhaven when Vinnie received a call from the Army Corp. of engineers. "The boat has entered the canal."

"Thanks."

"Happy to help." The phone was disconnected.

Gretchen asked Vinnie, "How long to get through the canal?"

"Depends on the tides. I'm no expert, and certainly not a boat person, but based on the total distance from the beginning of the canal to open water on the south end, I would say it is twelve miles. I'd give her an hour and a half. Her boat is powerful and can handle the tides. From there to the opening of Narragansett Bay is about fifty miles. That is another three hours. After that it depends on how far up the bay she travels. Sunset is around eight twenty so she has a lot of daylight to work with. One thing I would bet money on is that if she enters Narragansett Bay, she has a specific destination in mind. We need to

wait on the Coast Guard to keep us up to date.
From her perspective it is a great place to hide. From our perspective it is a tough place for her to get out of. Wherever she ends up, it is where Khalid gets off. He doesn't need the boat and he doesn't want witnesses. No doubt he will be armed and he will have substantial cash since all luxury boats carry enough of both."

"Where will he go once he leaves the boat?"

"Have no idea. I'm not certain he knows. He is on the run. That's when you make a mistake."

"We need to deal with him before he leaves the boat. Maybe we can still help Kay and her crew."

"Maybe. It will depend on the setting and the timing. One thing is certain; Abdu Khalid is not leaving the area alive. Finally, we have the butcher where we want him. It will soon be over."

"We have nothing more to do until we hear from the coast guard. Let's grab a late lunch."

On board "Money Talks" Kay shared the content of William's phone call with Thomas. "With Lee in custody and William under pressure, it is best that we do not return to Boston tonight. I suggest we take the advice William has given us and proceed to Pomfret Landing, Rhode Island. I have been there and it is a delightful place to spend a day or so. That will give you time to sort things out. I know this incident has served to speed up your departure to England. I will miss you dearly, Thomas, but I do not want you to get involved with the CIA, or, those who attempted to kill you. You should be able to fly out of Providence using a charter service to some other departure city. If you are short of cash, I have plenty on board to give you. I don't suggest you use a credit card since the government will quickly identify the point of sale."

"I never stop being amazed at your ability to sort through these matters. I think it best that we continue on to Rhode Island. It will be great to spend another night with you."

"I cannot wait. Now, let's get up to the pilothouse and inform Don and Andy that we are to proceed to the Cape Cod Canal."

Having used the canal many times, Don eased "Money Talks" around and headed south. While first mate, Andy, took over the boat, Don and Kay plotted a route to Pomfret Landing. He estimated that they would still arrive with a bit of daylight, but not much. He would radio ahead for a berth.

About the time Gretchen and Vinnie had finished lunch, "Money Talks" had entered the waters of Buzzard's Bay on the south end of the canal and had been picked up by the Coast Guard cutter, "Eagle's Nest" whose skipper called Gretchen. "We have the boat in sight and it will be another hour before we can determine whether she will make port in Fairhaven. If the boat is trying to elude you, my guess is it's too early for her to call it a day. There is also the fact that the boat can be easily detected in Fairhaven. Narragansett Bay, with dozens of marinas, is a much better place to take refuge in. I'll call with definite information in an hour or so." The skipper ended the conversation before Gretchen could say anything.

"A man of few words. Looking at the map, once we leave interstate 195, it is a tough drive to the east side of Narragansett Bay let alone the west side. I say let's head there. We can always backtrack if the skipper thinks 'Money Talks' is headed to Fairhaven."

"My thought exactly." They headed west.

The left interstate 195 and were on route 24 when the skipper called. "They are directly on the navigable channel of the Intracoastal Waterway and headed away from Fairhaven. I will stay with it as long as no emergency arises. There are a number of harbors along the way, but the next one coming up shortly is Newport. It would be easy to locate a boat there. If they take a pass on Newport and head into Narragansett Bay, they will have multiple ports in which to take shelter. Once I know they are headed into the Bay, I will call harbor masters I know in North Kingstown and East Greenwich, two of the large and popular spots and request that they let me know if they have a visitor. When I know, you will know." Again, no conversation.

"Does he ever take questions?"

"He's a skipper. Skippers know best."

"Another damn macho man."

CHAPTER 80

POMFRET LANDING

On board "Money Talks" Kay and Thomas were sitting naked in the upper deck Jacuzzi. It was a bright afternoon with a beautiful blue sky. The Jacuzzi was shaded from the direct sunlight by a large, white retractable awning. While both were anxious to find a safe port, for the moment they were enjoying each other. Neither was aware that the Coast Guard cutter had them under surveillance. Although out of sight, "Money Talks" was on the cutter's radar screen. The steward, who was not fazed seeing them naked, took lunch orders. Fifteen minutes later, wrapped in silk robes, Kay and Thomas had lunch on the first level sundeck. Sitting on the deck facing the stern, they could see many boats on the busy Intracoastal Waterway, but not the "Eagle's Nest."

In the meantime, Gretchen and Vinnie drove into Newport, figuring it was a strategic location for them to wait until they heard from the cutter. If Kay turned into the Sakonnet River, they would backtrack on route 114 north and await further word from the cutter. If she turned into Narragansett Bay, they would take route 138 across the bay and then follow route 4 north to wherever they were directed. With nothing but time on their hands, they decided to act like a married couple and tour Newport, looking into the windows of expensive shops, walking the waterfront, stopping for an ice cream cone. Tired from the hectic pace that they had kept the past days and having had enough of window shopping, they found a bench near the water and sat.

While half dozing in the sunlight, Vinnie's phone rang. There was a familiar voice on the other end. "Where are you and what is happening?"

He explained their trip from Logan to Providence, the phone calls to the Corp of Engineers and the Coast Guard, the tracking of "Money Talks," their waiting on Kay to make a turn and the ice cream cones.

"Good work. You are close to the end. Take no unnecessary chances, either of you. Assuming he has had a change of plans, do you still envision a symbolic attack?"

"I do, but not necessarily by Khalid. Remember, he has a network operating. He believes in suicide bombers so most likely has someone prepared to act."

"How can he communicate? We have him monitored. And, who would he be contacting?"

"He only needs to make one call. By the time you intercept and take action, it may be over. Depends on the timing and the target. As for who he'd be contacting, it would be someone who is positioned to do what Khalid is unable to do because he is here and not in Boston. We need to assume he planned for this contingency and he needs only to make one phone call."

"Where are you going with this?"

"Gretchen and I are convinced that Khalid flew himself to Boston from Denver on a private aircraft. We don't believe it is a Silver Eagle because that would be too obvious. It could be any one of a number of private aircraft. What I'm thinking is that it must be stored near Boston so he could get to it fairly fast. I suggest you contact the FAA and have them give you the locations of airports inside the Interstate 495 corridor. The corridor is essentially a circumferential highway around Boston about thirty or thirty five miles out. We're looking for an airport inside the half circle with a runway that could handle a private plane similar to a Gulfstream 450. Then deploy agents to each airport and check landing records for a Thomas Gilbane. A plane like the Gulfstream could be over Boston in a matter of minutes and have a choice of multiple targets. Loaded with fuel, it is a missile. There would be no warning."

"When this is over, you need to come in from the field and become an analyst in my office."

"We can talk when this is over."

"Be safe Vinnie. Hello to Gretchen."

"Was that Elizabeth?"

"It was."

"Why does she call you more than me?"

"Hadn't noticed. May I rest for a bit?" He closed his eyes and quickly dozed off. Seven minutes later Gretchen's phone rang. She put it on speaker phone. It was the Coast Guard.

"The boat just entered Narragansett Bay. They are going to Pomfret Landing. The harbor master called around and learned that the captain of "Money Talks" made a reservation for an overnight at Wainwright and Hobbs Marina and Sales. You'll see it as you enter the channel to Pomfret Landing Cove. Call if you need assistance. We'll be on patrol at the mouth until midnight and then back to the canal. Nothing will leave the bay without our knowing it." He hung up.

"Let's go. I'll drive. Route 138 to route 4 north. It is a short drive and we could be there before they enter the harbor. We are going to get this bastard after all. He is part mine, Vinnie, so remember to share."

CHAPTER 81

HORROR

They arrived at Pomfret Landing ahead of "Money Talks" and decided to defer making any specific plans until the boat was in the marina. There was a good deal they didn't know including who was aboard besides Kay Horton, Khalid and the captain. Also not known was the layout of the boat, whether or not it carried weapons, what Khalid had for firepower and whose side Kay Horton was on. Not researching the layout of the boat could prove to be a problem.

On board the boat the captain was talking to the marina supervisor. Apparently, there was no docking space available within the marina and Kay's boat would have to take a mooring in the harbor. Upset at first with the accommodation, the more she worked with it the more she liked the idea of not being too visible until Thomas was ready to leave. The harbor mooring would also give her more private time with him. Once Don had secured the boat to the mooring, she had the steward go ashore to the marina mini-mart and purchase what was needed for a simple dinner aboard the boat.

Gretchen and Vinnie, not seeing "Money Talks" tie up at any of the docks, decided to talk to the marina personnel. Passing the mini mart on the way to the marina office Gretchen suggested they grab a couple of cold drinks. They were at the cooler selecting the drinks when they overheard a man, who turned out to be Kay's twenty five year old steward, talking to the store clerk who was an attractive nineteen or twenty year old college student. She asked what boat he was with. When he mentioned "Money Talks" Vinnie and Gretchen continued to examine the contents of the cooler, all the while listening. During the next seven or eight minutes of flirtatious conversation between the steward and the clerk, they learned that there was a captain and first mate, the steward, and Kay Horton and her guest on board. Also learned was that the boat was tied at a mooring in the harbor and would remain there all night. The steward mentioned to the clerk that Kay Horton was a skilled captain and regularly takes her shift on long hauls. Finally, they learned that the owner and guest would dine on board and following that, the three crew members would take the shuttle launch directly into the village and have dinner. As long as they were back on board before dawn, Kay would be satisfied. Nothing was learned about weapons or the layout of the boat.

When the steward left, they went to the counter and paid for the two drinks. In the parking lot they talked. "This is it, what we have been waiting for, Vinnie."

"It won't be easy getting on board without being detected. The launch, even with the motor shut down, is apt to hit the stern as we try to board. Sounds at night are jarring. We have to believe that Khalid has a weapon. It is also common practice for luxury boats to carry weapons to fend off possible drug traffickers and pirates. Usually they carry a long gun and a shotgun. We would not stand a chance against a shot gun at close range. Kay Horton may also have a handgun."

"What are you saying? We don't try boarding after coming this far?"

"When the odds are against you, then change the odds. The only way to board is from the stern; the bow and sides being too high off the water. Even if we could board, we are too exposed. There are no walkways on the sides of the boat. I'm thinking that we use local law enforcement officials to hold the first mate and steward in custody overnight and we take the shuttle back to "Money Talks" with the captain. We have him talking to us as though his crew is with him. Once we board at the stern, he shoves off to safety. If he believes that his boss is in danger, he will be cooperative."

Darkness was beginning to settle in and lights were being turned on around the shore of the harbor and on board boats that were occupied. Vinnie and Gretchen, neither being a boating person, were surprised at the number of large luxury boats that were anchored, wondering how so many people could afford them. If they worked well into retirement, they would never have the money to own one.

"If nothing else, Gretchen, we get to board a luxury boat."

"The plan is to get off the boat alive and with Khalid dead."

"That will happen. Now, we need to lay out the logistics for the night. There is a lot to do. First, another call to Elizabeth. She needs to get things lined up for us by calling the Massachusetts State Police to bring them up to date. The State Police then needs to call the Chief of Police in this jurisdiction and repeat the story and request that he hold the steward and first mate overnight, making certain they have no cell phones and no way to get a call to the boat. We need to be there to deal with the captain, making it clear that Kay Horton's life is in danger."

"The timing has to be such that we do not try to board until we think Horton and Khalid are asleep, although I don't think that is what she has in mind. At her age, she can do it all night. Using your plan, we get to learn the layout of the boat from the captain. In the meantime, we have nothing to do but wait until the crew comes ashore after dinner. We follow them into town and wait until the local cops find a reason to hold them. You had better get started with Elizabeth. She has a lot to do to make this work."

He dialed her secure number and put the phone on speaker so Gretchen could hear. Expecting the call, she answered after the first ring. "Tell me what you need."

Vinnie explained the plan and she agreed with all of it and would make the call as soon as they ended the conversation. She did have a concern.

"Vinnie, I am having a difficult time believing that Kay Horton and Khalid are not aware of what is happening. Are you certain that the Coast Guard cutter was not spotted? If Kay knew enough to avoid returning to Boston and is smart enough to travel to a small port in Rhode Island, doesn't it make sense that she would know you would process the information the same way and do likewise?"

"What are you driving at?"

"Don't be surprised if when you board the boat they are not there."

"What?"

"You heard me. A boat that size must carry its own Zodiac or something similar in case of emergency. They could leave the boat and, instead of going to the marina, head directly to a town dock, steal a car and be gone."

He was silent for a few seconds. "Instead of my coming inside it may be time for you to come back into the field. Thanks, Elizabeth."

"Before you hang up, I'll give you an update on airports in Massachusetts. The state has many of them. There are thirty seven public use airports of which twenty four are owned either by a municipality or the Massachusetts Port Authority. Eight have regular commercial service making their runways long enough for a private jet of any size. The other twenty nine may or may not have runways long enough for a jet. Five of the eight with commercial service are located on the Cape or the Islands off of the Cape. The three remaining ones are Logan International, Worcester and Bedford. All three are inside the circle. If that is not sufficiently complex, the state has another one hundred and eighty four private landing areas and two seaplane bases. The odds are that one or more could accommodate a jet."

"Any suggestions from FAA?"

"They suggest we contact the Air National Guard, explain the situation and ask that they keep interceptors on high alert 24/7 for the next two days and hope for the best."

"We plan on boarding at one a.m. If Khalid is there and senses danger, he will make a call to whoever has control of his plane. My suggestion is that the Air National guard be especially vigilant beginning at midnight."

"Gretchen, anything to add?"

"Be glad when it is over."

"Stay safe." End of call.

The next several hours went as planned. The crew, instead of coming to the marina, took the shuttle directly into town. Vinnie and Gretchen saw the boat headed for the town dock and drove into town. They arrived at the dock ahead of the men. They followed them until they entered a restaurant on the main street in Pomfret Landing after which they met with the local Chief of Police and informed him of the crew's whereabouts. He had been fully briefed by the state police and was anxious to assist. His men would maintain watch outside the restaurant and at the appropriate time make a move. The police station was only a block away. Vinnie and Gretchen then went to the same restaurant to make certain the crew did not change its mind and go elsewhere. At ten thirty five the crew left the restaurant and as soon as they were on the street, two local cops approached them.

"Are you the crew on 'Money talks'?"

Don spoke up. "Yes. Why do you ask?"

"Our chief would like to have a word with you."

"What about?"

"The chief will explain. Please follow us."

"Whoa! Are we under arrest?"

"No. This has nothing to do with the three of you. It is the boat that is of interest. Now, please follow us." Which they did.

Once in the station, the first mate and the steward were separated from Don who was taken to the Chief's office. The Chief stood at six two or three, thin, ramrod straight. His face had a chiseled look and was weather beaten. He uniform was freshly cleaned and starched and the only item on his belt was a holstered Berretta. He gave the impression that Pomfret Landing was a no nonsense town. Don was motioned to take a seat and before he could say a word, the Chief spoke. "You and your men have done nothing wrong. We are going to hold your crew overnight and ask you to assist us in a government mission that has some element of danger to it."

Don was momentarily speechless. When he did speak, he asked, "What kind of mission and why me?"

"I want you to meet Agent Iverson and Agent Pagano of the Central Intelligence Agency. They will explain."

Gretchen displayed her credential to Don. "Captain, you do not have to do this, but your boss is in danger of losing her life. If you agree to help us save her and take her guest into custody, then you will be operating under several federal statutes and are sworn to secrecy under the penalty of imprisonment. Do you understand?"

"Yes. But if Kay is in danger, I'll help. As captain of a luxury boat, I learned early on to keep my mouth shut. Tell me what you want."

For the next few minutes, Vinnie and Gretchen explained as best they could without revealing too much information. They explained what they wanted Don to do including his drawing a diagram of the layout of the boat. Don told them that the British guest asked a lot of questions about the boat. Then, as discretely as possible, explained the sexual connection between Gilbane and Kay, and the nude Jacuzzi scene. He explained that the guest was physically fit and looked as though he could take care of himself. When asked about guns, Don said that he kept a shotgun in the pilothouse and Kay kept both a shotgun and handgun in her stateroom. He went on to explain that luxury boats usually kept weapons on board, especially when traveling in the Caribbean. Kay's stateroom had a hidden safe and significant cash was kept in it. When asked if he thought the passenger was armed, Don said he had no evidence he possessed a gun.

Gretchen asked, "What was the passenger carrying when he boarded the boat?"

"A suitcase, a carry-on and a lap top."

"Anything unusual about them?"

"No."

They spent the next hour going over the layout of the boat and working out how Don could get them on board without raising an alarm. They exchanged cell phone numbers. They were about to relax for fifteen minutes until it was time to leave when Vinnie asked an unexpected question. "Captain, from the time your boat entered the Cape Cod Canal did anyone suspect that the Coast Guard was monitoring your movements?"

"Funny you should ask. When I exited the canal and entered Buzzard's Bay, I could make out a Sentinel class cutter moving slowly as though looking for suspicious activity. I didn't think anything about it since it is common strategy for the Coast Guard to look over the traffic, so I did not mention it to Kay who was below. There is no view from the pilothouse to the rear unless you step outside. The side view is a ninety degree one so I had no idea if the cutter was still behind us. When we made the starboard turn into Narragansett Bay, we had a view to the starboard side. I thought I saw the cutter some two or three miles out. Kay was with me and I mentioned it to her and then shared what I had seen in Buzzard's Bay. The guest was below and didn't hear the conversation."

"What was Kay's reaction?"

"She asked if I was certain it was the same boat. I told her I had no way of knowing, but it would be unlikely that two Coast Guard boats would be patrolling the same small body of water. She simply nodded and went below. Later, when I was tying up she asked if I had seen the Coast Guard boat after we entered the bay. I hadn't and told her so. She didn't raise the issue again."

"Anything else?"

"I was surprised she gave the entire crew the night off. Usually one of us remains on board in case of an emergency."

"Do you think she simply wanted privacy with her guest?"

"No. She's been alone with guys before. I love working for Kay, but sometimes I wondered about her judgment in men. Maybe it has to do with being rich, but they are never embarrassed if there are witnesses to their sexual escapades. It's as though we don't exist. So, no, I doubt if giving us the night off has anything to do with having a guest aboard."

"Thanks, Don." Then turning to Vinnie, "Are you thinking what I am? She got rid of the crew so she and Khalid could leave the boat without being seen?"

"Or, to move the boat without the crew. Don told us that Kay is a capable captain. The question is where would they go?"

"They could not move the boat very far. The Coast Guard is at the mouth of the bay. I say they have left the boat or plan to leave the boat and get Khalid out of here. She put two and two together and figured the

Coast Guard was following 'Money Talks.' Let's make our move now! They may still be on board. The question is whether she is alive."

Gretchen turned to the Chief, "We have a change of plans. You need to get us to the boat as fast as you can. Don, we can use you once we are on board if you are willing. Chief, it's your call as to whether you want to come along."

"I'm with you. Now let me get us some firepower." With that he unlocked a gun case and removed two Colt M4A1 assault rifles and handed one to Vinnie. He kept the other.

The town dock was immediately behind the police station and a police launch was tied up. The Chief got in and the others followed. He started the engine and once the lines were released by Vinnie and Don, he headed for "Money Talks." Ignoring the harbor speed limit he turned the throttle to full power. From a distance they could make out the boat. Interior lights were on. Addressing both Vinnie and Gretchen and talking loud over the sound of the engine and movement of the boat, "What is your call, agents?"

Vinnie first, "Given what we have learned, take us straight in to the stern."

The Chief slowed the boat as it approached "Money Talks" and eased it towards the stern. Before he had made contact, Vinnie was out of the boat with Gretchen on his heels. They crouched and made their way into the main saloon. It was empty. "Gretchen, you go up and I'll go down."

Gretchen worked her way up and holding her automatic pistol in both hands, she checked all possible hiding places as she climbed. The pilothouse was clean with no charts or papers visible. Everything was normal with no sign of activity. She worked her way down to the main deck and descended the foyer stairs to the wardrobe areas below. She called out, "Vinnie, where are you?"

"In the main cabin. Don't come in."

She went in anyway and was horrified at the scene. Kay Horton was in a sitting position on the floor, naked, propped up against the foot of the bed, bound hands and feet. Her throat has been sliced from side to side and her head was barely attached to her body. Both of her thighs were bruised as thought pressure had been applied to them. Blood covered her bosom. Gretchen walked over to Vinnie who stood motionless looking at Kay Horton, took his hand in hers and began to cry. He placed his arm over her shoulder and held on to her.

Vinnie had seen worse in Iraq and Afghanistan, but mutilation of a body is something you never get used to. He knelt down and examined the body as Gretchen watched him, appreciating his strength and resolve. A few minutes later, he stood, and his eyes betrayed his silent rage.

Gretchen put her arm on him. "What is it?"

"Not only was she helpless being tied hands and feet, the bastard sat on her legs and was looking at her while he slashed her throat."

"How do you know that is the way it happened?"

"I saw it in Iraq. It was the Taliban's way to discourage the natives from cooperating with us."

"Why, why murder her this way? She wasn't a combatant!"

"He is a butcher. I think in a way he knew he was being comprised by western values and had to prove he was Abdu Khalid and not Thomas Gilbane. He'll pay for this."

The Chief entered and when he saw the scene, whispered, “May God have mercy.” Don saw the horror and ran from the room to the stern where he deposited his dinner. He sat on the deck and wept for Kay Horton.

The door to one of the wardrobes was ajar and inside the wall safe was open. Gretchen regained her composure and looked inside. It was empty. Khalid’s suitcase was still in the wardrobe and his lap top was sitting on the dresser. She opened it, booted it up and checked the last few sites he visited. One that caught her eye was a list of airports in Massachusetts, Connecticut and Rhode Island.

By this time Vinnie had found Don, “We need your help. Do you carry a Zodiac or other small boat on board, something the murderer could use to get off the boat?”

“Yes, a fourteen foot Boston Whaler was strapped to the top deck. I’ll see if it is missing.” He regained his composure and ran up to check. He called down, “It’s gone.”

“Don, when we spoke earlier, didn’t you tell us that Gilbane had a carry-on when he boarded?”

“A suitcase, a carry-on and a lap top.”

“Vinnie, the carry-on is missing and the last site he visited on his lap top was a listing of airports in the three states. He must be armed, that is why he took the carry-on. He is on his way out of here by air. This time he is not going to evade us. I want him dead.”

“Let’s talk to the Chief.”

All four stood on the stern deck. Don was still in shock, and Vinnie and Gretchen were angry over Kay’s murder. If only she had listened to them. If only her sister and Worthington had not been so fucking secretive.

The Chief had already called the State Police. A forensics team was on the way. Vinnie asked the Chief to call his own office to see if anyone in town reported a stolen vehicle, and to then call the marina to see if whoever was on duty had seen any suspicious activity. Gretchen called the Coast Guard cutter to report what happened. Although it was unlikely that Khalid would be leaving by boat, the Coast guard was to watch for anything unusual.

Vinnie called Elizabeth and reported. She had little to say in the way of a response knowing what he and Gretchen were experiencing. The bad news did not stop with Kay Horton's murder. Elizabeth reported on two more attacks in the Seattle area. Both a fire station and a television station were firebombed. Multiple deaths were reported. The total number of attacks had risen to twenty three and there was no stopping them.

"I need to go Elizabeth. Make certain that the Air National Guard is on alert."

With most of the logistics out of the way, Vinnie and Gretchen waited for the Chief to get off the phone with his deputy. "A couple who lives in Pomfret Landing reported their car was stolen. It was parked in the town lot adjacent to the dock and behind a restaurant where they dined. It is a late model Toyota Forerunner, white. When my men went to the lot to check for any clues, they reported that a Boston Whaler was moored there. It has 'Money Talks' painted on it. Your guy is on the run. Tell me what more I can do to help you two get this madman."

"The only way he can get out of the area fast is by plane and we have reason to believe he can pilot a plane. Where is the nearest airport?"

"Newport, but Providence has more flights."

"Chief, you need to get us to Newport." Turning to Don, "Stay with the boat until the body is removed. Then once your crew is back, wait here until the Chief gives you clearance to return to Boston. Chief, you will have to contact the family in the morning. Don has the name of the victim's sister and employer."

The Chief started the car and then asked, "Why do you think your man is going to Newport rather than Providence?"

"Given how recently Kay Horton was murdered, he knows we have time to set up roadblocks on all roads. Providence is also the obvious destination. But, all he wants to do is get out of the immediate area and go underground until things quiet down. The best way out is by air. If he does nothing more, he has still accomplished what he came to the states to do. Newport is close and at this time of night, or early morning, he will have no trouble stealing a light plane. He will kill to do so. When we get there, drive directly to the private plane area."

"Look, if you want to get there ahead of him, let me call the state police and ask for their helicopter. It would be here in twenty minutes or less and in another fifteen we will be in Newport. Remember, they are already plugged into this affair and would want to participate in nailing this guy."

"Do it."

The Chief made the call. Twenty five minutes later the helicopter was at the town parking lot next to the dock. The door opened and Vinnie, Gretchen and the Chief got in and were greeted by the pilot and co-pilot, both of whom wore side arms. Anticipating what Vinnie and Gretchen were thinking, the Chief leaned over to the pilot and shouted above the noise, "Stay low and as far away from the road as possible. We don't want to be seen by the murderer who is driving to Newport." The pilot nodded his head and slowly lifted the helicopter off the dock. When they were airborne, Vinnie checked out his MK23 then placed it in the small of his back. He reached down and pulled out his ankle gun and checked it. He put it back. Finally, he reached to his side to make certain his KABAR knife was secure. Gretchen checked the Sig P228 that she kept in the small of her back, and the MK23 in her shoulder bag. The chief watched and knew what they were thinking. The end was near.

In Bedford, Massachusetts, a lone man walked through the semi darkness that lingered between night and dawn. The Dassault Falcon was parked among equally beautiful aircraft. It was fueled and ready for flight. Soon, but not in time, federal agents would be swarming into airports identified as having runways long enough for a twin engine jet and located inside the Interstate 495corridor. By the time they arrived in Bedford, his mission would be completed. Imar Suhari had dedicated this mission to Allah and all the oppressed people of the world who, in his mind, had been robbed of their culture and their future by American diplomacy that condemned the Middle East to continued poverty, war and despair. This was a flight of revenge. He was carrying a full load of fuel.

Imar Suhari had called ahead with a flight plan that would allow him to be airborne at five thirty a.m. His plan called for him to land at plum Island, thereby giving him cover for his true destination. He had no idea if Plum Island's runway could handle the aircraft, but it made little difference since he had no intention of going there. No one at FAA questioned his flight plan.

He sat in his plane with fifteen minutes before takeoff and studied the map. The USS Constitution was docked such that her bow was pointed at two hundred and twenty five degrees. Hitting her broad side was impossible given her position, but he could strike her in the rear port quarter which would easily sink her. In order to get into that position to strike, he would have to approach Boston Harbor from the East/South East, come in low over the harbor itself and then enter the inner harbor. A slight turn to starboard at the last minute and he would have his target where he wanted it with the sun to his back.

He made his last minute cabin checks and waited for the tower to give instructions. With five minutes to go, he reviewed his flight plan. Once airborne, he would be picked up by the Boston Air Route Traffic Control Center in Nashua, New Hampshire. With surveillance aircraft in the air, he decided to avoid flying over Boston until he made his final approach. He would maintain a heading due east to Marblehead and continue over open ocean for twenty miles, then turn directly south and line up with the Scituate Lighthouse. When he was three miles off shore from the lighthouse, he would make his final turn to two hundred twenty five degrees, drop to one thousand feet above the water, and make his final approach flying over Cohasset, Nantasket Beach, Hull and then into Boston Harbor with the USS Constitution straight ahead.

The tower called, the tail number confirmed, and Imar Suhari was cleared to taxi to the designated runway. There were no other aircraft waiting. He made the turn on to the runway, held the brakes, moved the throttles forward, and once he reached peak power for takeoff, he released the brakes and the Falcon roared down the runway, gaining speed with every passing second, and finally soared into the heavens and turned to the East on its way to do Allah's work.

CHAPTER 82

FALCON DOWN

Following Elizabeth's call to the Air National Guard, F-15 fighter pilots at Barnes Air National Guard Base in Westover, Massachusetts went on high alert. It was five fifty two a.m. and Colonel Daniel Surette and Lt. Colonel Mike Steward were having coffee. They were assigned to the 104th Fighter wing of the Massachusetts National Guard. They were fully dressed and their two F-15's were on the tarmac, fueled, armed with air to air missiles and Gatling guns and ready for flight at a moment's notice. Theirs had been a quiet, uneventful shift and they were looking forward to seven a.m. when a new crew arrived.

Surette and Steward were carrying their coffee cups to the counter for refills when the pulsing blare from the horn broke the silence in the ready room. Ten seconds later the horn stopped and the loud-speaker came on. "Priority One." Both men grabbed their helmets and raced to their planes. Ground crews were at the ready and assisted the pilots into their air-craft. The twin engines ignited and slowly the cockpits closed. Colonel Mike Surette was first to move, followed by his wingman, Lt. Colonel Mike Steward. With permission from the tower, they rolled on to the run-way, positioned themselves two abreast with Steward slightly behind Surette, and propelled their aircraft down the runway. Once the wheels left the ground they did a quick climb to fifteen thousand feet and turned east towards Boston. They had been briefed earlier as to the threat and the areas to be covered. Flying between mach 1.1 or 1.2, they would be over Boston in a matter of minutes.

As Surette and Steward were lifting off the tarmac at Westover, Imar Suhari was looking at his watch. It was five fifty seven and he had made his turn off Marblehead and was headed due south for the Scituate Lighthouse. His air speed was three hundred seventy five mph. Traveling at six miles a minute, he would be at the lighthouse in less than four minutes at which time he would drop his altitude dramatically and make his turn to the west for his final approach. Four minutes later he would be at his target.

Boston Air Route Traffic Control radar identified Suhari when the Falcon made its turn over open ocean off Marblehead. There was no flight plan for a non-military plane to be at its altitude and bearing. The controller at Logan International attempted to contact the plane but there was no response. After a fifteen second delay, the controller initiated a second attempt to contact the Falcon. When the second attempt failed, the controller called for the shift supervisor. The supervisor made a third attempt and simultaneously sent an alert to Westover. When Colonel Surette and Lt. Colonel Steward received the alert, Imar Suhari was approximately two minutes from his lighthouse turn.

The two F-15's left Barnes Air National Guard Base in Westover and headed directly for Boston for an intercept. There was no contact over or near the city so they then made a turn to the north. It was when they were over Cape Ann that they received an update from Boston Air Route Traffic Control. They made a hundred and eighty degree turn and flew the same route as Imar Suhari towards Scituate. They intercepted him as made his final turn toward Boston harbor. He was less than four minutes from his holy grail. There was no stopping now. Yelling at the top of his lungs, "Allah is great, Allah is great" and intent on his target, he did not see the F-15's but felt the tremendous vibration and rocking of his aircraft as Colonel Surette made a pass over the top of the Falcon, literally feet from its fuselage. Suhari had hardly processed what had happened when the second F-15 practically scorched his plane as it flew over him. The vibrations from both aircraft led to his losing temporary control of the plane. He looked both left and right and he saw Surette beside him on the port side waving him to move off to the north toward open ocean. Suhari ignored the command. Surette moved off and Steward, on the port side of the Falcon, made a turn and came directly at it. Suhari looked to his left and saw the F-15 flying directly at him and that's then he saw the flash from Steward's Gatling gun as a burst of shells flew over the top of the Falcon. It was a warning, but there still was no indication that the Falcon would alter course.

It was less than two minutes to the target. Surette, who had circled around the Falcon, repeated what Steward had done and fired his Gatling gun at the Falcon. No movement.

"Eagle One to Eagle Two. We take it down now before it is over the city. Attack is from the port side. I'll make the first run. That should do it. If not, you get seconds."

"Roger, Eagle One. Let's do it."

Both aircraft made sharp turns and flew over the top of the Falcon. When less than a mile past it, they both executed one hundred and eighty degree turns and headed straight back toward the Falcon. Surette was first and Steward a half mile behind him and prepared to fire if needed. Surette had the Falcon in full silhouette and once he had it in firing position, he triggered two air to air missiles. The first struck the Falcon in the cockpit area and the second just to the rear of the port side wing. The Falcon erupted in a ball of fire and disintegrated. Surette then pulled the F-15 into a steep climb away from the explosion. Steward made a turn well before the Falcon. Both pilots came abreast of one another and watched the debris fall to the ocean. The Falcon was well inside the inner harbor and only a minute from its target when Colonel Surette blew it from the sky.

Wingman Steward moved up next to Surette, tipped his wing and they headed home.

CHAPTER 83

REVENGE

It was dark when the helicopter set down at Newport State Airport, located three miles northeast of the Newport business center. The three passengers exited and the copter lifted off and moved to a remote section of the airport where it would be out of the view of Khalid. It cut its engines and all was silent. The pilots remained with the aircraft.

As they stood in the helicopter landing circle, the Chief spoke to Vinnie and Gretchen. "If you look to the left and slightly south you can barely make out the terminal building. There is no commercial air service out of here, but the building is still in use. A small number of private and business aircraft are parked in front. Most of the aircraft are parked to our right in a larger lot that is parallel to the runway. If you look closely, you can see the outline of some of the planes. The entire left side of that lot, for its entire length, drops off into a wet area, dense with scrub, high bushes and rotting trees. The ground is swamp-like. Something of a mess."

"Thanks for the layout, Chief. It works to our advantage to understand the area better than our man does."

"One other thing. My understanding is that most planes refuel when they land so that they are ready to fly at a moment's notice or at times when there is no fueling service available. The runway is long enough to handle most business jets. Given the time of night, it is unlikely anyone is here. There is no night watchman. Your man will have a free hand in finding a plane that is unlocked, fueled and ready to fly. Knowing what I do about people, you can be assured that several of the planes are unlocked. I wouldn't let him get to the runway."

"No chance of that happening, Chief."

"I didn't think so."

"What is the approach to the airport from the highway?"

"The access road is behind the terminal building and it empties into a parking lot back there. Just behind the parking area and across the access road is a storage shed. The chances are good he will park at the top of the back lot where he will have a view of the upper lot where most of the planes are tied down. The access road ends there. It is anyone's guess whether he will check out the planes in front of the terminal building or go directly to the upper lot where there are more choices. Any thoughts?"

"Since he has no familiarity with the airport, I think he will first check the planes in front of the terminal to determine if anyone is here. Since he is in a hurry, he will most likely look for a single engine plane that has a decent range. If someone is around, he will kill that person and take the plane. If no one is here and the planes are secure, he will make his way to the upper lot and take the first plane that is unlocked and that has the range to get him to wherever it is he intends to go. This man is a survivor and we believe he knows exactly what his next move is once he is airborne."

"I think you are right, Gretchen. I suggest we put our phones on vibration and that you cover the terminal area while I cover the upper lot. If it looks as though he has found a plane at the terminal, signal me and I will be get there. If he moves towards me, signal me, hang up, then repeat it a second time. If you follow him, be careful. There doesn't appear to be any cover between the two lots."

"And, what do you want me to do?"

"Chief, you have done enough. This is not your fight."

"Murder in my town is my fight. I don't want to interfere with your strategy, so I will stay with Gretchen as backup."

"Makes sense. Thanks."

"I suggest we take cover and wait." With that Vinnie walked to the upper parking area and Gretchen and the Chief took cover behind a storage shed on the left side of the access road directly across from the terminal. Vinnie would have no cover unless he was inside one of the unlocked planes. He checked the first row and found two of them unlocked, one of which was a good candidate for Khalid's needs. Nevertheless, he passed on both and found an unlocked plane in the second row. Once inside, his line of sight made it possible to see Khalid if he was checking any of the planes in the first row. Satisfied with his plan, Vinnie sat in the darkened plane and waited.

An hour passed before Gretchen and the Chief saw the lights of an approaching car. It was moving slowly. It hesitated behind the terminal building, then moved forward and parked on the north side. From that location the driver could see the upper lot and the aircraft. Gretchen and the Chief had a clear view of the car. There were no outdoor security lights on the building. It was dark. The door on the driver's side opened but there was no light inside the car. Whoever was in the car had turned off the interior lights before opening the door. One person, a man, stepped out, looked around and then carefully nudged the door closed without making a sound. Once he had his bearing, he walked around the corner to the front of the terminal and seeing four aircraft, checked out each one. None were unlocked. He then turned to his left and moved toward the larger lot to the north of the building. When he made this move, Gretchen, who was still behind the storage shed and who now had a clear view of the man, alerted Vinnie. His phone vibrated. He waited. It vibrated a second time. Khalid was moving towards him. Vinnie wanted to confront Khalid before he killed him. He had a score to settle.

Khalid walked slowly to the larger lot. Once he passed the terminal, Gretchen and the Chief had him in full view. They also had cover from behind two cars parked on the north side of the terminal where Khalid had parked his car. They decided to wait until he well into the first line of aircraft at which time they would move quietly to the lower edge of the lot and wait for Vinnie to make a move.

Vinnie could see Khalid making his way to the lot. He removed his gun from the small of his back and held it in his right hand. When he had entered the plane, he did not shut the door completely in order to exit without any noise. He also turned off the interior light switch. With his left hand, he opened the door, got out and crouched under the belly of the plane and behind the shield of the nose wheel. He did not have a clear view of Khalid who found the first unlocked plane, but decided it would have limited range. When he reached the second unlocked plane, he got inside. The interior lights went on and for the first time Vinnie saw the butcher who had slit the throat of an innocent woman and who was inflicting pain and death throughout America. A minute later, the plane's engine turned over and started. With a limited warm up, Khalid advanced the throttle and the plane slowly moved ahead a few yards and then turned to the right on the way to the end of the lot where he would turn left and proceed to the runway. When the plane was at ninety degrees and in full profile, Vinnie took aim and shot out the left tire. The plane sagged to that side. Almost by the numbers, Gretchen and the Chief came out of the brush on the right side of the plane, fired several rounds and shot out the nose tire. Knowing he was not about to fly, Khalid leapt from the plane, the engine still running, and took cover behind the row of aircraft in the first line. The propeller continued to rotate.

Knowing that he had shooters on both sides, Khalid had to clear one side of the lot if he hoped to avoid capture. Having heard only one shot from his left, he decided to take on the single shooter who happened to be Vinnie. He fired three rounds in Vinnie's direction while he ran to the second row of planes where he took cover. When Gretchen and the Chief saw Khalid run across the parking lot to the second row of planes, they took cover behind the first row. Seeing movement on his right, Khalid fired off several rounds, all of which missed Gretchen and the Chief. Knowing that he was caught between two lines of fire, he decided to move to the opposite end of the lot, away from his attackers. As he ran a zig-zag route among the planes, Gretchen and the Chief fired but missed. Half way up the lot Khalid turned to his left, slid down the embankment and sought shelter in the brush and trees where he would have time to think.

Vinnie moved quickly and followed him to the edge of the lot. He was determined to look Khalid in the eyes when he killed him. The area Khalid moved into was three feet lower than the parking lot and was comprised of scrub trees, shoulder high brush, tangled bushes and high grass. The ground was covered with leaves, twigs and broken branches and was wet and slick. It was difficult to move without getting caught on the underbrush. It was also pitch black.

When Gretchen and the Chief arrived, Vinnie was waiting on the edge of the wooded area. He put his finger to his lips signaling them to be quiet. Then he put out his hand like a stop sign and then moved it down signaling them to stop and drop to the ground out of the line of Khalid's fire. He whispered to Gretchen and the chief, "I want you to move to the very end of the lot staying close to the edge of the woods. When your phone vibrates, I want you to fire two full magazines into the brush at shoulder height and at a forty five degree angle back to where Khalid entered the woods. Then stop firing and wait." She nodded her understanding of his plan. The next moves were his.

He put his MK23 in the small of his back and then reached to his side and checked to see that his KABAR knife was in its sheath. He dropped down on to the wet ground and slowly made his way into the brush walking a straight line from the lot. A short way in, he stopped and listened. This was Wardak Province and the Taliban all over again.

There was no movement or sound. Khalid had stopped. Running his hand on the wet ground, Vinnie found a baseball size stone and lobbed it overhand and forward to the left of where he believed Khalid to be. When it hit the brush, two shots were fired in its direction. From the gun flashes, he knew that Khalid was roughly forty yards in front of him. Given the dense growth it was impossible to see him. He crouched low, moved ahead a few yards and stopped. He stooped and felt around for another stone. This time he lobbed it forward and again to the left of Khalid. This time Khalid did not respond. It was a trick that worked only once. Instead, Khalid turned to the right away from the sound. As he did so, Vinnie advanced another ten yards, closing the gap. Although the sky was beginning to lighten just a bit, the level of darkness made it difficult to see any distance. Anticipating Khalid's next move, he knelt on the wet and dirty earth. He reached up as high as he could without standing and grabbed the trunk of a sapling and shook it vigorously. Hearing the rustling of the leaves, Khalid turned and emptied his magazine in the direction of the sound. Bullets flew dangerously close to Vinnie's head but he was able now to pinpoint Khalid's position. The firing stopped and it was quiet except for the sound of Khalid ejecting the empty magazine and slamming another one into the gun; sounds that Vinnie knew all too well. All was quiet again. Vinnie dialed Gretchen, waited for her phone to vibrate and then closed his phone. A fuselage of gunfire broke the night silence as Gretchen and the Chief fired two magazines into the woods in the direction Vinnie designated. Seeing the flashes of gunfire coming from far to his right and well ahead of his position, Khalid wondered if his pursuer had moved ahead of him. He looked toward the direction of the gunfire, uncertain what his next move should be.

Vinnie had moved forward quickly and could just make out Khalid with his back to him crouching low to avoid the gunfire. Khalid heard the crunching of underbrush and turned to see Vinnie running at him through the brush and high grass. Before he could get off a shot, Vinnie dove into him head first and both fell to the ground. Khalid landed on his back and dropped his gun from the impact as he struggled to rid himself of the powerful man on top of him who held his arms pinned to the ground. Khalid kicked Vinnie in the genitals with his right knee and then a second and third time. He tried to lift his body up from the mud, but was unable to move his attacker who had him pinned to the wet and slippery ground. Unable to use his arms, Khalid continued to kick in the darkness, hoping to release his arms from the grip of the man who was intent on killing him but who held no gun. The man on top of him was going to kill him with his bare hands. Even in the dark, Khalid saw the eyes of an assassin, a man not unlike himself.

Holding Khalid's arms to the wet and muddy ground with his knees, Vinnie quickly swung his left arm fully across his body to the right, and then powered it to the left and smashed his left elbow into Khalid's nose. Blood spurted over both men. He swung his right arm to the left and then powered his elbow into the right eye of Khalid, then repeated the movement a second time and crushed his jaw. Khalid moaned from the pain knowing that he was facing death at the hands of a man whose name he did not know. There was vengeance in the man's actions, a coldness that sent a chill through Khalid. This was no ordinary man; this was an assassin whose mission was to kill him. With Khalid lying immobile on the ground, Vinnie stood and kicked his right foot into Khalid's crotch, then again and again. The crying did not faze or deter Vinnie. Khalid pleaded with him to stop by partially raising his hands in surrender.

Vinnie could hear Gretchen and the Chief moving along the edge of the woods. It was time to finish his work before they arrived. He knelt over Khalid, his legs straddling him with the weight of his body pressing on his thighs in much the same way Khalid had sat on his victim. Fear and panic filled Khalid's eyes as he realized that the man whose name he did not know was reenacting the cold bloodied murder of Kay Horton. Knowing what the next and last step was going to be, he shook his head back and forth as a way to ask for mercy. Not to be deterred, Vinnie drew his KABAR from its sheath with his left hand and before Khalid could utter another word, carefully placed the blade on his neck and sliced it open from left to right. As blood spurted from the cut and before death took Khalid, Vinnie whispered, "There are no virgins waiting for you, Khalid, only the fires of hell for eternity."

Vinnie wiped the blade on Khalid's shirt and then got up. With the knife still in his left hand, he started back to the lot with blood on his hands and shirt, and clothes covered with mud. Gretchen and the Chief met him at the edge of the woods. The Chief looked at Vinnie, saw the knife in his hand, nodded and without a word, went into the woods.

"Gretchen, what's in there is for the Chief to deal with. What I did will not bring Kay Horton back to life, but Khalid will never kill again." He placed the knife into the sheath.

Sensing the enormous emotional pain he was experiencing in murdering another human being, and the guilt that overtook him for not being able to save Kay Horton, Gretchen put an arm around his waist and walked with him in silence to the waiting helicopter. Once they were aboard, the pilot started the engine; the blades began a slow turn and when they reached optimum revolutions the helicopter began its lift off the tarmac. Once airborne and over open ocean, Vinnie pushed open the window and dropped his knife and sheath into the sea.

The first light of dawn and a new day appeared on the eastern horizon.

EPILOGUE

PRESS CONFERENCE

Anthony Mallory, Director of the Central Intelligence Agency, held a press conference this morning to clarify a number of issues. His most important announcement was the confirmation that Abdu Khalid, the world's most notorious terrorist leader, was killed by CIA covert agents who had been tracking him for several months. Khalid was the al-Qaeda leader responsible for multiple terrorist activities in the United States. Director Mallory stated that he had given a directive to his agents to take Khalid alive to stand trial but the nature of the gun battle was such that the terrorist and three of his operatives were killed. The four bodies were buried in keeping with Muslim tradition. The location was being withheld for security reasons.

Although not confirmed by the Director, a high ranking unnamed government source stated that two CIA agents were injured during the gun battle and were receiving medical care at a military hospital. The unnamed government source further stated that it was believed the action took place in rural Wisconsin, but was unable to confirm this.

When asked about the makeup of the covert team and its objectives, Director Mallory stated that for security reasons the identity of team members would remain secret as would the site of their training. He acknowledged that the team would continue to seek out and immobilize terrorists wherever they were active. Because of the sensitive nature of what had occurred, he would not identify other individuals or agencies that assisted the team in locating and neutralizing Abdu Khalid.

Several questions were raised about recent incidents that appeared to be the work of military and government intelligence agencies. When asked if the destruction of a private aircraft over Boston's inner harbor by the 104th Fighter Wing was linked to Abdu Khalid's terrorist activities, Director Mallory stated that the CIA had no role in the downing of the aircraft. He believed the action by the Air National Guard was related to the increased trafficking of drugs in Massachusetts in recent months and that the 104th most likely was working in support of a Coast Guard mission.

A reporter stated there was a rumor circulating that the recent storming of an apartment in an upscale Boston neighborhood was a CIA effort to capture al-Qaeda operatives involved in the murder of the Chief of Police in Merritt, Massachusetts and who were hiding out in the apartment. Did the director have any comment?

To quote the Director, "The CIA does not respond to rumors. If I were to make an exception to that rule, I would tell you that more than likely the Beacon Street incident was an attempted robbery in a wealthy neighborhood. The illegal occupants of the apartment were confronted by the well trained Boston Police Department Swat team."

A reporter for a leading Boston newspaper asked the Director if the socialite who was murdered on her yacht in Pomfret Landing, Rhode Island and who was seen a few days earlier in Boston with a man who bore a striking resemblance to Abu Khalid, was a CIA agent who got caught in a failed mission?

The Director made clear that except for the two agents wounded in the gun battle with Abdu Khalid, all of his agents were accounted for. He said that at the time in question, Khalid was being pursued in the mid-west by his agents and could not possibly have been in Boston. He expressed sympathy for the family of the murdered woman and was confident that the Rhode Island State Police and the Federal Bureau of Investigation, working together, would apprehend the murderer. To quote the Director, "The resources of the CIA have been offered to both agencies."

In separate action it was learned that the Securities and Exchange Commission was conducting its own investigation into the death of the murdered woman in that she was also the director of a large hedge fund that was recently charged with irregularities.

The Director noted he was aware that Al Jazeera reported that al-Qaeda sources had contacted major news organizations and promised retaliation for the murder of Abdu Khalid and that it would seek out and kill members of the CIA team responsible for his death. Mallory emphasized, for the second time during the press conference, that the covert team that neutralized Abdu Khalid would continue to pursue enemies of the United States anywhere in the world and that no terrorist was beyond the team's reach.

He ended the press conference with a warning to al-Qaeda; "There is No Where to Hide."

Made in the USA
San Bernardino, CA
27 November 2013